HUNTERS IN THE SEA

They were already dead, they just didn't know it yet...

During the dog days of the USSR, desperate Russian scientists modified one of the oldest killers of all, smallpox, and turned it into a weapon so destructive even they realised it could never be used. Codenamed Hunter, it was left to rot in an obscure lab in the heart of Russia. Now, on a rusty freighter full of so-called freedom fighters is a disgruntled scientist with one test tube of this new plague. Commander William Steadman of the USS *Portland* and Captain Rem Reonov of the Russian submarine *Gepard* hold the fate of the world in their hands...

HUNTERS IN THE SEA

HUNTERS IN THE SEA

by

Robin White

Magna Large Print Books
Long Preston, North Yorkshire,
BD23 4ND, England.

British Library Cataloguing in Publication Data.

White, Robin
    Hunters in the sea.

    A catalogue record of this book is
    available from the British Library

    ISBN   978-0-7505-2725-5

First published in Great Britain 2006 by Orion
an imprint of the Orion Publishing Group Ltd.

Copyright © Robin White 2006

Cover illustration © www.carrstudios.co.uk

Published in Large Print 2007 by arrangement with
Orion Publishing Group

Magna Large Print is an imprint of Library Magna Books Ltd.

Printed and bound in Great Britain by
T.J. (International) Ltd., Cornwall, PL28 8RW

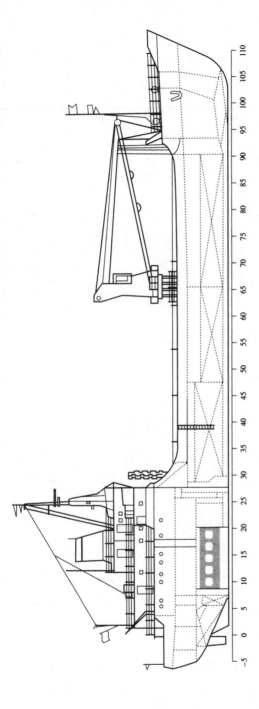

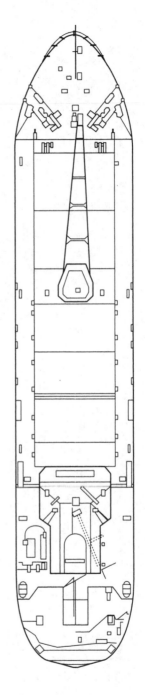

MV Cristi/Nova Spirit

I am indebted to the many submariners, active duty, retired, American and Russian, who helped make this book accurate, but not too accurate. You know who you are.

The brotherhood of submariners is small, and some names may sound familiar. But this is a work of fiction. Any similarities between real crew and the men (and the woman) in this story are purely accidental, except for one. Some of you will recognize that gentleman, and, I hope, smile.

Robin White, 2006

'NTINS…'

FOREWORD

Officially, the smallpox virus remains alive in only two places: inside a maximum-security laboratory at the Centers for Disease Control in Atlanta, Georgia, and in a similarly guarded repository near Novosibirsk, Russia. But recent reports indicate that in the early 1980s, the former Soviet Union created a vast network of facilities – all of them illegal – to grow large quantities of the deadly virus.

According to Ken Alibek, the former deputy director of the Soviet bioweapons program, the Soviet Union was capable of producing *tons* of smallpox virus each year and was researching ways to produce more virulent strains right to the very end.

Are these stockpiles still safe? Many laboratories in Russia are financially strapped. Specialists in the field of bioterrorism worry that underpaid or unemployed Russian scientists and researchers may sell – or have already sold – their expertise to the highest bidder.

No one, not even the Russians, can be sure what remains inside these derelict smallpox production and storage facilities. American intelligence officials say they have no specific evidence to suggest that mankind's worst scourge is in danger of falling into the wrong hands, that men who profess to love death as much as Americans love life would never release a weaponized virus meant, quite literally, to end the world.

They could be right.

CHAPTER ONE

DEMONS WAKE

4 OCTOBER
Pokrov Plant for Biopreparations
Vladimir Oblast, Russia

Dr Aslan Makayev pulled the curtains aside and watched the shift bus clatter off in a cloud of brown diesel smoke. It carried away the last of Pokrov's remaining workers. Only the nightwatchman and Makayev were left in the empty, echoing administration building. He let the curtains fall and picked up a gleaming leather briefcase.

It was a Vuitton *Moskova;* exactly the sort of flashy accessory favored by Moscow *biznismenyi* of a certain rank and far beyond the means of the head of an all-but-abandoned laboratory. Two weeks ago it had belonged to a far wealthier man. His initials, SS were engraved on the gold lock. The interior still carried a hint of his pungent cologne.

Exactly how the briefcase had come to belong to Makayev was, like many things in post-Soviet Russia, *trudna skazat;* a complicated matter difficult to describe. What it stood for was simpler: this glorious piece of olive leather was Makayev's ticket out of Pokrov, forever.

Years spent working around lethal organisms

had left their mark on the Chechen-born micro-biologist. His full black hair was streaked yellow from peroxide mists. His skin had been tanned by sterilizing ultraviolet lamps. His sense of smell was dimmed, his taste buds dead. It was a tribute to the House of Vuitton that he could still register the rich, heady aroma of leather rising from the fancy briefcase.

Makayev pressed the stud and the lock popped open. Inside were two papayas and a silver flask. The fruit was for Raisa and Gorby; a pair of rhesus macaque monkeys kept down in Pokrov's Zone Three isolator. The flask had been a present from his wife and bore the inscription *S'lubvyu ot Verie;* From Vera, with love. He turned it and the light fell on the engraved words. He read them, trying to remember the smell of her hair, the sound of her voice. All ghostly fragments now.

Vera's father was an engineer posted to the hinterland of Grozny, and she was everything Chechen girls were not: pale, exotic, modern, full of light and humor, free of the suffocating religion that smothered the region beneath a grim, medieval cloak. Makayev thought of himself as a modern man; he'd never seen the inside of a mosque in his life. When Makayev was offered a position in Russia, they left Grozny and moved north together.

They'd just settled into a new flat in Pokrov village when word came that two apartment buildings near Moscow had been blown up by 'Chechen bandits'. Tanks were poised at Russia's southern border. Vera's father still lived in

Grozny, and so she flew south, hoping to bring him out in time. Then tanks rolled across the border, and Grozny became a graveyard of alleys and rubble. Vera and her father vanished. The illusion that Makayev had a life, a future in the homeland of Vera's murderers died with them.

Makayev unscrewed the cap and filled the flask to the brim from a bottle of *Zarnitsa* vodka; it was the new batch, brewed and bottled in the annex that once housed Pokrov's anthrax fermenters. The cheap, potent drink – named after the first light of dawn – was Pokrov's sole source of revenue. He capped the flask, then picked up a framed photograph of his graduating class at the Grozny Institute for Biomedical Sciences.

The faces in the photo were still bright, still full of hope. *Why not?* They'd just taken the Oath of a Soviet Physician. They'd even believed it.

I swear to dedicate all my knowledge and strength to the preservation and improvement of the health of mankind and to the treatment and prevention of disease.

Makayev put the photo down, tucked the two papayas into a plastic biological sample bag and left for the basement.

The apartment empty, the memories painful and fresh, Makayev had tried to find solace in his work. Pokrov was an outpost of stability. It had done its secret work in rural isolation for decades. Wars and empires came and went. The Pokrov Institute for Biopreparations was forever.

19

But he was wrong. First, the money from Moscow stopped. Then the local farmers started demanding cash for food. Electricity became unreliable. Staggering bills piled up. Someone dismantled the security fence for scrap and no one stopped them. The small army garrison that once patrolled the grounds had abandoned Pokrov, too.

The former director, a dour Jewish academician named Aranov, traveled to Paris with his daughter to 'examine' French pharmaceutical equipment and never returned. Makayev knew three good microbiologists driving taxis in Moscow. The rest of the staff began to drift away, leaving behind only the stubborn, the lazy, or those too old to start over. Makayev called them *gribi;* mushrooms. They survived off Pokrov's decay, and by process of elimination, he'd become their leader. The Mushroom King, who at least had the entrepreneurial sense to convert the anthrax brewers to a more profitable purpose: distilling vodka.

The stairwell down to the basement was filled with the cold, dank smell of uncured cement. The treads were gritty with dirt tracked in from the autumn rain. He paused at the door to the lobby, peering through a small window.

The watchman at the front desk had his own bottle of *Zarnitsa* open. Old Savva had been here forever. *What would become of him after he left?* The Mushrooms would find a way to go on, of course. Pokrov might not be eternal, but vodka surely was.

He descended the final flight of stairs to the basement.

Most of the light bulbs down here were missing and the corridor was dim. He came to an unmarked green door distinguished from all the other green doors by an elaborate cipher lock. The door was fabricated from armor plate, and when he entered this week's code, it opened with the ponderous grace of a bank vault.

Makayev switched on the lights, revealing a white tiled tunnel. His nose tingled with the familiar, clinical smells of peroxide, ozone, bleach. At the end was a room equipped with gray steel lockers, where he traded jacket and jeans for full-body biohazard gear: a 'Moon Suit' made from two layers of blue plastic, a transparent hood, heavy yellow gloves he carefully taped shut at the wrist, and a briefcase-sized 'walkabout' box with its own supply of filtered air. Finally, a small pouch made of plastic netting. He placed the sealed bag with the papayas inside it, then turned a valve on the air box.

The Moon Suit inflated with a soft hiss. But then he reached to close his locker and caught his sleeve on something. He froze and checked for damage. There was nothing but a faint white streak where the outer shell was creased. The suit was made with two layers for this very reason. Still, a Zone Three bioweapons isolator was no place for trust. Not when a single virus meant death, and millions of them could fit in the dot at the end of a sentence.

To his left was the autoclave used for sterilizing instruments. To the right was a scrub sink and mirror. He walked over and pumped liquid soap onto his sleeve, then let water trickle over it. An air bubble would mean a breach. No bubble meant the suit was safe. As he waited, he looked in the mirror.

In his suit, his hood, his gloves, he could be anyone. Even the man he'd once been. Makayev was forty-two and wore his black hair as he always had, long and swept back over his head in a single, defiant wave. He still thought of himself as the young wolf from the wilds of Chechnya who'd arrived at Pokrov with a fresh degree in microbiology in his pocket and a beautiful Russian wife on his arm.

He looked down at his sleeve. No bubbles. No leaks. He walked to the back wall of the dressing room. It was fitted with an oval steel door that might have been taken from an atomic submarine. Beyond it was Pokrov's 'library'; a viral repository known as the Capsule.

Like a nested *matryoshka* doll, the Capsule was a building within a building, a room within a room, a vault within a vault. Makayev went over to it, spun a locking wheel and pulled. The door opened. Ultraviolet lamps blazed an unearthly blue. He stepped inside, shut the outer hatch and pulled a chain. A flood of peroxide washed over him. He reached out for the stainless-steel grab handles and let the decontamination cycle come to its end, then pushed open the last door.

A soft hoot greeted him from the darkness.

'Raisa? Misha?'

Pokrov means 'veil' in most Slavic languages. It's a feast day in the Orthodox Church commemorating the mysterious appearance of Mary in Constantinople. With barbarians at the city's gates, she'd spread a protective veil over the believers, rendering them invisible. Perhaps

Moscow knew that when it went looking for a quiet place to produce biological weapons.

Pokrov had never been a facility of the first rank; instead, its purpose was to produce military viruses after all the larger, more modern plants had been bombed into radioactive ash. Somehow the world had danced along the rim of that abyss for decades without falling. Makayev came to believe the contents of Pokrov's Capsule had helped keep the balance.

He reached in and flipped the lights on.

The Capsule was the size of a large walk-in closet. The walls, the floor, the ceiling were stainless steel. A large freezer chest stood to the left and a pair of wire cages to the right. In between was a narrow aisle barely wide enough for a man in a Moon Suit to pass.

Inside the cages were Mikhail and Raisa. Pokrov's staff had named the monkeys for the two criminals deemed most responsible for their unhappiness: Mikhail Gorbachev and his wife Raisa. It made life slightly more bearable to see them behind bars. They were small animals furred in sleek coats of silver and rust. They'd been born at Pokrov and had known no other life. Tonight, they were dying.

'I've brought you both a treat.'

The male was unresponsive, sprawled face down on the floor of his cage. He might already have appeared to be dead except for the rise and fall of his labored breathing. The natural shape of his ears were obliterated under clusters of hard, yellow blisters.

Raisa was in slightly better shape. Her face was

clear, she was alert, her eyes open. Then Makayev saw a thread of bloody drool slowly drip from her lips to the floor of her cage. She opened her mouth. Her tongue was cobbled with blisters.

In nature, smallpox takes the better part of a week to develop and macaques were naturally immune to its worst effects. But nature didn't stockpile weaponized viruses. Pokrov did, and the entire room was filled with an invisible, lethal cloud of contagion.

Makayev approached Misha's cage, careful to keep away from the bars. Dead animals had an alarming way of coming back to life, grabbing needles, tearing suits, biting with desperate strength. He unzipped the plastic bag, took out a papaya and pushed it through the feeding door. It rolled off the monkey's back.

He thought of Nina, the former director's wild, young daughter. What had she said? *Monkeys are smarter than people.* Then why was he on the outside of the bars in a Moon Suit looking in? Makayev moved to Raisa's cage. Her dark, almond-shaped eyes followed him. She saw the bag and like a child begging for coins, she held out a small, remarkably human hand, fingers curled, palm up. He dumped the papaya into it.

The monkey snatched it and took a great bite. She chewed, tried to swallow, but her tongue was swollen and the fruit made the hard blisters pop. With a cry, she spat out blood and pulp. She tried another bite. The same thing happened. Frustrated, she screamed, picked up a handful of wooden chips and feces and hurled them at Makayev.

He looked down. His suit was flecked with brown and red splotches, each one a hot viral colony. This was what the suit was for. He'd done it a hundred times before. He could do it once more. He turned away and walked three steps to the freezer.

A clay seal and a double strand of safety wire was all that guarded it. He yanked on the handle. The wire broke, the door swung open. A billow of icy nitrogen mist poured out around his booties. The fog settled, revealing rows of small, frosted glass tubes in metal racks, cushioned with towels soaked in disinfectant. Each sample vial was an inch long. Each contained a ball of gray, waxy 'telltale' that would turn bright red should a seal break. They were all sealed with a color-coded band.

The brown banded tubes contained *Yersinia pestis;* plague bacteria. Green was for tularemia, a debilitating respiratory disease. The black bands marked *L-4* indicated military-grade anthrax. At the far right were two rows of red-banded vials, twelve labeled *N1-I,* twelve *N1-O.*

N1 was the Soviet military code for *Variola major,* smallpox. The I stood for *India.* In 1967, the Soviets sent a medical team there to help the World Health Organization combat one of its last natural outbreaks. They were accompanied by KGB agents who quietly obtained samples.

India made an ideal weapon. It killed over half its victims, retained its virulence in freeze-dried storage and was stable in aerosol form. Under a powerful microscope, *India* looked like a rounded brick with an ominous hourglass nucleus surrounded by a wild, cat's cradle of hollow filaments.

25

The N1-O tubes also held smallpox, but of the *Ohotnik,* or Hunter strain. Under a microscope, Hunter looked less like a rounded brick and more like an iron manhole cover. The characteristic hourglass of viral DNA at the core was shielded behind thick plates of protein armor.

Military biologists combed Siberian graveyards for frozen victims of old epidemics. Hunter was discovered in the body of a native Yakut dug out from the tundra near the Russian village of Pohodsk. The village had been wiped out in the nineteenth-century smallpox epidemic. The hunter's body was found in a shallow grave, heaped with stones, wrapped in skins and buried with the tools of his trade: traps, snowshoes, a bone-handled knife.

Pohodsk is in the high Arctic where the earth freezes to a depth of more than a kilometer. But Siberia's short, hot summer thawed the upper layer and the hunter's corpse became a kind of laboratory for breeding viruses. Each winter the cold killed off most, but not quite all of them. Each summer the survivors multiplied in the warm, moist grave.

A century of natural selection yielded an organism able to withstand extreme conditions. *India* could survive outside the human body for only short periods, but the Hunter strain was much tougher. You could heat it, freeze it, dry it or drown it. Hunter survived.

Makayev reached into the freezer, removed four vials of Hunter and dropped them into the net bag. The glass crinkled and popped as it warmed.

Raisa was still shrieking when he re-entered the

airlock. Then he sealed the hatch and could no longer hear her. He pulled the chain and let the hurricane of chemicals wash over him once, twice. He headed for the locker room, stripped off the wet plastic suit and dressed in dry, warm clothes. He checked his watch. *Time.*

Makayev went back upstairs to his office. He placed the vials into the leather briefcase and carefully wrapped them in towels soaked with powerful disinfectant. It was a shame, because the chemicals would surely ruin the leather. He locked the briefcase and sat down to wait.

The call came forty minutes later.

He picked up his phone. 'Makayev listening.'

'Mister Director?' It was Old Savva. 'There's someone to see you. He says you're expecting him, but he's a foreigner and–'

'He represents a group of investors interested in our brewery.'

'Forgive me, Mister Director. I was only doing my job.' Then in a whisper, 'He's got two *byki* with him.' The word meant bulls. Bodyguards who offered the sort of protection no wealthy Russian would dream of traveling without. 'Is it all right to let them in?'

'It would be suspicious if he came alone. I'll be right down.'

He grabbed the briefcase, walked to the door and slipped the silver vodka flask into the pocket of his coat. He folded it over his arm, then paused, looking around one last time, and then he left.

With any luck, he would never see this place again.

Makayev took the stairs down to the lobby,

wondering what would happen when the morning shift arrived. Old Savva would tell everyone about the rich foreigner who wanted to pour bags of money into the plant. Where was Makayev? Had he sealed the bargain? Had he entertained this *biznisman* and his two bulls so well they needed the day to recover? Eventually they'd start to wonder.

By then, Makayev would be in a brand-new laboratory in a quiet suburb of Riyadh, Saudi Arabia. A lab filled with the best equipment money could buy.

He came to the lobby door and pushed it open.

Savva jumped up and stood at something like attention, arms straight at his sides, his thin chest puffed out. His dog, a gray-muzzled Alsatian named Sobel, lay curled at his feet. 'Director Makayev!' The dog lifted its silver muzzle and stared through eyes milky with cataracts.

The two bulls stood at the front door, flanking a shorter, stockier man dressed in a long, black wool coat: Sami Salafi. His initials, *SS*, were the ones engraved on the briefcase.

Salafi's guards wore the usual uniform of leather and jeans, snowy white shirts and blunt menace. They were hawk-faced, dark-skinned and angular. One had a full, bushy beard; the height of fashion among Muslim fighters the world over. The other was bearded too, though it was sculpted into a narrow line like a chin strap and so sparse it looked as though it had been painted on. He had some sort of tape player clipped to his belt, and a wire ran up to a tiny earpiece. Makayev knew at once they were Chechens.

Salafi's skin was the deep brown of a tropical hardwood. It made his straight, silver hair seem to glow with its own light. His eyes were glittering onyx, his face a mask of permanent appraisal.

'Welcome to Pokrov,' said Makayev.

'*Da, da, konyeshna,*' Salafi said. It meant Yes, yes, certainly, as though here was a matter already decided, goods already bought and paid for and unworthy of anyone's time, least of all his. 'You're ready?' His Russian was thickly accented, almost syrupy. 'You have everything?'

Makayev patted the briefcase. 'All the production figures.' He glanced at Savva. 'We'll be in the annex looking at the brewery.'

'Will you need an escort, Mister Director?' asked the old guard.

'No. I'm quite sure we can keep the bears away.' He turned to Salafi. 'Ready?'

'As you like,' said Salafi, and they all went out the front door with the bodyguards leading the way.

Outside, the sky was hammered with bright autumn stars. The forest was dark and heavy with the deep stillness of the oncoming Russian winter. Makayev could see his breath. The sharp-horned moon shed just enough light on the uneven steps to keep them from stumbling, but enough to reveal an old truck parked next to Salafi's black BMW sedan. It was an ancient GAZ-51, prehistoric with its rounded fenders, vented hood and canvas-covered bed.

Makayev looked at it. 'What's that truck doing here?'

'We've got a long journey ahead. We're driving

to Tula.'

'In *that?*'

'Of course not. We'll fly from Tula to Sochi.'

Tula was a grim, industrial city a few hundred kilometers south. Sochi used to be the Kremlin's playground. Now it was an unlovely, crime-infested port on the Black Sea. 'And from Sochi?'

'To Riyadh. This is Adnan,' he said, nodding at the bushy bearded guard. 'And his brother Musa.' The one with the sculpted beard and tape player. 'They're from your country. You probably knew that.'

'Yes.'

Without asking, without waiting to be told, the bushy-bearded Chechen began patting Makayev down. Adnan found the flask at once. He slipped his hand into Makayev's coat and fished it out. He cracked open the screw top and sniffed, *'Haram'*. Forbidden.

Salafi took it, smelled it. 'You were told to bring nothing else.'

'It was a present from my wife. It's all I have of her.'

Salafi shook it and felt the heavy slosh. 'It's illegal to bring alcohol into Saudi Arabia. Good Muslims avoid it.'

'I thought you were looking for a good biologist.'

Salafi chuckled. He glanced at the briefcase. 'The samples?'

'Four.'

'They're potent?'

Makayev thought of Gorby and Raisa. 'Very.'

'Then I suppose we should forgive you your

30

souvenir.' Salafi handed the flask back. 'Give the briefcase to Adnan and we'll be going.'

'No.' Makayev slipped the vodka flask back into his coat. 'I'll keep them safe until we arrive.'

'Adnan and Musa are here to keep us all safe.'

'And they have no idea what I've brought. I should tell you a few things before we leave.' Makayev gripped the briefcase to his chest. 'If the seals are broken, the organism will escape. What happens after that is a kind of biological explosion. First, we become infected. Then, those we come into contact with. One victim becomes thirty, thirty becomes nine hundred, then thirty thousand. The waves keep growing larger. AIDS took twenty years to kill fifty million.' He held up the briefcase. 'Hunter will reach that mark in twenty weeks if you let it escape.'

Salafi seemed surprised and not entirely pleased, as though an innocent tourist had come in to buy a rug and had cursed him in street Arabic. 'Is there something else?'

'I asked about the truck.'

'It's here because it must be. We can't have them following us every step of the way, Doctor Makayev.'

So. A bomb. 'You know what's stored in that building? Demons,' he said, brandishing the attaché case. 'Kept asleep, thanks to the fact that we can still produce our own liquid nitrogen. You don't want to wake them. And there's an old man in there who has done nothing. I won't allow it.'

'No one asked you to allow anything,' said Adnan.

Makayev ignored the guard. 'There's no need

31

to cover our footsteps in rubble and blood. We can be gone before anyone wonders where I am.'

'Sure. We'll drive straight to Sheremetyevo,' said Salafi, meaning Moscow's main airport, 'and when they ask you why you're flying out of the country we'll just tell them you're unhappy.' He snorted. 'You'd have the *entire world* know where you've gone. They already think my country is in bed with the terrorists. You'd hand them the proof.'

'The world needs Saudi oil. Who cares what they suspect? I'm a biologist, not a terrorist.'

'The kingdom is rich with enemies, and you're a biologist with a weapon beyond the dreams of any terrorist.'

'Enough,' Adnan reached into his belt and pulled out a bright, wicked blade. It had sharp, serrated teeth. 'If he cares more for protecting the old Russian than his own wife then let them die together.'

'Put it away.' Salafi seemed more than a little frightened of these two guard dogs, as though they might suddenly remember they weren't dogs at all, but wolves. Then his expression changed. A sharp, focused look. 'You can't blame Dr Makayev for what happened to his wife. He wasn't even there.'

Makayev's face tingled. 'You know *nothing* about it.'

'I know your government opened an inquiry into her disappearance,' said Salafi.

'And found nothing!'

'No. They told you nothing. I have the full report. Would you like to know what they did to her before she disappeared?'

Makayev felt the pull of the Saudi's words; the same force you felt standing at the lip of a chasm. Your life depends on staying back, but the empty space has a kind of fatal gravity. It pulls you nearer, nearer.

'Your wife and her father were stopped at the Central Railway Station by soldiers. Her father was allowed to board the train. Because of her name, *your* name, she was not. He refused to leave without her, so they were arrested. Prisoners were to be taken to Minutka Square, but they made a little stop first.'

Makayev turned his head aside. 'No.'

'Yes. There were four soldiers,' Salafi continued calmly, evenly. 'The commanding officer was Colonel Yuri Budanov. He was first but they all took a turn. They made her father watch every-thing before they shot him. One soldier broke down and confessed. He was sent to a psychiatric hospital. The colonel was never convicted. This is the truth.'

Makayev found it difficult to breathe, 'I demanded answers!'

'You asked embarrassing questions. Why would they reveal anything? They told you nothing because to them, you *were* nothing.'

'But the truck—'

'Adnan and his brother have arranged a diversion to allow us to travel safely. A cell-phone call will trigger it.' Salafi came close and lowered his voice. 'Now let me tell you something. If they had done to my wife what they did to yours, I would *demand* to place the call.'

33

Makayev looked back at the worn, brick facade. The lights burned in the lobby. All else was dark.

Salafi opened the back door of the BMW. 'Well?'

Makayev saw a folder on the back seat. It carried the seal of the Caucasian Military District and was signed by the Chief Procurator. A cell phone sat beside it. He felt the call of empty space, the open window, the horror of the past, the promise of a future, the vertigo of possibility.

'I'm coming,' he said, and slipped in next to Salafi.

Savva unscrewed the cap on his bottle of *Zarnitsa*. He was about to take a drink when the dog shoved a muzzle under his elbow. 'What?'

The dog wobbled over to the front door.

'All right.' Savva put the bottle down and grabbed his wide-brimmed officer's cap and pulled it down low on his head. He opened the door and saw the truck pulled up to the front steps. Those black shits from who knows where hadn't come here in some old truck. Were they hoping to steal Pokrov's production equipment? Where were they? He drew the ancient Nagant revolver from his holster. 'Go find them, boy!'

Sobel took the stairs slowly, painfully. At the bottom, he turned in the direction of the old truck, listening.

Savva heard it, too. A tinny string of electronic tones, a rising stairway of notes that he'd heard before but couldn't identify. It was Beethoven's *Ode to Joy*. He only had time to think of what it meant, of what they'd done to Director Makayev,

34

when the music ended in a white flash. It scalded his eyes, bleaching the building, the stairs, the trees in dazzling light. The blast wave arrived an instant later. It picked him up off his feet and threw him back through the front door in a blizzard of shattered glass, falling bricks and fire.

CHAPTER TWO

THE BELL RINGER

5 OCTOBER
USS *Portland*
Great Meteor Seamount, Mid-Atlantic

The navigator looked up from his chart table aft of the periscope stand. 'Deep water ahead, XO,' said Lieutenant Commander Pardee. He was huddled over a chart with his assistant. 'There's nothing between us and the Azores. We can put on as much speed as you want now.'

And it won't do a damned bit of good, thought Watson. Six men were riding a life raft in the middle of a monster hurricane, and Watson knew they were doomed. Not that he could say it. Tony Watson was *Portland's* executive officer, one short step away from captain; a rarefied realm where appearances ruled as much as reality, and possibly more.

Lieutenant Commander Watson was a small, serious man with thinning brown hair, pale blue eyes, a narrow face and prominent jaw. Some of the crew called him 'Choo Choo,' though never within earshot. It was an apt nickname, for Watson was first and foremost an engineer, a 'nuke'. There was little a Westinghouse S6G reactor could do to surprise him. Not so the men who ran it, nor the admirals who ran everything else. *Especially* the admirals.

In a Navy that prized engineers, Tony Watson was always one of the best. He'd ranked third in his graduating class at the Naval Academy and disputed the calculation so effectively he'd ended up sharing number two. If his personnel file required glowing fitness reports, his cast shadows. When Naval Reactors scheduled a dreaded Operational Reactor Safeguard Exam (ORSE), Watson took on a determined, radioactive glow himself No one was going to find anything wrong with his plant.

Now ORSE teams always found *something* wrong. For Watson, sending them back empty-handed was a kind of holy mission. And necessary, too, for the Navy only handed out boats to its best engineers.

Portland's previous captain had picked him to serve as the boat's executive officer. Then a Guam-based submarine collided with an uncharted seamount and the Navy sent Watson out to check the integrity of her reactor. When he returned, the XO slot was taken.

And so he went to sea instead as *Portland's* engineer. The old captain tried to make it up by recommending Watson for command school and a fast track to his own boat. All the planets were lined up, and then, catastrophe. His sponsor was relieved of command while underway, sidelined so brutally he eventually took his own life.

That catastrophe had a name: *Lieutenant Rose Scavullo*. The first woman ever assigned to serve aboard an American submarine. That young XO who took Watson's job had a name, too: William Steadman, Watson's boss and skipper of the USS *Portland*.

He glanced at the submarine's control station in the forward portside corner of the control room. The displays showed them at a depth of four hundred feet, running southeast at a healthy twenty-six knots. The sonar repeater mounted directly ahead was a blizzard of white lines; sound generated by storm waves, not ships, or, as submariners prefer, *targets*. 'What's our current time on-station, Nav?'

'Two and a half hours,' said Pardee. 'But we can cut thirty minutes off if we get the nukes to row a little harder.'

Row harder? It offended him that the navigator would use such a mundane phrase to describe the incredibly complicated process of extracting power from a seagoing nuclear reactor. The nuclear plants of the United States Navy had a *perfect* record, and with good reason: they were operated and maintained by men with the same dedication to absolute perfection.

Yes, the reactor could drive the boat a lot faster and they could arrive half an hour sooner. What would they do with the time? How could they surface in a hurricane? And if they did, how could they find those men? And if they found them, how could they be brought on board with-

37

out dashing them against the hull? Would speeding up change any of these simple physical facts? *No.* Could he say it? No. 'Helm. Make your depth five hundred feet. All ahead flank.'

The *click click click* of seat belts being fastened was louder by far than the distant hum of the engine.

Two sailors at the ship's control station sat in bucket seats before a pair of aircraft-style yokes. The helmsman seated at the inboard station controlled the rudder, the planesman at the outboard seat the boat's diving planes. In between was the knurled knob of the engine telegraph.

With the boat safely at depth, the helmsman spun it until its pointer indicated *FLANK*.

Aft in the Maneuvering room, the duty throttle-man acknowledged the order and adjusted the propulsion turbine valve to send more steam to the engine. Control rods were shimmed up to expose the primary coolant to more radioactive fuel. Cooler, denser water was drawn through the sizzling nuclear fires, generating more heat, making more steam, smoothly spinning up the great pinwheel of *Portland's* screw.

No sound, no vibrations hinted at the unleashed energies, but USS *Portland,* the newest and final *Los Angeles*-class nuclear submarine in the fleet, was accelerating like a barracuda chasing down a meal.

'Maneuvering answers all ahead flank,' said the helmsman.

Above the helm, a large flat screen displayed an electronic copy of the paper chart spread out on Pardee's table. It resembled a hiker's map of rugged, mountainous terrain. Instead of peaks and passes, there were fracture zones and mountains towering over deep abyssal plains.

Portland had just crossed the crest of the Mid-Atlantic Ridge south of the Azores. A magenta line connected her present position with a small red circle near an undersea mountain called the Great Meteor Seamount; the spot where an Air Force WC-130 hurricane hunter aircraft had ditched.

Watson glanced at the display mounted at the ship's helm. The digits flickered, then began to rise. *Thirty knots ... thirty-one ... thirty-two.* Like all 688-class boats running on a flank bell, the deck heeled two degrees to port. To hold her depth she needed to hold a 'down bubble' and Pena was slow. 'Half a degree down, Dive. Get with it before we start porpoising.'

'Aye aye, sir,' said Lieutenant Pena. Pena sat immediately aft of the two men at the helm. He was a junior supply lieutenant on his first run aboard a submarine. His black hair was cut high and tight to the scalp – 'whitewalls' in naval parlance – with an aggressive promontory over his forehead. Pena's sole duty was to carry out Watson's commands quickly and precisely.

Most surface officers found submarines confining, the living conditions primitive, the sense of danger constant. But Pena was built small. The living conditions on *Portland* were austere, but there was a camaraderie you didn't find on a surface ship. The crew of a submarine was a *family.* Best of all, a close friend from his East Los Angeles high school, Lieutenant Felix Ortega,

39

was *Portland's* junior weapons officer. They'd volunteered to put some authentic home cooking on the wardroom table on halfway night; the midpoint in *Portland's* cruise. No one but the captain knew when that might be, but he was sure it would be the most popular meal of the run.

Watson felt the boat come level for a moment, but then she began to roll off. 'Pay attention, Pena. You've got wave action to contend with.'

Pena looked back. 'At five hundred feet?'

'If the waves get big enough up there, we'll feel them down here.' How big did waves have to be to feel them down here? *Too big.*

Hurricane Vince was a weird late season storm that had skirted the Bahamas before turning back east and, as landsmen say, passing safely out to sea. Out over the warm waters off Africa, it merged with a tropical depression and blew up into a monster. An Air Force hurricane hunter was dispatched to take its measure. Something happened inside the hurricane's eyewall, and the plane had been spit out with fuel streaming from split-open tanks.

They tried to stretch their dwindling gas supply to make the Azores, but the headwinds were ferocious and inexorable mathematics allowed for no appeals. The plane went into the water with the pilot using the final few pounds of fuel to maintain some control.

Portland was two days out of Groton, Connecticut, heading for a special operations run in the Barents Sea off Murmansk, where something very odd – even unprecedented – was happening.

After a decade of inactivity, the Russian submarine fleet was finding its sea legs again. With the help of a gusher of oil currency flowing into the Kremlin's coffers, new boats were being built and old ones refurbished. A Northern Fleet *Akula* had departed its base at Gadzhievo. A British submarine picked it up and began trailing it. Then, the *Akula* vanished. No one knew where it had gone until it was discovered off the American shore near Norfolk.

Portland was to go to the Barents and find out how the Russians were doing it. Instead, a flash message bent her course south. No surface ship could fight its way through a hurricane to rescue six men adrift. *Portland* could, though once she arrived no vessel made a worse rescue platform.

Portland was designed with submerged stealth and speed in mind. She had no real keel, no wave-taming stabilizers. She wallowed like a hot dog in the smallest seas. A serious wave would wash right over her, and even the open bridge atop her sail – and anyone in it – would go under.

It was this thought more than any other that convinced Watson that those six men were doomed. He was an experienced submarine officer and engineer. He could drive *Portland* to the correct latitude and longitude. But he had no idea how to get those men aboard once he got there. He could only hope that *Portland's* young captain, the man he'd nicknamed *Hollywood*, would see the logic of that before the sea proved it to them all.

Aft of the boat's control room in an overheated, locked compartment stuffed with electronics, a light began to flash on the ELF receiver console.

Portland's trailing wire antenna had picked up a 'bell ringer'; a signal to come up to the surface for an unscheduled broadcast.

Radioman Matthew 'Banjo' Gant had the watch. Officially, he was an Information Systems Technician First Class but he preferred the saltier *radioman*. He looked at the light and swore. *Shit. Now?* Coming up to the surface seemed like a *very* bad idea. Banjo had read the weather reports, the storm warnings. He knew what it was like up there.

Radioman Gant was tall and gangly, with wheat blond hair and the open innocence of a North Dakota farm kid. He'd brought an electronic banjo on board and loved to spend hours playing it through a pair of headphones. He played only for himself Like the poster down in the mess area said, *Noise Kills!* If not by betraying your position to an enemy, then by annoying the shit out of your shipmates. He shared the radio shack with the communications officer and Lieutenant Rose Scavullo, who wasn't a submariner but a Russian-speaking linguist; a spook.

She noticed the flashing light and the look on his face. 'Message?'

'Yes ma'am,' he said, wondering if she knew just what was about to happen. 'You'd best stow your gear and strap in. It's rough up there.'

Lieutenant Scavullo sat before a flickering blue display. A gremlin had taken up residence somewhere in *Portland's* new communications gear. But where? Today, she was trying to determine if it might be hiding inside her signals intercept system. If so, she had only a few days before they

42

arrived off Murmansk to evict it.

This was her second run aboard *Portland*. Indeed, it was the second time *any* woman had served aboard an American submarine. The men of *Portland* could make mistakes and chalk it up to experience. Everything she did had to be perfect. Any flaw, any fault, would give ammunition to those who hated the idea of women serving aboard the boats. If that gremlin was in *her* gear, it was going to die.

Gant saw she hadn't clipped her seat belt. It was the rule when the boat was steaming at flank. Getting a junior officer to behave wisely was hard enough, but a *female* JO? He was tempted to let her find it out by herself, but then he figured, *They'll blame me if she cracks her head.* 'Ma'am? I'm serious. You'd best belt in.'

'I'll be fine, Banjo.' She had two binders open over the keyboard and a third on her lap. The belt would get in the way. The boat was rock steady. They weren't about to go flying and neither was she.

'Okay.' Banjo figured he'd done his job. *The stupid shall be punished.* He reached for a microphone and growled the control room. 'Conn, Radio. We've got a bell ringer.'

Watson looked up at the gray overhead. The textbook formula said the roots of a forty foot sea reached down two hundred feet. To feel them at five hundred meant there could be *hundred* foot waves up there. Enough to send green water clear over an aircraft carrier's flight deck. No submarine had any business in seas like that.

43

It was a matter of physics. A ship's keel kept it floating upright. On the surface, *Portland* was the same: her center of buoyancy was above her center of gravity. The problem came when she was neither surfaced nor submerged, but in between. At some point her centers of buoyancy and gravity would merge, and *Portland* would have no stability at all. She'd float upside down, right side up, on her side; a steel pipe three hundred and sixty feet long and thirty-six wide, filled with nuclear fuel, chemical poisons, weapons, superheated steam and not the least, one hundred thirty men. *And one woman.*

Watson briefly wondered which gods he'd offended to end up serving under the very captain who'd taken his slot at Command School, and alongside the woman who was most directly responsible for that travesty. Whatever he'd done, it must have been a real *doozy.*

Go up, or stay deep? There were no right answers. Nor for an executive officer who couldn't afford any errors pinned to his name. *That's what captains are for.* He smiled and turned to the messenger of the watch. 'Go wake the skipper and tell COB we need a walk-through for stow for sea.' By that he meant Chief Hank Remson, the Chief of the Boat, *Portland's* senior enlisted man.

'Aye aye.' The messenger vanished through the forward portside door to officer's country.

Banjo glanced at Scavullo. 'You were out on *Portland's* last run. You hit any heavy weather?'

She started to answer, but then stopped. Submariners don't talk about where they went and

44

what they did. And she had signed a secrecy agreement about that last cruise, promising never to discuss it with *anyone*. 'You really think it'll be rough, Banjo?'

'My last boat, we had a bell ringer in weather that wasn't anything like this and you never saw so many guys puking their guts out.' Banjo fished out a small plastic bag from under his console. 'You might want this just in case.'

'No thanks. I grew up around boats.' That was so, but the truth was, *Portland* hardly seemed like a boat to Scavullo. More like a small, over-crowded basement, a lab experiment to see how one sane woman handled the stress of being sealed up in a living space the size of a modest three-bedroom house with 130 men.

On a good day she felt like a clay pigeon at a convention of skeet shooters. True, they'd installed 'privacy blankets' on her bunk down in junior officers' berthing. But a couple of blankets didn't change the fact that on a submarine, sights, sounds and smells were community property. Theirs, and hers.

Just the same, the three swivel chairs solidly bolted to the deck plates had safety belts. It wouldn't be showing weakness to use them, would it? Scavullo put her binders aside and fastened hers.

The twenty-three-year-old linguist had her mother's glossy raven hair, her father's blue eyes and a Four/Four qualification in Russian she earned for herself at the Defense Language Institute in Monterey, California. Five was the highest rating DLI awarded. No other student had come close. She'd broken new ground by requesting submarine duty. Women had never served aboard a United States Navy submarine and never would. Where would they sleep? Where would they pee? How on earth could you lock up one woman with a hundred or so young men?

But Scavullo was from Maine, and so was the senior senator on the Senate Armed Services Committee. And that senior senator was a woman. Outgunned, the Navy retreated. She'd gone up against the whole damned Navy and though it still surprised her, she'd won. A gremlin who kept her from doing her job, that was scary. But a little rough water?

No *way*.

Watson keyed the 1MC microphone. A hum sounded. Throughout the boat, everyone stopped whatever they were doing and looked up at the nearest speaker. 'This is the XO. Secure all gear adrift. Chiefs report your spaces to the Chief of Boat and stand by for heavy rolls. I say again, stand by for...' He stopped as a tall, young-looking officer wearing the silver oak leaves of a commander strode into Control.

'Captain in Control,' the helmsman called out.

'Okay, Tony. I've got the conn,' said Commander Steadman.

At thirty-eight, William Steadman was barely a year older than his XO; unusually young for the commanding officer of a fast attack, but his path to command had been anything but usual.

Steadman had been forced to relieve a very senior captain who'd suffered a mental break-

46

down under the Arctic ice cap. They'd come within a whisker of going down and Steadman handled the situation. Though *Portland* was badly hurt, he went on to rescue nearly the entire crew of a sinking Russian boomer, a *Typhoon*.

He'd expected to lose his head over relieving the captain. To his amazement, the Navy sent him to Prospective Commanding Officers School in Hawaii. *Portland* went to the yard for extensive repairs. When she was ready, another surprise: instead of sending him off for 'seasoning' at some shore billet, they gave her to him.

At first he felt like he was holding the fort until the *real* captain showed up. But now, a few days out of Groton, a new feeling had grown inside him. It wasn't in the books on command and leadership the Navy encouraged junior officers to read. In a way, it was like the moment he looked at himself in a mirror and realized that his khaki uniform no longer seemed like a costume for a part he was playing. Indeed, it was civilian dress that now seemed strange.

He'd developed a new set of nerves that fanned out into *Portland's* every nook and cranny. As though seven thousand tons of low-magnetic steel had become a physical part of him, silencing his doubts and whispering that for all its technical brilliance, its fearsome weaponry, *Portland* was a ship that needed a captain and that he, Commander William Steadman, was that captain.

Steadman's hair was the shade of light brown that turns golden under the summer sun. He had a runner's physique that straddled the line between skinny and lanky. Summers spent working as a lifeguard on the beaches of Rhode Island had brought him to the service as tanned and fit as a recruiting poster. Submarines changed that fast. They were more challenging, more interesting, but between the good food, no exercise and no sun they were a lot less healthy. He glanced at the contact evaluation board and then said, 'What's the situation, Tony?'

'Banjo copied a tone.' He paused as the deck rose. 'Feel that?'

Steadman glanced at the depth repeater. *Five hundred feet.* He looked at Watson and said nothing. He didn't need to. 'Maybe someone picked those Air Force guys up. Wouldn't that be nice.'

'We'll have to put up an antenna to find out. I don't know how we'll maintain depth control in these seas, Captain.'

Steadman weighed the words and the source. Watson's concerns were real. But he was also a bit like a librarian who hated the idea of sticky fingers on the books. He was an engineer first, a leader second. 'Norfolk wouldn't send us a tone unless it was important.'

'Roll the boat and they won't get bilged. You will.'

Steadman thought, *That's not exactly true.* His orders said to pick up six men in a raft. They didn't say if it was convenient. *No. We'll have to try.* 'Let's take her up. If we can handle periscope depth we'll copy the broadcast. If not, we'll dive back down to review what we've learned.'

'The boat doesn't belong up in those waves, Captain.' It came out almost before Watson knew it, and heads turned throughout the control

48

room. 'It's not safe.'

The last thing Steadman wanted was to put himself above criticism. Submarining was dangerous enough. But here was a challenge that required an answer. 'A ship riding at anchor in a harbor is safe, XO. But that's not what this ship is for.'

There was a silence in the control room, broken only by the steady hum of the engine, the soft click of the depth repeater.

Watson finally broke it. 'Then I'd like to go aft and make sure the engineering spaces are ready.'

'Good plan. Report back.'

That's not what the ship is for? thought Watson. No. Grandstanding a rescue and hazarding the ship was not what a 688 was for. The XO stepped into the aft passage and disappeared down the ladder to the middeck. There, a hatch opened into a tunnel that ran aft through a shielded bulkhead to the reactor spaces. He opened the watertight door and stepped down.

It galled him to think Steadman would be writing his fitness report. Steadman had evicted a good captain from his own bridge with only the thinnest veneer of legality. He'd taken sides with a woman unqualified to serve aboard submarines against one of the most experienced commanders in the fleet. A woman whose very presence on board *Portland's* last run had very nearly put her on the bottom. In a Navy where officers got benched for dragging a keel in a sand bar, that was a screw up of the first magnitude. And yet the admirals had given him *Portland*. What would they hand him for taking his boat up into a hurricane to stage a rescue attempt?

49

Watson couldn't imagine what benefits could outweigh the obvious risks, but he'd lay odds Steadman had them calculated out to five decimal places.

He's not entirely wrong, thought Steadman as he walked to the small, padded seat set in the forward rail of the periscope stand; the oddly informal throne from which a modern nuclear attack boat was commanded. He leaned back and took a deep breath, watching the dot of light that was *Portland* move across the electronic chart above the helm. He had to think through his next moves very carefully.

It was possible the message had nothing to do with the downed crew. But no one would call a boat up into a hurricane sea for routine communications. So it was *something* important. Something Admiral Sam Graybar, Commander Submarine Force Atlantic, was willing to risk the boat for, too. 'Helm,' he said, 'Left five degrees rudder. Steady on course of two nine five.'

'Left rudder five to two nine five,' said Pena.

Portland swung her bow around to the northwest.

A ghost from a WWII diesel submarine would find the control room of a modern nuclear boat lavishly roomy. But in truth it was more akin to an airliner's cockpit enlarged to the size of a two-car garage, packed from linoleum floor to gray metal overhead with ducts, conduits, controls, instrumentation and, depending on what was going on, as many as twelve men. Every square foot contained at least one thing too many. It looked

50

disorderly, but like the organs of some great undersea predator, nothing was here without a reason. Nothing, and no one.

At its center was the periscope stand; the wide-angle search scope and the high-power attack scope sitting side by side and surrounded by the one item that suggested *Portland* was a ship at sea and not the basement of some crowded industrial building: a polished chrome railing. But the true center of the control room, indeed, the entire ship, was not a place at all, but a man.

Steadman took another deep breath. *Portland* had spent the better part of a year in the yards in repair and still had a 'new boat smell'; an amalgam of fresh paint, hydraulic oil and floor wax. The darker odors of sweat and hot electronics a hull took on with time were detectable, but not yet overpowering. A civilian might come here and wrinkle his nose at a stink reminiscent of dirty socks moldering inside an oil can. To Steadman, it was the smell of home.

Electric Boat had replaced or rebuilt her equipment, her sonar processors, her onboard computers, her controls, with gear intended for the new *Virginia*-class boats just coming down the ways. She was one of the most advanced ships in the world, yet nowhere else did the title of *captain* echo the age of oak and canvas.

Back then a warship might be out of touch for months at a time. Like a thirty-gun frigate, Steadman had only his officers and crew to rely on; a blend of old hands who knew everything, younger petty officers and sailors who thought they did, junior lieutenants who'd never sailed aboard a submarine before and at the bottom of the pecking order, eager young boys who hadn't yet earned their dolphins.

The surface fleet was different. The skipper of an aircraft carrier was like the branch manager of a huge corporation. Never out of touch with the home office, never beyond their oversight, their questioning. Virtually every step, every decision he made was the careful product of a large and amorphous committee; rehashed, reconsidered, and finally, when the weight of the paperwork grew to some magical figure, carried out.

Not so *Portland*. Submarines still operated alone, out of touch, their captains *fanatical* about not radiating *any* sign of their existence. While at sea, his word was law and everything that took place, good, bad and indifferent, was his to own.

The boat shuddered, heeled over slightly, then came right.

Steadman glanced at the depth repeater to make sure they were still deep. He thought of his crew. One hundred and thirty of them, from the machinery and reactor spaces aft to the torpedo room forward. And Lieutenant Rose Scavullo, too. All depending on him to come up with the right answers every time. For one wrong answer was all it took to make headlines. He looked up as though he could see through the hull to the maelstrom raging overhead. *Now this.*

Steadman turned to the helm. 'All right, Mister Pena. Make your depth three hundred feet. Turns now for ten knots. Sonar? Let's go open mike.' It put Steadman in touch with all the boat's critical stations without having to reach for a microphone.

Chief Farnesi, the chief of the watch, sat at the ballast control panel just behind Pena, facing outboard. His job was to manage the submarine's weight and balance through a complex system of interconnected tanks and valves. His life was about to get very interesting. 'How heavy you want her, skipper?'

'Forty thousand pounds,' said Steadman. 'If something doesn't feel right I want the boat moving downhill.' He looked to his right.

The weapons consoles controlling the boat's torpedoes and Tomahawk missiles were all dark. The missiles were all nestled in tubes forward of the pressure hull. If one of their hatches came loose the tube would flood and the missile would drown. That would be expensive, but not fatal. The twenty-four Mark-48 ADCAP torpedoes down below in the torpedo room were another matter. Each of them weighed two tons, and they could not be allowed to move so much as an inch.

'Conn, Radio Room is ready for incoming message traffic.'

Steadman said, 'Torpedo, Conn. Report.'

The answer came at once. 'Conn, torpedo room.' It was COB Remson. 'All the chiefs have checked in. We're rigged for sea. I've gone through the forward spaces myself. We might see some skin books flying around berthing but we should be okay.'

Should be okay, or will be? Steadman caught himself wondering how Chief Jerome Browne, *Portland's* old COB, would have said it. 'It's automatic' was Browne's favorite expression. It meant don't worry. Everything's taken care of

53

'The fish secure?'

'We've got a bad skid bolt we're replacing. Give me another couple of minutes and we'll be ready to rock and roll.'

'If you don't like the looks of something, I want to know.'

'You won't need the intercom, Captain.'

'Good. Engineering, Conn. Report.'

'Conn, Engineering.' It was Watson. 'We're ready aft.'

The XO was precise by nature. If he said *ready* he meant it.

The growler buzzed. 'Conn, Torpedo,' said COB Remson. 'Got the new bolt threaded. We're good to go.'

Steadman turned to Lieutenant Pena. 'Helm, make your depth two hundred feet. Turns for six knots.' It was as slow as he could go and have control authority, as fast as he dared take on those seas. *Here we go.*

CHAPTER THREE

ICELAND SKULL HOCKEY

Black Sea Port of Sochi

An elderly twin engine turboprop roared aloft, scribing two trails of sooty exhaust across the sky that Makayev found suspiciously tropical. The sun was unnaturally warm for early October and the air was spiced with the heady smell of pine resin. It made him uneasy, and he grasped the leather attaché tightly to the heavy coat he no longer needed.

He watched the airplane longingly. That was how they should be traveling. Not on the ground like some helpless insect waiting for the boot. If they'd done what he'd suggested that night in Pokrov they'd be in Riyadh now. Instead, they were waiting for a *bus*.

Adnan and Musa gazed up at the plane as though measuring the right moment to launch a missile. Salafi simply sat down on a bench.

Makayev turned to him. 'This is your idea of traveling discreetly?'

'It's been planned,' said Salafi, though even he looked annoyed. A truck was to have met them at the air freight terminal building.

Makayev had had it with Salafi's plans. The entire journey south from Pokrov had been a kind of exquisite torture that combined the fear of being stopped and arrested with the even greater fear of traveling so slowly even *Russian* police stood an excellent chance of finding them.

A good highway connected Pokrov with the industrial city of Tula. Did they use it? No. They'd gone by dark back roads, with Adnan driving so fast they'd pitched into a deep rut almost before they'd seen it. It felt like the car had run off a cliff. They'd left a muffler behind and clattered into Tula making enough noise to rouse even the sleepy local traffic police to action. They'd been pulled over twice on their way to the airport. Each time Salafi had handled the matter with a

55

twenty dollar bill.

Once at Tula airport they found the charter plane that was supposed to take them to Sochi grounded with 'technical problems'. It took four hours and a thousand dollars from Salafi's bottomless supply to solve them, but they were late in leaving and late in arriving at the Black Sea port. Now Salafi expected them all to ride the old city bus to the docks like a group of wayward factory workers on their way to a spa.

That was Salafi's plan? He heard a motor and looked up.

'You see?' said Salafi as he stood. 'I told you. No problems.'

A red and white city bus rounded the curve from the terminal and wheezed to a stop in front of them. Adnan and Musa got on first. There were a few passengers who'd boarded at the terminal and three young women dressed in the smudged blue and gray smocks of cleaning girls. Their hair was covered in plain white scarves.

Adnan gave the signal and Makayev and Salafi climbed aboard.

Makayev looked at the faces of the other passengers. The young girls in their smocks, especially. Their faces were tanned with the strong southern sun, but their expressions were weary, even beaten. All of them were younger than Vera had been when he last said goodbye, and yet they looked what? Ten years older. *Hopelessness,* he thought. It was a disease Makayev was not about to contract. He turned away and looked out the dusty window as the bus entered the outskirts of Sochi.

Pokrov had been Old Russian. Sleepy, agricultural, wooden churches standing sentinel by mercury-gray rivers. Tula was Soviet Russia: a grim, industrial city dedicated to making guns and samovars. But Sochi was the first place Makayev had seen since leaving that seemed foreign. The streets were crowded with men and women in light, airy clothing. The stores had bins filled with fruits and vegetables. Outdoor cafes were busy.

Salafi stood up.

'What's wrong?' asked Makayev.

'Nothing. We're here.'

The bus stopped across from the ferry docks. It was early afternoon and it was obvious from all the activity that a ship had just arrived.

'Wait,' said Salafi, and taking both bulls, he left Makayev on a nameless street corner.

He watched them go and wondered whether he'd see them again. What if something had gone wrong? What if they were leaving him behind? Where could he go? All he knew for certain was that he was thousands of kilometers from anything he'd ever known, that night would fall in the next few hours and that he was supposed to board some ship. But how? There would be passport controls, militia officers, customs police. Surely they didn't expect him to walk up and buy a ticket?

A flat bed truck with Turkish plates stopped across the street from where he stood. There was a steel shipping container painted with the word SEALAND lashed down in the back. Adnan drove. Salafi was next to him. There was no sign of Musa. The Chechen motioned him on board.

The cab smelled of rotting fruit. A layer of squashed apricots decorated the floor, leathery and black.

The road to the pier was blocked by a customs control gate. A line of trucks was waiting to pass through, each of them heaped with drifts of small, red tomatoes. As each truck bumped up the ramp at the gate so the driver could present his documents, a few tomatoes would cascade off the full beds. Children darted in to collect what they could before the truck started up again and its wheels mashed it all to pulp.

The line thinned, and finally the last truck rolled by. A uniformed policeman turned his attention to the one vehicle waiting to go the other way. He wore the usual wide-brimmed officer's cap, was armed with the usual Kalashnikov. He waved them to hurry up and come forward.

The air brakes hissed, and Adnan slipped the truck into gear. They began to roll.

Makayev's pulse pounded. It was the first actual checkpoint of any kind he'd encountered since leaving Pokrov.

Adnan leaned close as he braked to a stop. 'Say nothing.'

The officer came to the driver's window. He looked directly at Makayev, then Salafi, and finally Adnan. 'Dokumenti.'

Adnan handed over a package of papers. Passports, transit visas, travel authorizations, and slipped within, a hundred dollar bill.

The militiaman opened them, licked his thumb and examined the packet closely. 'What ship?'

'The Cristi.'

'Cargo?'

Adnan nodded back. 'Used furniture.'

The officer made a mark on a clipboard, then handed back the transit papers, less the hundred dollar bill. 'Move!'

They drove out onto the pier, by the gleaming white Turkish ferry, to a rather less imposing ship tied up at the very end.

At least, Makayev *thought* there was a ship. *Cristi* rode so low to the water that all he could see was a yellow loading crane and a slab-sided box of steel punctured by a few portholes that wept red rust. *We'll be lucky not to sink.* 'We're supposed to take *that* to Saudi Arabia?'

Salafi smiled. 'You'd prefer your own yacht?'

'I'd prefer to arrive in one piece.'

A thin, lithe black man dressed in oily khakis clambered up onto the pier from the ship's deck. He wore an officer's cap set at a jaunty tilt, and pink plastic sandals on his feet. He walked straight to Salafi. 'You're late.' He looked at Makayev. 'I'm Captain Warsame, master of the *Cristi*. You will be our guests until we dock at Malta.'

'Malta?' Makayev turned to Salafi. *'Malta?'*

'It's been planned,' the Saudi said wearily.

Makayev could see no evidence of a plan, well thought out or otherwise. He regarded the captain, who had to be African. Russians called Chechens blacks, but they clearly didn't know what they were talking about. This captain wasn't just *dark*. He was almost purple black. The African reached for something at his belt and for a moment, Makayev thought he was drawing a pistol. Instead, he clicked a handheld radio on

59

and spoke a few words in a language Makayev could not begin to identify.

A moment later, the big yellow crane mounted on *Cristi's* deck swiveled out over the pier, then dropped a hook onto the roof of the SEALAND container. Adnan climbed up, attached it, then gave a signal. With one hand on the cable, he rode it up, over the pier and onto the ship.

Captain Warsame watched, then spoke a few more words. A gray cloud belched from the smokestack. Tarry lines were singled off. A warbling siren sounded from somewhere in the city. The *thud thud thud* of a big helicopter made the air shudder. He looked in the direction of the sound, then said, 'It's time we sailed.'

USS *Portland*
Atlantis Basin

As *Portland* swam up from the deeps, the subtle dips and rises grew stronger and less predictable; hardly noticeable to a sailor accustomed to a destroyer, but unsettling to submariners used to rock-steady decks.

Steadman glanced at the electronic chart above the helm. They'd left one drowned mountain astern. Another, the Atlantis Seamount, lay dead ahead. He turned his attention to the sonar repeater. Steadman was sharp for an officer, but it was a time to consult the expert. 'Sonar, Conn. Any close contacts?'

Directly forward of control, in a quiet space lit by blue lights from above and the glow of CRT screens below, four men wearing black head-phones sat staring into octagonal screens. Though the sonar division was nominally led by a young lieutenant named Kelso, when Steadman needed to know something he went straight to the sonar supervisor: Petty Officer First Class Steve 'Bam Bam' Schramm.

The crew called them 'sonar girls' because they didn't seem to do much in the way of real work. But Bam Bam knew there was a damned good reason why every good submarine book featured a smart sonarman who saved the day. That was just being *accurate*.

Schramm sat at the sonar supervisor's console wearing a homemade headphone made with his own speakers and a pair of thick, red engine-man's ear muffs. 'Conn, Sonar,' he said. 'All I hear is a lot of ocean. If there's a ship up there I'm glad not to be ridin' her.'

Born in Tennessee, Bam Bam had dark brown hair, a narrow face outlined in sideburns that skirted legality, and the finely calibrated ears of a concert pianist. At his fingertips was acoustic data gathered by three different sensor arrays: the front-mouthed, spherical array, the side mounted hull array and the 'towfish' that trailed behind the boat.

Bam Bam's sonar displays were the next best thing to a window. Acoustic information was ana-lyzed in different ways for different purposes. Passive broadband sonar, the classic 'waterfall' display, was good at detecting and tracking targets. Narrowband sonar could distinguish the unique frequency signature of a particular vessel. The

61

DEMON display (demodulated noise) determined the speed of a contact and the number of blades on its screw. Last was his active intercept sonar, which is what Schramm figured he'd be listening to shortly before he met Elvis. It analyzed the frequency and location of active sonar pings hunting for *Portland*. All of these systems operated passively, listening rather than emitting energy. The boat did have an active sonar; the thundering SADS-TG set. At high power it was capable of boiling seawater.

Schramm could pick up a whale singing a thousand miles away. He could hear a surface ship sixty miles out and most Russian submarines from forty. It was the finest sonar suite in the world, and though this was his third run on *Portland,* his first as sonar chief, he'd never seen, heard, experienced anything like the sonic storm raging across his screen.

A shudder coursed through the boat, as though the bow had plowed into something more solid than mere water, something that only reluctantly yielded to the thirty-five thousand horses driving her forward.

'Depth now two hundred feet,' said Pena.

Steadman spoke over the 1MC, sending his voice throughout *Portland.* 'This is the captain. Commander Submarine Force Atlantic diverted us to rescue six Air Force crewmen forced down in a hurricane. Heavy weather turned all surface ships back. Only a submarine can do that job, and *Portland's* that submarine. We've just been called up for an unscheduled broadcast. It's possible somebody picked those guys up, in which case we'll all have something to celebrate. To find out we have to put up an antenna and it's going to be rough. Secure all loose gear and hang on. Dive officer,' said Steadman, 'make your depth now one hundred feet.'

'Anybody here ever ride the Iceland Elevator?' asked Chief Farnesi as he pulled his own seat belt tighter. 'You'd catch one of those bastards up in the North Atlantic in winter. Stand at the bottom of a ladder, grab the rails and when the boat drops out from underneath you let go and fly up a deck. Makes a sound like a xylophone as your knees hit the rungs.'

'Sounds like Iceland skull hockey,' said Pardee. There was no seat for him to strap into. Instead, the navigator wedged himself between a chart box and a nearby bulkhead. He looked like a crab in a crevice, waiting for surf to break over him.

'Depth now one hundred fifty feet.'

The deck heeled five degrees to port, then ten. The motion was eerily smooth, like a cork riding a vast mid-ocean swell. Someone chuckled nervously. Fifteen degrees. The control room looked normal except that everyone had a serious case of the leans. An amusement park fun house where the rules of gravity were temporarily revoked.

Eighteen degrees now on the inclinometer.

'Jesus,' someone whispered. The invisible wave rolled by and the deck slowly returned to its normal place underfoot.

'One hundred twenty five feet.'

'BRA-34?' asked Steadman. It was one of *Portland*'s communications masts.

'Ready,' said the petty officer seated at the elec-

63

tronic support measures (ESM) console, though he thought extending anything now was a good way to lose it.

'Depth now...' Pena began, but suddenly the numbers on the fathometer started to unreel, and fast. *Ninety ... eighty ... seventy.*

'Full down on the planes, Mister Pena,' said Steadman.

'They're full down already!' Pena could see that shoving the control yoke against the stops made no difference. They were in the grip of a greater power, one that was drawing *Portland* up against its will.

This isn't working. 'Make your depth four hundred feet!' But even as he spoke the sudden rise ended with an eerie, weightless pause long enough for Steadman to see fifty feet on the repeater.

Then the submarine began to roll.

Portland's hull was filled with a chaos of crashing coffee mugs, flying pencils and lost wrenches. The computer monitor down on the mess decks where off-watch sailors played video games broke free and fell to the deck. An avalanche of frozen pizzas blocked the door of the cold box. A fifth of Jack Daniel's that absolutely no one in the Auxiliary Machine Room recognized shot out from behind the diesel generator and shattered against the opposite bulkhead. A thousand unsecured objects slid across the deck until they were stopped by something that *was* secure.

Steadman grabbed the railing of the periscope stand and looked uphill at the helm. The inclinometer read forty degrees starboard. At some point they would go all the way over. He had to get the bow turned into the seas before that happened. 'Turns for eighteen knots! *Left* full rudder!'

Portland's bow struggled around to meet the swells. Propelled by the furious slash of her screw, she punched her bow into a wall of green water.

'Hang on!'

The bow held its up angle, then *Portland* pitched forward into the following trough. Steadman heard the fast *thud thud thud* as the screw rose clear into the air, and then the hull slammed back down.

He saw the sailor at the helm pull back on the yoke to bring her level, and with the bow pointed steeply down it was an understandable reaction, but not a good idea. Down was where the seas were calmer. Down was where *Portland* was designed to survive. Down was where he very much wanted to be. 'Dive! Take her down to four hundred *smartly!*'

'Depth now fifty feet!' said Pena. 'We're diving!'

Thank God they're belted in. 'Make turns for ten knots,' said Steadman.

'Conn, Radio,' said Banjo Gant. 'We lost the floating wire up there. The screw musta' chopped it off.'

Rigging a new wire was a dirty, wet job under ideal conditions. It would have to wait. 'We'll worry about that later, Banjo,' Steadman switched to the torpedo room circuit. 'Torpedo room, Conn. Report.'

'I thought that last wave was coming right through the tubes,' said Remson. 'We got white-caps in the bilge but nothing's busted.'

Steadman switched to the IC circuit. 'Engineering, Conn. Report.'

'No issues,' Watson said dryly.

Simple words and not bad news, thought Steadman. But Watson's triumphant tone said more. *We're all professionals back here ... not like you 'coners;* the derisive term used by nukes for anyone who worked forward of the engineering spaces.

'Skipper?' It was Farnesi at the ballast control panel. 'Those seas are spaced at twenty-two seconds.'

Steadman looked back. 'You actually timed them?'

'Only thing I could do with my eyes shut.'

Twenty-two seconds, thought Steadman. It might be long enough if the message was short and they didn't try to acknowledge it. The words of a salty old instructor in shiphandling came back to Steadman, rising up from deepest memory: *The object is to control the movement of your ship and not yield to the elements. We may not be able to control the forces of Nature, but we can use them to our advantage.*

The Iceland Elevator. You stepped up to the bottom of a ladder and let the sea launch you up. What if he put *Portland* into a similar position, kept her heavy, and used the sea to his advantage? Could it work long enough to grab that message? *Maybe.*

Radioman Gant looked at Scavullo. Her face was waxy and sweaty. *Oh shit. She's gonna' spew.* In the hot, sealed radio room that could turn contagious. 'You doin' okay, lieutenant?'

'Fine.' She closed her eyes and tucked her

66

shoes under her console.

Gant pulled out the plastic barf bag again. 'You sure?'

'I already told you. I...' But then she opened her eyes and the radio room was not where her brain had left it. Something clicked, and she grabbed the bag from Banjo and turned away just in time.

'Helm,' said Steadman. 'Make your depth one hundred feet. Raise the BRA-34. Let's try this one more time.'

'One hundred feet and three one zero aye,' said Pena. He thought *What's with this try shit?* You tried something when you didn't know what was going to happen.

Pena's feeling was shared down in the torpedo room.

A red-haired torpedoman with the sleeves of his blue coveralls rolled up to expose bulging biceps yelled, 'Hey COB! What the fuck is Hollywood trying to prove?'

Good question, thought the Chief of the Boat. Hank Remson had chewed the soggy stub of his unlit cigar to shreds. It was a sure sign that he wasn't happy. The skid bolt they replaced was loose again. 'Jesus Christ, you worthless, scum-sucking sonofabitch. Show some respect. Even if he drills us into the side of a fucking pier and your dental work ends up in your colon, he's the skipper, not Hollywood. Got it? Now quit wasting air and hand me that new bolt.'

Remson was a small, wiry man seemingly custom-built for a submarine's cramped spaces.

He had thick black hair, dark eyes, a razor-sharp black mustache and a disarming smile that no enlisted man believed for an instant. The cold cigar was a permanent fixture. The torpedoman handed Remson a new bolt for the torpedo hold-down strap. The fastener was as thick as his thumb and coated in white grease. 'If he takes us up there again we'll need more than a new bolt. You tell him. He's got to listen to you.'

'Red, when your hat size gets as big as your shoe size, I'll take your concerns to the captain.' He started screwing in the new bolt by hand, careful not to cross-thread it.

The torpedo on the loading tray was a gleaming green cylinder twenty feet long, twenty-one inches across and weighing three thousand eight hundred pounds. Enough high explosive was packed into its bullet nose to break the back of an aircraft carrier. Five straps secured the torpedo to the tray, and each strap had five steel bands bolted to a massive casting at the base. In any other sea state he'd say forget it. But today, Remson wanted *everything* tight.

Remson slapped a wrench on and began to torque it down. At first it seemed to work. The bolt grew tighter, tighter, then, as before, something gave way. The head turned. *The fucker's stripped.* He turned to the torpedoman. 'Tell ya' what, Red. Let's you and me throw some straps around this fish.'

The instruments at the helm were in constant motion, depth, speed and deck angles all changing in ways Steadman had never seen.

Pena watched the depth repeater flash a stream of digits, slow, then come to a brief rest. 'One hundred feet, skipper!'

Any second now, thought Steadman. He was baiting the ocean, daring it to catch them. Only this time, he would use it. *There!* Steadman felt the familiar acceleration press up against the roles of his shoes.

'Depth now sixty feet!' Pena shouted.

'I'll be damned. The mast is exposed,' said the chief at the ESM console. 'We've got multiple signals!'

Multiple? Steadman was about to ask who was sending them when *Portland* slammed to a stop as a sea rolled over her. The bow burst through into the air, then pitched down. 'Chief! Start counting!'

Farnesi clicked his stopwatch. *Twenty-two ... twenty-one...* When the count reached zero, the next wave would be on them. *Eighteen seconds ... seventeen ... sixteen...*

Emptying her stomach left her feeling much better. Scavullo had her heavy black headset on and she was jacked into the aircraft band that Banjo was handling. It gave her something else to think about. She pressed her headphones to her ears. A very anxious voice was coming through loud and clear.

'Lobsterman, Lobsterman, this is Coast Guard Rescue Six guarding the push. How do you read?'

Lobsterman was *Portland*'s call sign. She glanced at Banjo.

'I got it,' he said. 'Conn, Radio. New message

traffic received. It's coming through crypto. And we're being hailed by a Coast Guard aircraft.'

'Fifteen seconds,' warned Chief Farnesi.

Steadman said, 'Put him over, Banjo.'

Gant lined up his switches. 'You got him!'

Steadman clicked his microphone. 'Coast Guard aircraft, this is Lobsterman. How do you hear?'

'You're a sight for sore ears, Lobsterman. Rescue Six is a Charlie-130 orbiting some guys who are real anxious for a ride. When do you estimate on station?'

'Stand by, Rescue Six.' Steadman grabbed hold of the railing with one hand and an overhead handle with the other. 'Nav! I need an ETA.'

Once more the bow rose skyward, then plunged down with a hard smack that rang through the hull. *Portland* was buried under an avalanche of green water and foam, then slowly reemerged.

'Twenty minutes out!' shouted the navigator, then retreated back to his brace position.

'Rescue Six, this is Lobsterman. Twenty minutes. What's the sea state and what kind of winds do you have?'

'The swells are *huge*. Winds up here are fifty-eight knots from the southeast, gusting seventy.'

'Rescue Six, we're on the way. Lobsterman out.' He slammed the microphone onto its hook. 'Retract the BRA-34! Diving officer! Make your depth three hundred feet! Ahead two thirds!'

With diving planes deflected down, *Portland* nosed deep into the long trough between the mountainous seas. The bow went under, then the sail. The radio mast slipped back into its well intact.

70

Chief Farnesi kept track of the time as he opened up *Portland's* ballast tanks to the sea. The next wave was due. 'Here it comes.'

Remson was in trouble. The first wave had opened a hairline crack in the steel block securing the hold-down strap close to the torpedo's nose. The second impact broke the block clean through, and now two tons of Mark-48 were straining against a thin nylon strap as Red frantically ratcheted it tighter and tighter. Remson had his arms around the nose of the weapon, trying to steady it, hugging it for all he was worth.

The deck pitched decisively down.

'About fucking time,' said Remson. 'Hang onto this thing with me, Red. I think we got it beat.'

Red dropped the ratchet bar and positioned himself on the other side of the torpedo tray. He braced his broad back against the loading ram and the shifting weapon steadied. Then, he looked up. 'What's that noise?'

The great wave was hollowed by the screaming wind, ripping its crest off and filling it like an enormous black sail. It grew taller. Sixty feet, sixty-five, and then it began to topple.

An avalanche of green water buried *Portland*, driving the stern down and, the bow up and out of the water. As the wave foamed south, *Portland's* bow fell in a seven-thousand-ton belly flop.

The impact doubled Remson's vision. His wrench levitated off the deck, then tumbled away and struck a torpedo tube drain line. The pipe

71

broke, sending a jet of salt water across the room. The nylon strap holding the loose torpedo parted with the twang of a snapped piano string. It whipped over the top of the Mark-48 and caught Red full in the face, sending him sprawling to the decks with blood gushing from his mouth.

Remson saw the torpedo shift. He threw his whole body at it.

The Mark-48 rose clear off the tray. It stopped, suspended in midair, and then, two tons of steel, torpedo fuel and high explosive came down on Hank Remson's hand with the soft, muffled crunch of bone. His wedding ring guillotined off his finger swiftly and cleanly.

Remson had no sense of pain, no awareness of anything beyond the smooth steel skin of that Mark-48. There was no way he would let it go. No way. With his hand under its mass, he threw his shoulder against the torpedo to keep it from falling off the tray. It would not budge because he would not allow it.

He still had the cigar wedged into the corner of his mouth, he was still holding on when Red stood up, wiped the blood off his chin with the back of his hand, and with four other torpedomen, rolled the errant weapon off him.

An urgent call rang out through the submarine: 'Corpsman lay to the torpedo room! Corpsman lay to the torpedo room!'

Portland dove deep and fast. At three hundred feet it became possible to walk her decks without caroming off bulkheads. At four hundred nervous smiles reappeared. Though her air was

72

tainted by whiffs of spilled battery acid, vomit and ammonia, the submarine was under control, responding to the helm, in her element.

A line of sailors with sprains and bruises waited for the duty corpsman outside a makeshift sick bay set up on the mess deck. But Chief Cooper, *Portland's* only doctor, was too busy with Remson to see them.

'You know what kept that fucking torpedo from dropping off that fucking tray?' said Red. 'The COB.' His face still dripped sea water and blood.

Chief Cooper and the torpedoman helped Remson down to his bunk in the Goat Locker, the senior chief's lair. The chief of the boat still had the soggy stub of his cold cigar clenched in the corner of his mouth. 'COB,' said the corps-man, 'You know what I gotta do, right?'

Remson looked up as Cooper prepared a hypodermic. 'Quit blowin' smoke. You got other guys waiting to hold your fucking hand.'

'You'll sleep now.' Cooper found the vein and slid the needle in. He was preparing Remson for a major operation. He was preparing himself, too. He was trained to handle everything from heart attacks to food poisoning, even depression and minor surgery. One look at Remson's left hand told him that this would not be minor.

'Fucking Hollywood,' said Red.

'Skipper doesn't make the waves, Red,' said Cooper.

'He took us into them, didn't he? COB told him there was a loose fish. Did he fucking listen?'

'I need your help, not your opinions.' Chief Cooper was a serious man in bright, steel-framed

73

glasses. His blond hair was so closely cut it resembled a kind of white bristle. He exuded confidence, which experience had taught him was as therapeutic as anything in his small pharmacy. 'Get my bag and open it. Try not to bleed on anything.'

Red unzipped the medical bag and placed it gently beside Remson's thigh. COB's eyes were still open. 'There's something *evil* living on this boat, chief. I tell you what. We've seen nothing but shit ever since she came on board.'

'Who?'

'The skipper's girlfriend.'

'She's not his girlfriend, asshole.'

'And *Portland*'s not a fucking jinx boat, either.'

Cooper cut Remson's shirt away and tossed it to a nearby bunk. The soggy mass of red and black lay wadded against a bulkhead. He erected a small curtain to keep Remson from seeing the shredded flesh and crushed bones. 'Feeling okay?' When Remson didn't answer, he plucked the sodden cigar and tossed it to the deck. He turned to the torpedoman who'd helped carry him up from below. 'The knife.'

'Shit,' said the torpedoman as he passed the scalpel to Cooper. 'You can't put it on ice or something and sew it back on?'

'Hand me that knife or find someone who can.'

There was a knock, and the door to the Goat Locker opened.

Cooper turned. It was the captain.

Steadman came in and spotted the bloody rags, the two men standing over Remson. *My God*, he thought, *Is there this much blood in the world?* He

74

shut the door behind him. 'How is he?'

'In shock and sedated,' said Cooper. 'His ring cut off a finger and the bones in his hand were crushed.'

'I guess we musta' hit a wave or something,' said Red. 'Sir.'

Steadman could see the fury in the torpedo-man's eyes. 'COB said there was a stripped bolt. Did you get it replaced?'

'Yeah,' said Red. 'Twice. But the whole block came apart on us. I had a nylon web around the fish and it let go in my face. The only thing keeping that fish from rolling off the tray was the COB.'

Steadman turned to Cooper. 'Can you save his hand?'

'I'm trying to save his life. Excuse me, but I've got to cut.'

Remson swiftly finished the amputation begun by the errant torpedo, cutting through flesh and sinew fragments. One white spur resisted the blade. He looked up at Red. 'Bone saw.'

Steadman tried to shut his ears against the grating of the saw.

Cooper grunted once as he leaned over Remson. When he straightened, he had a something in his hands that resembled a waterlogged wool glove, heavy and limp.

The intercom chirped. Steadman picked it up. 'Steadman.'

'Captain?' said Banjo. 'Eyes only message from COMSUBLANT.'

'Okay, I'll be right there,' said Steadman.

CHAPTER FOUR

FORWARD DEPLOYMENT

USS *Portland*

Steadman went aft along the mid-deck, stopping to check in with the injured men waiting outside the mess area. Submarines aren't built with violent motion in mind. They're full of sharp, dangerous objects. One machinist mate from the boat's Auxiliary Gang had been thrown against a lubrication pump hard enough to knock himself out. Steadman could see he was still more than a little dazed. *Concussion?* He detailed someone to take him forward to the Goat Locker, then hurried up the ladder to the top deck and the radio shack.

The radio room's door was always kept locked. The idly curious were discouraged by serious security warnings. Even the captain had to knock. The bolts were thrown open and the door cracked wide. Steadman went in.

The small space smelled of hot electronics and half-digested breakfast. Steadman didn't need to ask any questions. He could see Scavullo's face.

'Hot off the printer, skipper.' Banjo handed it to Steadman.

There were just six lines, and they changed everything. For Steadman, for *Portland*. Most of all for six men waiting for a rescue.

76

There was a knock at the door, then Tony Watson leaned into the radio shack. 'I'd like a word with you, Captain.'

'Something wrong?'

'I'd prefer to speak to you privately.'

'Okay. In my cabin.'

There were four doors in the portside passage forward of the control room: one to the captain's stateroom, the officer's head and the XO's cabin to the left, and a single door to the sonar shack to the right. At the forward end, a ladder guarded by a chain dropped to the middle deck.

Steadman's cabin wasn't much bigger than a walk-in closet, paneled with imitation wood and with a bunk that could be made up into a booth and table. The chrome trim, the blue vinyl, the paneling gave it the feel of a cheap motor home, not a billion-dollar warship. A multifunction display mounted near the bunk was crowded with data; depth, course and speed projected onto a map of the Atlantic.

Steadman shut the door. 'All right. I'm listening.'

'We're not the search and rescue arm of the United States Air Force. You know about the torpedo block. It'll take us days to figure out what else got broken.' He glanced at the orders in Steadman's breast pocket. 'You know how many *miles* of pipe are on this boat?'

'I know who to ask.'

'You heard the Coast Guard pilot. The winds are pushing that raft so fast we'd have to chase them on a flank bell to catch up. And then what?

Wallow around up on top and lasso them as they surf by?'

'Tony...'

'Commander, bottom line is if you take us up into that storm again, I'll have no choice but to put my recommendations against it in the log.'

'Here.' He tossed the paper down onto the table. 'Read.'

Watson picked it up.

Z090043Z10OCT2005
NLOB*NLOB*NLOB
FM: COMSUBLANT
TO: CO USS PORTLAND
SUBJ: SPECIAL OPERATIONS

1: ABORT RESCUE OPS EFFECTIVE
    RECEIPT THIS MESSAGE
2: TRANSIT GIBRALTAR SUBMERGED
    BEST SPEED FOR FORWARD
    DEPLOYMENT E. MEDITERRANEAN
3: REPORT O/S CAPE SPERONE 8E 38N
    NO LATER THAN 00z 12 OCTOBER
4: PORTLAND TO RDV WITH HELO CALL
    SIGN SOURDOUGH SIX FOR
    INSERTION DET ONE, PLATOON
    BRAVO, SEAL TEAM EIGHT
5: PORTLAND TO COMMENCE VBSS OPS
    E. MED
6: UNODIR PORTLAND WILL TAKE ALL
    PRUDENT MEASURES TO AVOID
    DETECTION BY SUB/SURFACE UNITS
    DURING MED OPS
7: THIS IS NOT NEGOTIABLE – MOVE

Watson looked up. 'These orders are screwy.'

They sure are, thought Steadman. It was one thing to be 'forward deployed' and another to be sent into an entirely new *ocean.* And VBSS stood for Visiting, Boarding, Searching and Seizing; stopping suspect ships and checking them for illegal cargo, immigrants, drugs or weapons; duty more suited to a third-world patrol boat than a nuclear submarine. Sending *Portland* out to inspect suspect cargo was akin to assigning a billion-dollar stealth bomber to report traffic conditions.

The intercom buzzed.

'Captain, Conn.' It was Navigator Pardee.

Steadman picked it up. 'Go.'

'Skipper, we're fifteen miles away from where that Coast Guard pilot last saw the raft. They've probably gotten blown another couple of miles since. I recommend we put on some turns and get ahead of them before we surface. That way the wind will push them back at us. We can shoot a line and drag them into our lee.'

Fifteen miles. He looked at the orders, seeking some maneuvering room. He wanted to grab the admiral by his stars and demand an explanation. But to radio his misgivings would require surfacing, and surfacing *once* had proven too costly. 'Stand by, Nav.' He looked to his XO. 'What else do you want to say about these orders?'

'First, where's the chart package from Squadron? They can't just send us into the Med without a deconflicted route. How do we know there won't be another submarine in our way?

And there's no chop line. The Med is Sub Group Eight's sandbox. They can't send us in there without Naples knowing we're coming.'

'Apparently they can.' Steadman had noticed this omission, too. The usual 'change of operations' chop line that spelled out who he'd report to in a new area was missing. The Med was *supposed* to belong to Rear Admiral Steven Stanley, Commander, Submarine Group Eight.

Slinking through Gibraltar submerged and not letting him know was odd, but for Watson to focus on it was like noticing peeling paint in a house that was on fire. 'That's all that strikes you as screwy?'

'No.' Watson waved the orders in the air as though dispelling an odor. 'This whole deal is irregular. It doesn't just violate good practice. It violates Navy regs. They can hang us if we *accept* these orders.'

'What would you do? Tell the admiral thanks but no thanks?'

'I'd request *in writing* that they clear the way with SUBGRU Eight and make sure there's an up-to-date nav package ready for us at La Maddalena. That way it's on *Norfolk's* head, not yours. *Or mine.* But there is one good thing. These orders get us off the hook out here.'

'I doubt those six men would agree.' He read the orders again. *This is not negotiable – Move your boat ... Graybar sends.* Steadman took a long breath, let it out, then clicked the intercom. 'Nav?'

'Captain?'

'Plot a course for Gibraltar.'

'Gibraltar? But–'

'Do it.' Steadman slammed the microphone into its cradle. He turned to his exec. 'Survey the boat for damage. I want your report by the end of the watch.'

'There's a lot to check out, Captain.'

'Then you'd better get started.'

As Remson slept, Chief Cooper held doctor's hours in *Portland*'s mess deck. An old wooden sign hanging over the entrance proclaimed it the 'Captain Dan's'. On it, an old toot of a fisherman in yellow oilskins stared across a rolling sea with a red pipe clamped in his teeth. Someone must have found it in some tourist shop and thought it looked appropriately Down East for a boat named *Portland,* though no one would admit to it.

The Captain Dan's was the largest single open space in the boat, and between sailors coming off watch looking for something to eat and those needing medical attention, every one of its thirty seats was filled. Cooper bandaged sprains, checked for broken bones and treated minor burns while the cooks tried to clean up and get ready for a meal.

For once the mess area lived up to its name. The decks were splattered with spilled orange and purple bug juice, straws, wooden stir sticks and condiment packages. An avalanche of frozen pizza threatened to spill from the deep freeze every time the door was cracked. The best the cooks could do was throw piles of sandwiches and sweet rolls up on the counter while they tried to restore some kind of order.

Sonarman Second Class Ron Niebel took in

81

the scene and almost decided to turn around when he spotted Banjo Gant. Niebel was known as 'Socks' to his crewmates, though only a few knew why. He grabbed a sweet roll, splashed a ceramic mug full of coffee and slid into a booth across from him. 'Jesus. That was some ride.'

'I knew it was gonna' be bad but not *that* bad.'

'Our div officer was yelling like he was riding a bucking bronco or something,' he said, meaning Lieutenant Kelso, the sonar division officer. 'I think the bastard *enjoyed* it.' He took a bite of his bun. 'You heard one of the fish broke loose? COB wrestled it down. The XO is pissed.'

Banjo raised an eyebrow. 'Because the COB got hurt or because a fish broke loose?'

'Yeah. A nuke's a nuke. If it ain't glowing they don't give a slit.' Niebel took another bite of sweet roll. 'You get the radios fixed?'

'We have a serious case of the gremlins.'

'Gremlins are what you get on a jinx boat. Which is what *we* are in case you didn't know.'

'What jinx?'

'Like *Jacksonville*. They did this burial at sea ceremony for some rag hat diesel submariner. They were supposed to scatter his ashes at sea, only they ended up getting sucked down the snorkel. The next night? *Bang!* She gets run down by a tanker. *That* kind of jinx.'

'What's *Jacksonville* have to do with us?'

'Who were we tied up next to in Groton? *Jacksonville*. If you ask me, that gremlin got bored and jumped ship. Or got himself invited.'

Banjo was not inclined to believe in dark spirits. But he *had* spent a lot of time running down a radio problem to no effect. 'I hope not.'

'I hear we're going to put COB off in the Azores.' Socks was fishing. Banjo wasn't biting.

'Come on. What's the deal? Where are we going?'

'Skipper will announce it.'

'Hollywood will be lucky if they let him keep his job after that little performance. But then, he's the guy who brought the jinx on board.'

'By docking next to *Jacksonville?*'

'By pulling strings and having Scavullo ride the boat with him again. When did bad shit start to happen to us? When she showed up.'

'That was a year and a half ago.'

'And I was here for *that* ride. You heard what happened.'

'Sea stories.' *Sea stories* were the naval equivalent of fairytales, only less truthful.

'Now this is a no shitter. She was shacking up in the XO's stateroom and playing around with the radioman at the same time.'

'No way.' Neither one was the sort of thing he could easily imagine from Lieutenant Scavullo. And of course, that XO was now *Portland's* captain. 'Are we talking about the same lieutenant?'

'You know another rider with tits? She played with Tincher's head so bad he put a *gun* to it and pulled the trigger.'

'Tincher? I went to A-school with the guy. Had a pirate's mustache and called himself Pasha?'

'That's him. Or was.'

'He *shot* himself?'

'In front of everyone right up in Control. *Bang!* I mopped up his brains. Can you imagine what

83

she had to do to make a bullet look better?'

Banjo had heard some crazy talk about *Portland's* last run, but not *that* crazy. 'Where'd Tincher get a gun?'

Got him. Niebel ate the last of his sticky bun, then washed it down with coffee. 'I might tell you the whole story some day. You know. Trade.'

'Sure.' Banjo looked at his watch. 'I gotta go.'

'Go.' Niebel waved. 'Before you do think about this: you could get her yanked off the boat and take our bad luck with her.'

'Me?'

'What do you think would happen if she went crying to the CO that you grabbed her ass?'

'I'd be gone *yesterday.*'

'Correct. Now run it backward. What do you think would happen if a guy said *she* was making moves on *him?* An officer *harassing* an innocent radioman? You don't think someone would jump all over that?'

'But she's not harassing anyone.'

Niebel sighed. 'Well, just think about it is all I'm saying. So where's it gonna' be? The Azores or Groton? A or B?'

'C,' said Banjo, and he got up and left.

It was like those hot summer days at Old Orchard beach, a hundred degrees and humid, water in the fifties. Scavullo would run straight into the icy ocean and dive in. She'd rise, spluttering with cold, then race back out to the sand to bake. Her skin would be numb, prickled with goosebumps, with a throbbing ice-cream headache.

The air-conditioned breeze blowing down on

her from the radio shack vents felt arctic. She smelled of vomit. Her limbs were trembling. She had to get out of her soiled overalls and into something clean and warm.

She left the radio shack, turned aft and climbed down the ladderwell to the middeck. She hurried by the mess area and wardroom, hoping no one would see her. Sailors were not predisposed to kindness when it came to weak stomachs. They'd show up at her bunk with open tins of sardines smothered in chocolate syrup and marshmallows if they thought it would get to her. And it would.

Her bunk was in the front row of junior officers' berthing on the bottom, starboard side. It was six feet long, three wide and two feet tall; in other words, the size and shape of a cheap casket, with barely enough room to climb in and sleep. There was no question of sitting up in bed, though it was possible – just – to change clothes in there with some determined acrobatics. The rack was equipped with a light for reading, an audio jack, a few shallow cabinets and an air vent she kept tightly closed.

Underneath the mattress pan was a shallow steel tray for her clothes and gear. Instead of the usual single blue thin curtain, a heavy fabric blanket enclosed her entire bunk. It was supposed to be a bit less prone to 'accidentally' open.

Scavullo knelt down, pulled out the clothes tray and automatically reached in for a fresh set of khakis.

And stopped.

Atop the neat rows of pants and blouses, beside the orderly rank of socks and underwear, was a pair of gray Jockey Hipsters with *Scavullo* written in indelible ink inside the waistband. Someone had cut away the cotton fabric to transform the plain and deliberately unerotic panties into a thong. Then, to make sure she understood, they'd taken a red marker and drawn a crosshaired periscope circle on what remained of the crotch.

She stared at it as though it might vanish if she looked away. The old captain would have laughed this thing off. Everything was supposed to be different now, except that it wasn't. She slammed the steel tray shut and stood, furious. Half of her hoped she'd spot some snickering sailor, the other half worried that if she gave in to that it would be the end of women riding the boats forever.

She saw, instead, the boat's Executive Officer.

Tony Watson was heading aft. The passage was narrow and Lieutenant Scavullo was in his way. He seemed surprised to see her, as though a piece of unrequisitioned equipment had showed up at pierside without operating instructions, without NAVSEA documentation, without any obvious reason at all. Finally, he said, 'Is everything all right, lieutenant?'

No! The XO was *supposed* to be the officer you took your problems to, but Scavullo didn't trust him. 'Yes, sir.'

'Your radio gear make it through those aquabatics?'

'I ... I don't know. I haven't had a chance to check it all out.'

'I'm making an inventory of damaged equipment so I'll need something in hand. But

86

between you and me you can take your time. You won't be needing any intercept gear. Not where we're going.'

'But ... why is that?'

'Your mission got canceled. We're not going north. I can't tell you where we *are* going,' said Watson. He tried to keep even a hint of smugness from his voice and very nearly succeeded. 'But I can say there won't be any Russians to listen to. You'll be a passenger until we manage to put you off the boat.'

Scavullo thought about what she'd found in her tray. She was plenty anxious to leave, but not under fire. It was one thing to turn your back. Another to run. 'Do you know when that might be, sir?'

'No. You're just lucky I'm not captain. I'd have you washing dishes for the duration.'

You bastard. 'Well sir, I've washed dishes before,' she said, trying to keep even a hint of disrespect from her voice and very nearly succeeding. 'And besides, you're not the captain.'

His face turned hard and icy. Her words seemed to ricochet right off, though they did not. 'And I have you to thank for that, don't I?'

'I don't screen prospective commanders, sir.'

'You just sink them. I don't expect you to understand this, but *Portland*'s last CO was a good submariner. You got him thrown right out of the Navy.'

'Sir, a good submariner doesn't order an enlisted man to assault an officer. He did and he was caught.'

'You saw those orders, lieutenant?'

'You know they weren't in writing.'

'A good engineer believes only what's proven. You haven't made the case. Get that damage report to me, and lieutenant?'

'Sir?'

Watson took a sniff, then wrinkled his nose. 'You might want to change.' He tried to pass her and when she didn't step aside fast enough he snarled, 'Make a hole.'

'Yes, sir,' she said. She slowly eased to one side and Watson stormed by, heading aft for the sanctity of the reactor spaces like something was chasing him.

The officers' wardroom is just forward of the crew's mess. It was more than just a place for *Portland's* thirteen officers to take their meals. It was their office, their classroom, an emergency operating room in a pinch, and their sanctuary. The bulkheads were paneled with imitation ash. The deck was aggressively waxed linoleum, though most of it was hidden by a large table. The table was covered with a blue, non-skid pad on which USS *Portland Officers' Wardroom* was stenciled, as though someone might look in and mistake it for anything else.

The wardroom was nearly always bustling. Not now. Other than a sailor from the A-Gang busy mounting a large plasma video screen that had broken free in the storm, Steadman had the place to himself.

He sat at the table with a mug of coffee. The lighting was cool and fluorescent. Green plants chosen for their ability to survive neglect hung from hooks secured up in a maze of wire bundles, air ducts, diffusers and yellow battle lanterns. Steadman pulled the orders out of his pocket and reread them.

'Almost finished,' said the A-ganger. 'It'll be good as new, skipper.'

Steadman looked up. What had he just said? He was about to ask when there was a knock at the door.

Lieutenant Scavullo opened it and looked in. Her face was waxy and pale, her dark hair stuck to her forehead with sweat. 'I'll come back.'

'Come ahead.' He folded up their orders and put them away. 'I want to hear what you've done about nailing our radio problem.'

She glanced at the A-ganger. Inside ten minutes the word would spread through the boat that she and the captain were having a private chat. But she stepped into the room and closed the door. 'Very well.' She walked to the urn and poured a mug of hot water.

'Rough ride?'

She looked down at her stained blue coveralls. 'I was going to change, but...' Scavullo stopped. 'Banjo tried to warn me. I didn't listen.'

'When a petty officer first class speaks it's wise to pay attention.'

She sat down across from Steadman. 'Is COB going to be all right?'

The sailor repairing the screen bracket stole a quick glance at them, then turned away as though he'd accidentally seen something forbidden.

Steadman chose his words carefully. 'He's stable. What he needs most is a real hospital.'

'Done,' said the A-ganger as he rolled up a cloth bag of tools. He hurried out into the passage and closed the door very, very gently.

'Then it's just as well we aren't going north,' she said.

Steadman cocked his head in surprise. 'Who told you that?'

'The XO did.'

'Mister Watson should know better than that.'

'He wanted to make sure I knew my mission was over.'

'I see.' Steadman turned to make sure the door was truly closed. 'Well, whatever he thought he was doing, he's right. We're going east.'

'To the Azores?'

I *wish*. 'No.'

She put her steaming water down. 'But you said COB needed a hospital. The nearest one *has* to be in the Azores.'

It was. *Ponta Delgada, and from there to Lajes Field and a fast flight back to the States.* They'd have to sail *right by it* on the way to Gibraltar. 'I drive the boat. Norfolk says where it goes.'

'But you're the captain. You can decide to...'

'A captain's word used to be law, lieutenant. Now I've got admirals sitting on my shoulders second guessing every move. Even in the middle of a goddamned hurricane.' He took a swallow of bitter black coffee.

'But what about COB?'

'Don't you think I told the admiral about him?' he snapped. 'If it were up to me we'd be steaming towards the Azores right now. If it were my call we'd have those six men on board. Or a *damned*

90

good reason why we couldn't.'

'I'm sorry. Of course.' His tone told her to back off, and she did. She sipped from her mug. 'The XO said I'd leave the boat when we put in. Can you say if that will be soon?'

Steadman was surprised. She seemed to like the idea of leaving *Portland*. 'Why? Are you in a hurry?'

She stiffened. 'No, sir. But there's not much reason to send a Russian linguist where there aren't any Russians to listen to. And it might make everything go easier. For me and for you.'

'For me? How is that?' *Let it be something in the radio system.*

Now she was the one compelled to choose words carefully. 'Captain, do you ever think about what happened on our last run together? Hitting that *Typhoon* under the ice and following her all the way to the Pacific...'

'Yes I do. Why?'

'When we got back, after the investigation, I figured, that's it. One way or the other it was over. They might not throw me out of the Navy, but they'd never let me back on board another boat. They surprised me.'

'They surprised me, too. Still, I'm glad that's over with.'

'Yes sir.' She paused, then said, 'But it's *not*. I went to my rack to change. Someone tampered with my personal items.'

'Oh?' Steadman's eyebrows bunched as though he'd taken a bite out of something unpleasant.

The door to the wardroom opened, a nuke lieutenant from the engineering division started

91

in but then he saw Steadman and Scavullo. 'Sorry,' he said, quickly backed away and closed the door.

'What kind of tampering, lieutenant?'

'Someone cut my underwear up and wrote a message on them.'

Not again. 'Have you told the XO?'

'I don't think it would do much good.'

Steadman might have differences with Tony Watson but he was not going to undermine him. 'The XO's a straight shooter, lieutenant. You just have to prove yourself. If you can he'll respond correctly.'

'I just saw him and with all due respect, you're wrong. Even if I had all the evidence in the world. He thinks he missed selection for commander because of me.'

'He actually said that? In *words?*'

'Yes sir. Believe me. The last thing I would want is to hand him my head as a trophy. But you two have to be able to work together. *Portland* depends on that. If you try to stamp out whatever is brewing among the crew over me being here, it could turn into...' she paused, 'something like the last time. And nothing is worth running that risk, sir. Nothing.'

'You think there's something brewing then?'

'Maybe it's an isolated prank. But if there isn't something going on now there will be if I stay aboard.'

'You'd let them run you off? I'm surprised.'

Her eyes flashed. 'Nobody's running me anywhere. But there's no mission for me now, no reason to be the center of this kind of attention.'

Her argument made sense, though whether Admiral Graybar would agree was another matter. 'Very well. I'll forward your request with my recommendations. In the meantime, I'd like you to go back to work.'

'What work is that?'

'Take on the intermittent problem we've been having with our radios. Find it and eliminate it. That's your new assignment.'

'But I'm a linguist, not an electronics tech.'

'As you said, we don't need a linguist where we're going. We *do* need someone who knows their way around our radios and this way you won't be sitting on your hands.' *Or wondering what people are whispering.* 'If you nail that glitch you'll earn everyone's thanks, mine especially. That will make another submarine slot possible. You want that, don't you?'

'Of course, but...'

'In the meantime I'll send up your transfer request. Fair enough?'

He didn't understand. She wasn't just looking out for herself. If something blew up now it would be *his* skin, too. 'I guess so.'

'I'm glad that's settled.'

Scavullo nodded and got up. But as she left the wardroom she thought, *You may be the only one who thinks so.*

CHAPTER FIVE

SHELL GAME

10 OCTOBER
MV *Nova Spirit*
Off Fil Burnu Lighthouse, Turkey

Though most of the world's maritime freight rides immense container ships, there's still work for small, unscheduled vessels carrying mixed cargoes to out-of-the-way ports; molasses to Spain, scrap steel to China, rags to Egypt, or undocumented people fleeing poverty or war for anywhere else. Like the old tramp steamers they resemble, these 'break bulk' ships have no regular routes. They fly a bewildering array of flags of convenience. Their ownership is kept deliberately opaque.

Eleven of them rode at anchor a mile off the lighthouse marking the northern terminus of the Bosporus Strait, waiting for the mandatory safety inspection required for passage to the Mediterranean. Painted in faded colors and rust, they were all one honest inspection away from the scrapper's torch.

At the head of the line was a 2000-tonner, owned by Lebanese and launched from a Polish yard in the 1970s. She had the blunt icebreaker bow of a ship built for northern seas. A blocky gray deckhouse was set aft. A freshly painted gold stripe on her single funnel gleamed like a bracelet in a battered toolbox. The stack was raked in a jaunty way that suggested speed and efficiency. The painted shell hid two corroded pipes, one the engine air intake, the other its sooty exhaust. A hatch in its bottom led down to the 'fidley'; a raised half-platform in the engine room.

Her main deck was buried under piles of salvaged drill pipe taken from a stripped-out oil field near Baku. A yellow loading crane towered amidships, giving her a dangerous, top-heavy appearance that shouted *capsize*. She flew the red and white flag of Tonga; a Pacific island nation favored by ship owners who found Panamanian registry overly restrictive.

She'd sailed from the Georgian port of Sukhumi as the MV *Nova Spirit,* bound for a scrap metal yard on the island of Malta. Out in the middle of the Black Sea, far from ship and shore, she received a radio message from her owners in Beirut. Her single diesel clattered to a stop. She drifted before a light southwest wind while the crew broke out buckets and brushes and painted over the name on her stern. The red and white flag of Tonga came down. The white, gold and green banner of Cyprus was raised. *Nova Spirit* was gone. She was now the MV *Cristi.*

Three ships up the line was another 2000-ton tramp owned by the same Lebanese syndicate. She'd departed the Black Sea port of Sochi as the MV *Cristi* with forty thousand sacks of powdered cement, six cargo containers lashed on deck and four passengers: Makayev, Salafi and his two Chechen bulls. She was crewed by eleven

95

Pakistanis and captained by a Somali.

Like her sister ship up the line, she'd been built in the same Gdansk yard, had the same aft deckhouse, same false stack, the same midships crane. She'd also steered for a quiet spot in the middle of the Black Sea, shut down her engines and drifted. Then she shed her name and flag. Down came Cyprus. Up went Tonga. For a few hours there were two *Cristis* adrift on the Black Sea. Then balance was restored, and the *Nova Spirit* was reborn.

The new *Nova Spirit* had been designed and built by Communists but her layout conformed to a more traditional maritime hierarchy. From the small bridge set atop the 'iron house', the ship's Somali captain could look over the roof of the cargo crane all the way to the wave shield at the bow. Open wings extended to port and starboard, overhanging the main deck below. The radio and chart cubicle occupied a tight passage aft of the bridge. It ended at a watertight door that opened onto the lifeboat deck. The wooden boat was once brilliant orange, but salt and sun had faded it to pastel.

An interior ladderwell from the bridge dropped down to the cabin deck. The captain's stateroom was forward. Makayev and Salafi occupied the two middle cabins, with Adnan and Musa sharing one of the smaller ones aft. The door to the last cabin, an armory stuffed with enough weapons to equip a hundred men, was kept locked.

The galley deck below was a large space equipped with an ornately carved wooden bar. In deference to the Muslim crew, it was kept draped with a white sheet useful for showing movies. A forward watertight door opened out to the main deck, another aft led directly to the fantail where five times each day the entire crew, from lowliest oiler to Captain Warsame, gathered for their prayers.

Belowdecks was the hot, oily realm ruled by Engineer Assad, who sat at his gray metal desk on the fidley deck like a king on a throne. In response to the engine telegraph he could reach back to the controller, twist knobs, flip switches and alter the flow of fuel and air to the Polish-built MAN diesel. The Pakistani crew lived and slept forward of the three cargo holds in a warren of bunks built into the ship's bow, and below all were the oil tanks that spread their smell and taste into the old ship's every crack and cranny. In Russian, the oil was called *mazut;* the cheapest, heaviest, dirtiest fuel that could be coaxed to burn.

The air inside Makayev's stifling cabin smelled of fuel oil. The water that reluctantly spurted from the tap at his small, steel sink tasted of it. Makayev's sweaty skin was slick with it. In military biology, absolute cleanliness was a matter of life and death, but what options did he have? Salafi had told him to stay here, hidden, until the Turks conducted their safety inspection.

Now here he was in a hot, airless cabin, alone and waiting for some bright future to materialize. It reminded him of his last days in medical school.

The graduating class of the Grozny Institute for Biomedical Sciences had few choices. They could apply for a position in European Russia and be turned down or they could 'volunteer' to work at a local clinic where the local religious chief, the *imam,* held more authority than any doctor. Places where a physician who dared to conduct a physical examination of a pregnant woman without her husband present could reasonably expect to have his throat cut.

The Russians had an expression for such places: they were *where the Devil throws pancake parties.* Wild territory marooned in the past, where ancient, primitive demons ruled.

Makayev was a modern man, a man of evidence and reason and a militant atheist. He listened to Russian music. He had a Russian girlfriend. He was determined not to wait around to learn of his fate, but to grasp it, to steer it. And so when a notice was posted asking for volunteers to participate in a special national program in 'military medicine', he sensed new possibilities and signed his name.

The interview took place two weeks before graduation. It was May in Grozny. Spring, by the calendar, but a cold rain was trying hard to gather up enough enthusiasm to solidify into sleet. Naturally, the district heating plant that supplied the whole neighborhood had shut down three days before and the office he was shown to was cold as a crypt.

Like everyone else, Makayev wore heavy clothes meant for the weather, not the calendar; a thick wool coat, sweater, felt pants and boots. He sat down and waited, sending the occasional indignant puff of steam at the iced over window.

Finally, as the sky darkened and the streetlights

began to sputter on, as Makayev was starting to think that Mozdok might be a terrible place to practice medicine but it was better than Khasavyurt or Borozdinovka, the door opened and a tall, erect man dressed in dark suit and tie came in.

His clothes were unremarkable, but his hair and face instantly caught Makayev's attention. It might be sleeting in Grozny, but this fellow looked like he'd just come back from a long holiday in the tropics. His skin was deeply tanned, his wheat-blond hair streaked and sun-bleached. Even his bushy eyebrows. He hadn't known enough at the time to recognize the effects of sterilizing ultraviolet and peroxide.

The recruiter threw a briefcase onto the desk and sat down across from Makayev. 'So. You want to work on important matters?'

'Absolutely.' Makayev had just spent the winter holed up like a gopher. Here was a man from a *very* special national program indeed. A man who seemed to belong to a different species of human; a variant that enjoyed vacations at government spas, plentiful food and sunshine.

'I work for an organization attached to the Council of Ministers. We're looking for a few professionals on a test basis. I will tell you, it has nothing to do with hospitals, clinics or health care in the conventional sense. The cures we work on are more *international*. Still interested?'

The Council of Ministers? That was in *Moscow!* Makayev felt like one of Pavlov's experimental animals. The bell had just rung and it required great discipline to keep from salivating. 'Yes!'

The tanned gentleman chuckled, then proceeded to sketch out the broad outlines of a vast and secret government project to 'create biological defenses for the Motherland,' but he still hadn't told Makayev his name or rank. Who cared? Sign the papers the man slid across the desk and Makayev and Vera would be on their way to *Moscow*.

'One thing more,' the man said as Makayev reached for the pen. 'This is not a normal research position. This work is highly classified. You won't be able to discuss it with your family. You're married?'

'Not yet. But–'

'Do it soon. It makes life easier. You understand, there exists an international treaty that bans all work related to making or storing biological weapons. The Soviet Union signed this treaty and so did the United States. We know they're lying. They have an entire arsenal of germs. Now, do you have any doubts that they would use them to destroy us? That we must be able to defend ourselves no matter what form such defense might take?'

As children they'd all been taught that the capitalist world would stop at nothing in its mad quest to destroy the Soviet Union. But Makayev prided himself on believing nothing without a firm evidentiary chain. What did he know about the Americans? Less than nothing. Still, this was a test and he was not about to fail. 'No doubts.'

The interviewer passed the pen across the desk. 'Then sign.'

A week later, Makayev was called to the school's administrative office. A letter of authority had arrived. He was to exchange it for a train ticket and travel immediately. Not to Moscow, but to a place he'd never heard of before, a rural village southeast of the capital named Pokrov.

There, Makayev was issued with a white coat and given flasks to clean.

The director, a dour academician named Semyon Aranov, told him to forget the oath he'd taken as a Soviet physician. Making bioweapons was an industrial enterprise; a matter of formulas, processes and technique. 'You're no longer a doctor,' said Aranov. His face was tan, his dark hair streaked with yellow just like the man in Grozny.

This no longer seemed like the glow of health to Makayev. Aranov – a Jew, he noted – looked more like a photo that had been left in the developer too long. 'Then what will be my position?'

'This is a factory. You're a factory worker.'

Makayev nodded, wondering what he'd gotten himself into. He found out soon enough: when the spring 'testing season' arrived, he was assigned to the ten-man team bound for an island set in the middle of the Aral Sea in Kazakhstan; Rebirth Island, a testing site for bioweapons so loathsome, so utterly remote the Devil himself would think twice before throwing a pancake party there. The staff at Pokrov called it *Tmu Tarakhan:* the Kingdom of Cockroaches.

There was a sound from the passage outside his cabin. Makayev turned just as the door opened. It was Adnan, the bull with the quick, dark eyes and full bushy beard. 'Bring your briefcase.'

'Where are we going?'

Adnan grabbed Makayev and shoved him out the door. *'Hurry!'*

CHAPTER SIX

INTO THE MOUSETRAP

11 OCTOBER
USS *Portland*
To Gibraltar

Steadman couldn't ignore an admiral's orders without good reason, but he sure as hell could *bend* them. He took *Portland* well north of the direct route to Gibraltar. From here, above the submerged foothills of the East Azores Fracture Zone, he could make fast passage to Ponta Delgada and see Remson off to a good hospital.

All he required was a green light from Norfolk.

Steadman ordered the boat back up into the shallows. From a depth of fifty-eight feet, the satellite antenna atop the communications mast broke the surface and beamed up an urgent request to divert. It took less than six minutes for COMNSUBLANT to deny it. Chief Remson was not going to be put ashore at the closest port. And Scavullo's request to leave the boat received the same summary dismissal.

Steadman ordered *Portland* back into the deeps, turned his bow east and stepped on the gas. The submarine rocketed across the eastern Atlantic at nearly forty knots, putting 1200 miles of ocean astern in a day and a quarter. If Norfolk was going to force him to turn away from the Azores, from those six men in a raft, Steadman was going to burn atoms like it was the opening move of World War Three. He could only hope that when he arrived in the Mediterranean, he'd find a compelling reason waiting there.

He slowed down only long enough to put up the antenna and send Norfolk a second message requesting a medical divert. Scavullo would have to ride the boat a while longer, but the *instant* they found calm waters, Steadman wanted a helicopter standing by.

It took two attempts to get this message sent, for Scavullo had been no more successful in ousting the gremlin in *Portland's* radios than Banjo Gant. It was almost irritating that Admiral Graybar's reply came back so clearly: the only helicopter *Portland* could expect would be the one bringing out eight US Navy Special Warfare operators; the famous Sea, Air and Land Force known as SEALs. Remson, or his body, could ride it back out.

In any event, waters calm enough to surface and take Remson off by helicopter proved hard to find with a hurricane spinning in the Atlantic, and when the seas finally did ease they were hard by the gates of Gibraltar. Here, the ocean was churned not by storm, but by an armada of commercial shipping converging on one of the busiest maritime zones in the world.

The Strait is a thirty-six-mile-long waterway connecting the Atlantic with the Mediterranean. It divides southernmost Spain from northernmost Morocco. Its entrance to the Atlantic is twenty-seven miles wide, but like a funnel, it narrows to barely eight at Gibraltar itself. Two hundred vessels of all sizes and descriptions thread this needle each day. International rules of the road are supposed to prevail, yet it remained a battle for position. Who goes first? Who is faster, bigger?

Supertankers barreled east and west, certain that no ship would dare contest passage. Freighters nosed in where they could while small cross-Strait boats, tugs and ferries darted among the crowded sea lanes like boys running through rush-hour traffic on a dare.

Steadman looked at the sonar repeater mounted in the control room and could see no way in. 'Sonar, Conn. Any gaps?'

'Conn, Sonar. None.' Bam Bam was looking at a solid wall of sound. 'I've got a conga line of targets from here to Bermuda.'

Gaps or no, they would have to find a way through, and soon. They had a date with a SEAL squad off Sardinia and it was just a day away. 'Keep track of the intervals. We may have to cut in line.'

'Aye aye.' Though Bam Bam didn't like the sound of that. *Portland*'s sonar supervisor was used to hunting for the faint beat of a nuclear submarine's heart, finding targets hidden by the fireworks of snapping krill shrimp, the rumble of distant undersea earthquakes, the eerie songs of whales. Now his world was filled with the slash of high-speed propellers, the majestic rumble of big ones, the rattle and squeal of bad shaft bearings and the endless, cataract roar of great ships plowing the sea; some of them large enough to carry *Portland* as deck cargo. Making sense of it was like trying to count cattle by listening to the thundering hooves of a stampede.

As Steadman prowled the hundred-fathom line off Cape Trafalgar, the contact evaluation plot on the forward bulkhead of Control became a spaghetti tangle of targets and ranges. He sat back against the rail of the periscope stand, listening to the heavy *swish ... swish ... swish* of big screws passing overhead.

'Sonar, Conn. Who was that, Bam Bam?' asked Steadman.

'Sierra Forty-Eight. She's got two screws turning for twelve knots, course zero nine three. Range four hundred yards and opening. And she's running empty, skipper.'

Empty? 'How can you tell?'

'Her mechanicals sound kinda' boomy and she's riding so high her screws are half out of the water. They're splashin' something fierce.'

Sonarman Niebel sat at the console next to Schramm. He pushed his headphones back and said, 'Boomy?'

'What can I say? It's a gift.'

'If the going rate for bullshit ever hits ten cents a pound, you're gonna' be rich, Bam Bam.'

'Never make ten cents a pound if you keep flooding the market. Your Sonar First Class test is coming up. Doing any studying at all?'

'I've been busy.'

With what? Schramm gave him a sour look. It was his job as sonar supervisor to make sure all his guys were making progress up the ladder. Niebel was smart enough to make first class, but

105

even lazier. 'You remember when old Iron Ass caught me pulling watch barefoot?' *Iron Ass* was their name for *Portland*'s former captain.

Niebel chuckled. 'He had the fucking Chief of the Watch call me out of my rack to relieve you 'cause,' and here Niebel's voice assumed a stiff, formal tone of reprimand, 'you can't stand a professional watch without your socks.' He grinned. 'What about it?'

'You took off your shoes, balled up your socks, threw them at me and walked away while Iron Ass sputtered like bacon in a fire.'

'What does that have to do with making First Class?'

'You ever think that might have been the high point of your Navy career?'

Niebel's grin vanished. 'Hey, I've got bigger worries than tests. Like living long enough to see the beach.'

'You got some disease I should know about?'

'Yeah,' said Niebel. 'You got it, too. We're both riding a fucking jinx boat.'

Steadman looked at the sonar repeater and thought, *It's amazing.* You could fill a dozen computers with an encylopedia of sound and never match what was inside a good sonar operator's head. The crew called them *sonar girls* because they thought sitting behind a green screen was ridiculously light duty. But there were times Steadman felt his main job was pointing *Portland* where Bam Bam would have her go.

'Conn, Sonar,' said Bam Bam.

Steadman picked up the microphone. 'Go.'

106

'There's something funny goin' on. Sierra Forty-Nine is inbound from the west, course zero eight five at twelve knots. But there's a gap opening up behind her. It was four thousand five hundred yards a minute ago. Now it's six thousand to the next target. And cross-Strait traffic to the north and south is pulling back, too. Like they're linin' up for a show.'

'What kind of ship is Sierra Forty-Nine?'

'Sounds like a big tanker with lots of hull under the water masking her screw and plant. Range is now fourteen thousand five hundred yards. The gap to Sierra Fifty is now *seven* thousand yards.'

Seven thousand yards. That was enough to slip *Portland* through. But what was spooking everyone? He said, 'Helm. Take us up to sixty feet. Turns for eight knots. All stations make ready for periscope depth.'

The approaches to Gibraltar were too shallow for deep running and so it didn't take long to reach sixty feet. When Pena reported ready, Steadman turned. 'Up the search scope.'

The wide-angle number two scope rose from its well. An enlisted Nav ET trained it west as Steadman did what submariners call 'the dance with the one-eyed lady'. He crouched, rising with the scope, ready to stop it the instant it broke the surface. The view was black, then green, then white. A wave drowned the lens, and then, frighteningly clear, Steadman saw the oncoming ship.

Her wide hull was black and her bow wave white. Looming above her deck was a huge, orange sphere. She looked like a domed stadium incongruously set out to sea. The giant's name,

Norman Lady, was clearly visible. *LNG tanker!* thought Steadman, LNG stood for liquefied natural gas, and from her size she likely held enough to turn the Strait into a sea of fire if someone put a hole in her side. 'Down scope!' Steadman snapped. 'Nav! Sounding!'

'Three hundred eighty feet, skipper,' Pardee replied.

'Helm! Take her down to three hundred feet *smartly!*'

'Three hundred feet smartly, aye!' said Pena. The young lieutenant didn't need to waste time wondering what the rush was about; the captain had just seen something bad.

Portland planed down away from the mottled light. He couldn't put *Portland* on the bottom without fouling water intakes and he couldn't stay shallow without getting run over. Nor was being run over the only risk. Hull suction from the deep-bellied *Norman Lady* could pull them up into a collision.

'Two hundred eighty feet.'

Steadman listened as the thump and thrash of the tanker's screws grew. He didn't need sonar to hear it.

'Three hundred feet. Leveling off.'

The rumble grew deeper, becoming less like machinery and more like the cataract crash and boom of a great waterfall.

'Permission to enter Control?'

Steadman turned aft. It was the XO, and from the thick file folder he was carrying, Tony Watson's post-hurricane survey of the boat's condition had uncovered some problems. 'Come.'

Watson nodded to Pardee as he passed the navigation table. He glanced at the charts, then walked forward to where Steadman was standing.

'Conn, Sonar. Here she comes.'

The sound of the laden tanker swelled. It became a heavy vibration cut by the whine of high-speed turbo-generators, the groan of thousands of tons of steel flexing under immense load.

Though she had nearly two hundred feet of water overhead, *Portland* was drawn up into the tanker's swirling wake, bobbing like a toy before settling back down to her proper depth.

'Sierra Forty-Nine's passing off the bow,' said Bam Bam.

Watson stopped, looked up. 'What the hell was that?'

'LNG supertanker. Everyone on top is giving her a wide berth. We're going to trail her through Gibraltar if Bam Bam approves.' Steadman clicked the intercom. 'Sonar, Conn. Do you have a good enough fix on Sierra Forty-Nine for us to remain well clear?'

Bam Bam thought long and hard before he answered. He knew what Steadman wanted to hear. He also remembered something the skipper had told him before they'd sailed from Groton: *The day will come when you get to tell me I'm full of shit. If that day comes and you don't, you've let us all down.* 'Conn, Sonar. If you're willing to take rudder orders from the sonar shack I can do it.'

Steadman smiled. 'Proceed.'

'Come right five degrees to zero nine five.'

Steadman said, 'Helm! Right five degrees rudder. Come to zero nine five degrees. Ahead

109

one third. Follow that tanker.' He looked back to Watson. 'What did you find out?'

'A couple of minor items, a few that aren't so minor and a lot we won't know about until we put in to take a look outside.'

That wasn't the answer Steadman was looking for, even if it might be strictly true. An XO was supposed to be more than just a spare captain ready to take over the helm in an emergency. A good XO makes a boat hum. Right now, Tony Watson wanted to play word games.

Steadman opened the folder. There was a cover page, an executive summary, a time line and a breakdown by department: Navigation/ Operations, Weapons, Engineering, and Supply.

One odd entry stopped him: a broken computer monitor that had come loose and crashed to the deck. It might be a problem in a fire-control console. But this was the machine in the mess deck the enlisted men used to play endless rounds of Doom.

Now that he was looking he found more oddities: a bow plane grease fitting that leaked, a pump that squealed, an annoying glitch in the radio system that came and went and no one could isolate. All of them were real, but each one had been written up in their presail inspection back in Groton. None of them had *anything* to do with surfacing in the middle of a hurricane. He closed the file and looked at Watson. 'I see some old squawks here. Why?'

'I thought it would be best to be complete.'

No, this is a bill of particulars against my judgment, and you wanted it as long as possible. 'Will anything

110

here keep us from making rendezvous off Sardinia tomorrow night?'

'That depends on how much risk you're willing to live with.'

'I want your engineering evaluation, XO.'

'My engineering evaluation is we need yard time to inspect the items we can't physically put our hands on.'

'Has the safety of the boat been compromised?'

Watson batted the ball right back, low and hard over the net. 'Any time we sail with something broken we compromise safety.'

'How does a broken video game compromise safety?' asked Steadman. 'No. Forget I asked. Unless you say otherwise, I'll assume there's nothing standing in the way of carrying out our orders.'

No one in Control actually turned to listen to them spar. And no one missed a single word.

'That's your call to make, Captain,' said Watson.

'And I just made it.'

And so with the way east guarded by a floating bomb of a ship no one wanted to get near, *Portland* merged into the flow of traffic, leaving the Atlantic behind for the sea German U-boat captains once called *The Mousetrap:* of the 62 U-boats sent to the Mediterranean via Gibraltar, not one ever made it back out.

In the half century since WWII, everything about the technology of submarines had changed, but the sea had not. The Mediterranean was very salty, and a deep, saline flow surged west through Gibraltar, spilling into the Atlantic abyss. Fresher, lighter water from the Atlantic rushed in along the surface. Knots of turbulence spun away in great whorls where the two currents met.

Portland squeezed through the eye of the needle, with Gibraltar to the north and Mount Acha to the south, bobbing in the turbulent wake of a gas tanker, trying to keep from broaching above and off the mud below. Finally, the *Norman Lady* turned northeast. Steadman listened to her sounds fade, then said, 'Nav? What course to Cape Sperone?'

'One one five, Captain.'

'Helm!' said Steadman. 'Right give degrees rudder. Come to one one five. All ahead *flank*.'

CHAPTER SEVEN

THE KINGDOM OF COCKROACHES

AFTERNOON, 12 OCTOBER
PK-16
Bosporus, Istanbul

The helmsman of the Turkish maritime patrol cutter *PK-16* checked his printed list. 'The last one today.' It was a little ship and very late. They would be within their rights to put her safety inspection off until tomorrow. 'We could let them wait.'

Inspector Aykul Erol glanced at his watch, then at the growing smudge of a freighter riding at anchor. There was an inverse but reliable rule: big ships were easy, little ones were trouble. A big ship with real owners and a legal cargo, you hardly needed to go aboard. But a small tramp flying a flag of convenience, stuffed with who knew what? They could be difficult. 'Who is she supposed to be?'

'*Nova Spirit*. Powdered cement for Alexandria. Tonga registry but Lebanese-owned.'

'Wonderful.' At least Tonga was a real island. Erol had inspected a Ukrainian freighter earlier in the day that was flying the flag of Mongolia; a country without a coast, without a river to the sea, without even a decent *lake*. You'd have to cut the ship apart and carry it by camel to its home port of Ulan Bator.

'Tomorrow, then?' asked the helmsman.

Inspector Erol considered his options. Board this tramp tonight and there was some chance the inspection would go smoothly. Put it off and he'd start tomorrow behind schedule. 'Let's tempt fate. Take us in.'

The helmsman swung the wheel over and steered the small, red and cream cutter for the anchored *Nova Spirit*. The sun was barely above the undulating line of the Levantine Hills, and the Maslak skyscrapers and Faith Sultan Mehmet Bridge were already scattered with lights.

Aykul Erol had been looking at ships all his life. It had been his profession for the last eighteen years as an inspector with the Turkish Maritime Police. To Erol there were good ships and problems. A good ship was a G-Class tanker owned by a real company with a real address. The

113

ship would be clean, the paperwork perfect. Her machinery would work. The crew would be competent and her master truthful.

Problems were more common. A problem would lose her steering and go aground, smash up a waterside mosque or worse, collide with a *good* ship and fill the Bosporus with burning oil. Arab ships were problems. Russian, Ukrainian and Romanian ships of the Black Sea fleet, they were problems, too. The crew would be thieves, illegals and worse.

'At least they're ready,' said the helmsman. 'You see it?'

'Yes.' A Jacob's ladder hung down the old freighter's side. Erol could see great scabs of rust on the freighter's sides. 'Come in easy. We don't want to put a hole in her.'

'She's going to sink sooner or later.'

'Later, and somewhere else I hope.'

The Montreaux Treaty allowed commercial ships free passage through the Bosporus, even though the Strait had become a kind of narrow alley running through the heart of Istanbul; a city of more than sixteen million. But it allowed Turkey to set certain conditions: pilots for large ships, and mandatory inspections for all.

Nova Spirit sat low in the water, but in reasonable trim. Aykul Erol could see a few containers lashed to her deck and his heart sank. Did they hold Japanese televisions? Poppies from Afghanistan? Stolen cars? Albanians hoping to swim to Italy? A nuclear missile? He'd have no choice but to look, for if he didn't and it turned out there was something a bit too interesting in them it

114

would be his neck.

The helmsman throttled back and swung the wheel. The cutter scraped to a stop against the dark hull.

He stepped out of the wheelhouse. *Nova Spirit's* load lines were in sight. *Check.* He grasped the tarry ropes of the Jacob's ladder and climbed. It turned his fingers brown. No doubt he'd be covered from head to toe before this was through, and his wife would shriek at him.

Five rungs up and he swung his legs over the rail and onto *Nova Spirit's* deck. He came face to face with four men. A tall, slender black man dressed in oily khakis and pink plastic sandals. A short, silver-haired businessman in a suit stood next to him. He might have been Lebanese or a dozen other Mediterranean possibilities. Behind them stood two common sailors, except Erol knew they weren't. Not from how they returned his gaze. Not from how they stood. One with a bushy beard, the other one's almost fancifully barbered. Escaped convicts? Army deserters? Bodyguards? If they were sailors then Aykul Erol was a ballerina.

He slipped a laminated checklist from his uniform jacket. 'I'm Inspector Erol. Where is the captain?'

'I am.' The tall black man stepped forward. 'Captain Warsame, master of the *Nova Spirit.*' Erol's doubts must have showed, because Warsame said, 'You haven't run across too many Somalis?'

'No.' Erol looked at the businessman. *Who was he? A passenger?* 'You've sailed through the Strait before, Captain?'

115

The African glanced at the businessman then said, 'This is my first passage south.'

'Ah.' *Why did you have to check?* He took out a pencil. 'Cargo?'

'Powdered cement from Sochi.'

'Destination?'

'Alexandria, Egypt.'

'An interesting port.' He always said that. 'Main and auxiliary engines?'

'Working,' said Warsame.

Check, and check. 'Emergency generator and steering gear?'

'Ready and standing by.'

Rusted and frozen in place. 'Windlass and anchor?'

'You can see for yourself' said Warsame. 'We've been riding at anchor for a long time now.'

Erol could make them wait a good deal longer if he felt like it. 'Any sickness to report on board? Any rats or rodents kept as pets?'

'Thank God, no sickness,' said Warsame, though he gave the silent businessman another questioning look. 'My crew work. They don't have time for pets.'

'Did anyone go ashore at Sochi?'

'No.'

Odd, thought Erol. It was hard to keep a tramp's crew on board in any port, much less one that promised so many interesting and illegal opportunities. What else would this black captain lie about? He decided to press him. 'You understand that if this inspection reveals dangerous cargo or contraband your ship may be seized and the crew imprisoned?'

'We understand that the Strait is an international waterway and that commercial ships have free passage,' said Sami Salafi. 'Naturally, if assistance is required we would accept any offers of help.'

Now we hear from you. 'You are...?'

'Abdul Hakeem. I represent the ship's owners,' said Salafi. 'Since this is the captain's first trip into the Black Sea, we thought it best to have someone look over his shoulder. You understand, I'm sure.'

Not really. *Abdul Hakeem* might as well be Arabic for John Doe. *And those two sailors are your bodyguards.* That made some sense, though not quite enough. An owner's representative riding a ship like this? 'Are you a ship's master, Mr Hakeem?'

'I'm a businessman. Import and export.'

'Then what advice are you qualified to give?'

'Only common sense. To do all that is required, obey the rules and keep the ship safe from unnecessary troubles.'

Erol looked at the containers lashed on deck. *Like those?* 'The deck cargo came on board at Sochi, too? What's in them?'

'STC used furniture,' said Captain Warsame.

STC meant *Said to Contain;* a manifest entry that was the legal equivalent of shrugged shoulders. Inspector Erol looked at the locks and chains on the containers. 'Perhaps we should go have a look.'

'As you like,' said Salafi.

As I must, thought Erol. He turned to the guard with the bushy beard. 'Open the inspection door on the forward starboard container.'

Adnan glanced at Salafi. The Saudi nodded,

and the Chechen started for the nearest box.

'Perhaps the *other* starboard container would be better?' Erol suggested. He wanted them to know that dressing two monkeys in sailor suits didn't teach them the difference between port and starboard. It wasn't a police matter, or more accurately, it wasn't going to be one. No. It was more a matter of professional pride.

He followed Adnan across the deck and over a fore and aft catwalk. With each step a ringing bell grew louder in his head. A company representative on a derelict ship no one could possibly care about. Some last-minute cargo loaded in a port where pirates, thieves and politicians were all the same. Two thuggish sailors who couldn't tell port from starboard. A master unwilling to speak a word without clearing it ahead of time. There was something going on, though Aykul Erol had little desire to personally solve this mystery.

Only last year a maritime policeman was killed in an inspection accident. He fell down a ladderwell into an empty hold. Aykul knew the man was famous for 'paper' inspections. He would never step foot belowdecks to examine a full hold much less an empty one, and yet there he was, his head on one side of a watertight door, his body on the other, his neck quite broken. It was difficult to imagine how he'd fallen to the deck, then made his way to the door and then managed to break his neck, but then, accidents could be mysterious.

Adnan took out a key and slipped it into a padlock securing the inspection door. It opened easily, and he stood back.

Erol put his hand to the flashlight hanging from a web belt. A good soldier develops survival instincts. A maritime inspector doesn't spend years looking at ships without developing some, too. He could go to that small metal door, point his light in and see what sort of used furniture the Egyptians were buying these days from Russia. He could also stick his hand into a basket of cobras. His instinct told him it would amount to the same thing.

He moved his hand away from the light. 'You've been delayed long enough.' He turned to the African captain and said the words that ended every inspection: 'Have a safe passage.'

'And thank you for *your* cooperation, inspector,' said the African.

Aykul Erol had done his duty. *No. Not quite.* There was one final administrative chore to see to: he'd write up a suspicious activities report from the safety of his office, first thing in the morning.

Makayev's shoulder ached where Adnan had grabbed it. Salafi would hear of this. Someone had to remind them who was in charge. He stopped and listened. What was going on outside on deck.

Adnan had hustled him to this dark cargo container and locked the door. It was only by accident that Makayev had found a flashlight in among plastic bags filled with dried fruits and nuts. Then, the inspection panel swung open and the low afternoon sun beamed straight in. If someone had bothered to look they would have seen Makayev blinded by the glare, hands up, retreating back into the dim interior. His first thought had been, *It's over.* And his next was a hope that the police would let him shower before they threw him into a cell.

But there were no shouts of alarm, no police, no arrest, and he was left more puzzled than afraid. Then the small inspection door swung shut and the darkness returned. Was it possible they'd missed him? Why was he still locked in? Though Makayev had to admit that if he had to be held a prisoner in a windowless steel box, this was not such a bad one.

The shipping container with SEALAND painted on the outside was roomier than his cabin. There was the light he'd found, a cardboard box full of preserved foods, ventilation holes that drew fresh air from underneath the container's floor. A pair of stacked bunk beds, a chemical toilet. In short, other than that locked door, it was business-class accommodation for any illegal immigrant.

There was even a change of clothes, and given the state of his own he was tempted to change into them. Two dark blue dock worker's uniforms hung from pegs on the bunk bed, both with photo ID security badges. The badges carried the golden compass rose of the Malta Maritime Authority. One showed Adnan's face, the other Musa's. Makayev left them alone. He assumed they were to help get them all off the ship when it docked.

He sat down on the bottom mattress of the bunk bed. It sagged nearly to the floor. He tried to stretch out, to find some comfortable position, but his back ached no matter which way he twisted. He gave up, leaned against the wall and drew in a breath. The stink of fuel oil was masked by the musty, mildew smell of old bedding. It instantly brought back a memory, and then, a surprise: a smile.

Back when the Aral Sea was a sea and not a dead cesspool, Rebirth Island had been a star-shaped spit of sand fifty miles from the closest shoreline. It bore an odd but appropriate resemblance to the spiked, three-lobed international symbol for biohazards, for the Soviets had turned Rebirth Island into the world's first open-air biological weapons test site.

Then the rivers feeding the Aral were diverted to feed thirsty cotton crops. As the water level dropped, the arms of the island grew broader and the bays filled in. In the three visits Makayev made there, it had transformed itself into a true peninsula joined to the mainland at its southern cape; the very site where the most dangerous experiments had been conducted.

The grandly named 'Science City', a complex of sun-scalded wooden barracks overrun with indestructible cockroaches and small lizards, occupied the northern tip of the star. When Makayev first saw the camp it was almost a real town, with a power plant, cinema, school, even a small library stocked with western scientific periodicals. A military base sat at the center of the island star, along with a series of intersecting dirt runways. The testing areas were set reliably downwind on the star's two southern arms.

Makayev had been assigned to a six-man bunk

121

room that had exactly the same, musty bedding smell as the SEALAND cargo container. The other men were off preparing for the evening's test shot. Makayev was the junior on the team and his work – hauling full anthrax bomblets to the military squad that would fire them – was finished. It was hard, manual labor in the furnace of a desert noon, and he collapsed onto his cot too hot to sweat, too hot to think, utterly spent.

Though the window was wide open there wasn't a breath of wind. The air was heavy and silent. Not even flies could survive the heat. Then, as the long hours and the physical exertion pulled his eyes shut, something heavy thudded onto his chest. He opened an eye, then sat up.

A single, perfect orange rolled onto the floor. Now, back then a fresh orange was like a diamond; exotic, beautiful and rare no matter the season. He looked around. The room was empty. The door was shut. The window, it was open.

He rose from his bunk and went to it. Outside, down on the ground was Nina Aranova; the director's twenty-year-old daughter.

Nina was small, with short, reddish blonde hair, widely-spaced gray eyes and freckles that made her seem even younger. She wore boots, a soldier's floppy 'Afghan' hat, a green sleeveless shirt and baggy shorts the color of Rebirth Island's dust. Her legs, her arms her cheeks were red from too much sun. She was a graduate student in veterinary medicine; a career choice her academician father apparently hated. He rarely spoke to Makayev about anything, but he'd complained to him about her throwing her future away curing cows and chickens.

Makayev held up the orange. 'You?'

'Do you see anyone else?'

'Where did you get it?'

'The monkeys.'

'Taking food from test animals is forbidden.'

'It's a bigger sin to let a good orange go to waste.'

Well, there was that. Makayev knew the experimental animals on Rebirth Island ate better than he did. More than once he'd overheard the others joke about stealing their rations of fresh fruit and vegetables. After all, the monkeys were only here to die. 'Why throw it to me?'

'They made you work in the sun like a *zek*.' A prisoner. 'You'll need some energy for your tour.'

A tour didn't seem so appealing just now. But she was right about how they'd treated him. He looked to see if someone might be coming back up the road, but there was only swirling dust. 'What tour?'

She gave him a triumphant smile and waved for him to join her.

He followed her down the gravel road that lead to the military camp. 'You've been here before, Miss Aranova?'

'Every summer since I was a child. My father thinks that his work is communicable. I developed an immune reaction.'

'To test organisms?'

'No. To murder.'

They came to a fork. The soldiers were to the east, she took him west to a flat, shingled beach. Though it was a beach in only the most technical

123

sense. It was more a kind of pavement made of crusted salts and evaporated minerals. Nothing could live in such a hostile environment. There were no birds, no waves, no sounds. A wide, shallow bay shimmered and steamed in the sun. The dead water reflected the skeletal remains of an airplane that had landed short of the island's runway. The bent spars and ribs sprouted weird salt-flowers that took on the colors of the underlying metal: iron red, green copper, titanium blue.

Their feet left no prints in the hardpan. They skirted the airstrip, keeping out of view below its gravel berm, and arrived at the back door of the monkey house. A machine was humming.

She produced a key and opened it. The windowless block building was deliciously air conditioned, and cool, fresh air spilled out. 'This is where they screen for disease. They can't have sick monkeys. They have to be perfectly healthy to die.'

He followed her into the monkey house. It was dark, and the cold air smelled of sweet fresh cedar, and something else. Some lighter, organic note. 'And cool. I'd move here if they allowed it.'

'I'm sure they'd let you volunteer. For science.'

She was mocking him, mocking Pokrov and of course mocking her father, too. Here was a complication his instincts told him he would be smart to avoid.

She flipped on the lights.

Cages to the left and right, and even the corridor between them had a roof of wire mesh. Makayev looked around and saw where the organic smell was coming from: the food dishes brimmed with oranges, melon sections, even papayas. He'd never tasted a papaya. Actually, when had he even *seen* one?

She popped open a wire door and grabbed an orange from a steel tray. She bit into the skin, then began peeling it, tossing the skin to the ground.

'*This* is where you got my orange?' he asked her.

'Does that shock you?'

'But why didn't the animals eat them?'

'They're too smart.'

'Smart?'

'Monkeys live in the world of their senses. What they see, smell, feel. We live with what we *know*. We ignore our senses and tell ourselves stories, like what we're doing is important. Or that if *we* don't grow poisons then someone *else* will. Or the biggest one of all, that what we do doesn't matter. Monkeys are smarter. They know what this place is all about. Why would they bother to eat?' She split the orange in half and took a great bite. Juice spilled down her shirt. 'What will it be tonight? Q Fever? Anthrax? Brucellosis?'

The citrus smell was intoxicating. 'You know I can't say.'

'That bad?' She offered him the uneaten half. 'Here.'

He took it, sniffed. Was this a test to see if he could be trusted to follow the rules? He decided *No*. He popped it into his mouth. It was sweet and tart and very juicy.

'Do you know what my father calls you? His pet Muslim.'

The orange soured. 'I'm not a Muslim and I'm

125

not his pet. And you're also wrong about our work not mattering. It's a life and death struggle.'

'For the monkeys.'

'For the nation.'

'You're not that stupid, *Doctor* Makayev. Or are you?'

She said *doctor* as though she'd caught him pretending to be something he was not. It was the first time he noticed how much Nina enjoyed weaving words into a tangle, though not the last.

'Other countries have these weapons,' he said. 'Have you considered the possibility that our program is the only thing that keeps them from being used against us?'

'Have you considered the possibility that everything you've been told is a lie?'

'We should go back, Miss Aranova.'

'It's a furnace outside and my name is Nina.' She stepped closer to him and looked closely at something at the open collar of his shirt.

He looked down. Was there an insect? A piece of orange peel? But there was nothing. 'What?'

'Your pulse. It dropped below 100 beats per minute in the first few minutes here, but it's up now. I'd say, 110. You're angry?'

'No,' he said, a bit too quickly. Makayev touched his sweaty neck and felt the throb of his heart. 'How can you tell just by looking?'

'Count for yourself.'

He let his hand fall. 'I think it would be best if they didn't catch us stealing from the test animals. I'm not interested in practicing medicine in Grozny.'

'Better to cure one case of pneumonia than

grow what you grow in Pokrov. Anyway, don't worry. You're not going anywhere. Unless you run. Would you do that? Run, I mean?'

Even using oblique language to talk about leaving a classified program was enough to put you on the watch list. Makayev was not about to make that mistake. 'Where would you run to?'

'Anywhere.'

'You've never seen Grozny.'

'I told you not to worry. You're exactly where they want you.'

He thought of how her father treated him. 'How can you know?'

'Let me tell you a few things. You've heard of Lysenko?'

'Of course.' Lysenko, the geneticist who spurned genetics as a bourgeois hoax. Who used dubious experiments to 'prove' that a giraffe got its long neck through exposure to tall trees, that selfish, capitalist mankind could alter these traits through exposure to Marxist materialism. It had been a very popular notion in Stalin's Kremlin, and one that set back Soviet science generations before it was finally stamped out.

'My father was chosen to study under Lysenko,' said Nina. 'It was considered an honor. You're his Muslim? My father was Lysenko's Jew.'

'I'm not Muslim, Nina.'

'That's what you think. Lysenko used to brag that he never reported results that went against his theories. My father still believed in the purity of science. He kept all the data even though it never was published. The police found it, of course, and he was sent to Pokrov to work on

127

veterinary vaccines as his reward.'

Makayev thought, *No wonder he doesn't want you to follow in those steps.* 'Pokrov? Punishment?'

'It's a matter of perspective. He was one of the leading biologists of his time, sentenced to a life with cows, pigs and chickens. You see to them, a man who speaks truth can never be trusted.'

'I'm sorry, but how does it apply to my situation?'

'Can you be trusted? That's all they want to know. And so far I would say yes. Too bad.'

'You're wrong, Nina. I'd never do anything I thought was wrong.'

'Like poisoning half the world?'

'Those organisms will never be used. The world is different.'

'Not at Pokrov.' She put her finger to her lips and let her voice fall to a whisper. 'I'll tell you a secret. At Pokrov it's still 1947. Nothing has changed.' Her eyes fell to his neck. '120 now.'

Makayev reached for his throat, pretending to swipe away the sweat. The air handler switched off. The silence felt heavy, impending. 'It's time to go.'

'Sorry. Deviations are not allowed.' Nina stepped close and moved his hand away from his throat. She traced the pulsing ridge of his internal jugular with her finger, down its length from below his ear to where it joined the subclavian vein. 'Can you be trusted, Doctor Makayev? Or can you begin to think for yourself?'

'Miss Aranova...'

'Nina.' She moved against him, pressing her face against his neck, letting her tongue follow the same course her finger had just traced, leaving a cool trail of wetness behind. She was small and the top of her head barely grazed his chin. Her breasts pressed against his chest. She made a soft, satisfied sound somewhere deep in her throat. When she looked up she saw faint gold rings in the gray of her eyes. 'Honest sweat?'

Before he could protest that this was not what he had in mind, that he was newly married, that even if he was trapped inside a factory dedicated to death it was still better than treating syphilis in Grozny, she stepped back, pulled her shirt over her head and tossed it to the ground.

It was an agreeable invitation, but saying yes could be dangerous. Saying no to the director's daughter might also be dangerous. 'What if they find us?'

'I think you're more intelligent than you know.' She reached behind her back to unhook her bra and let it fall. Nina stood with her hands on her hips. Her breasts were small and pear-shaped, her waist narrow. She balanced on one foot and stepped out of her baggy shorts.

'Nina, the rules say...'

'*Enough* about the rules. Look at a map. This island doesn't appear. What rules are there in a place that doesn't exist?' She took his hand and pressed it to her skin.

The air conditioning had cooled her, but it flushed under his touch. She was right about a lot of things. It *was* fifty miles over water to the nearest settlement and twenty three hundred back to Makayev's new wife. Some of the other men drank away the hours here. Surely this was a healthier alternative? Her nipple hardened against his palm, and when she looked up, he saw that old triumphant smile on her face.

'128 beats. I think you're ready.' She stepped away from him, put her thumbs into her panties and slid them down.

There was a simple metal table with two metal chairs tucked in between the cages. On it, a dusty record book filled with numerical entries and dates. She spun the chairs around and placed them almost, but not quite, together. She climbed onto the chairs, one knee on each, then reached out and gripped the table's edge. Her sun-pink legs were spread, her pale bottom thrust up in open invitation.

The posture was straight out of a primate physiology class. It was called *presenting*. She didn't look back to see what he might be doing. Nor did she need to.

She was right about Pokrov but wrong about the rules.

That night, a small, metal sphere was launched on a low trajectory over the heads of a hundred screaming rhesus macaques chained to a double-row of stakes. It spun and sparked like a party favor. When it was directly above them, it exploded.

The monkeys tugged furiously at their chains. Some put their heads to the ground, eyes shut. A few covered their mouths as a dark cloud of finely milled anthrax powder descended. Too late, for this was L-4, Pokrov's 'premium' strain. The animals had already breathed in three times the necessary lethal dose before the cloud even touched the ground.

In nature, inhalational anthrax takes days to develop. L-4 was a weaponized variant and much more efficient. The monkeys developed lung lesions in hours. By midnight, the lesions had released a flood of toxins into their blood. There were no survivors to greet the rising sun.

After the night's slaughter, Director Aranov returned with the other men from Pokrov. Nina was still in her dusty shorts and shirt. Makayev had managed to change into a somewhat cleaner outfit. They were in the commissary eating a late dinner, careful to sit at separate tables.

Aranov came in. 'Stay away from the animals.'

But when he said it, he was staring straight at Makayev.

Makayev thought about where she lived now, and what she was doing. Giving private tours to Israeli biologists visiting Nes Dimona for the first time? Married to a soldier?

His thoughts were interrupted by the rattle of anchor chain, followed by the chuff and clatter of the ship's engine. He got to his feet and felt the deck tremble. *Finally.* He heard the *click!* of a key and the big door at the front of the container opened.

It was Adnan's younger brother Musa. The surgical precision of his sculpted beard was softened by a generous growth of dark stubble. The hawk-faced Chechen was dressed in the oily shirt and filthy khaki trousers of an ordinary sailor, though it was hard to imagine how anyone could mistake him for one.

131

'Salafi wants to see you,' he said.

Not Mr Salafi? 'What about?'

Musa snorted in a way that suggested there was nothing Salafi might say that could possibly interest him.

CHAPTER EIGHT

THE HIGH WALLS OF KAFFA

**MV *'Nova Spirit'*
Bosporus, Istanbul**

Makayev gripped the leather briefcase with its four vials of Hunter as though it were chained to his hand. He slept with it. He went to the toilet with it. He never let it out of his sight. He followed Musa up a ladder and into the galley, then up another deck to the cabins. They passed the locked fifth cabin and came to Salafi's door. Musa knocked, then pushed it open without bothering to wait for an invitation.

Both of Salafi's portholes were open and the air was fresh with a salty evening breeze. He sat sprawled like a pasha on a metal cot cushioned with blankets and pillows. His black shoes were lined up on the floor at his feet. A black pistol sank deep in the blanket folds. A small table held bowls of almonds, raisins, a thermos and two glasses.

Makayev eyed the food and drink. He was

terribly thirsty. His throat felt dusted with fine particles of glass. But he'd missed a meal, too, and his stomach was rumbling about it.

Salafi dismissed Musa and turned to Makayev. 'I'm sorry we had to keep you out of sight. Some inspectors inspect. Ours was more sensible.'

Makayev went straight to the sink and opened the tap. It hissed, then spat rusty water. He put the briefcase down and cupped his hands.

'I wouldn't drink that,' Salafi warned.

'I *am* a biologist.' Makayev splashed his face, careful to keep the foul-smelling water out of his mouth. He gazed at Salafi's thermos.

Salafi twisted it open, filled a glass and handed it to Makayev.

Makayev drank it down in a single gulp. Only when it was empty did the taste of sugar and mint register. He helped himself to a handful of raisins, then held out the glass. 'More.'

Salafi refilled it. His gaze fell to the attaché. 'The samples are safe?'

'Let's both look.' Makayev pressed the stud. The briefcase popped open and Salafi stood back as though it might explode in his face. He removed a disinfectant-soaked towel. It gave off a potent chemical smell that swiftly filled the cabin. Salafi wrinkled his nose but Makayev wasn't bothered by it. It was a *good* smell. A *reassuring* smell. He unrolled the towel.

The four vials were intact, their caps were in place, the dry flakes inside gray, not the bright red that would indicate a broken seal. He rewrapped them and snapped the case shut. 'Satisfied?'

'Let's go breathe a bit of fresh air.'

The ship was entering the narrow Turkish Strait. The hills to each side, Europe here, Asia there, were dusted with lights. The waterway was filled with darting excursion boats, ferries and lumbering ships. A great silver bridge spanned the water, its towers catching the last red glow of the setting sun. A large stone fortification beneath the bridge's eastern terminus was bathed in brilliant, almost theatrical, floodlights.

Salafi leaned against the rail. 'That's Rumeli Hisary Castle. Mehmet the Conqueror launched his final assault on the city from there. It was the beginning of a Muslim empire that went from Mecca to the gates of Vienna. Can you imagine such a thing today?'

'No.' And that was just as well, for when Makayev thought of a Muslim empire, all he could imagine was a bigger Chechnya, filled with men like Adnan and Musa. *No thanks.* 'When do we dock in Malta?'

'Three days. There's an afternoon flight to Riyadh. If we catch it we can be in Saudi Arabia by dinner. If not, we'll wait a day for the next one.'

'All of us?'

'Adnan and Musa won't be coming.'

'Where will you send them?'

Salafi seemed to find this funny. 'I don't send them anywhere.'

Makayev remembered the two uniforms hanging inside the container. *They're not going to work for the Malta Maritime Authority, either.*

Salafi turned. 'You've been to Istanbul before?'

'Never.'

'It's a remarkable place. This city was once the center of the world for culture, art, science and philosophy. The Caliphate ruled the civilized world from right here.'

Makayev watched the Asian shore scroll by so close the sound of families at dinner carried across the water. He could smell cooking.

'Have you ever wondered,' said Salafi as the ship sailed into Istanbul's heart, 'what the Caliphate might have given to the world if it had survived?'

'The thirteenth century?'

'You make a joke, but when Mehmet conquered this city, Europe was like our third world, ruled by uneducated, uncivilized kings who spent their brief lives fighting each other, living in filth and ignorance.'

Makayev felt strangely lightheaded. He needed more water, yet the thought of drinking left him nauseated. He gripped the rail tightly. 'But in the end those kings won.'

'Not with better ideas or better values. All they had were better weapons.' He reached into his jacket and shook a cigarette from a silver case. 'God willing, you're going to change that.'

With a better weapon? Makayev hoped Salafi wouldn't light that cigarette. His stomach was turning inside out. 'You're wrong. A virus isn't a weapon. It will kill you just as happily as your enemy. A virus can only be a shield to keep others from using *their* weapons against you.'

'Really? Do you know the story of Kaffa?'

'No.' Makayev was finished with stories. What he wanted now was to close his eyes, to sleep.

'I'm surprised. In 1347, Kaffa was a Genoese fortress city, occupied by Christian traders and guarded by high walls. Again and again the city was attacked. The walls always held.' He lit the cigarette.

Makayev moved upwind. The smoke seemed to track him.

'Then Tatars laid siege to Kaffa with catapults and Greek fire, but they began to sicken and die. You see, they'd also brought Black Death.'

Makayev thought of the refrigerator down in the Capsule filled with *Yersinia pestis:* the brown tubes.

'The disease swept through the Mongol army. The Genoese looked down and laughed. Then Khan Janibeg, the Mongol general, loaded corpses onto the catapults and fired them over the walls. In a week, Kaffa fell. The survivors fled. Plague traveled with them. First every port city, then up every river valley. Like an invasion. It took three years to spread across Europe. Twenty million dead. In Italy, they stacked corpses like lasagna, one atop the next. People thought the end of the world had come. So tell me, Doctor Makayev. Was plague a weapon or just a shield?'

'Millions of Muslims died, too. It was just another suicide bomb.'

'You don't approve of martyrs?'

'I'm no religious scholar, but a civilization that blows up schoolchildren is the one that's committing suicide. Not these martyrs.'

'And yet sometimes it take a great sacrifice to achieve a great end. Remember the Japanese kamikazes.'

136

'I remember they flew their airplanes into warships, not buildings full of civilians. And what great ends are you talking about? What great books have these *martyrs* written? What discoveries have they made? All they produce are severed heads and toppled buildings.'

'Not all Muslims are terrorists, Dr Makayev.'

'Then why is it that all terrorists seem to be Muslim?'

'Saudi Arabia is a Muslim land.'

He held up the briefcase. 'We developed this ... *material* only because we knew it could never be used. Then everything fell apart. Poor Russians would like to be rich. That's a dangerous situation.'

'But you trust the Kingdom,' Salafi persisted.

'The Saudis are rich and they want to stay that way. They have no reason to use military viruses. They have more to lose by letting them out. The *jihadis* are crazy but I'm not. If I thought Hunter would fall into the wrong hands, I never would have come out with you.'

The wake roiled up brown and muddy as the ship slipped between the two continents.

Salafi seemed to weigh his words out carat by carat before speaking them. 'Many of us think in this way, but I would advise you to be more careful when we arrive. The Saudis look solid, but then everything looks solid until there's an earthquake, yes?'

'Saudi Arabia is earthquake country?'

'Some of the *jihadis* are crazy. It's like we're locked inside a cage with two hungry tigers. One tiger wants our oil, the other our souls. That's

137

where you come in.' The cigarette flared, the cloud of pungent smoke wreathed his head as though it were on fire, then drifted away. A mischievous look came over his face. 'You're going to make Saudi Arabia indigestible.'

A tendril of smoke followed Makayev. It merged with the stink of diesel, the curry, rotting garbage and sewage rising off the water. He felt his stomach contract, and he lurched away from the rail and headed for his cabin at a run.

'Dr Makayev?'

Makayev fled to his cabin, caroming between the wall of the iron house and the rusty rails. He went in, slammed the door and staggered to the metal sink. He barely had time to lean over before he vomited. Once, twice, again until nothing came.

He pressed his forehead against the cool steel. Emptying his stomach left him feeling better. He turned on the tap. A spurt of oily water shot out. He let it clear out the mess and rested his head against the smudged mirror. *The water,* he thought. He must have swallowed some in Salafi's cabin. Who knew what was swimming in the ship's filthy tanks?

The faucet was still running. He reached to twist it off and saw the last pink streaks swirl down the drain. *Pink?* He looked at his hands. No cuts, no scrapes. He spat it into the sink.

Not pink, but red.

He opened his mouth. His gums weren't bleeding. He tipped his head back and let the light fall more deeply. He saw something far back in his

138

throat, small and round. Had he swallowed an insect with the raisins?

He opened his mouth wide to let in more light, to see better. *There!* It was a pale yellow tick, attached and engorged. He remembered something about not pulling them, about how the head came off and remained embedded to cause infection. But it was too horrifying to think of a parasite feeding on him. He reached in with a finger to touch it and felt it pop, releasing a warm gush of bitter-tasting fluid. The tick's body went soft. *Now what?*

He tilted his head to let the mirror bounce light more deeply into his throat. Makayev hoped to see the dying tick crawling away. Threads of blood streamed from a pea-sized blister, not a tick, that wept a thick, clear fluid. There was a strong, metallic taste utterly unlike blood.

Nausea. Thirst. A slight fever. A sore back. These were symptoms that might lead to any one of a thousand diagnostic destinations. But add a weeping yellow blister and they led to just one.

He cracked open the briefcase. His hands shook as he unwrapped the four vials. A sharp, chemical smell emerged with full potency. The seals were absolutely intact. No. This was not the way. He counted the days since leaving Pokrov, and then he knew.

He'd snagged his Moon Suit on a sharp metal edge in the changing room. He'd checked it for damage but somehow a virus had managed to find its way into the fabric. Perhaps when Raisa threw that clod of blood and shit. Hunter had sheltered in it from the blast of sterilizing

139

chemicals and light. And when he walked out of the Capsule, Hunter had come with him and ... he stopped.

That Turkish inspector! Was Makayev shedding virus when he boarded the ship? Probably not. But if he *had* been infectious, if that Turk had inhaled a particle of Hunter, then all Istanbul was in danger. When had Makayev turned contagious? A minute on the wrong side, a particle of virus drifting on a breeze could doom a city. Or more.

Whatever the answer, it no longer mattered that the Kingdom of Saudi Arabia was a safe harbor in a dangerous world, that rich sheiks had more to gain by keeping it than using it. Hunter was loose. Salafi, his two bulls, the crew. All of them would come down with it and most of them would die. It put their arrival in Malta in a very different light.

Docking would be enough. Death would drift invisibly on warm, Mediterranean breezes among happy vacationers heading back to Rome, Berlin, Paris, London, New York. One victim would become thirty, then nine hundred. Twenty seven thousand. Three quarters of a million. And then? The mathematics of contagion were well understood.

Makayev had treated deadly viruses as though they were so many invisible bullets; start with the correct biological materials, add the proper nutrients *here*, follow the correct industrial steps and extract a finished product *there*. So many bullets, harmless unless loaded and fired. And with Hunter, that would never happen. Who would fire a bullet that would turn around and

140

blow a hole in your own head?

He'd forgotten that viruses weren't bullets. They were *alive*. They could fire *themselves*. What were the fine words he'd spoken so long ago?

I swear to dedicate all my knowledge and strength to the preservation and improvement of the health of mankind and to the treatment and prevention of disease.

He'd taken this demon from Pokrov's freezer. He'd allowed it to wake. Now it was up to him to find a way to stop it before the ship reached Malta. *Three days.*

In Salafi's story, Kaffa's high walls had been made of stone. The walls that shielded the modern world of swift and universal travel and porous borders were nothing but cobwebs.

CHAPTER NINE

OSCAR

12 OCTOBER
USS *Portland*
Algerian Trough, off Cape Sperone, Sardinia

Scavullo took her yellow highlighter and marked off the last circuit on the schematic drawing of *Portland's* radio systems. 'That's it,' she said to Banjo. 'It's not here.'

'Maybe it's gone.'

'Radios don't fix themselves, Banjo.'

Banjo shrugged. *Spooks don't fix radios, either,* he thought.

They'd checked out every transmitter, every receiver. The Black and Red circuits, the crypto gear that kept *Portland's* secrets, even the old legacy teletype that chattered out emails, Family-grams and nonessential message traffic. The gremlin wasn't hiding in any of them.

Or perhaps, it was in *all* of them. Each of those systems had been afflicted at one time or another. Each had suddenly frozen up and gushed out streams of unintelligible garbage. Yet when she tried to find the common fault, the displays turned maddeningly clear.

It was almost enough to make her start believing in gremlins. *Or jinxes.* She glanced over at Banjo. What was he making of all this? *Probably wondering why the captain sent a linguist to do a radioman's job.*

'What do you want to do now, ma'am?' he asked.

'Quit.' She threw her marker down. 'I'll be down in my rack. Call if the radios start speaking in tongues, okay?'

'You got it, lieutenant.'

She unlocked the radio shack door and walked out into the passage. A junior nuke lieutenant named Pat Boserman was heading the opposite way. He was short and noticeably well fed, and so the passage was not wide enough to let them pass without knocking knees.

She pressed her back into the bulkhead to give

him more room. 'Everything okay in the neutron department?' she asked, trying to cover up *frustrated and tired* with *perky and pleasant.*

'Why?' He seemed alarmed.

'Take it easy. I'm just making conversation.'

'About what?'

'Never mind.' *Nukes.* She turned slightly, letting one shoulder protrude so that when he passed by he'd feel her bones and not the softness of her breasts. Though she wore a sports bra that was sexy as armor plate, she knew the effect even a glancing encounter had on men who ached for a woman's touch.

He went forward to Control. She went aft to the ladder and climbed down to the middeck.

The smell rising from the crew's mess hit her before she stepped off the ladder. The cooks were busy setting out lunch. A bleached gray wooden sign mounted above the doorway proclaimed the mess the *Captain Dan's.* The leathery old fisherman with his red pipe and yellow sou'wester irked her, but then she was a real Mainer. Not the cartoon variety. *What would they call the mess on the USS* Princeton? she wondered. *The Tuck Shop?*

Inside, the first rush of sailors coming off watch were lined up at the serving counter. A messmate was slicing hunks of meat off a prime rib roast the size of a big Thanksgiving turkey. One of the sailors noticed her, whispered, then nodded in her direction. The line came to a stop. Then, as though heeding a command, the men turned their backs to her.

Same to you. She hurried forward. She could

143

always stop in the wardroom for some tea. The door was open and she spotted the XO at the table. *Nope.*

The radio room was occupied by a gremlin. The wardroom was enemy territory. Rose Scavullo was running out of places to hide.

She'd always fought to make her own way. Her father had been a Navy man. Her brother worked at Bath Iron Works building ships. The University of Maine had an NROTC program. The Navy recruiter thought she was a 'hot commodity'; a smart young woman with straight As in Russian. She could give something back to her country and the world. It was a feeling that only grew after 11 September 2001.

But the more she saw of the United States Navy, the more she realized it was a crazy quilt of feudal principalities. The 'brown shoe' aviators were divided into fighter pilots here, transport and helicopter pukes there. They *all* looked down on the 'black shoe' surface fleet.

The aviators needed linguists; they flew EP-3s to eavesdrop off hostile coasts. But Scavullo had an inner ear that was spring-loaded to the *vertigo* position. The Navy wanted her to spend her career in some windowless building in Washington listening to intercept tapes.

The submariners she met were quieter and less boastful than the pilots, and they seemed smarter, too. They sailed unseen to interesting places because they *could*. Go along and she'd be *making* those tapes, not just listening to them. The problem was, women were allowed to fly, they commanded ships at sea, but serve aboard a submarine? Never.

Scavullo fought. She'd argued her way out on a limb, then a branch and now onto a very slender twig. She wondered if that had been their plan all along: reduce her options, give her what she wanted, wait for her to fail, then hold her up as an example of why women didn't belong on the boats. It wouldn't be the dumbest idea the Navy ever cooked up.

The bright lights of the mess area dimmed as she continued forward to the berthing areas. On a submarine, no matter the hour, someone is always awake and on duty. That meant someone was always sleeping, too. She could hear enthusiastic snoring coming from behind drawn privacy curtains as she eased her way down the narrow passage. She couldn't press her back against someone's privacy curtain. She couldn't do the 'shoulder shuffle' without putting an elbow into some sleeper's face.

The only space that still felt secure was her small, curtained-off bunk. It was the very last place she could climb into and escape the looks, the whispers and, not least, the unpleasant fact that she wasn't wanted on *Portland,* and now that they weren't headed north, not needed, either.

Scavullo's rack was in the forward row on the bottom, starboard side. It was dead quiet, which was good news. The boat had three audio channels; country, rock and Christian. A few quiet hours of *none of the above* would improve her outlook on everything. She got down on her knees and pulled the heavy blue curtain aside.

She gasped and jumped away.

145

Someone was already in her bunk.

'Lieutenant?' She turned. It was Pena, the young supply officer.

He stood at the forward end of berthing and said, 'Anything I can do?'

'Yes. Have you seen Commander Steadman?'

'I just left him up in Control.'

'Go back and get him.'

Pena chewed on that for a few seconds, then said, 'You want me to go *get* the captain?'

'Get him.'

Lieutenant Pena was a 'chop'; a surface fleet loaner new to submarines and far down nearly anyone's seniority list. They were the same rank. Indeed, he could have told Scavullo to go take a dive into the sanitary tanks, but he had eyes. He could see something was up. He had ears and they could hear the fury in her voice. And so the young lieutenant nodded and said, 'Sure. Whatever. Okay.'

She stood rooted to the deck.

'Uh, I need to go forward, okay?'

She moved, but only just enough to let Pena pass.

When he did, he didn't feel the softness of her breasts, nor the sharp bones of her shoulder, but two hard fists.

'Permission to enter control?'

Steadman looked up. *Pena?* He'd just gone off watch. 'Forget something?'

'No sir. It's Lieutenant Scavullo. She, ah, she'd like a word with you. She's down in lower JO berthing.'

146

'She wants *what?*'

'A word, Captain. She's waiting.'

Steadman was about to say she could damned well wait until he had nothing better to do, but there was something in Pena's nervous stance, something in his face, that said that might not be a good idea. *Jesus. I've just been summoned off my own deck by a non-qual lieutenant. What's next?*

He took one last look at the sonar repeater. *Nothing.* The screen was filled with the noise of their own swift passage. The electronic chart above the ship's control station showed the El Mansour Seamount safely astern. The deep, open waters of the Algerian Basin lay before them. At four hundred feet there was nothing in the world they could hit but another submarine. That was always possible, though the ocean – even the Med – was still a big place. He hoped.

He turned to Lieutenant Commander Pardee. The navigator was busy at his table trying to keep up with the boat's rapid advance across his paper charts. 'Nav? You've got the conn. I'll be right back.'

Steadman slid down the forward ladderwell and stalked aft. *This had better be worth it.* Then he saw Scavullo standing in the passage and if eyes could emit X-rays, he would just have absorbed a fatal dose. 'What is it, lieutenant?' He walked up to her. Her eyes were red.

Assault. It had happened once before on *Portland's* previous run and he was sure it had happened again. Only this time, *Steadman* was the commanding officer. 'What happened?'

She turned, grabbed the blue privacy curtain that shielded her bunk and yanked it open.

At first all Steadman saw were legs and feet and he thought, *Suicide?* But then he pulled the curtain open all the way and let out a sigh of immense relief. *Oscar?*

Oscar was a 'crash test' dummy used for their man overboard drills, weighted down with scrap metal until he approximated a real sailor's heft. And from the look of things, Oscar was in the mood for love: his crotch bulged with an impressive erection a real sailor could only dream of and only a piece of steel pipe could explain.

'It's happening again,' she said. 'Whether you want it to or not.'

Her words had scarcely left her mouth when Steadman's feeling of relief at not finding a dead sailor in her rack was replaced by anger. Not at the prank, for that was clearly what this was. But something larger, something far more serious. He spun on his heel.

She grabbed him by the shoulder. 'Commander? I want...'

Steadman felt her touch. Six words filled his mind and every one of them was *No.* He twisted away. 'If you're going to ask me to find a way to get you off the boat, forget it. I have more faith in you than that.'

'No!' she said, surprised. 'Well, before, maybe. Not now. Not after *this*. They'll have to throw me over the side,' she said. 'I just want to warn you.'

'Warn me about what?'

'If I find out who did this, who's *doing* this, I'm not going to keep it quiet. Not for the sake of the boat. Not for anything. You understand? I've got places I can take it and it won't be pretty. Not for *them* anyway.'

Great. A civil war. That's just what we need. 'I'm sure you've got people looking over your shoulder, lieutenant. Now you're not a member of this crew so I can only advise you on this, but if you let me handle it I don't think you'll be disappointed with the results. Are you willing?'

'With all due respect, sir, I'd like to see some before I answer.'

'You will.' *And more.* He yanked a microphone off the bulkhead intercom. 'XO lay to junior officer's berthing on the double.'

Tony Watson bustled up from the wardroom, face flushed. From the sound of Steadman's voice he'd expected to find a broken weld spraying high-pressure water into the boat. Instead, he found Steadman and Scavullo. 'What's going on?'

'Take a look in her rack, XO.' He stood back. 'What do you see?'

Watson leaned over, chuckled. 'A sailor's prank, Captain.'

'You're an expert when it comes to assessing risk. That's the best you can do? A prank?'

'I don't think Oscar poses much of a risk to Lieutenant Scavullo,' he said. 'Might be the other way around.'

'Wrong answer. Think. Where was Oscar stowed?'

'Ah.' *Now* Watson got it. 'The sphere.'

The inside of the boat's sonar sphere was used to store all manner of rarely needed items: mooring lines, life jackets. And Oscar, the man-overboard dummy. The only access to the sphere was through a long tunnel whose watertight hatch in the forward elliptical bulkhead was kept sealed for a very good reason: if the tunnel flooded with the hatch open, there was nothing to stop the ocean from filling *Portland*'s hull all the way to the reactor compartment hatch. Nothing.

'Someone cracked that hatch, XO. They broke our rig for dive while we were underway. You don't think that's risky?'

'Yes, of course, but...'

'No buts. Someone endangered my boat. I want his name *today*. Find out who did it and I will send him up a rope when those SEALs arrive tomorrow. By the neck, if I can figure out how to get away with it.'

Watson nodded. 'All right.' He saw a look of victory on Scavullo's face. *It's you again.* 'I'll get on it right away and report back.'

'See that you do.'

CHAPTER TEN

INVASION

12 OCTOBER
USS *Portland*
off Cape Teulada, Sardinia

Threading *Portland* through Gibraltar proved easier than finding the sailor behind Oscar's midnight movements. When they arrived at their rendezvous point off Sardinia, Watson had no names to offer up in sacrifice at the feet of a seething captain, nor Steadman any results to show Scavullo. Civil war would have to wait; Steadman was too busy.

He ordered the boat to make ready for periscope depth. The sea was quiet and the contact evaluation board showed only the distant grumble of big ships heading for the port of Cagliari. But more than one captain had learned to his regret the difference between *should be* clear and *is*. Only when they'd made a full circle to check 'baffles' did Steadman say, 'Helm. Make your depth sixty feet. Radio? Stand by to transmit our on-station message.'

'Conn, Radio,' said Banjo. 'Message is formatted and ready.'

Lieutenant Pena watched the numbers on the fathometer click as the boat swam up from the deeps. It stabilized at exactly sixty feet. 'PD, Captain.'

Steadman walked to the periscope island. 'Raise the search scope.' Then he remembered the gremlin. 'Raise *both* BRA-34s.'

Two masts, both dedicated to long-range satellite communications, slid up from their wells inside the sail. The top of the search scope's optical head bristled with receivers to sniff out signals aimed in their direction. It quickly found some.

'Ship radars to the north, east and south, skipper,' said Petty Officer McAllister at the electronics support console. 'Signal strength is low to very low.'

Steadman swung the periscope around in a full sweep. The eyepiece seemed shrouded in blackout cloth, but then he caught a brief yellow flash of light from the crescent moon.

'Message sent and acknowledged,' said Banjo. A coded transmission reporting *Portland* on station and requesting medical evacuation at first light radiated up into the soft, Mediterranean sky to a relay satellite in low orbit. The signal ricocheted across the world to Norfolk in seconds. Their answer was, if possible, even swifter.

'Conn, Radio,' said Banjo. 'New message traffic received.'

Tony Watson stepped into the doorway to the forward portside passage. 'Permission to enter Control?'

'Down scope.' Steadman waved the XO in as the messenger of the watch appeared with Norfolk's new message. He read it, then handed it to the XO.

1: READY YOUR DECK FOR IMMEDIATE
   HELO INSERTION DET BRAVO SEAL
   TEAM EIGHT ... GRAYBAR SENDS

'He's sure in a hurry,' said Watson. 'I'd vote to take Remson off in daylight.'

So would Steadman. Submarines and helicopters were a difficult mix in the best of conditions. *Portland's* decks were narrow and rounded and the smallest seas made her pitch and roll. A helicopter had to contend with all that motion, plus the wind, all while hovering at a constant height over a fixed point. Hard enough when you could see. Dangerous when you could not.

Steadman remembered how Norfolk had ordered him off the rescue mission in the south Atlantic. Once more, he was being told to ignore what he thought was right and he wasn't in the mood. 'Nav,' he said to Pardee. 'What time is local sunrise?'

A quick consultation of the charts gave Steadman his answer, and he drafted a reply to Graybar's terse message:

1: PORTLAND WILL HAVE A READY DECK
   FOR HELO OPS 0710 ... STEADMAN
   SENDS

The answer came roaring back.

1: SOURDOUGH SIX NOW INBOUND
2: SURFACE YOUR BOAT IMMEDIATELY,

153

Steadman turned to his XO. 'We're outvoted. Have Chief Cooper get Remson ready.' He clicked the 1MC microphone. A hum went through the submarine, and everywhere men paused and looked up.

'This is the captain. All stations prepare for surface operations.' He nodded to his XO. 'Tony? Have the deck division rig some work lights. I want it bright up there.'

Even though they were far from ship or shore Watson clearly didn't like the idea of *bright*. It went against a submariner's instincts for stealth. 'How bright?'

'Like high noon.' Steadman turned. 'Dive officer. Surface the boat.'

The raucous horn of the surface alarm echoed three times through the steel hull. An instant later, a storm of compressed air forced tons of water from *Portland*'s ballast tanks. She grew lighter, rising up to where water met sky.

Steadman turned to his XO. 'You've got the conn.'

Steadman went forward, passing the doors to the sonar shack, his stateroom, then Watson's cabin. He noticed the officer's head sign: NO KNOCK! NO ENTRY! Flip it over and it simply said MEN. The A-gang made it up for Scavullo's use to replace the old one that had said MEN on one side and WOMAN on the other.

Everyone knew putting a woman on a

submarine would be complicated. Who would have guessed that the physical hurdles would turn out to be the easy ones to solve?

The captain came to the ladderwell, unchained the safety guard, checked to make sure no one was coming up, then slid down to the middeck. He landed lightly, then turned forward and made his way to the Goat Locker. A bleached goat's skull, complete with horns, was wired over the door marked CPO QUARTERS KNOCK THEN ENTER.

Remson lay on his bunk, gazing at the gray metal overhead through morphine-dimmed eyes. The soggy stub of an unlit cigar flicked up and down in his teeth like the tail of an agitated cat. Word had filtered down to the Goat Locker that his ride was on the way, and Chief Cooper, the corpsman, was already busy packing his seabag.

Steadman glanced at Cooper.

'I'll come back in a minute, Captain,' the corpsman said, and then eased out of the Goat Locker.

Steadman walked over to where Remson lay. 'We're sending you to a real hospital, COB.'

'Yeah. In the middle of the night. Tell you the truth, skipper, I'd just as soon stick around till sunrise. What's the big rush?'

I don't know. 'There'll be plenty of lights. Before you go, I want to talk about what happened back there.'

Remson had known some officers who would say, *I want to talk to you about what happened* and mean *Let's get our stories straight.* He'd sailed under this captain for less than a week but he knew Steadman wasn't like that. 'Waste of time,

155

skipper. A sailor doesn't have to like how his orders taste, he's just got to swallow them. You told me to secure that fish. I thought it was and I fucked up. What's more to say?'

'This: you saved this boat. And when I find out why they called us up to the surface just to turn us around, you'll know too.'

Remson shifted and winced. 'And when they won't tell you, come see me. Remember, old chiefs know everything.'

'I'll remember.' The deck tilted, then steadied as *Portland* broke the surface. For a moment both men were lost in thought, remembering the storm. But this was no hurricane sea, just the gentle rocking of the calm Mediterranean.

'XO make any progress finding Oscar's pal?'

'None.'

'It wasn't just one moron. A job like that, it would take a minimum of two,' said Remson. 'One to dive the tunnel and one to stand lookout. If I were on my feet I'd have them at mast.'

But not Mister Watson. 'I believe you would.'

'I guess I let you down again.'

'How so?'

An odd look clouded Remson's face, as though whatever he was chewing on was a lot more bitter than the soggy, unlit cigar stub. 'You know, this boat had a rough year. It started before I even came aboard. That last WESTPAC run you guys made, getting laid up in the yard for repairs. What just happened with the loose fish. The guys have been flapping their lips about how *Portland*'s jinxed.'

'You believe in jinxes, COB?'

156

'I believe that ever since our rider reported aboard, bad things keep happening. It's easy to see how rumors start. Once they do they can turn into...' Remson paused.

'A self-fulfilling prophecy?'

'Yeah. It's like you lose your edge and *expect* bad stuff to happen, so it does. Jinx talk can spiral out of control. You start off with little deals that build up into *big* deals. That's where we're headed.'

'And the crew blames Scavullo.'

'I'd stake my anchors on that. Whoever they're sending out to take my place is going to have a real job turning this around before it gets serious.'

'We'll see.' Steadman stood back. 'Any way I can help you ashore?'

Remson's eyes shut, then opened. 'Well, there's one thing. I don't need two good hands to take a class of non-qual nubs and turn them into good submariners.' Remson meant Sub School in Groton, where *Portland's* last COB had been assigned.

'I've never known a chief who needed *one* hand to do that.'

'Yeah. But see, the Navy, they might want to declare me disabled. I figure you might be able to put a word in for me and set them straight.'

'I'll sit on the admiral's desk until he says uncle.'

'I kinda' thought you would. Of course, kids, they're different these days. Tattoos, piercings. No discipline. No determination. You need some kind of a hook to get their attention.'

157

'What kind were you thinking about?'

Remson grinned and raised his wounded arm. 'Something made of submarine HY-80 stainless steel. Think that'll keep their attention?'

'Count on it.'

CH-46E *Sourdough Six*

The tandem-rotor helicopter showed no lights as it thundered over the coast of Sardinia at Cape Teulada. They'd flown south at a nice safe altitude of two thousand feet, but then the pilot, a Marine Corps captain, nosed the big Sea Knight over.

The windshield was filled with nothing but black sea and black sky.

'My altimeter's tits up,' said Capt Carroll Lane, the aircraft commander. He tapped the glass face of the instrument and the needle bounced a bit more enthusiastically. 'What's the radar say?'

'One thousand nine hundred,' said Quill. He was a United States Navy lieutenant. He was accustomed to resupply missions, though he'd only flown out to meet a submarine once, and then in broad daylight. 'It might not be too accurate in a flat sea state.' He paused, then, 'We would never fly a night op without a functioning altimeter.'

'Yeah. Marines do things their own way.'

They're nuts, thought Quill. 'One thousand five hundred.'

The Sea Knight and Lane's crew had been sent from a desert base in southern Iraq to La Maddalena, Sardinia. Naturally, the first thing they did on arrival was sample the local night life.

158

Lane's co-pilot had gone out with a Russian belly dancer who took him to her favorite seafood bar. He'd gone one on one with raw octopus and the octopus won. Quill was his replacement.

'One thousand feet,' said Quill, wondering how low this crazy jarhead was going to fly.

Captain Lane kept the helicopter in a steep descent. He was a Marine, and for a Marine, all flying was tactical flying. The sort where you didn't just see the ground, you tasted it. Of course, that was in the nice, flat deserts of Iraq. Not that it would make much difference here. Both sand and water were hard as concrete at 150 knots. 'Go on and give the boat a call.'

'Manhole Manhole, this is Sourdough Six. How do you read?'

There was no answer.

Lane pushed over more steeply, watching with satisfaction as Quill's hands made a furtive grab for the collective. 'I got the helicopter, lieutenant. A couple of minutes and you can let the cargo know to get ready.'

Their 'cargo' was an eight-man SEAL squad carrying enough gear to equip a Marine Expeditionary Force, a medical corpsman to deal with an injured submariner and one Navy chief. The cavernous bay in the back of the chopper was filled with dozens of waterproof boxes, weapons cases, a deflated rubber boat, an outboard engine, explosives and ammo. All that loose ordnance in the hands of non-Marines made Lane nervous. He'd be happy when they were off his aircraft, the sooner the better.

'Radar shows *two* hundred feet,' said Quill.

The intercom came alive.

'Hey Captain?' It was Lane's crew chief. 'We got eight action heroes back here anxious to kill something. How long before we can drop 'em someplace?'

'Tell them boots on deck in ten minutes.'

A red light flashed on Quill's panel. The radar altimeter put the ocean a scant hundred feet below them. *'Watch it!'*

Lane waited a second, then leveled off. They were pounding over the ocean at better than 160 knots; a lot of speed for something as big and ugly as Sourdough Six. 'Try 'em again.'

'Manhole Manhole, this is Sourdough Six. How do you read?'

This time, there was an answer.

'Manhole reads you five by five. Authenticate Bravo, India, Foxtrot, over.'

'Roger Manhole,' said Quill. 'Can you show a light?'

Lane pressed the foot switch for his cabin intercom. 'Eight minutes out.'

'Hey Captain,' said the crew chief. 'The cargo wants to get dropped off as close to the sail as possible. They have a lot of shit to...'

'What in hell is *that?*' said Quill.

At first, Lane thought it was an explosion. Here, far from ship and shore, a brilliant white glow erupted from the featureless dark of the sea. As Sourdough Six thundered in, he could see the geometric silhouette of a submarine sail rising from the heart of it. The brilliance caught the foam riding up against the black hull and turned it tropical green. 'Now *that's* what I call showing a light.' As he circled the glare and came in from astern, he said to his loadmaster, 'Gunny? Pop the doors and rig for roping. Tell the froggies I'm dropping them off at the corner of Broadway and Times Square.'

USS *Portland*

The helicopter was a rumble, a whine, then a ghostly white belly and a blast of wind that swept over the submarine's slick hull.

Steadman kept watch from the tight confines of the open bridge atop the sail. Two lookouts rode the rounded roof immediately behind him. He looked back over the brightly lit afterdeck. The lights the XO rigged on improvised mounts poured down enough wattage to turn night into day. The aft escape hatch stood open, and Steadman was glad the sea was calm.

Chief Cooper and his injured patient squatted on the aft deck under a torrent of rotor wind from above. They were both clipped into the recessed safety track and Remson wore a horse collar harness, too. A sailor stood behind them with a long wooden pole. He turned and gave Steadman the thumbs up signal.

Steadman picked up a microphone. 'Sourdough, this is Manhole. You're cleared to lower the discharge line.'

A braided steel wire unwound from the rescue hoist of the roaring helicopter. The whirling blades of a helicopter generated a tremendous static charge that had to be dissipated. Neglect

161

this and the first person to touch that line would never forget it again.

The sailor caught the cable with his pole, let the metal hook on the end make good contact, then guided it down to the steel safety rail on the deck. There was a bright flash where it touched.

Steadman was about to tell Cooper to hook Remson on, when a forest of black lines snaked down from the open doors of the hovering Sea Knight. *Portland* looked like a big fish caught in the tentacles of a menacing jellyfish.

An instant later, dark bodies in black suits, helmets and goggles hurtled down the ropes so fast Steadman couldn't tell if they'd jumped or fallen. Large rubberized bags thudded to the deck, then more bodies. Five, six. Eight.

In the midst of this invasion, Chief Remson was hoisted up and the SEAL squad moved forward bearing padded crates and bundles, some of which would plainly never fit through *Portland's* hatches. A moment later, Steadman caught sight of Remson's replacement being gently lowered onto the deck.

The cables and ropes were drawn back up and as suddenly as they had come, the helicopter roared off into the night, leaving only the sounds of the sea lapping against the hull and the voices of the men.

The peace was broken by a loud, metallic *bang! bang! bang!*

'What in hell?' Someone was pounding on Steadman's submarine. He knelt down to the deck of the open bridge to the small 'ice door' set into the port side, undogged it and pushed his head out.

Below, a SEAL with a big bushy beard paused in his labors, looked up, then went back to swinging a small sledge at a reluctant locker hatch.

While Electric Boat had worked to undo the damage from *Portland*'s last arctic patrol, the yard crews had installed a curved fairing at the base of her sail to help direct – and quiet – the flow of water. Inside the fairing was unclaimed space, which never stays unclaimed on a submarine. A hatch had been installed, and even though the resulting locker wasn't watertight, it was big enough to accommodate a couple of life rafts. It was this hatch the SEALs were trying to force open.

'Belay that hammering!' Steadman hollered.

The bearded SEAL didn't even pause. He took another swing and the door came free. He reached in and yanked a heavy, flat package out and promptly tossed it over the side.

It was one of *Portland*'s two life rafts.

'Stop that!' Steadman roared.

He might as well have shouted at the ocean. The second raft followed a moment later. They floated off beyond the perimeter of light. The SEAL motioned to the others, and something that looked like a big, deflated rubber sausage was passed up the line and stuffed into the open hatch.

Steadman squeezed through the ice door and jumped down to the deck, putting himself between the SEAL and the hatch. The special ops trooper was dressed from helmet to boots in black.

He seemed to notice Steadman for the first

time. 'You're in the way.'

'What do you think you're doing?'

'Offhand I'd say your deck division's job.' His eyes were hidden behind shooting goggles.

Steadman jabbed his finger into the SEAL's chest. 'You're one funny remark away from Captain's Mast. What's your name?'

'Sanders. Bravo Two to my friends. You can call me Kernel with a K.' The SEAL took in the silver oak leaf pinned to Steadman's collar. 'So I'm guessing this is your boat?'

'Get your CO up here.'

A voice from further down the line called, 'What's the holdup?'

'I got a commander who wants to talk to somebody in charge.'

'That would be me.' Another black-clad figure strode forward carrying an outboard motor. It was a matt-black pump jet with no propeller and must have weighed well over a hundred pounds. He had it balanced over a shoulder like a fishing pole. He pushed his goggles up over his helmet and handed off the motor to one of his men. 'Lieutenant Jameson. Bravo's CO. Kernel's my XO.' Unlike most of his other men, Jameson was clean-shaven. His eyes were the deep blue of glacier ice.

'I'm Commander Steadman.'

'Pleasure to make your...'

'Number one,' Steadman interrupted, 'nobody tosses my gear over the side. Two: nobody bangs on my hull with a hammer unless they work for Electric Boat. With me so far, lieutenant?'

'Sure,' said Jameson. 'But some of our gear won't exactly fit down your cute little trunk

164

hatch, will it?'

'Three: don't patronize me. Ever.'

'Wouldn't think of it. Sorry about ditching your rafts but we're bringing our own Zodiac and it's got to get stowed someplace. The boat we were supposed to meet had a drydock shelter. You don't. So if you'll just let us get our gear squared away, we can button you back up and go below. I'll fill you in on what's going to happen.'

Steadman was about to tell the impertinent lieutenant that going for a swim and retrieving those life rafts was what was going to happen, but then he heard a new voice, and an old one.

'Just what in *hell* is going on around here?'

Steadman turned.

'Who's the freak in charge of this circus? And what *dink dunk* let those rafts go over the side?'

It was Command Master Chief Jerome Browne. He'd been *Portland*'s Chief of the Boat for her last run to the Arctic. There, trapped beneath a solid overcast of ice, her sonar blinded, her hull flooding from a collision with a Russian *Typhoon*, Browne's cool determination helped save them. It also nearly cost him his life. He'd taken a much-delayed assignment as an instructor at the Submarine School in New London.

'*You're* Remson's replacement?' said Steadman. He was both surprised and delighted. 'You said once you hit the beach you'd never go out again.'

'I guess I made some *unintentional* enemies.' Browne was a small, wiry black man with a razor-sharp mustache and touches of gray shading his temples. He'd spent more time in submarines than anyone on *Portland*, including her captain. His

165

eyes twinkled in the bright work lights. He straightened and saluted and said, 'Command Master Chief Jerome Browne reporting aboard.' He made a point of noticing the float vest Steadman wore over his uniform. 'And may I say it's a true pleasure to see you on deck properly equipped with a float coat.'

Steadman saluted back. He knew what COB was talking about. Browne had hauled him out of the sea after he'd gone over the side without his float vest. He didn't give Steadman a piece of his mind or whisper to the other senior chiefs that their captain had a death wish. That wasn't COB's way.

Master Command Chief Jerome Browne never yelled, never raised his voice except when at quarters pierside, and only then to be heard above the normal shipyard din. He never got angry, not even annoyed. Instead, he had a God-given talent for letting sailors, and officers, know when they'd disappointed him. And with very few exceptions, it was enough. When COB Browne spoke, things happened.

One of the lookouts riding the top of the sail put his glasses down and noticed who had replaced Remson. 'Hey COB! What are you doing back?'

Browne scowled up at the lookout and recognized an A-ganger who'd been aboard for *Portland*'s ice run. 'You still a knuckledraggin' A-ganger? What's wrong, son? You gettin' lazy on me?'

'No way, COB. I just like fixing things.'

'Good answer. How's the boat?'

The lookout grinned and gave him a thumbs up. 'It's automatic.' But then the smile faded. 'Well, *almost*.' He glanced at Steadman, then away.

'I see.' Browne squinted at the glare of the work lights. 'Looks like Christmas came early this year.'

'You can thank the XO for the lights.'

'I'll be sure to do that.' Browne turned his attention to the deflated raft and outboard motor on deck. 'Hey Smooth Dog,' he said to the SEAL lieutenant, 'quit losin' gear and get your ass below. This ain't the Staten Island Ferry you're riding.'

'Aye aye, COB.' He looked at Steadman. 'Where do we rack?'

Smooth Dog? Steadman wondered. 'The torpedo room. Get settled and then come meet me in my cabin.' Steadman looked aft. The deck division was breaking down the lights, coiling up the wires that streamed down the open escape trunk. 'Make a smooth hull!'

The decks were cleared, the work lights stowed, the hatches closed and locked, and eight minutes after Steadman had issued his command, *Portland* sank out of sight beneath the waves.

The SEALs transformed the torpedo room into a chaotic dorm filled with boisterous young men with voices set to *loud*. Mattresses had been set out for them among the torpedo racks. The squad chief, Senior Chief Petty Officer Harry Wheeler, pronounced them all wimps and deliberately selected a steel shelf spanning a pair of gleaming green Mark-48 ADCAP torpedoes. The other five enlisted men, Petty Officers Anders, McQuill, Battaglia, Stepik and Flagler claimed the others.

The eight SEALs were all specialists. Anders and McQuill were top-ranked marksmen. Battaglia was the squad 'breacher'; an expert in opening doors with a bang. He was also Bravo's strongest climber. Hand Stepik a radio and he could field strip it, rebuild it and not only would it work, it would work better. Petty Officer Flagler was the squad corpsman. His training and experience outstripped *Portland*'s Independent Duty Corpsman, though with an understandable emphasis on gunshot trauma.

But the SEALs were also generalists. They could all shoot a tight pattern inside a kill circle at long range. They were all powerful swimmers and expert combat divers. Their CO spoke passable Russian and his XO was rated 3/3; not quite up to Scavullo's 4/4, but good.

As the equipment cases were opened and their contents distributed, the torpedo room began to resemble an arsenal. The burly torpedo-men stood back and watched as their compartment filled with an astonishing collection of MP5 machine guns, shotguns, sniper rifles, Sig Sauer side arms, grenades, explosives and enough ammunition for a month of shooting. Out came radios, climbing gear, wet suits, Draeger breathing apparatus and electronic equipment the SEALs called computers but looked like nothing any of the curious sailors had ever seen before.

Two cylinders drew the torpedomen's special

interest. Their serial numbers were noted and a manual consulted: the tanks contained welding gas. Welding gas?

The SEALs tossed a black rubber case on top of the gas tanks. It contained bricks stamped PBX-IH-135; a total mystery until someone pointed out that each and every Mark-48 torpedo contained a warhead composed of PBX: plastic bonded explosive. Put welding gas and explosive bricks together and you had the raw materials for a powerful fuel-air bomb. Not the giant 'cave busters' pioneered in Afghanistan, but plenty big enough to crack *Portland's* tough steel hull like an egg.

And then there were the small pouches containing folded yellow fabric. Once again the serial numbers were memorized and sent aft to the nukes in the reactor spaces. They ID 'd them as quick-donning biological hazard suits, and not the low-bid junk *Portland* kept on hand against chlorine gas and battery spills. They were the best commercial equipment money could buy, rated for a Level Three biocontainment lab.

A torpedoman ambled up to Stepik. It was Red, the TM who'd helped Remson wrestle the errant Mark-48 back into its tray. SEAL or no, the radioman that could intimidate him had yet to be born.

Stepik was checking out a secure radio, untangling cords and making sure the pouch labeled SPARE PARTS-HEADSETS still contained them when Red kicked the big waterproof fiberglass case he was using as a stool. It was the size and shape of a small refrigerator.

'What's this thing anyway? A backpack nuke?'

Stepik rose up and shoved Red back against a torpedo rack. The torpedoman came up swinging. Two SEALs pinned Red's hands without much in the way of visible effort. Moving torpedoes around had made Red strong in an amateur sort of way. The SEALs were professionals.

'Take it easy,' said Stepik. 'What we got here is a portable diagnostic ADN device. That stands for Antibody-Doped Nanowires and each one is a thousand times smaller than your little red cunt hairs. So lookee, but no touchee, okay sailor?'

CHAPTER ELEVEN

DARK WINTER

USS *Portland*

Steadman gave the conn to Watson and retreated to his cabin with Browne. He shut the door. 'What do you know, COB?'

'Me? I'm just an old chief.'

'I thought old chiefs know everything.'

'That's usually the case. Not always. I did see *Oklahoma City* sitting in La Mad. Her rudder was covered with tarps and scaffolds. She had a dry-dock shelter on her back that was all banged up.'

'What did she hit?'

'Nothing official but if someone were to bet they came to PD in Gibraltar and found a ship already there I believe they'd collect.'

That would explain our sudden change in orders. 'You know we diverted here to take her place.'

Browne nodded. 'I heard about those six Air Force guys. They're calling it a *recovery* operation now.'

'We were their last hope, and then SOM-SUBLANT pulled us out to play war games with SEALs.'

'I don't know what they're all up to, captain, but those frogmen aren't out here to play games. They're packing *serious* horsepower.'

'Weapons?'

'*Authorization.* I hear Jameson's got a sheet of paper signed by the President of the United States. He's got himself a real 007 license to kill.'

'Who gets killed?'

'I don't know. Jameson will have to tell you *something* but I wouldn't expect much. See, to him, *Portland's* the bus, you're the driver and *he's* gonna' say where it goes.'

'No lieutenant is giving me rudder orders.' *Though one did call me off my own deck!*

'Well, I know Jameson and his exec were chattin' up a storm in Russian, so maybe that tells you something about who they're after.'

'Russians? In the Med?'

'Too bad Scavullo wasn't around. She might be able to fill in some of the blanks.' Browne paused. 'She doing all right?'

'No. And that's a problem I need you to solve right away. Some of the crew thinks she's why bad things seem to be happening.'

'A jinx.'

171

'I don't believe in jinxes, COB. And they're trying to run her off the boat. She's got her back up and feels like fighting.'

'Good for her.'

'Not good. She's got heavy hitters back in Washington waiting for someone to screw up. I *refuse* to give them that opportunity. Not on my boat.'

'Our boat, commander. What did they do to her, exactly?'

'Two nights ago some idiot opened up the sphere tunnel, dragged Oscar out and put it in her rack.'

'With the boat *dived?*'

'Correct. Mister Watson can't seem to identify the guilty party.'

'Like it says in Isaiah 42, *I will lead the blind in a way they know not.*'

'I'm counting on you. If some idiot is willing to do that to play with Scavullo's head, what next?'

'He's got more to worry about than Scavullo now. I'm here.'

'Remson thought there could be more than one.'

'You know, it might just be easier to get Scavullo reassigned.'

'No deal. I don't know why but CONSUBLANT wants her out here. I can't make the Navy take Scavullo off the boat but this crew *will* behave. I'll fry them if they don't. Make sure they know it.'

'Aye aye, Captain. A little fear can be a beautiful thing.' But Browne remembered their last run, and how even he'd been shocked to find Lieutenant Scavullo in Steadman's stateroom.

172

Sure, there was a very good reason. It was innocent, even necessary. The captain had sent a maniac radioman out to hunt her down. But that was Browne's mind talking. His gut had reacted in a different way entirely. What would someone *looking* for trouble find to report? 'She got any work to keep her busy?'

'I gave her the job of fixing a glitch in our radio system.'

'Glitch?'

'It makes hash out of some messages, some of the time. It seems like it's inside both the transmitters and the receivers. We've been fighting it since we set sail from Groton.'

'I see.' Blueprints and systems diagrams were rushing through Browne's mind as he stood there. Finally, he said, 'Well, no boat of *mine* is going to have a *glitch*. Other than that, how's *Portland?*'

'The XO would say she's ready to sink.'

'And what would her *captain* say?'

A look of pride came over Steadman's face. 'We took a serious beating up in that hurricane, COB. We came through.'

'Remson's a good man.' Browne could see there was something more. 'That's all?'

'For now,' said Steadman.

There was a knock at the door.

Steadman turned. 'Come!'

It was Lieutenant Jameson. He'd stripped off all the hardware down to a green flightsuit and a pair of old sneakers.

'Speak of the devil,' said Browne. 'How you gettin' on, Smooth Dog? Find your accommodation to your liking?'

'We're settled.' Jameson looked smaller without his harness, his body armor, his helmet, goggles, webbed belts and gear. But he still managed to fill the open doorway. His short brown hair whorled to a peak at his forehead. His eyebrows were bleached almost white by salt water and sun, and a scattering of freckles surrounded a nose that had almost, but not quite, been set after a bad break. He was carrying a manila envelope. 'Sorry, COB. I'll have to ask you to leave.'

'Us rag hats can't spend much time with you O-gangers,' Browne said with a wink. 'We tarnish your brass.' He eased out into the passage.

Jameson shut the door. 'Lieutenant Jameson reporting aboard.'

Steadman flipped up his bunk and turned it into a table. 'Coffee?'

'I'd prefer to get you oriented first.'

'Okay.' Steadman sat. Jameson did not. 'Orient me.'

'Sir, what I'm about to share with you concerns a Special Access Project code named Yellowstone. I'm authorized to read you into it but it doesn't go anywhere else. Not to your XO. Not COB. Your navigator knows where we're going and how fast we get there. Not why. Okay?'

A Special Access Program explained why not even the senior submarine chiefs knew what was up. 'Go on.'

'Two weeks ago, a Russian biological warfare facility about fifty miles southeast of Moscow was hit by a truck bomb. The place had a stockpile of bad bugs left over from the Cold War.'

'Just sitting around?'

174

'Pretty much. People have this idea that bio-weapons are kept locked up and guarded around the clock. Not in Russia. They've got a dozen old plants like this one protected by a rusty fence, if someone hasn't stolen the fence. Anyway, they aren't funded any more and Moscow doesn't know what's out there. They figure if they forget about them everyone else will, too.'

'Somebody remembered. Who?'

'The Russians say it was a Chechen job. They always say that, but they might be right this time. The plant's director was Chechen. He was photo-graphed on an airport security camera with a Saudi national. We know this guy. His name is Salafi and he travels on a diplomatic passport. He's got two *jihadis* riding shotgun. They're brothers, Chechens, and both of them are wanted by NATO.'

Security camera? 'We're watching Russian airports now?'

'We watch the Russians watch Russian air-ports.'

'What did the two brothers do to make NATO's most-wanted list?'

'They shot a couple of American women in Bosnia. The ladies were running a high school for girls. The brothers capped them right in front of the kids. Lesson learned. The school closed.'

'Are the Saudis willing to help us with their guy?'

'Oh, sure, but remember, they gave Salafi his diplomatic passport to start with. They'll feed us stuff that suits them and play dumb when it doesn't. I wouldn't put it by them to be behind this in the first place.'

'They've got oil. Why do they need bio-weapons?'

'To keep someone from grabbing the oil. These guys wired their own fields for destruction with that in mind. If they think someone's about to move in, they push a button and *boom*. Oil goes to a couple hundred bucks a barrel. Then Saddam tried the same thing. We had the fires out in what? A month? So maybe the Saudis went looking for something a little more permanent.'

'And they sent this guy Salafi to find it.'

'Buy it, more likely. He works for an Islamic charity based in Riyadh. On the ground it's more like an ATM for terrorists,' said Jameson. 'When the House of Saud needs to pay some protection money to the *muj,* Salafi's their bag man. When the crazies need to hit up the royals, he's their go-to guy. Sometimes the money builds a mosque. Sometimes it pays off the widow of a suicide bomber. Salafi takes his cut either way.'

'All right. It's a Russian weapon. What are they doing about it?'

'The usual. Pretending nothing happened. Day one they put out the word Pokrov was a vodka distillery that had a little industrial accident. The next day it was a natural gas explosion. Day three they sent out troops to throw a ring around the place. The only people allowed through now are wearing serious biohazard gear. Keep in mind, these are the same clowns who sent guys into Chernobyl with gas masks soaked in vodka for radiation protection. When they're scared, we're scared.'

'Scared of what?'

'Smallpox. Pokrov was set up to brew it by the ton.'

By the ton?

'Here's what we're looking at,' said Jameson. 'Johns Hopkins simulated a bioterrorism attack a few years ago. They called the game Dark Winter. What would happen if a terrorist released smallpox in Oklahoma City? It took two weeks for the disease to spread across twenty states and fifteen other countries. Containment proved impossible. The Soviets fooled around with a bunch of other agents, but when you want to pull the curtain down smallpox is the way to do it. The last natural outbreak of the virus was back in the 1970s, so the world is pretty much dry tinder. One spark starts a big fire.'

'And Yellowstone is about putting out the sparks.'

'Yes sir. The Russians tracked the Saudi and his Chechen friends to the port of Sochi on the Black Sea. They stood up a goat grab...' he stopped when he saw Steadman's expression. 'Search and seize,' he explained. 'They dropped some operators on a ferry that had just sailed from Sochi. They were wearing full biohazard gear, head to toe. They came up empty. No goats. No Chechens. No bioweapons.'

'All right. The Saudis are liars and the Russians are incompetent. What exactly is *Portland*'s role?'

'We believe the men who hit Pokrov, its director and the stolen bioweapons are still at sea. Our job is to find them, see where they're going and intercept them before they get there.' Jameson opened the manila folder and fanned a series of black and white enlargements across the table. 'This is the Pokrov Plant for Biopreparations. What's left of it.'

It showed a cluster of buildings. The roofs were studded with special ventilators. The big building in the middle of the campus had collapsed in on itself.

'That image is fresh. Notice you aren't seeing vehicles. No patrols. No checkpoints. They're holding everything back twenty miles. So far we haven't monitored anyone screaming outbreak, so the containment structure probably wasn't breached in the explosion. Next.'

It was an overhead view of a port; a series of jetties and piers, a few ships docked, a few riding at anchor. The picture was so detailed it might have come from a low-flying airplane. You could see ripples on the water.

'You're looking at the port of Sochi,' said Jameson. 'The white ship is the ferry the Russians raided.'

Steadman noticed the other vessels. 'What about these three?'

'Good question. By the time the Russians asked it they were gone. One east to Costanza, one north to Sevastopol, the last one south for the Bosporus. Two were intercepted and checked. Nothing. Our target is the southbound freighter. She's the MV *Cristi*, registered in Cyprus. She's already cleared Turkish inspection. Last shot.'

Steadman looked at the final photo. It was a side view of a small freighter painted in black, white and rust. She had a heavy crane amidships.

'You don't need a submarine to stop an old freighter.'

'You do if you want to keep her under covert surveillance 24/7. Or if you want to find out where she's going without them knowing we're watching. A satellite can only take a snapshot. What happens in between passes? No one knows. And an airplane will give away the game. If they know we're onto them what's to keep them from running the ship up on the nearest beach and cracking open a few vials? A submarine with a team of special operators is the *only* platform that can carry it off.'

And Steadman knew the submarine mafia was desperate for new missions. When boats cost billions, you needed an enemy worth the price of admission. It would seem they'd found one. 'All right. Tell me your plan for keeping smallpox off *Portland.*'

'We're immunized and we brought plenty of vaccine.'

Steadman made a mental note to talk with the boat's corpsman about that. 'I buy that you need a submarine. Why mine?'

'You're our backup. The DDS boat we were supposed to meet got herself dinged.' DDS stood for Drydock Shelter; a pressure-tight chamber that rode piggyback on a submarine's deck and allowed SEALs a quick way in and out of the boat with all their gear.

'*Oklahoma City.*'

Jameson didn't elaborate. 'There was only one other boat under way with a Russian-speaking linguist. *Portland* was it.'

179

So that's why they won't let Scavullo off.

'This renegade Chechen biologist speaks Russian,' Jameson said. 'Any documentation he brought out will be in Russian, too. We'd like to get our hands on them and your rider can help us out. Who is he? I went to language school with some of them.'

'I'll make sure you meet,' said Steadman. He picked up the intercom phone. 'Radio? This is the captain. Have our rider come to my cabin immediately.' He hung the phone up. 'What about *Cristi's* crew? This is a submarine. We don't have a brig for prisoners.'

'We're not taking any.'

'Nobody authorized me to raise the Jolly Roger.'

Jameson reached into the envelope and brought out a sheet of paper. 'I believe this speaks to your concerns.'

Presidential Order 2005-22: On Enemy Combatants and the Use of Lethal Force

By the authority vested in me as President, Commander in Chief of the Armed Forces of the United States and by the Constitution and the laws of the United States of America, it is hereby established:

(1) International terrorists have carried out attacks on the United States. To protect the United States and its citizens, terrorists and those who support them must be deterred and disrupted prior to carrying out new attacks.

(2) That having fully considered the magnitude of the potential deaths, injuries, and property destruction that would result from such attacks, I have determined that an extraordinary emergency exists, and that issuance of the following orders is necessary to meet this emergency:

(1) Individuals engaged in activities that threaten the citizens or interests of the United States shall, for the duration of this state of emergency, be identified as enemy combatants.

(2) As such, I have directed the Secretary of Defense to authorize the Armed Forces of the United States to use lethal force against any and all enemy combatants engaged in terrorist acts.

(3) When such authorization is not operationally feasible, or when timely and immediate intervention is necessary to deter or disrupt a terrorist attack, lethal force may be employed at the discretion of the commander on the scene to carry out the provisions of this Presidential Order.

(4) This order shall be published in the Federal Register.

THE WHITE HOUSE
March 2005

Browne was right. Here was a hunting license

that appointed Jameson judge, jury and executioner. 'This turns the whole world into one big free-fire zone, doesn't it?'

'It acknowledges the fact that it already is one. And it puts war back into the hands of warriors.'

'I'm not worried about warriors fighting wars,' said Steadman. 'I don't much care for the idea of them *starting* them, though.'

'With terrorists, waiting for the chain of command to respond is suicide. This fight has to take place on the dark side of the law, commander. Otherwise, we'll be sweeping up bodies back home.'

'The dark side means what exactly?'

'The American people will forgive us if we go too far defending them. They won't forgive us if we fail.' Jameson went over to a large paper chart of the world's oceans. '*Cristi* will have to sail by Crete on her way almost anywhere. If she's bound for Europe or Africa she'll take the western sea lane by Kithira. If it's the Middle East she'll run the eastern pass at Karpathos. If we stand off the island and wait, we can follow her no matter what her destination turns out to be.'

Steadman joined him at the chart. There were fancier, more detailed classified charts but when you needed a quick look at the big picture, it was hard to improve on Heezen's *World Ocean Floor.* 'That's shallow water and it's full of traffic. *Cristi* could put in anywhere.'

'That's why we've got to get moving. The sooner we watch her movements the better. If she's heading for an island, or for somebody's territorial waters, we'll take her down. If it looks like she's making rendezvous with another ship, they both go down. *Portland* will be responsible for area security.'

'I won't order a torpedo fired at a ship that just happens to cross the wrong bow.'

'Yellowstone gives you that authority.'

'Not from that piece of paper I saw. I read the *on-scene commander* makes the call. Now, when you're out in your raft that's you. But on these decks the on-scene commander is *me*.'

'Nobody's going to tell you how to run your boat but you've been detached from the fleet. You don't even report to the *Navy* except personally through COMSUBLANT and all he knows is that you're inside Yellowstone. When it comes to operational matters, I call the shots.'

'Like hell.'

'Call the admiral. He'll confirm everything I've said.'

In other words, Steadman could act on his own best instincts or he could fire a message to COMSUBLANT, Admiral Graybar, and risk being told to obey this young lieutenant. Either way, he might gain cover but he'd lose whatever maneuvering room he still retained as the captain of a warship at sea. *No.* 'As far as I'm concerned while you're embarked you're a division officer. You report to the XO and he reports to me. If that's not to your liking you'd better start looking for a new submarine.'

'Which side are you on, commander?'

'The side that says you don't stop terrorists by becoming one.'

Jameson chuckled, as though Steadman had said something hopelessly quaint. 'I almost forgot.' He reached into a pocket and withdrew a black computer disc. 'It's an Ocean Systems sound file on *Cristi*. Screw, flow, plant noise, electricals. Everything.'

Steadman took the disc. He knew there were sound files on every warship and submarine that sailed, friend and foe alike. But tramp steamers? That was news. He picked up the microphone hanging from the bulkhead. 'Nav? This is the captain. Plot a course for Crete by way of the Sicilian Strait. Have the XO get us moving at flank.'

'We headed for liberty in Athens, skipper?' asked Pardee. You could hear the anticipation in his voice. Athens wasn't as much fun as Brisbane, but it was a hell of a lot better than most liberty ports.

'I said Crete, Mister Pardee.'

There was a knock at the door.

'Come!' said Steadman.

'Sir?' It was Scavullo. 'You...' She stopped when she saw Jameson.

'Rosie?' said the SEAL. 'How'd *you* get a submarine posting?'

She composed herself quickly, but not without a lot of effort. 'I passed my exams. Unlike you.'

'You know each other?' said Steadman.

'We overlapped at language school,' said Scavullo.

Steadman eyed her, then him. There was more to this. 'He may need your help translating documents.'

184

'Actually, sir, I don't know that there *will* be any documents,' Jameson said. 'It was just a contingency and...'

'It was important enough to pull my boat out of the Atlantic,' said Steadman. He looked angry and he was. 'I left behind six men on a raft in a hurricane because of this *contingency.*'

'Sir, we're not reading her into a Special Access Project. It's...'

'If the linguist on *Oklahoma City* was authorized then so is she.'

Jameson considered the matter and decided on a tactical retreat. 'Okay, if something low-level comes up she can help. But if we run into anything hot we'll have to haul it back to Washington.'

'How will you know what's hot?' Scavullo asked innocently. 'Did you bring somebody who reads Russian?'

'I went to the same school you did, Rosie,' Jameson snapped.

'Moy kote govorite pa rooskie luscha chem ti.' My cat speaks better Russian than you.

'Ya pominyu, shto oo tebya ochen talantlivaya koshka!'

Scavullo reddened. He'd just told her she had a very talented pussy.

'You two practice your Russian someplace else,' said Steadman. 'I've got a submarine to attend to. Take off.'

'Sir,' said Scavullo. 'I only wanted to...'

'Out,' said Steadman. Scavullo moved. Jameson did not.

'Both of you.'

CHAPTER TWELVE

SPRINTS AND DRIFTS

13 OCTOBER
K-335 *Gepard*
Port of Tartus, Syria

Heat was the enemy, and the enemy was winning. Russian submarines were built to survive cold Arctic waters. They were never meant to broil under the incandescent glare of the Syrian sun, simmering in water warm enough to poach a fish.

'Single all lines!' Captain First Rank Rem Leonov's command sounded crisp. The deck detail's movements were not. They moved listlessly, drugged by the oppressive heat, their pale northern skin flushed with incipient sunstroke. And hot as it was up here, it was worse below.

'Engines astern, slow,' said the captain.

Starpom Stavinsky, *Gepard*'s first officer, acknowledged the order normally, as though nothing out of the ordinary was happening down in the brutal oven that was the boat's Central Command compartment.

Gepard's single pinwheel screw churned the filthy harbor water to a muddy froth. A gap opened between the submarine's tapered stern and the wooden pier where a thin crowd of the curious watched from whatever shade they could claim.

Leonov was a small, dark-eyed Muscovite with black hair, trimmed mustache and the high cheekbones of a Tatar. Short and compact like a fighter pilot, he was all spring and no slack. He wore his dress uniform, jacket, wide-brimmed hat and sweat-soaked white shirt, fully exposed atop the submarine's rounded black sail. 'Right full rudder!'

Gepard – Russian for 'Cheetah' – was an advanced *Akula* nuclear attack boat. Laid down in the Soviet Union's final year, she'd languished unfinished for almost a decade while the Russian Navy went bankrupt. Then *Kursk,* the newest submarine in the Northern Fleet, sank in the Barents Sea, threatening to pull down a score of admirals with it. If *Kursk* could be lost, what Russian ship was safe? And if no ship were safe, what good was a Navy?

They went hunting for something to prove the Russian Navy still had a reason for existence and found *Gepard* sitting in a pool of rusty water in the Severomorsk yards. She looked more like a half-dismantled hulk than a warship. But oil money was flooding the state coffers, and a great deal of it was dedicated to *Gepard.* When she finally left drydock under her own power, she was the newest and most advanced submarine in the Russian fleet, incorporating an 'active silencing' system not even the Americans had. Leonov had tested the device under the harshest imaginable conditions: playing cat and mouse with the American Sixth Fleet, and it had worked.

'Rudder amidships,' said Leonov.

The intercom squawked Stavinsky's acknowledgement.

Leonov had shadowed the Americans, slipping among them like a wolf. He proved the Russian Navy was good for more than rusting and sinking. The Americans he'd shadowed were alive only because it was practice, not war, and because he, Rem Leonov, allowed it.

Gepard was different, and so was Leonov. Like the commanders who sailed the other 'big cats', the *Tiger, Cougar, Puma, Ocelot* and *Leopard,* he was confident and aggressive. After Leonov had trailed an American *Los Angeles* and remained undetected, the captain had ordered an all-hands celebration. The men of the engineering section fashioned an ornate titanium crown, painted it gold and presented it to Leonov. It was inscribed *LYV.* Russian for 'Lion'.

Not all *Gepard's* crew were so admiring of their commander. Most of the enlisted were draftees; here only because they were too poor to pay off their military obligation and intelligent enough to avoid the Army. It was considered an unfortunate twist of fate to be assigned a captain who took his duties seriously. They nicknamed him *Lyvonok* and Executive Officer Stavinsky *Cherepakha.* 'Little Lion' and 'Turtle' from a mocking children's song.

Leonov might not be universally loved, but he did solve a large problem for the admirals of the Northern Fleet. Here was *proof* that Russian submarines were as good as American submarines. And so, instead of recalling *Gepard* home after her successful cruise, the admirals sent her back to Syria to take on provisions at Tartus for 'extended operations in the Mediterranean zone,' and, while there, to serve as 'goodwill ambassadors'.

Leonov didn't like the sound of *extended operations* in this samovar of an ocean any better than he liked the idea of dispensing goodwill to the sly, thieving Syrians. No Russian submarine had called on the old Soviet base at Tartus in ten years, and a decade of local ownership had turned it into a pirate's cove of smugglers and corrupt officials. Dealing with them absorbed Leonov's supply of goodwill as fast as the Syrian heat sapped the ship's already inadequate cooling system.

Leonov picked up the intercom. 'What is the temperature in Central Command?'

'Forty three degrees, Captain,' said Stavinsky.

'You should have brought a banana tree instead of a birch.'

Stavinsky had brought along a sprig of green birch from his home in Gadzhievo. It sat in a glass of water in his cabin. So long as it remained green, he could imagine a world beyond *Gepard's* gray steel walls. 'Or pineapples.'

'What about Engineering?'

'Worse.'

'We'll find cool water soon enough,' Leonov said encouragingly. But there was danger here. The ship's air conditioning was running at maximum and falling behind. Systems would start to fail in the heat, resulting in more heat, more failed systems. At some point a runaway bootstrap reaction would take place. And the heat affected more than just machinery. *Akulas* were highly

189

automated warships. An American *Los Angeles* could sail with a crew of a hundred and thirty. An *Akula* dedicated more space to weapons than people, and so *Gepard* sailed with just seventy men, each one of them necessary.

When the stern of the eight-thousand ton submarine cleared the bumpers at the end of the pier, Leonov said, 'Line handlers below!' The sweaty men sullenly moved in the direction of the main trunk. No one rushed. 'Engines all stop.'

'All stop,' came Stavinsky's reply.

Leonov gazed across the hazy waters of the inner harbour. He could feel the heat radiate off his coal black deck. To send him and his ship to a place like this! 'Ahead slow.' He looked astern as the port of Tartus slowly receded into the steamy haze. 'Oleg? How deep is the channel?'

'The chart says it was dredged to twenty meters in 1980.'

'Small boat dead ahead!' shouted one of the two lookouts posted atop the open bridge.

Leonov raised his binoculars. A fishing boat was sailing across the sea channel. By eye she was just a fleck of dirty white confetti. In the glasses, he could make out her low barge hull, a red wooden shack on her deck, a lateen sail. As Leonov watched, she slowed, then stopped, he saw the splash of an anchor heaved over the side. He snatched the microphone. '*Starpom!* Sound the horn. Three blasts.'

Bah-wah... Bah-wah... Bah-wah!

Leonov watched through the glasses. 'The idiot has his fishing net out.' He grabbed the microphone. 'Helm. Ahead one third.'

'Captain?'

'Ahead one third!'

'Understood!'

Leonov felt a shiver of power vibrate through the deck plates as *Gepard* accelerated. Ahead, a glass-smooth skim of water sheeted over her spherical bow and cascaded back across her black flanks in a tumble of foam. The first fresh breeze in what seemed a lifetime cooled his face. The most modern Russian submarine in the fleet and the captain who could stick his thumb in the eye of the Americans was not about to be delayed by a fisherman and his net.

'Ship's status?' he asked.

'Ready to dive, captain,' said Stavinsky. 'We'll have a hundred meters of water under the keel beyond the last sea buoy.'

Maybe, thought Leonov. It wouldn't do to get his belly stuck on a shoal. He had no desire to negotiate a tug from the Syrians while his ship sat in the mud. 'The horn again, Oleg.'

Three more blasts echoed across the outer harbor.

Leonov kept his glasses on the little boat. The horn had not motivated them, but the sight of a low, black warship charging at them with a curling white wave in her teeth did the trick. One second the half-naked fishermen were pulling in their net, the next, they leaped like fleas for the wheelhouse. A chuff of black soot rose from the fisherman's stack as two men raced back to her stern with axes to cut away their net while a third did the same for the anchor lines.

'We'll pass very close,' warned a lookout.

'We failed in our mission to bring goodwill to Syria,' Leonov said. 'I think we may leave a few of them cleaner.'

The lookouts laughed as *Gepard* charged ahead. The little boat swiftly grew from a dot to a toy to a real vessel as the submarine rocketed by a scant fifteen meters away.

Gepard caught the fisherman's net. There was a *twang!* then the crackle of splintered wood as the stern ripped away from the Syrian's hull, spilling debris into the water while her crew swam for their lives.

Leonov watched his wake swamp the settling barge. When it passed, only scattered boards and bobbing heads remained.

'They look cleaner already, Captain!' called out the port lookout.

'Good bye and good will to you!' called Leonov. Then, he turned and said, 'Clear the bridge! Lookouts below! Prepare to dive!'

A raucous dive bell sent the men of the surface detail scurrying to the main trunk hatch. Standing at the top of the ladder, Leonov could feel heat rising up like a chimney. The rungs of the ladder were painfully hot to the touch. He stepped inside and started down. Soon all his sweat dried to streaks of salt. The clamshell hatch clanged shut overhead.

The ladder ended at the aft end of Central Command. The instant Leonov's boots touched the green tiled deck, he said, 'Kiselyev!' He barked at the radio officer. 'Make the necessary departure signals. Tell Moscow we're prepared to accept new orders.'

Radio Electronics Lieutenant Kiselyev was lumbering and slow, and the heat did little to speed him up. When he finally brought a sheet of thin translucent paper to Leonov it was damp and smudged from his sweaty hands.

Leonov studied the onionskin for a moment, then smiled.

1: American Los Angeles-class submarine transited Algerian Trough 12 October and proceeding east at high speed.
2: Make best speed 16E 36N and intercept SSN vicinity Straits of Sicily
3: Track and trail SSN in combat range
4: Determine SSN area of operations and mission.

The Americans were 'proceeding east at high speed'. An interesting urgency, and it would also make finding them easier: speed meant noise. The Sicilian Strait was a day and a half away. The waters there were narrow and difficult, but it was also the neck of a bottle through which the Americans would have to squeeze. And when they did, *Gepard* would be there.

'Passing the first sea buoy, Captain,' said Stavinsky, who was very curious about any orders that could make Leonov look so happy. 'Depth under the keel now one hundred meters.'

'Make your depth seventy meters. Dive.'

The deck angled down as tons of water filled her ballast tanks. It grew quieter, and slowly, painfully slowly, cooler.

'Have the navigator plot a course for the Straits

of Sicily.'

'We're going home?' the starpom asked hopefully.

'No. We're going hunting.'

USS *Portland*
Straits of Sicily

Portland's radio shack was just aft of Control, its door kept closed and locked. COB Browne gave it three hard knocks, then stood back. The bolts slid aside and the door cracked open.

'Hey, Banjo,' said Browne. 'How's that clawhammer coming?'

Gant was trying to learn the clawhammer style of banjo picking, and so far it had eluded him. How did the new Chief of the Boat know about that? 'Not so good, COB. I've been kinda busy.'

He peered beyond the radioman's shoulder. 'Mind?'

'Sorry. Come on in.'

'Why thank you, Banjo,' he said politely, but with the look of an admiral invited to board his own launch. 'I understand you've got yourself a little problem in here.'

Banjo turned to see if Scavullo had heard.

'Not that one.' Browne strode in. 'Well,' he said to Scavullo. 'I see you found your way back onto a submarine. How'd that happen?'

Scavullo pushed back her headset. She'd heard Browne was back, and it was welcome news. He'd been prickly and particular with her on their last run together, but absolutely fair. 'The Russians

194

have a word for it, COB: *Sudba.* It means *fate.*'

'I understand you've had some problems on this run.'

'It's an experiment. The Navy wants to see how long I can take being locked up in a submarine before I kill someone.'

Banjo listened and thought, *Did she just admit to something?*

That wasn't the problem Browne meant but it was on his list. 'I was under the impression you *requested* this duty.'

'I did.'

'And you also requested *off.* Why?'

'I'll tell you, COB. Imagine you're walking into the Plantation Club. It's 1920 and you aren't carrying a tray. Does that give you an idea?'

Senior chiefs rule in mysterious ways. Some are red-faced screamers able to make the veins in their necks throb on demand. Browne's approach was different and no less effective: he let you know that if you screwed up you were *personally* disappointing him. Most sailors who experienced it felt about as high as a grease mark on the deck, and all sailors knew he held himself to the same high standard.

'Let me clue you in on something, lieutenant,' he said quietly. 'No one in *this* Navy looks at me and says what a good job I do for a *black* man. They look at these,' he pointed to his dolphins, 'and these,' his chief's anchors, 'and they say here's the sailor who has *all* his shit in one bag. Now if you want to cut and run away that's your affair.'

'You see someone running?'

'Just checking. And there will be no *personal*

crusades on my boat either. You got a problem with a crewman, you come see me and I assure you it will be addressed.'

'What about officers?'

'About the *radio* problem,' said Browne, choosing not to answer her question. 'What progress have you made in isolating it?'

'None. Every time I think I have it cornered to one system it jumps.'

'Computers check out?'

'First thing we did. We went scorched earth and reformatted and reloaded everything except the crypto programs. But it can't be in those. The decoding gear is just reacting to what the receivers pick up.'

'What else have you checked?'

'Everything.'

'That's a physical impossibility,' said Browne, this time with a different, cooler tone. 'I guarantee there's *something* you missed because *that* is where your *problem* is hiding.'

She stiffened. 'I don't skip things, COB.'

'You haven't found what you're looking for so by definition you skipped *something*. Okay? School of the boat is now in session,' said Browne. 'Banjo? You will come up with a *thorough* systems checklist. Find one, adapt one or write one. *Leave nothing out* or you'll be a while getting back to your banjo picking.'

'Aye aye, COB.'

'Lieutenant? I don't expect you to know these radios so your job will be to *follow* Banjo's checklist *exactly*. I'm sure you'll be more thorough this time.' He turned to leave, then stopped. 'By the

196

way, Banjo. I understand we've got some pranksters on board.'

Banjo started to say something, then stopped.

'Don't worry, son. I'm not asking for names. Not *yet*. But if you *happen* to run into someone who *might* fit that description, I hope you'll let him know that he is now *officially* retired. There will be no more pranks on *my* boat.' COB didn't explain himself nor did he need to. He smiled at Scavullo. 'Welcome back, lieutenant. It'll be a real pleasure to see what you come up with. Bring your results after you come off watch.'

'But that's just two hours from now.'

'In the Goat Locker,' said Browne. 'And don't be late.'

Portland sprinted across the central Mediterranean, covering the five hundred miles from the coast of Sardinia to the Straits of Sicily in sixteen hours. COB Browne sat before the ballast control board as Chief of the Watch. He was reasonably pleased with the world: a green board, boat in trim, plenty of air, hydraulics up. Lieutenant Pena was Dive Officer, and the two sailors at the ship's control station under his watchful eye kept *Portland's* depth good to within ten feet.

Navigator Pardee knew when they'd pass south of Malta to the minute, and they cleared the island right on schedule in the afternoon of 13 October. The shallow saddle connecting Sicily with North Africa passed astern, and the Malta Trough announced itself in the swift unreeling of numbers on the bottom sounder; eight hundred became a thousand, then two, then three thousand feet before finally steadying. The trough was an undersea channel that led east to the Ionian Sea, where the bottom plunged to nearly sixteen thousand feet. Indeed, if the Med had been a bathtub, the Ionian Sea would be the drain.

Though *Portland* had put a lot of sea miles astern, Steadman was uneasy. Nothing screwed up passive sonar like a high-speed run; the torrent rushing across her hull rendered her totally deaf. All captains pay attention to procedures. Good captains also listen to their instincts, and racing through the sea blind and deaf was raising the hairs on the back of his neck. He picked up the microphone that hung at his seat on the forward rail of the periscope island. 'Sonar, Conn.'

'Sonar, aye,' said Bam Bam.

'We're going to check baffles. Report all contacts, all noise levels.'

'All right, skipper. It's been kinda' boring up here anyways.'

Boring? No. Boring was not holding any targets inside thirty miles. Boring was knowing you weren't about to drill the boat into an uncharted gravel bank at thirty plus knots. Steadman knew a skipper who had done just that, and brought his boat home with his torpedo tubes full of rocks. The last eleven hours had *not* been boring. Steadman hung the mike up. 'Helm? Left five degrees rudder. All stop on the engines. Hold your depth at three hundred feet.'

The afternoon meal had been served and dinner preparations were underway. Tony Watson and Lieutenant Jameson had the wardroom to

198

themselves. Watson wore khakis with dangerously sharp creases. Jameson had on a pair of grungy sweatpants, a stained T-shirt and Teva sandals that looked like they'd been worn to run a marathon over a lava field.

It was eerily quiet in the wardroom. Even more so given that the reactor was putting out a sizable percentage of its rated power to propel the submarine at near-torpedo speed.

'You look like you've settled in,' said Watson disapprovingly.

Jameson grinned. 'There's only one thing to say to a SEAL in dress blues, XO. *The defendant shall rise.* Hey. I wanted to thank you guys for flogging the boat for us.' He'd pegged the XO as a Mark-One geek submariner, and though SEALs rated them a particularly low order of life, staying on the XO's good side had some advantages. 'I hope we're not using up too many atoms.'

'The tank's full,' said Watson. He had a mug of coffee and a pile of technical manuals in front of him. Usually the SEALs seemed like crude gladiators interested in only the 3-Ms of movies, meals and mattresses. But if this unkempt gorilla expressed an interest in the reactor he'd try to educate him. 'Actually, the more power we pull from the plant the more it's ready to give. The faster we circulate coolant the cooler and denser it becomes. Dense coolant is able to absorb more energy. The more energy it absorbs the hotter the steam, and so...'

'The hotter the steam, the faster we go?'

'That's right. We'll hit limits in thermal transfer, hull drag and screw efficiency long before we run out of atoms.'

'So flanking around is no big deal?'

'For the reactor,' said Watson. 'Keep in mind we're making a lot of noise, our situational awareness is degraded and there's less margin for error in navigation. You look like you're on vacation, lieutenant. I hope it isn't contagious.'

'Being a SEAL? No sir. It's definitely nothing you can catch.'

'I meant your uniform. We *are* in the same Navy, I think.'

'Same Navy, different rules. Submariners can only do what the book says they can do. SEALs can do everything the book doesn't say we can't.'

'I'm surprised there *is* a book.'

'Yes sir. And we can read it, too.' He'd sucked up enough. 'I don't think we hit it off too well with your skipper. Any way to improve that?'

'The raft business.'

'Your CO was ready to throw us over the side to get them back.'

'Let me give you a tip about how to get along with Commander Steadman: keep his reflection buffed and you can write your own ticket.'

Jameson thought *weasel*. A SEAL who said that about his CO would end up with broken bones. But he gave Watson a rueful smile. 'There's a few like that in every community, I guess.'

'Make him look good and you'll have no worries from our CO. The one you need to watch out for is our rider.'

'Lieutenant Scavullo? Why?'

'She's got special status on board. The Navy doesn't want any complications. They're willing to go to *extraordinary* lengths to prove that putting women on fast-attack boats can work. It means she can get away with pretty much anything she wants to.'

'The captain can rein her in, can't he?'

'Can. Won't. You see, the CO and Lieutenant Scavullo have a complicated relationship. You know what the typical career path is for a submarine XO? He spends two years ashore *before* he can think about Prospective Commanding Officers School. Our captain was *Portland's* XO on Scavullo's first run. *Eighteen months ago.* Now he's her captain. Enough said?'

'Wow. He must be a hot runner with the admirals.'

'Hardly. He's not even an Academy graduate. He's riding a political wave.

'Scavullo?'

'You might say that each of them is the reason why the other one is here.'

Jameson was about to ask how Steadman could get away with having a 'complicated relationship' with a junior officer when he stopped and looked up.

The hanging plants were tilting. The distant rumble of the screw fell silent.

'We're slowing down,' said Watson. 'We've got to give sonar a chance to do something useful now and again.'

We're not here for neighborhood tours. Jameson stood. 'Excuse me, sir, but I think I'd better go have a little chat with your CO.'

'Just remember what I told you,' said Watson. 'And if you need any more help with anything, come see me.'

'Aye aye, sir. I sure will.' With that, Jameson took off for Control.

Steadman glanced up at the sonar repeater. The picture was coming into focus like a landscape emerging from behind snow. 'Sonar, Conn,' he said. 'Anything yet?'

'Stand by.' Bam Bam thought, *That's the good thing about the skipper.* There was no Mickey Mouse. The old captain, the one they called *Iron Ass,* would make you *pretend* to listen even when the boat was on a flank bell and there was *no fucking way* anything – shy of a depth charge going off close aboard – was going to make it into the sonar arrays.

Bam Bam had put away his portable CD player, stashed the library of George Strait albums he'd entertained himself with for the last two watches, and was now paying very close attention as the world of undersea sound reappeared on his screen.

It was a world of white vertical lines against dappled green. Each line looked like a fine thread of sand being poured from above, and represented a distinct sound. Their brightness, their steadiness, their pulsing rhythm expanded inside Bam Bam's brain to become shrimp and ships, undersea volcanoes, lovesick whales and, now and again, submarines.

A faint line appeared. He quickly identified it as a ship far to their north. Bam Bam watched it, letting the turns of its screws, its progress across the surface, the sound of its engines, grow into an identity. 'Conn, Sonar. I got a small, single-screw surface contact bearing zero four zero. Designate him Sierra Sixty-One. Sounds like a fisherman headed northwest. Probably making for Palermo with the catch of the day.'

'The fish biting good up there?' asked Niebel.

Bam Bam pressed the headphones tight to his ear, then said, 'You like calamari?'

Gepard
Straits of Sicily

'New contact, Captain.' It was Lieutenant Kureodov, *Gepard's* sonar officer. The other officers treated him with a certain respect, for he had an uncle who was a senior admiral in Moscow. But privately they called him *Termite;* a creature who burrows in and once ensconced becomes exceedingly difficult to evict. Who knew what would happen to them when their tours ended? But the Termite? It was generally recognized that he would die in an admiral's uniform.

Kureodov sat behind a large circular screen tucked into the forward corner of the Central Command compartment where it could easily be seen by the captain. Three separate targets could be automatically tracked. A pulsing spike of light illuminated the 300 degree radial. As he watched, the radial shifted north to 305 degrees.

Leonov walked over from the captain's chair; a swiveling leather throne set dead center in the compartment. He stood behind the lieutenant's shoulder. 'How would you evaluate it?'

'A submarine moving at high speed. Most probably a *Los Angeles*.'

'Why a *Los Angeles?*'

A simple enough question, though Kureodov didn't have an immediate answer more convincing than *what else could it be?*

There were times like this that Leonov wished he could pick his men. Unlike the United States Navy, only officers were permitted to operate a Russian warship's critical systems, only to leave their ships at the first opportunity for shore duty. The enlisted men, the common *matros,* were useful for hauling in lines, cleaning bilges and doing the many distasteful things required to keep a submarine at sea. The old warrant officers, you could rely on them, but they were in short supply. He'd quietly pulled some strings to get Stavinsky assigned to *Gepard.* He only wished he could have selected a real sonar officer, too. 'Why a *Los Angeles*, lieutenant?' he repeated. 'You must have some reason.'

Kureodov was on his second and last patrol as sonar officer. He had no great love for sea duty except that it was a necessary check mark to collect for his personnel file. Since Leonov was always trying to be the teacher, it was best to play the student. 'What else could move so fast?'

'A cigarette boat filled with rich Italians and topless blondes.' A chuckle went around Central Command. 'And how can you be sure of its speed without also being sure of its range?'

'One moment,' Kureodov said coolly. His ears burned at being laughed at. Kureodov looked forward to waving goodbye to him once the ship returned home to Gadzhievo. He used a trackball to move a cursor over the spoke of light. He clicked a button and waited.

Establishing an accurate sonar range was as much a patient art as a science. It required careful, painstaking ranging legs and experience. Instead, a simple computer program used signal strength to estimate distance, and projected its guess up into a small box at the bottom of the circular screen. 'Fifteen kilometers.'

'Where did that come from?'

'The system calculated the...'

'The system makes assumptions, Kureodov. It's up to you to interpret them correctly. What if this contact was noisier than normal?'

'What kind of submarine would be so noisy?'

One commanded by a captain who doesn't care who hears him. 'What about his blade count?'

'Two hundred sixty revolutions per minute, Captain.'

'At 265 revolutions a *Los Angeles* will make thirty-four knots. Forget the system. Use that speed and bearing shift to calculate a range.'

Kureodov might be lazy but he could add and subtract. He scribbled the equation down on a notepad, then solved it. 'Thirty-nine kilometers,' he said, surprised it was so far off the computer's estimate.

'If this were war and we'd used the wrong range to launch a torpedo, we would miss. But the enemy would have heard it and fired back at us and we would now be dead. You see my point about assumptions?'

'Not even a *Los Angeles* can hear us from thirty

205

nine kilometers.'

'Don't bet your life on it.' Though Kureodov was likely correct, for *Gepard* was equipped with both passive and active silencing systems. She was very quiet, especially between six and ten knots. Perhaps even more so than the typical *Los Angeles*. 'I want to know the *instant* he passes abeam eastbound. Understood?'

'Understood!' Kureodov wondered if a negative mark from Leonov could really impede his progress to a staff position. *No. He's only a ship driver.* By definition, operational officers were at a disadvantage when it came to promotions. But then he noticed that something had changed on his sonar display. 'Captain? The contact appears to be turning. And his blade count is falling.'

Leonov took a look for himself. The spike of green light had stopped its steady march to the east. It was veering north, and the blade count was down to 100. Then ninety. Then sixty. *What are you doing?*

A speeding *Los Angeles* making enough noise to wake the dead had almost no chance of detecting his ship. But a silent, drifting one, that was a different matter. He turned to the electronic countermeasures officer. 'Arm the *Sirena*,' he said. 'But do not activate it yet.'

USS *Portland*

'Sonar, Conn. Anything?' asked Steadman.

'Clear screens,' said Bam Bam. 'But we're getting multiple reflections and all kinds of distortions off the layer. Sonar conditions are down-right *squirrelly* out there tonight.'

Steadman hung the microphone back up and watched the course gyro click its way around from northeast to north, then northwest.

'Permission to enter control?'

Steadman turned.

Lieutenant Jameson filled the forward portside passage. 'Sir? Could I have a word with you in private?'

Now what? Steadman glanced at the helm, saw that they were holding three hundred feet, passing through north and decelerating through eight knots. He crooked a finger. 'Come.'

They made their way aft, passing the periscope stand, the navigation plotting tables where sailors were kept busy with *Portland's* curving, north-ward path. Past Pardee, who was checking the issue dates on Mediterranean charts he'd never had reason to use before.

Steadman stepped into the passage leading by the radio room and further aft to the stout, watertight door emblazoned with placards about security and radiation hazards. Beyond it and half a level down was 'nuke alley'; the reactor spaces. *Watson's realm.* 'Go,' he said.

To any SEAL, a Presidential Finding that said *go get 'em* was like God Almighty telling you to kill them all and let Him do the sorting. But for some reason Jameson didn't understand, Steadman didn't seem to share that view. 'Sir, there are a couple of points I didn't cover the other day. I thought I'd better do that now while there's time.'

'I'm listening.'

'I know it's standard practice to do a sonar sweep after a high speed run, but we aren't out here to conduct standard operations. You're not in the United States Navy any more. Your *only* job is to find that freighter. Time is of the essence. We can stop them, but not by dicking around out here doing sonar sweeps. If we don't intercept *Cristi,* or if we intercept her after she's handed off that Chechen biologist and his weapon, someone's going to ask who let it happen.'

Steadman stiffened. 'If someone asks I'll answer for it.'

'No sir. It will be you and me and every other officer in your command and that's the truth. Think about what could happen if they use that bioweapon. It will make the investigations into who let 9/11 happen look like a birthday party.'

Jameson wasn't wrong. The decisions might be Steadman's to make, but everyone on *Portland* would be saddled with the results.

'One more thing,' said Jameson. 'I've reconsidered your offer of Lieutenant Scavullo. She's right. Her fluency could be a real asset to us. I'd like her operationally reassigned to Yellowstone.'

'She's not riding any rubber assault boats.'

Would you be saying that if she were just another guy? 'No sir. But we can link her up to the boarding party by radio. That way if we run into a language problem she can help solve it right on the spot.' *Get it? I'm offering a slice of glory to your girlfriend.* 'But none of that will matter if we don't rendezvous with *Cristi.*' He stood back. 'You're driving the boat. But I hope you'll consider what I've said very seriously.'

'I've heard you.' Steadman spun on his heel and re-entered Control. In four long strides he was back at the small, padded seat at the forward end of the periscope stand.

He scanned the contact evaluation board, then glanced up at the sonar repeater. There was nothing close by. Just a few, distant surface contacts. They'd circled around from due east to north and now the course indicator showed southwest. He unclipped the microphone from the bulkhead. 'Sonar, Conn. I'm not seeing anything out there.'

'We haven't swept out the southeast sector yet,' said Bam Bam.

Steadman checked the Contact Evaluation Board. Nothing. And southeast was the African coast. *Portland* had no business down there, nor was it likely that anything threatening would be found. 'We're going to have to let it go. Helm? Left full rudder. Steady on course zero nine three. All ahead full.'

Jameson stood at the aft passage and smiled. The XO might be a weenie who couldn't fight his way out of a juice bar without a manual to tell him how, but he had Steadman *nailed.*

Gepard

'Contact bearing three five nine,' said Kureodov. 'True range is twenty kilometers and still closing.'

Here he comes thought Leonov. A *Los Angeles* had very sensitive sonar, and the most acute of all was built into the spherical bow. *And his bow is turning in our direction.* Captain Leonov pulled down a microphone dangling from a coiled wire. It was called a *kashtan* for the walnut it vaguely resembled. 'Rig the ship for quiet operation.' He turned to the lieutenant at the electronics support console. 'Switch on the *Sirena*.'

The annoying *thud thud thud* of the *Sirena* masker assaulted his ears. A computer was now monitoring every noise made within the submarine, and sending out pulses of energy in the form of sound waves to precisely counteract them.

The masker was effective at quieting his submarine; not totally, for it could do nothing about flow or screw noise. But it dramatically decreased the range at which an enemy would detect him, and in the game of cat and mouse that was submarine warfare, where the margin between victory and defeat, life and death, was small, Leonov could put up with a bit of annoyance.

'Captain? Contact shifting east again and showing turns for sixteen knots,' said Kureodov. 'Now twenty knots.'

'East?' said Leonov.

'And turns now for *twenty-two* knots,' said Kureodov proudly, a student glad to surprise the master. He turned away from his big, circular screen. 'He didn't see us!'

CHAPTER THIRTEEN

ABYSS

MV 'Nova Spirit'
Sea of Crete

Makayev opened his cabin door. It once seemed so terribly flimsy. Now it moved slowly, heavily, like the hatch that had guarded the Capsule back at Pokrov. He thought of that night, the explosion, the way Salafi had pushed him right to the edge where the vertigo of possibility had whispered *jump*.

A disease like smallpox progresses like a pebble down a slope. One rock dislodges two, then four, sixteen, and then? With Hunter, the first rock moved when he'd entered the Capsule. Somehow, a virus had taken root inside him, hijacking the cells of his own body, turning them into miniature factories for producing more Hunter. At some point, one day ago, or two, they'd reached a critical mass. Salafi, the two brothers. The ship's crew. *Avalanche.*

He put his hand to his neck, to the scattering of small, hard beads beneath his skin, all of them malignantly rich with virus. He should be glad he was still on his feet. There would come a moment, tomorrow, the next day, when the slope would steepen to the vertical. And then?

If Hunter had escaped the ship with that Turkish inspector, there was nothing he could do but sound a warning. Now.

The central passage was empty and the door leading out to the fantail was open. He could hear the murmur of voices, the sunset devotions, the *Salatu-l-Maghrib*. The entire crew would be assembled back there. Who was steering? Who was operating the engine? The same person who would be sitting at the radios: God.

He took the ladderwell up to the bridge. One step, pull, another. His head felt hot and tight, a balloon ready to float away. He paused, sniffing the smell of cardamom and curry from the galley. Makayev tried to remember when he'd last eaten, and decided it didn't matter. Every sip of water, particle of food, breath of air, only meant more viruses churned out from those factories.

He came to the small bridge atop the iron house. A soft, irregular tapping filled the small space like an old grandfather's clock with a bad case of arrhythmia: *click ... click click ... click.*

The compartment was small, dirty, metallic and gray. Steel tables were welded to the bulkheads. Angled panes looked down over the foredeck. The sun had nearly set, and the rugged coast of a large island was turned to silhouette by the low slant of golden light.

The helm was at the forward starboard corner and lit by a single red lamp. The clicking sound came from there. The wheel? He imagined it large, wooden and spoked, but found a small metal disc the size of a dinner plate instead.

It moved with a sharp and definite *click.*

Automatic steering? A laptop computer sat open on the console next to the wheel. It was plugged into a power receptacle. The screen was lit with a blue nautical chart. A tiny ship's symbol was at the center, tracking faithfully along a magenta line that marked a convoluted course through the islands of Kea, Yiaros and Kithnos. Cables from the computer snaked through a propped-open porthole to a black, puck-like antenna strapped to a railing outside.

Switch the computer off, spin the wheel and he might run the ship aground. It might attract help. It would surely keep them from reaching Malta. But the crew, Salafi and his two bulls, would walk away. And with them would go Hunter. What he needed to find was deep water, not shallow. Dark blue, not pale.

He found the zoom feature, and clicked it once, twice, a third time. The islands receded and the view expanded to encompass the whole of the central Mediterranean from Greece to Italy to the north African coastline. Makayev let his finger trace the magenta ship's intended course, then stopped at a triangular zone of dark, dark blue halfway between their present location and their destination of Malta: the four thousand meter deep Ionian Abyss.

Yes. Shout a warning to the world about Istanbul, then put the ship on the bottom *there* and Makayev could die a fool, not a mass murderer.

He turned away from the helm and made his way aft.

The radios were tucked into a tiny, windowless alcove at the back of the bridge. Just a steel desk and a wall of ancient tube radios, their glass dials dark and dusty. A calendar was pinned to the wall, open to February 2001. Sitting on the desk was a tiny, modern short-wave set connected by a cable to the ship's main antenna. A microphone lay beside it on a nest of black coiled wire. A bright red button on the face of the short wave was labeled *distress*.

Makayev punched the red button. The numbers 2182 and CH16 popped up in the radio's display and began to flash. He reached for the microphone, pressed what he hoped was the transmit key and said, in a frog's croak, '*Kto nibout sluchayet?* 'Is anyone listening?'

He waited, then saw the volume was turned down. He twisted the knob up full until the small alcove crackled with the static sound of frying bacon. 'Any ship, any ship. Please answer.'

A new voice boomed surprisingly clear and strong, and even more, it was a *Russian*. '*Baltic Conveyor* listening. Who is on Channel Sixteen?'

'This is an emergency! My name is Makayev!'

'What's your emergency and where are you?'

Makayev paused. 'The ship is *Cristi*. We are near Kithira Island.'

'What's your problem, *Cristi?*' The disembodied voice was starting to sound annoyed.

'The ship passed through Istanbul. There is a disease on board that might have escaped, it must not be allowed to...'

A hand clamped over Makayev's mouth. Another grabbed his shoulder, spun him away from the radio and slammed him against a bulkhead. A healthy man might bounce off and come back swinging. Makayev dropped to the deck as though he'd been struck with an ax.

'*Cristi*, this is the *Baltic Conveyor*. Say again?'

Adnan snatched the microphone and handed it to Salafi.

'This is the motorship *Nova Spirit*. Do you speak English, sir?'

'*Da*. A little.'

'Sorry if my first mate worried you,' said Salafi. His was an English accent spiced with Delhi. 'Our chap had a bit too much to drink. He can't even remember the name of his own ship. We're *Nova Spirit*.'

'Tell him to keep away from channel sixteen. *Baltic Conveyor* out.'

Salafi clicked off the radio, then stood over Makayev. 'What were you trying to do?'

Makayev sagged against the bulkhead, his chin against his chest.

Adnan felt Makayev's pebbled skin, took his hand away and looked up at Salafi. 'You said he was only seasick. Feel him.'

'I'm not a doctor and neither are you.' Salafi came up to them and crouched down, his knee bent. 'What is it, Makayev?'

'The ... ship,' Makayev said, though it came out a mumble. 'He can't ... go ... to Malta ... Pokrov...'

'Why not?'

'Like ... Kaffa ... Malta ... everywhere.'

'What are you sick with?' Salafi slapped him. '*Speak.*'

'What about Pokrov?' said Adnan.

Salafi shot him an angry glance. 'This doesn't concern you.' He leaned even closer to Makayev.

'If you're ill with something you brought there can be no question of continuing. The Saudis want a biological institute. Not an epidemic. So tell me the truth or I swear I will throw you over the side tonight myself'

'All ... of you ... sick.'

'No one is sick on board but you.'

Makayev shook as though he were freezing and not burning hot with fever, then said, 'Soon.'

Salafi let him go. Makayev collapsed to the deck.

He was a businessman, not some fanatic marching into a café with a bomb strapped to his waist. He was here to connect an interested party with some valuable merchandise. But catching some filthy disease, or dying from one, this was not part of the bargain.

Adnan peered at the Saudi as though gauging where to take the first bite. 'You know why he's sick.'

Salafi decided, *Riyadh. They'll know what to do.* Only then did he acknowledge Adnan's question. 'How can I?'

'Because I see it in your face. You said the samples were safe.'

'That's what *he* told me.'

'But they are not.'

'We were vaccinated for this very reason. You know all this.'

Adnan nodded at Makayev. 'He was vaccinated, too.'

'Stop talking. Let me think.'

Adnan felt the hard lumps at Makayev's neck. 'I think I know why you're so afraid. You have your beautiful houses, your bank accounts, your friends in the government. Losing all the world can offer terrifies you. It's not so frightening when you have less.'

'We're going to make a new arrangement. Forget Malta. We'll turn and put in somewhere where there's an airport. They'll send a jet and we'll all go to Riyadh. We can be at a good clinic in a matter of hours.' Salafi picked up the short-wave microphone. He thrust the disconnected plug into the jack. 'In the meantime, find the briefcase and bring it to me.' He looked down at Makayev. 'Throw him over the side. We don't need him now.'

'No.'

'What do you mean *no?*'

Adnan's eyes went cobra still. 'Talk on your radio. Walk off the ship or jump into the sea. It doesn't matter. You think you make all the arrangements? You forget that God is the best arranger of all.'

'This is not a religious question.'

'You're wrong,' said the bearded Chechen.

'Do as I say or the Prince will know!' *The Prince* was the Saudi royal who kept men like Adnan and Musa busily employed. And just as there was no place beyond his reach, there was also no place beyond his wrath.

'Tell him we will do as God commands,' said Adnan as he hoisted Makayev over his broad shoulder and left. Not for the side of the ship to throw Makayev overboard, but to the container lashed down on deck.

Adnan was a fighter, not a philosopher. But even he could sense the stirrings of something big and important inside him. Something far greater than just knocking down a few towers or blowing up a few embassies. A terrible blow that would turn a thousand years of weakness on its head and return the world to a state of purity, of righteousness. Let the Saudi have his briefcase, his vials. Adnan had something greater.

He stepped out onto the open cargo deck. He wasn't sure how he and his brother could use this *kafir* Chechen to serve God. Not yet. But he knew that when God handed you a weapon like this, He didn't mean for you to throw it into the sea.

15 OCTOBER
USS *Portland*
Ionian Sea

Like the fable of the blind men and the elephant, a submariner's view of his world depended on where he stood. The nukes aft looked down on the 'noseconers' in the forward spaces. The 'coners resented the special pay and privileges that nukes enjoyed and they *hated* the fact that nukes didn't put in much time 'messcranking' in the galley.

The senior chiefs stood above the two clans, settling arguments and calming jealousies from their throne in the Goat Locker. On *Portland,* it was located at the forward end of the middeck, next to the ship's office and hard against the elliptical bulkhead that kept the ocean out of the hull. Here all problems were heard and solved, all questions

218

answered, all deficiencies swiftly addressed.

Even senior officers hesitated at the door marked CPO QUARTERS: KNOCK THEN ENTER. Not Scavullo. She'd just spent two hours going through a mind-numbing search and destroy mission and had come up with *exactly* what she'd predicted: nothing. It was with these thoughts that she reached up and gave the door a good, hard knock.

COB Browne looked up from a printout of *Portland's* crew, their backgrounds, the boats they served on and the informal comments left by senior chiefs for the sole benefit of other senior chiefs. 'Come!'

Scavullo stepped into the Goat Locker. She had a binder in her hands and it was a big one.

She didn't find it, thought Browne. He could see it in her face. 'You're right on time, lieutenant. Come in and bring me the good news.'

Scavullo eased in and shut the door. 'We did our best. Banjo came up with a good list. We swept out the entire radio shack top to bottom, COB. That gremlin is not inside the submarine.'

'You mean you didn't find it.'

'*No.* I mean it isn't inside. The problem shows up as intermittent streams of garbage the crypto gear tries to decode but it can't. How could it? It's not code. It's just random noise coming down the antennas.'

'Coming down *all* the antennas?' *Portland's* radio systems were designed with a lot of backups. There were six separate antennas, seven counting the emergency whip. 'You want me to believe there's some kind of *bug* hangin' onto the hull

219

sending random signals down *all* the wires?'

'I know it sounds crazy, but Banjo and I are both convinced the problem is *outside* the hull. Maybe there's a break in a cable. Maybe even a chemical reaction with sea water that's generating stray current. But whatever it is, it is *definitely* on the *outside.*' She offered the binder. 'You can check for yourself All the tests. All the results. Right here.'

'I can see that won't be necessary,' said Browne. 'I'll let the captain know what you've found. We may want to surface and have a little *bug* hunt next chance that comes along.'

'Plan on spending some time. This bug is dug in deep.'

'I'm not sure I like the sound of a *bug* any more than I like jinx talk. You want to tell me what you know about those two little pranks?'

Her expression hardened. She thought of the crosshairs drawn on what was left of her panties. 'The men don't accept my being here, COB. I don't mean every last one of them. But a majority. And you know what? I'm not about to give in but I *am* beginning to see their point.'

'Let me offer a slightly different interpretation. The fact they're pulling these *pranks* means they just *might* be accepting you. You know, in the past, submariners were known for some crazy hazing. Getting your dolphins pinned to your bare chest. Drinking them at the bottom of a big glass of brew. I can't *begin* to tell you how many sailors got duct-taped to the overhead the day they qualified on the boat. It was a rite of passage.'

'The only rite of passage they want is to see me right off this boat.'

'And *that's* not going to happen. Meanwhile, you got a captain whose future depends on you coming home with a smile on your face. And you have a COB who's backin' you both a hundred and ten percent. So let me ask you a simple question: can you live with it?'

Scavullo felt the tension leave her face. The beginnings of a smile appeared. 'It's automatic, COB.'

'What I like to hear, lieutenant.'

There was a knock at the door.

'Come!' Browne commanded.

It was Banjo Gant. He saw Scavullo. 'I can come back later, COB.'

'The lieutenant and I are finished. She told me what you found. You agree this radio problem is outside the hull?'

'I don't know how it can be anything else.'

'Then you've done your jobs.' COB thumped the binder with the radio test results. 'I'll take a look at these and pass my recommendations to the XO. Good work. Both of you.'

A superior officer could just say *dismissed*. A senior chief had his own way of doing the same thing and Scavullo knew it. 'Thanks, COB.'

Banjo waited until Scavullo left, then said, 'COB? Some of the guys are pretty upset.'

'In what way, son?'

'Look, I work with her. I think I know her pretty well. She's no grape.' Submarine slang for *idler*. 'She's an officer, so sometimes she does dumb shit, but she's no jinx.'

'And they think she is?'

'And some of them are *real* anxious to see her

221

off the boat. One way or another.'

'I know about the *pranks*. Does it go any deeper?'

'Aye aye, senior chief. It does. For some of the guys, if she won't walk off the boat, they'll do something. You know what can happen.'

'I see,' said Browne. A submarine was a dangerous place to work on a good day. And a very dangerous place to work if someone had it in for you. 'Can I rely on you to do what's right?'

'Sure. I'll keep my eyes out when she's in the shack but I can't be everywhere.' Banjo paused, then got to the point. 'Can you do anything?'

'I'm the Chief of the Boat,' said Browne, insulted.

MV *'Nova Spirit'*
off the island of Paros, Aegean Sea

Black sea and black, starry sky divided as the east glowed with the coming dawn. Captain Warsame woke early and walked through the freighter, pounding on each cabin door, switching on every light belowdecks, rousing weary crewman with the call, 'On your feet! Prayer is better than sleep!'

It was time for the *Salatu-al-Fajir*, the dawn prayer held on the ship's stern. No arguments were allowed, and, other than the Russian, no exceptions were granted.

And so it was something of a surprise when Warsame looked over the faithful gathered in the fantail and came up one short. The light was dim, but he could see who was missing.

On his knees, with the red Tongan flag shifting in an uncertain southerly breeze behind him, Warsame led the crew in bowing their final *taslims*, then rose and said, 'Peace be on you and the mercy of Allah!' And with that, he rolled up his rug, slipped on his pink plastic sandals and went hunting for Salafi.

Warsame was of a Somali clan of fisherman and sailors. When civil war broke out and the streets of Mogadishu became a battlefield, it was only natural to escape to the relative safety of the sea. His younger brother was better with books, though, and he left Somalia for Canada, then America. He married, had children, went to an American university. He'd seen all the West could offer. Where had it gotten him?

Into an American prison, alone, cut off from friends, family, even lawyers. A terrorist, they said, because he'd made the fatal mistake of visiting Afghanistan at the wrong time and, foolishly, admitted it when the police came knocking on his door.

Warsame didn't need his brother's book wisdom to know that America was faith's mortal enemy. He'd seen them drop like locusts from their mighty helicopters into the streets of Mogadishu. He'd seen holy mosques defiled with filthy boots and women dishonored and searched. He'd also seen their machines in smoking ruins, children dragging their burned bodies through the alleys and their clattering helicopters flee for their ships at sea.

The world was shocked that a ragged Somali militia could throw the powerful Americans out, but Warsame was not. There were no accidents. It was the power of faith over faithlessness.

He found Salafi asleep, head down on a hard, metal table up in the radio cubicle. The fancy briefcase the Russian *kaffir* carried everywhere was at his feet. He didn't know what was inside it and knew better than to ask. As for Salafi, at first he thought he was dead, but then he saw his body slowly rise and fall. The shortwave set was on, the volume turned up high. The room crackled with static.

He gave the Saudi's chair a shake.

Salafi started, looking around in panic until his eyes focused and came to rest on the African. 'Did they answer?'

'Who?'

Salafi looked at the radio, then at Warsame. 'What do you want?'

'Is your soul too weak to rise for morning prayers?'

'I fell asleep.'

Warsame glanced at the radio. 'Is there a problem?'

'Yes. Something terrible has happened. We need to find a good airport. Which one is closest?'

'This is the sea. There are no airports. And I'm a captain, not an airplane pilot.' But Warsame thought, *Athens, if we turned around. Souda Bay is still ahead, but the Greeks run it, too.* 'What is this terrible thing that has happened?'

'The Russian. Your passenger. He fell overboard in the night.'

My passenger? 'How? And why was I not informed?'

224

'Who knew? He must have gone out on deck for some fresh air and...' Salafi shook his head. 'I should have watched more closely.'

'I thought your two men were here for that.'

'What's done is done. It's too late now for blame.'

'You've searched the ship? It's easy to get lost on even so small a ship as this one.'

'They have. I saw him last night. This morning I found this next to the rail,' he said, pointing to the briefcase. 'Makayev never let it out of his sight. Never. You can see why this changes everything.'

He left his luggage and went for a swim? 'For you, yes.'

'You don't understand,' said Salafi. He picked up the briefcase carefully. 'There are materials here that must be delivered at once.'

'Malta is only two days away.'

'I can't afford one extra day.'

'A ship like this is not free to stop anywhere. Drop anchor in the wrong port and the police would be waiting. If we sent out a distress–'

'No.' Do that and none of them would ever see Riyadh. The royal family lived by a set of iron rules. Not the laws of Islam, but of survival. They woke each morning with one thought: what must I do today to hold onto what I've got for another day? Another month? Next year?

Salafi had presented them with the ultimate insurance policy in Makayev. Own him and his bottles and no one would dare challenge the Kingdom again. *You want to take our oil? Take this plague with our compliments.* But now he'd told them that

225

something had gone wrong with that insurance policy, and what would Riyadh be thinking?

He looked at the silent radio. He'd have to play this one very carefully. *The vials.* They would be his *own* insurance policy, too. But then the radio static cleared, and a rich, honeyed voice said,

'*Calling Nova Spirit, Calling Nova Spirit. Answer.*'

Salafi lunged for the microphone. '*Nova Spirit* listening!'

'*We have found a new buyer for your cargo. Proceed to the port of Catania and meet the company agent there.*'

'What about the two other shipments?' *Adnan and Musa.*

'*The agent will be expecting them. Out.*'

The voice vanished. The static swelled.

Salafi turned the volume down and let out a long breath, then looked up at Warsame. 'You heard? Catania.'

Warsame switched the shortwave to the weather channel, listened to the recorded message, filled with reported winds, buoy pressures and forecasts.

'So?' asked Salafi.

'There's weather ahead. We'll put on a bit of speed while it's calm and get you to Catania.' He left the Saudi and walked forward to the helm, grasped the engine telegraph and shoved it to *All Ahead Full.*

CHAPTER FOURTEEN

PROPHECIES

USS *Portland*
off Akro Vouxa, Crete

The Med is small as oceans go, and it took only half a day steaming on a flank bell for *Portland* to arrive off western Crete. At that speed, her sonar was essentially blind, and Niebel used his watch to catch up on a submarine thriller written by a retired officer. He threw the paperback to the deck. 'Can you believe this shit? It's bad enough we have a rider with tits. He's got a woman *running* his fucking boat.'

Bam Bam pushed his headphones back. 'What's so bad about a rider with tits? I think it improves the scenery.'

'You striking for the fucking gender sensitivity committee?'

'No. I've just got better things to think about.'

'So do I. Like what happened the last time she was out with us. We were under the ice and on the fucking *bottom*. Or did you forget about that?'

Bam Bam hadn't forgotten. He'd heard the hiss of water rushing in under high pressure, the shouts of panic, the dimming lights. No, he hadn't forgotten. 'She wasn't driving the boat, Socks. Iron Ass was.'

'She was driving the XO is what she was doing.'

'You know, my father once told me that life's a whole lot simpler when you plow around the stump. You might want to consider that.'

'I'll tell you what *else* I'm considering: we're all going to end up in the ocean unless we get her off the boat.'

'She's got the captain, the COB and most of the Navy behind her. Don't corner something meaner than you are.'

'It'd be self defense if I did. What are you listening to anyway?'

'Sound cut.' There might be nothing to monitor with the boat flashing through the ocean at near-torpedo speeds, but Steadman had handed Bam Bam an unmarked diskette and told him it contained sounds of a surface target they would soon be hunting. He wouldn't tell him what kind of target, or why it was so important. Bam Bam loaded the files into his sonar system and studied them closely. For Schramm, what a target sounded like was all he needed to know most of the rest.

The bits and bytes of the digital file grew in his mind to become a ship. A small freighter, single screw, slow, plodding, and poorly maintained. If this 'target of interest' had been a musical instrument, it would be a battered trombone abused by a high-school marching band. Her shaft throbbed against a bad bearing, her pistons slapped. He heard the *thrum ... thrash ... thrum* of a bent propeller blade, the gurgle of water flowing over a hull that hadn't been cleaned of barnacles and weeds in a long time. After a few sessions with his headphones, Bam Bam knew as much about the ship's condition as her crew, and likely more.

'Sonar, Conn.'

Bam Bam jumped and picked up his microphone. 'Sonar.'

'Is that sound file up and loaded?'

'Aye aye, skipper. If that tub is around I'll find her.'

Any Chief of the Boat worthy of the name possessed powers easily mistaken for the magical. One of them was knowing the whereabouts of everyone on board the submarine, twenty-four hours a day. Browne helped his mojo along with a low-powered walkie-talkie. Hooked up with a discreet mouth-mike, he could sit at the ballast control panel managing the boat's trim and quietly finding out why a sailor hadn't shown up for his watch. And just *what was he doing* bullshitting in the engine room lower level anyway? Browne liked to say he had more rooms to take care of than a hotel manager and it was nearly true.

And so when Tony Watson left the middeck wardroom, heading for his cabin on the upper level, Browne knew exactly when to leave the Auxiliary Machine Room down on the bottom deck to meet up with him.

The door to Watson's stateroom was just closing when Browne stopped it with the toe of his shoe and knocked. 'Mister Watson?'

Watson looked out, annoyed, but then he saw Browne and the pinched look evaporated. 'Hey COB. What can I do for you?'

'If I might come in, I'd like a private word with you, sir.'

229

'Looks like you're already in.'

Browne took that testy reply as a *yes* and shut the door behind him. He respected Watson as a first-class engineer. But engineers had their own way of thinking. To a hammer, the world is studded with nails. Browne figured a *leader* needed a few more tools in his belt.

Watson's stateroom was smaller than Steadman's and lacked the display screens that permitted the captain to roll over in bed and take in the boat's status at a glance. It contained extra folding bunks for when distinguished visitors evicted the XO from his own space.

Watson had to step to the rear bulkhead to allow room for Browne to stand. 'What's on your mind, COB?'

'I think we've got a situation,' said Browne. 'I believe it's time to shut it down before it grows up. You know what some of the men are saying about Lieutenant Scavullo?'

'I hope you're not getting worked up over a few pranks.'

'No sir. I'm concerned about where that train is headed. And I don't consider breaking the boat's rig for dive a *prank.*'

'Okay. Point made. The obvious answer is to get her off the boat. She's wasting our air and eating our food. She's not contributing anything to the mission. At least, none that I know about. But we can't seem to get rid of her. What do you think we need to do?'

'First off, she did a fine job scouring out the radio shack for that intermittent comms problem. She's convinced me the fault is external to the pressure hull.'

'External?'

'Me, I'd check the antenna control unit in the sail. All the signal traffic gets routed through it.'

'We'll have to surface for that. What else?'

'I believe it would be wise to assign some people to keep an eye on her. To make sure there aren't any more pranks. Or accidents.'

'We don't have spare men sitting on their butts trying to look busy. This is a tough business, COB. Everyone has to carry his weight and more. Who are we going to shortchange so that Scavullo has a babysitter? She asked for submarines. Well, I've got news for her. Submarines are full of submariners. If she doesn't like that fact then tough. As for pranks, I trust you'll make it clear to the men that they will not be tolerated.'

'I've made that known, sir.'

'Naturally, if someone crosses the line I expect you to act accordingly and bring him straight to me.'

'If someone crosses that line she could end up hurt.' *Or dead.*

'You're blowing this up out of proportion, COB.'

'Maybe,' said Browne, 'but even a minor incident with the lieutenant is gonna' reflect badly on the boat.' *Including you. Get it?*

'There's no time for hand holding. We've got a squad of special operators on board. I don't need to read their orders to know this boat is going to see action. I expect you to keep the enlisted in line.'

'Yes, sir.' Lieutenant Scavullo could expect no

231

help from the XO. Other than Banjo and Browne, she would be on her own.

K-335 *Gepard*

'Blade count is down to one hundred revolutions,' said Kureodov. 'Range eleven thousand five hundred meters.'

What are you up to? Leonov wondered as he watched Kureodov's sonar screen. *What are you stalking?*

'Captain?' It was Kiselyev, the radio officer. 'We've got a scheduled seance in fifteen minutes.' They were Moscow's regularly scheduled broadcasts to the fleet. A low-frequency antenna farm in a field outside Moscow beamed out the usual smattering of ancient information and useless warnings on a precise schedule. He unfolded the sheet of onionskin paper with Moscow's orders and came to the fourth line.

4: DETERMINE SSN AREA OF OPERATIONS AND MISSION

The American's 'area of operations' would appear to be the inshore waters of Crete. Were they looking for something? A crashed bomber with an atomic weapon inside? A missile that splashed down in the wrong sea? 'Ahead slow. Come to periscope depth. And Kiselyev? Signal Moscow that we are tracking our assigned target.'

Portland swept the sea for a ship matching Bam Bam's sound file from the island of Kithira in the west to Santorini in the east. Rough, rocky islands, some inhabited, some not, they rose like stepping stones every thirty miles or so between the Greek mainland to Crete.

The sea off Crete's northern coast was busy with power boats, yachts, a couple of larger freighters. Even a wayward containership well off the usual transit lanes and in real danger of grounding. That would be her master's problem, not Bam Bam's, and he was about to go off duty and the boat was turning back west to retrace its course when he heard something different, and something familiar.

He listened, eyes shut, for a solid thirty seconds before he keyed his microphone. 'Conn, Sonar. Single screw ship bearing zero three two. Range is still...' he stopped. A flashing box appeared on his screen. The computer was trying to tell him something. He spun a trackball to move a cursor to the box, and hit SELECT.

'What?' asked Niebel. 'More squid boats?'

Bam Bam waved him quiet. 'Captain? The computer's got a possible match on that target of interest. Bearing now zero three zero. Range twenty-two thousand yards. Designate him Sierra Sixty-Two. He's headed southwest for sure.'

'Put it up,' said Steadman. 'I'll be right there.'

There was a hum over the 1MC shipwide intercom. *'Lieutenant Jameson to the sonar shack.*

233

Lieutenant Jameson to the sonar shack.'

Steadman was standing over Bam Bam in a few seconds. The SEAL commander had to climb up an entire deck from the torpedo room but he wasn't far behind.

Bam Bam had the contact's sound spectrum up on his screen. He put the stored file up beside it, and you could see why the computer was excited: the display showed the profiles of two jagged mountains. Both of them with identical peaks, identical valleys, identical shoulders. Each mountain represented the sounds of machinery, flow noise, the hum of a 50 hertz electrical system, the spinning of a three-bladed screw. One was the 'target of interest', the other Sierra Sixty-Two.

'That looks like our guy,' said Jameson.

It did to Steadman, too. 'What do you say, Bam Bam?'

'Could be, skipper.' Bam Bam put the sounds of Sierra Sixty-Two into his headphones and closed his eyes, letting this new contact play against the one in *his* memory. The outlines of these two peaks looked the same on the screen but there were subtle differences. Some sounds were new, others were missing. *Could be acoustics,* he thought. They were in warm, shallow water with all kinds of reefs and shoals to mess things up.

'Could be,' said Jameson, 'or is?'

Schramm looked up at the two officers. 'Could be. The ship on that sound file had a bad main bearing and a bent screw. This guy doesn't. The plant noise is kind of off key, too. I'd say half a note flat.'

234

'Are we talking about sonar or music?' said the SEAL.

Niebel coughed into his hand to keep from laughing out loud.

'They're pretty much the same thing if you know how to listen.' Schramm turned to Steadman. 'If that target's important I'd want to go up and grab a visual.'

Steadman didn't object to the look of frustration on the SEAL's face. He was a little too anxious to start blowing things up. He grabbed the 1MC microphone on the bulkhead and clicked on it. 'This is the captain. All stations make ready for periscope depth.' He hung it up, then crooked a finger at Jameson. 'Let's go up and take a look.'

Tony Watson had the conn as Steadman walked into Control. 'All stations are ready for PD, captain.'

'Okay, XO. I've got the conn.' Steadman said to Lieutenant Pena. 'Come to three four zero. Take us up to sixty feet.'

'Three four zero and sixty feet, aye, skipper.'

Portland planed up into shallows mottled with the strong green light of late afternoon in the eastern Med. They were in relatively deep water at the center of the pass, with the large island of Kithira thirty miles west, and smaller Andikithira twenty-eight to the east.

'Up the search scope.'

The number two scope rose from its well. Steadman crouched low as the eyepiece rose, making sure he'd know the instant the head broke through the surface. The view went from green to soft, luminous turquoise; a color he

235

could not recall ever seeing in the Atlantic. Steadman stopped the periscope's rise. *There.*

The freighter was sailing southwest; *Portland* was moving north. As the two vessels converged, the freighter grew larger, clearer.

Steadman increased the magnification and zoomed in. 'I'm looking at a small freighter, deckhouse set aft, a single stack and a loading crane amidships.' He stepped aside and invited Jameson to have a look.

Jameson put his eyes to the eyepiece. He swept the freighter from bow to stern, then returned to the open decks beneath the arm of her loading crane. *Pipes?* The last thing he wanted was to play gladiator games in a pipe garden. He elevated the scope. *And the crane cab will be a bitch if they're awake,* he thought. From that perch a decent shooter would be able to sweep the deck. 'That's our target.'

'The ship in the photo had bare decks.'

'But the timing's right, her course is right. The sound file is close. If you can maneuver us astern we could read her name.'

Steadman said, 'Helm? Left five degrees rudder. Ahead two thirds. Come to zero one zero. Down scope.'

The periscope slid back down into its well. *Portland* wheeled around to the north, and soon was directly astern the plodding freighter. The ship had scarcely moved two miles.

'Up the search scope.' Once more Steadman crouched down and let the rising instrument unfold his lanky frame to full height. He increased the magnification once, twice, a third time. At 25X, he could see a figure climbing down a ladder from her bridge, and by tilting the periscope's head down slightly, her name in bright white letters: *Cristi* across the top, with the name of her home port, *Limassol*, below.

CHAPTER FIFTEEN

STORM WARNING

MV *'Cristi'*
Kithira Strait

Captain Ahmed Khanji made his way down the bridge ladder to the freighter's stern. Some masters spent their sea time sitting at a desk like a factory manager. Not Khanji. He liked the clean, elemental smell of the ocean, so different from the rank odors of the shore. He liked outwitting thieving port authorities and crazy owners. But what he loved most was to come here, light a cigarette and watch the mesmerizing rush of water and foam of his wake. Seeing a course made good in a white, turbulent line that stretched all the way to the horizon gave him a sense of worth. How many men could say as much?

The sky overhead was deep indigo, but off to the northwest a building storm front caught the last rays of the setting sun. Billowing turrets of cloud glowed white and gold, their bellies black and full of rain. *Storm,* though he would never speak the word out loud. Foul weather could hear its name being called and it just might answer. Not a good thing on a ship this old and frail.

He'd commanded her for six years; an eternity in a world where cheap vessels changed hands at the turn of a card. The new owners, whoever they were, had even less commercial skill than the old; half the time he left port in ballast, empty of cargo, shuttling between one unpromising place and another. Fuel was expensive and the crew cost something to keep and feed, so Khanji figured he'd have some new owners soon. *Unless they scrap her.*

He didn't exactly love his ship, but he'd grown to know her and it was plain she was coming to an end. She was slow, her water tanks were fouled with oil and her oil tanks with water. Her diesel had an unhealthy cough. But he was her captain, her master. At sea only God himself had more authority, though sometimes he had to remind the owners of it.

They'd left the crowded sea lanes and First Mate Somebody's Cousin, whose real name was Dawish, was standing watch up on the bridge. Dawish was a young Egyptian who'd graduated from the Arab Academy for Maritime Transport the previous year. It was good most of the islands were astern. Dawish was a serious boy, but he could be trusted not to hit something only when there was nothing to hit.

Once they skirted the weather, the run down to Alexandria would be clear. That is, if the Israeli Navy didn't board him. They seemed to take special delight in harassing ships with Arab crews, and the green, gold and white flag of Cyprus wouldn't keep them away. Khanji shrugged. Some things he could control, others not. Politics were like that squall off to the north: rain that fell on someone else's head.

He sucked his cigarette to embers and flicked it into the sea. He was about to light another when he felt a familiar pressure against his ankles. He looked down. It was Osama, the ship's cat, passing back and forth between his legs. 'What are you doing here?' He scooped the cat up and scratched his chin. 'You're supposed to be on duty.'

Osama was a small, tawny cat with startling yellow eyes, named not for the terrorist hero but for the Arabic word for *lion*. He was a useful shipmate, for a tramp freighter was really nothing more than an ocean-going rat's nest. Not this ship, thanks to Osama. 'Look busy,' he said, and tossed the cat to the deck. He bounded up the ladder for the aft watertight door, but something made him suddenly veer off and leap into the lifeboat.

Dawish leaned out of the galley's after hatch. 'Captain? Message from the company.'

They'd already had him stop the ship and paint out her old name, her home port and change the flag at her stern. What did they want from him now? 'So? Bring it down.'

The Egyptian hurried down the ladder and handed Khanji a paper.

The message from Beirut was brief. The owners had found a buyer on Crete willing to pay more for their cargo. That meant profits and it was profits that kept the ship temporarily safe from the cutter's torch.

239

Khanji took note of the Kithira beacon. 'The Greeks close down at sunset. We'll never make Souda Bay in time. We might as well plan to arrive at first light.' Another distant flash. Khanji took its measure with a mariner's suspicious eye. How fast was the squall moving? It would be best to stay ahead of it with a heavy load of pipe up on deck. *Eight knots should do.* The storm would move faster, but it had to cover more distance. Could it catch them? *No.*

Dawish saw his concern and said, 'There's a weather warning on the radio. Do you want to listen?'

'Why not?'

They climbed back to the bridge where the captain disconnected the automatic pilot and spun the small, disc-shaped wheel. His ship's blunt, heavy bow swung around to the northeast. They'd pass close to the small, dark hump of rocks that was the southeast tip of Andikithira Island, then turn due east for Souda Bay.

'Is the crane working?' asked Khanji as First Mate Somebody's Cousin fiddled with the shortwave. The ship's big cargo crane had control problems. It had stranded a Turkish inspector in mid-air for nearly an hour before they'd brought him aboard. 'We'll need it in the morning.'

'The engineer says he fixed it.'

'Did you see for yourself?'

Dawish looked at his feet.

'Listen,' said Khanji, 'if the crane won't work, the Greeks won't let us dock. We'll have to anchor out in the harbor and try to fix it. Another ship will take our berth. Maybe this new buyer will decide he doesn't need our pipes. You want to go back to Egypt and drive a taxi?'

'I will go.'

'Good idea.' Khanji reached over to the engine room telegraph and grasped the metal handle. It was worn to a bright bronze by so many leathery hands. He shoved the annunciator forward to get the engineer's attention down, then pulled it back from AHEAD 2/3 to AHEAD 1/3. The ship seemed to sag wearily as she slowed. 'What about that weather?'

Dawish turned up the volume.

Khanji listened to a recorded warning of a deep *gregale* spinning northward from the African coast. *Gregales* were sudden, violent storms with flashing thunderstorms, hail, winds and heavy seas; a kind of small-scale hurricane, though plenty dangerous. The squall line bearing down on them was just its most northerly tentacle. But by the time it wasn't so distant Khanji would be safe inside the breakwater at Souda. He tapped the glass face of the barometer. The pressure was holding. 'Keep us two points off Andikithira Island and ahead of that squall line and we'll have a quiet night.' With that, Khanji left the bridge.

Khanji had spent twenty-five years of his forty years at sea. He was an experienced ship's master with an excellent weather eye. But his forecast for this night would soon be proven wrong.

USS *Portland*

'Fucking SEAL lieutenant swims oceans and

241

jumps tall buildings with a single bound,' said Bam Bam angrily. 'But he's no sonarman.'

Niebel looked around to make sure no one was listening, then said, 'The sound profiles looked pretty close.'

'That singing whale you found up under the ice last year looked pretty close to you, too.' It had turned out to be the clever ruse of a Russian submarine captain who didn't want to be found. He assumed, wrongly, that no one would come looking for an amorous bowfin.

'Hey, a recording of a whale and a whale are almost the same.'

'Someone's got to know the difference between almost and–' he stopped. The cluster of white lines that was their 'target of interest' was shifting. Sierra Sixty-Two had just turned around. 'Shit'. He grabbed the microphone. 'Conn, Sonar. Sierra Sixty-Two just turned northeast. Range opening to nine thousand yards. Speed is steady at eight knots.'

Did they spot my scope? Steadman wondered. That might explain the turn, but why slow down if you were making a run for it? He clicked the 1MC and sent his voice throughout the boat. 'Lieutenant Jameson to Control.' Then, he turned and looked aft to the chart tables. 'Nav?' he said to Pardee. 'How much daylight is left up there?'

'Two hours to full dark, skipper. No moon for three and a half.'

Two hours, eight knots. The ship could reach land before *Portland* could launch her SEALs under cover of darkness. 'I need ETAs to all the nearest ports.'

242

'Kithira is closest but there are harbors at Andikithira and Kastelli. And tons of inlets all up and down the coast. All of them?'

Where almost anyone in a small boat could be waiting. Or even a helicopter. Great. 'No, for Andikithira and Kastelli. Assume a speed of advance of twelve knots.' It left him with another, unpleasant, set of orders and he had no choice but to issue them. He took a deep breath, then spoke. 'XO? Sound general quarters.'

An urgent electronic tone sounded throughout the boat. Soon, it was accompanied by the muffled thud of running feet and Tony Watson's voice booming over the 1MC:

'Man battle stations! Man battle stations!'

'Torpedo room, fire control,' said Steadman. 'Make tubes One and Two ready in all respects but leave the shutters closed for now.'

'Torpedo room aye.'

'Ship ready.'

The gun was cocked, the safety slipped off. All that remained was to aim and pull the trigger. Steadman said, 'Firing point procedures, Sierra Sixty-Two, Tubes One and Two.'

'Firing point procedures, Sierra Sixty-Two, aye, captain,' said Lieutenant Ortega, though he was certain this was just another drill, wasn't it? The boat's central computer sent bearing and range data from Bam Bam's console into the electronic brains inside two Mark-48s.

Steadman turned to Pardee. 'What kind of bottom do we have?'

'Two hundred feet until we're well north of Andikithira. And Sierra Sixty-Two's ETA there is

243

forty minutes. Two hours thirty if she's making for Kastelli,' said Pardee.

'Very well,' said Steadman. If that ship was sailing for the harbor at Andikithira he would have no choice but to stop her with a Mark-48. If she kept offshore, she might still be heading for a landing on Crete. *Two hundred feet.* That wasn't much ocean to drown whatever bugs they might have on that ship. It was within the range of a determined diver. 'Sonar, Conn.'

'Sonar, aye,' said Bam Bam.

'Put a ten thousand yard no-sail zone around Sierra Sixty-Two. Let me know the instant it looks like *anything* might enter it.'

'Captain?' Jameson stood in the forward portside door.

'Your target just turned east.'

K-335 Gepard

Sonar Lieutenant Kureodov had been watching two spokes of light on his circular screen perform a kind of strange duet. One was bright and throbbing, the second faint and steady. The bright spoke was a small, noisy ship churning first south, then northeast. The faint one was a nuclear fast-attack submarine following her every move.

What could the American *Los Angeles* find so interesting about a noisy old freighter? It was like watching a cat stalking a piece of trash. 'Captain? I think the Americans are tracking that ship.'

Gepard's radio cubicle was screened off from the

rest of Central Command by a simple blue curtain. *Starpom* Stavinsky swept it aside and stepped in. 'What's taking you so long?'

'It's two pages,' said Kiselyev, *Gepard's* radio communications officer. 'Text and images.' He handed the sheets to Stavinsky.

Pictures? He looked into Kiselyev's face for some sign of what such a long message might contain. Kiselyev was a jolly bear of a man who ate for two and took nothing but his meals seriously, but he looked somber, even a little frightened. Of what?

Stavinsky took the message sheets and left. He could have read them, of course. Most *starpoms* would. After all, information was the most valuable currency on a submarine, except for the bottles of home brew the crew thought they'd kept hidden from him. But he thought of the look on the radio officer's face and thought. *No.*

Leonov was seated in his leather swivel chair and facing the sonar console. Stavinsky came at him from behind. 'Message received, Captain.'

Leonov held out his hand. He read the first page, examined the pictures on the second, then folded them up.

If Stavinsky was hoping for a hint of what they contained, he was disappointed, for when he was finished, the captain reached up and pulled down a *kashtan* microphone. He stood up and clicked it on.

'This is the captain. We have received new orders.'

A happy murmur spread through Central Command. Indeed, through the whole submarine, for by tradition a Russian submarine commander reads orders to his crew only twice: after their first dive on departure from base to let them know where they were going and when they turned around for home.

In each of *Gepard*'s eight compartments, from the torpedo room in her bow to the hot engineering spaces astern, men stopped what they were doing and looked up to the nearest speaker. Could they be home in Gadzhievo in time for an anniversary? Would the *dacha* garden still have a few hardy vegetables to harvest, or be stunned brown and dead by frost? All hands waited to hear the good news.

'Men of *Gepard*,' said Leonov. 'Thirty-two days ago we sailed from our homes in the far north. Our motherland, our ship was at peace.' He paused. 'The situation has now changed.'

What? Stavinsky turned to his captain.

Leonov's words seemed to suck the very air out of the hull. All the happy conversations, the homecoming plans, the joking, came to a sudden stop. The eerie silence was broken only by the soft whir of hydraulics, the flipping of switches, the occasional whispered orders from the diving officer to trim the boat.

'Two weeks ago, terrorists raided a strategic weapons depot in central Russia. They slaughtered the guards and blew up the building to cover their bloody tracks. These are the same criminals who invade our schools and murder our children. Who plant bombs in our apartment buildings. Who smuggle explosives onto airliners. Now they have stolen a weapon. A *strategic* weapon.' He paused, letting that word sink home. 'They have eluded our police, our security forces, our border patrols. They boarded a ship thinking they could escape into the sea. But they have made a fatal mistake. From now until further notice, you will consider yourselves at war.' He looked to Stavinsky. 'Sound General Quarters.'

Instead of the computer-generated series of tones used in American submarines, *Gepard*'s crew was called to battle stations with the grating buzz of a power saw biting into oak. Disappointment at not hearing the expected recall melted into a frantic rush. Everyone, even the off-duty men in their racks, sprinted to their assigned posts.

Stavinsky had his stopwatch out as the eight compartment commanders checked in ready for battle. When all was complete he said, 'Ship is at readiness Condition Two, Captain. How are we going to find these bandits?'

Leonov crooked a finger for Stavinsky to follow. They walked to the sonar station. He pointed to the screen. Two spokes of light, one bright, one faint, both evenly spaced, never varying. 'Kureodov? How long has the *Los Angeles* been trailing them?'

'Nearly an hour, sir.'

'A long time for a simple tracking exercise,' said Leonov.

'What else can they be doing?'

'I think it's our target out there.'

Stavinsky had served under the Little Lion long enough to know his mind. 'You'll have to sink it in front of the Americans.'

'The weapon was taken from us. The bandits murdered our citizens. Who better to administer justice?' said Leonov. 'We'll keep that island between us and the *Los Angeles*. We'll wait for them off the southern tip of the island, then move in. If it's our ship, I won't waste any breath asking the Americans for permission.'

'The stolen weapon. If it's atomic they might...'

'We'll use Type One Elevens.' The *Squall* rocket torpedo. They flew through the water at astonishing speeds; better than two hundred knots. But they were also temperamental. There were whispers – never confirmed – that *Kursk* had been trying to launch one when she blew up. 'We'll kill them before they have a chance to kill themselves. Or us.'

The two spokes of light shifted on Kureodov's screen and faded as the rocky island eclipsed them. 'Contact lost, Captain.'

'Helm,' said Leonov. 'All ahead full. Torpedo room?'

'Dobrin listening.' Anatoly Dobrin was the senior *michman,* or warrant officer, in charge of the torpedo room.

'How fast can you load a pair of Type One Elevens?'

'Start timing, Captain,' said Dobrin.

Leonov glanced at his second in command. Stavinsky clicked a stopwatch. Leonov was always pushing the torpedo gang for quicker times, and not without reason. What good was a weapon that swam at better than two hundred knots if it took too long to shoot?

The drumming of the noise cancellation system rose from barely audible to annoying. Leonov checked the sonar display to be sure the Americans could no longer hear them, and said, 'Turn off the *Sirena.*'

USS *Portland*

They say that the sea is a submariner's principal foe, but if so it was one that was surprisingly easy to forget. Boredom was different. The lights on a submarine are always on, the air is always 76 degrees. Other than in a few, sound-isolated compartments, the boat is as hushed as a library. The days are interchangeable rotations of sleep, meals, standing watch, studying and sleeping, broken only by drills to test readiness for disasters no one believed would happen.

Boredom grinds the sharpest blade dull, and now, after working back to back watches staring at the sonar traces of a decrepit freighter barely making six knots, Bam Bam was bored to the bone.

When the faint flicker of a fifty hertz electrical system appeared astern, he chalked it up to a reflection. After all, the tramp steamer off the bow was radiating a 50 hertz buzz, too. *Built in a Commie yard*, he thought, and wondered if that still meant anything. It was possible he was picking it up from a long ways off, the sea bounced sounds around, focusing some, diffusing others, and occasionally doing both at once.

But then came the muffled thud of a very big cavitating screw, not three-bladed like the freighter, but seven. It was followed an instant later by a sonic signature that cut straight through what was left of Bam Bam's lassitude: pumps, big

249

ones, the rising whine of turbomachinery and the fizz and gurgle of water slipping by a large, submerged hull.

'Conn, Sonar,' he said. 'Tonal contact bearing one nine four, possible submarine and he smells like a nuke.'

MV 'Nova Spirit'
Ionian Sea

The freighter's deck vibrated as her engine strained to make fourteen knots into building winds and seas. She was lightly loaded and rolled so enthusiastically Warsame had to hold onto the ladder rails as he made his way down from the bridge to the fantail. He stopped and looked off to the southwest.

He'd been keeping his eye on an oncoming wall of gray cloud all afternoon. It started off as an indistinct smudge on the horizon and now it covered nearly half the sky. *We'll catch it tonight.*

He stood at the open scuttle leading down to the engine room. The cool air that flowed down through it kept it from becoming impossibly hot, but in a storm it would have to be dogged down. A flooded engine room in a gale was a disaster from which few ships, least of all this one, could emerge. He climbed down to the hot, oily engine room, nodded a greeting to Assad the engineer, then stood at the base of the ladder, listening.

A good captain learns every noise his ship can make, and with her throttles up there were plenty of them: the crash of the distant bow hitting a sea, the thump and groan of the hull, the nervous, knitting-needle clack of intake and exhaust valves opening and closing.

'Intake pump is running a little hot!' Assad shouted.

Warsame nodded. It was a piece of information with a value that was as yet unknown.

The engine room occupied one and a half levels at the very bottom of the ship's stern. The crankcase, screw shaft, generator and steering motor were on the lower level. The engine controls, cylinders, exhaust, manifold, air intake and fuel injectors were on the raised fidley deck. A watertight door in the forward bulkhead opened onto the Number Three cargo hold; a ladder followed the exhaust and fresh air intakes up to a hatch built into the bottom of the false stack.

Warsame climbed down to the lower level and touched the sea water cooling pump. He spat on it and the casing sizzled.

The engine room was full of hot spots. In warm waters it could be one hundred and fifty degrees in places. The Mediterranean was a warm ocean, but even Warsame knew the pump was hotter than it should be.

He worked his way aft to the shaft casing. He watched it spin in the meager light of a naked yellow bulb. He listened closely to the irregular throb of a loose main bearing. It was a bit deeper and it would fail some day. But it had sounded like this for a long time. He climbed up to the steel mesh fidley deck, listening to the *whoosh* of the big pistons inside their sleeves, then walked back to where Assad sat at his desk.

251

The engineer had his big red ear protectors on. A logbook lay open on the desk. 'Watch that pump,' he said to Assad. With that, Warsame left for the bridge to see if there was any more word on the weather.

CHAPTER SIXTEEN

FIRING POINT PROCEDURES

USS *Portland*
Argos Escarpment

Jameson slid down the ladder to the bottom deck and jogged forward to the torpedo room. His men had been on five-minute alert ever since they'd picked *Cristi* up on sonar, but now the submarine was at General Quarters and the bubbleheads were finally getting with the program. Long, green Mark-48 torpedoes sat on their loading trays, and the breech doors on Tubes One and Two were hung with signs that announced WARSHOT LOADED.

'Hey Kernal!' he shouted to his XO from across the compartment.

Noise Kills! wasn't just a saying among submariners. It was engraved on their souls, and the shout earned Jameson a filthy look from the leading torpedo chief and his men.

Jameson ignored them. 'We got a COI.' A contact of interest.

'Are we interested?' asked Sanders.

'Very. But the hit's going to be a little complicated.'

'No like complications, kemosabe.'

Jameson looked up as his men collected their equipment into neat piles. 'Hey! Gather round, gents. We've got a boat full of *muj* bobbing around up there. There's gonna' be blood on deck and I'd prefer that it all belongs to them.'

Floyd Wheeler, the squad chief was a big, blunt man of thirty-six with close-cropped hair and deep lines etched onto his face by a career spent dealing with lesser mortals. His hands were paddles, his scars a history of wars declared and otherwise. He'd fought in places no one outside the tight world of Special Operations knew were even at war. His voice was tobacco-cured. He was a true Bullfrog SEAL. No one, not even Jameson, dared to call him Grandpa. 'What's the deal?'

'We've got a target with a walking deck buried under a shitload of pipe.'

Wheeler grunted. 'Nice place for a guerrilla war if you're the guerrilla.'

'Plus, we're going to have to board in a blackout period.' There would be no available satellite to provide a direct linkup with higher authority. 'So we won't have comms except relayed back through the boat. You okay with that, Steve?'

'I guess so,' said Stepik. 'I'll leave the satcom behind. That thing's a brick.' The satellite radio was a nice thing to have, but it was dead weight without a satellite. 'I sure don't like the idea of digging *muj* out of steel pipes, though. They could have firing positions set up behind them.

It'd be like assaulting a tank.'

'We'll flush 'em. And remember, they're rag-headed asshats, not shooters.' *I hope.* 'We'll jump off a thousand yards ahead of the target and hit them amidships where the main deck is low to the water. Chief? You have the Zodiac and the bug box.' The bioweapon detector. 'Anders? You climb point. I'll follow and rig the net for the rest of you ladies to climb.'

'How come I climb point?' said Petty Officer Tommy Anders. He was sinewy and slender, with curly blond hair and startling blue eyes.

'Because you *are* a shooter. I want you to hustle up that crane cab and cover the boarding before the Tangos realize we're there. Once you set security you can plink them as they leave the deckhouse. Rickie B? You follow me,' he said, meaning their explosives breaching expert, Petty Officer Richard Battaglia. 'Haul the gas and cache it somewhere safe on deck. I don't want it falling overboard.'

'No problem,' said Battaglia. He was called Pyro by the rest of Bravo squad, and he was built like a miner; short and powerfully wide, with black hair and a devilish sparkle in his brown eyes the girls in Virginia Beach found hard to resist. The 'gas' he'd be hauling and stashing was one of two acetylene cylinders they'd brought to the boat; the trigger for a massive fuel-air explosion. To Pyro it was just another load he'd have to strap to his overburdened pack next to a sledgehammer, a steel pry bar, a shotgun, ammunition and pouches full of specialized explosives.

'Kernal leads the second element. That's Stepik,

Flagler and McQuill.' Radioman, medic and another good shooter for rear security. 'Chief?' Jameson said to Wheeler, 'you cover our climb from below. When we signal, haul up the bug box and start sampling the air for smallpox. On deck, inside. Everywhere. The first element leapfrogs to the bridge. We'll get the ship stopped and secure the accommodation decks. The follow on element does the same with the machinery and cargo spaces. Remember, we are *not* authorized to waste widows and children, but any Tango dumb enough to come at you with a weapon is a target. And Stepik? You'll be linked back to the boat through the girl if we need something. Don't get chatty. I want clear channels.'

'I hear you.' Stepik was a little over six feet, sandy hair, heavily muscled, but with gentle eyes and a kind of slow, dogged persistence. He was the only married man on the squad; a fact that made him the object of scorn he usually took good-naturedly.

'Up on deck, if it's not one of us and it's un-armed it goes face down and tie-tied. Once we control the bridge we'll start a debrief. Just re-member, there are two Chechen *muj* up there who murdered some American ladies. They didn't like their looks and they probably won't like yours, either. Everyone down with this so far? Any ques-tions?'

'When do we go?' asked Kernal Sanders.

Jameson checked his watch. 'As soon as I go sing *Kumbayah* with the captain.'

The big video screen mounted in the officers'

wardroom was filled with a chart of the southern Aegean. The rocky fingers of the Greek mainland reached down from the upper left to snatch at the curved, leaping fish that was Crete. An arc of small islands linked the two, as though a few scales had slipped from its grasp and fallen back to the sea.

Cristi sat under a red cross hair with a blue cigar symbol of *Portland* in pursuit. Together, they'd made a sweeping turn around the northern tip of the island of Andikithira, then east along the drowned slopes of the Argos Escarpment. A second cigar shape, this one red, represented the unknown Russian boat off the southern tip of the island.

Steadman, Tony Watson, Rose Scavullo and the boat's independent corpsman, Chief Cooper, were already waiting when Jameson knocked on the door.

'Come,' said Steadman.

Jameson took in the group. He was not happy with what he saw. 'Sir, these people aren't cleared. I'll have to ask them to leave.'

'They're staying. You asked for Lieutenant Scavullo's help with communications and the XO and my corpsman are here because *I* want them here. It's reasonable and it's my decision. Now have a seat.'

'Okay,' said Jameson. His expression said, *It may be reasonable, but it's your funeral.* He sat down at the table.

'As you all can see on the chart,' Steadman began, 'we intercepted a surface target and have been trailing her. She's the *Cristi*, homeported in Limassol. But we're not alone. Sonar picked up a submerged target off Andikithira. Contact was too brief for a solid ID, but Bam Bam thinks she's a single shaft, seven-blade Russian nuke, either a *Sierra* or an *Akula*. Either one might be bad news.'

'I thought the Russians weren't supposed to be able to sneak up on you guys,' said Jameson.

'They didn't,' said Steadman testily. Though they very nearly had. And submarines didn't just appear out of nowhere. He'd ordered Bam Bam to review the last few hours of sonar tapes to see what he could find. 'The question is what they're doing here, and how does it affect us?'

'The Soviets used to maintain a small Mediterranean submarine flotilla,' said Scavullo. 'They rotated units in and out from the Northern Fleet to a base in Syria. It was considered vacation duty.'

'Thanks for the history lesson, lieutenant,' said Tony Watson. 'Right now I'd like someone to tell me what *we're* doing here.'

'Fair enough,' said Steadman. 'Sierra Sixty-Two is a two thousand ton-class freighter that *may* have a stolen weapon of mass destruction on board, along with the people who grabbed it from a Russian depot.'

'Jesus. Nukes?' said Watson.

'No. Bioweapons. The ship was headed southwest when we first identified her, but then she turned tail. Now she's running east.'

'Did they spot us?' said Tony Watson.

'Anything's possible, but if they did I'd like to hire their lookouts. In any event, Lieutenant Jameson and his men are going to board her, check her for the stolen weapon and if they find it, destroy it in place.' He turned to Chief Cooper. 'That's why you're here. If they find a bad virus up there, I'm depending on you to keep it off *Portland*.'

'What virus are we dealing with, skipper?' asked the corpsman.

Steadman looked to Jameson. 'Lieutenant?'

'*Variola major.*'

There was a pause, then Chief Cooper said, 'You guys are jumping a ship full of *smallpox?*'

'If we're lucky. We'll have to run tests to know for sure.'

'Not on board *Portland* you won't.'

'Relax, chief. We brought our own diagnostics. We can do it on the freighter.'

'Yeah, but can you *keep* it on the freighter? That stuff is wicked contagious and nobody here is immunized.'

'We brought a supply of vaccine. We'll make sure we come home clean, but if you're worried we'll let you know what we find. If it's smallpox, you can start rolling sleeves. And chief? This is a no-shitter: if you breathe a word of this outside this wardroom your next duty will be at the Baghdad Free Clinic.'

Cooper scowled. 'Captain, I can't immunize sailors without telling them what I'm sticking them with. There could be guys who have allergies, or compromised immune systems.'

'You have AIDS patients on board, chief?' said Jameson.

'I've got healthy submariners on board.' Cooper looked to Steadman. 'Sir?'

Steadman took a deep breath, then said, 'If they *confirm* smallpox on that ship, the crew will be immunized. That's my call.'

Jameson thought, *A regular Navy officer who takes responsibility?* Now *that* was refreshing.

Chief Cooper was less convinced. 'The lieutenant here said he *thought* it was smallpox. What happens if it isn't? Does he have vaccines for every bioweapon out there? Different agents require different containment protocols.'

Steadman said, 'Good point, chief. I want you to rig a decontamination area up on the weather deck. We'll have them strip down and do a full-spectrum delouse before they come back into the hull.'

'That's unnecessary,' said Jameson.

'It's also my call. Okay chief? Get going.'

'Yes, sir,' said Cooper. 'I'll have a chat with the nukes. They'll come up with some *serious* chemicals.' He got up and left.

Steadman waited until the door shut. 'All right. What do you need from us?'

Jameson glanced at the chart. 'The target is already beyond the harbor at Andikithira, but she could put in at Kastelli later tonight or Souda Bay by morning. There could be another boat waiting to meet them there. It's a big facility. There's usually a few of our ships riding at anchor in the military harbor, and a major airport close by.'

'Our ships could be the target,' said Watson. 'The freighter could maneuver upwind and drop anchor alongside a destroyer. By the time someone shoos them away we've got smallpox on board.'

'Possibly,' said Jameson, though if you had something like smallpox, you didn't use it against

259

a destroyer. You used it against a *country*. 'Once they transfer the bug off that ship we've reached a point of no return. For obvious reasons, we can't allow that.'

'Just how are you planning to stop it?' asked Watson.

'*Portland* will surface a thousand yards abeam her line of advance,' said Jameson. 'You don't have to blow your tanks dry. Decks awash is enough. We'll man up our Zodiac and intercept her. Just keep the target in sight, watch for surface traffic and monitor the frequency.' He looked at Scavullo. 'There won't be any reason to contact us. We'll signal you for recovery.'

'Excuse me,' said Scavullo. 'But aren't you forgetting that Russian submarine? If there's a stolen Russian weapon on board that freighter they might think it still belongs to them. They might even be out here trying to stop it. Shouldn't we let them clean up their own mess?'

'The *Russians* let this weapon get snatched from under their noses,' said Jameson. 'The *Russians* couldn't recover it. You think they deserve another shot?'

'What if they don't want our help?'

'*I* need some help,' said Watson, 'I heard something about destroying weapons in place. I'm still waiting to hear how.'

'The ship is going to the bottom in little sterilized pieces,' said Jameson. 'We brought a thermobaric weapon big enough to take a carrier down. The freighter will pretty much *vanish*.'

'What about the crew?' asked Scavullo.

'The same.'

'Wait,' said Watson. 'You're planning to *sink* a civilian ship flying a foreign flag? *With* her crew? *Without* any evidence except your say so?'

Steadman sat back and kept a poker face. There were times when he appreciated his XO's highly developed instinct for survival.

'Sir,' said Jameson. 'I'm not suggesting that we go carpet-bomb innocent civilians. These guys mean us harm and they've got a weapon that can do a lot of it. It's suicidal to waste time wondering if the evidence will pass in the Southern District Court of New York. Intelligence is information, not a legal brief. You collect it and when you have enough then you act. If there's stolen WMD on board, that ship is a legitimate target. We will board her, neutralize her cargo and take her down safely. That's the mission I'm authorized to carry out.'

Watson put out his hand. 'Show me your authorization.'

He looked to Steadman. 'I've shared my orders with your CO. He can tell you as much as he wants to. I can't.'

'Captain?' asked Watson.

'Lieutenant Jameson has all the authorization he needs. But only after he's off the boat. And Lieutenant Scavullo raises a very good point. We have to assume that Russian submarine could have orders to observe that ship, stop her, arrest the crew, even sink her. I don't intend to get caught in the middle. Suggestions?'

'One,' said the SEAL. 'Assault *Cristi* before the Russians have a chance to screw things up again.'

Steadman turned to the chart. Half of Andiki-

261

thira was behind them. In fifteen miles they'd pass South Point, and if that Russian submarine was waiting for them, that's where they'd be. *Fifteen miles.* It was two hours away at the freighter's current speed. *Portland* could be there in under thirty minutes. 'It won't be full dark yet.'

'I'll take dusk.'

'Captain,' said Watson, 'I wonder if we don't need some specific orders from Norfolk? Once the SEALs are off our decks we have no operational control over them.'

Jameson thought, *Submariners.* They just didn't have a fucking *clue* about life outside their checklists and manuals. 'Sorry, XO, but if you sit around playing sea lawyer, I can just about *guarantee* things will go wrong.' He saw Watson's sour look. 'If the Russians get involved, if *Cristi* escapes, we pass the point of no return and go straight to *failure.* That's unacceptable. To me and to our country. But Commander Steadman is right. It's his boat and his call.'

My call? Suddenly he'd been promoted from bus driver to the guy who'd take the fall if that ship was a legitimate target and they let it get away. Say *go* and *Cristi,* and everyone on her, would, as Jameson put it, pretty well vanish. Say *wait,* put up an antenna and request confirmation – or cover – from Norfolk and risk a delay that would add a lurking Russian submarine with unknown intentions to the equation. Or worse, allow a ship loaded with a nightmare weapon to make port, to transfer her deadly cargo, even escape. 'What if you're wrong?'

'If it's not our ship then some very bad guys

with a very bad bug are somewhere else.'

The captain of an aircraft carrier could order up a thorough briefing by his own personal intelligence staff. He could hold a conference call with his superiors and *their* superiors. He could pass everything up the chain and let them own the decision as well as the results.

A submarine is different. Steadman was alone. 'All right.' He pulled down a microphone from the bulkhead. 'Conn. All ahead flank.'

Jameson had sized Steadman short. Tackling dangerous missions and letting the consequences be damned was what SEALs were all about. But it was a gutsy move for Steadman. Jameson had thought he was dealing with a captain in love with his reflection and his weasel XO.

It seemed he'd only been half right.

MV *'Cristi'*
off Andikithira Island

First Officer Dawish took the catwalk to the deck crane. Heaps of pipe to either side made it a narrow corridor whose walls were tall enough to keep him from seeing the ocean.

The crane was parked with the jaws of the hookblock resting on the wave shield at the bow. The shield was meant to keep seas from sweeping the low cargo deck in a storm. Dawish climbed the four steps up to the control cab. The ladder was coated with oil and grime and soon he was, too. He took out his key.

The cab was kept locked because it made an in-

263

viting place for the crew to hide. It was surprising how many secret compartments could be found on such a small ship. The steering room aft, the stores compartment forward, in and hidden among the pallets and moldy sacks in the three holds below decks. The ship was a warren, some of them fitted with lights, all of them strewn with empty bottles, candy wrappers and pornographic magazines.

Dawish unlocked the door and the rancid smells of sweat, hydraulic fluid and scorched electrical wire spilled out. A pile of oily rags on the floor made the fire hazard complete. One tossed cigarette and the cab would go up like a Molotov cocktail.

He kicked the rags to the deck below and pulled himself into the operator's seat. It was cracked vinyl patched with sticky tape. The exposed foam crumbled to dust at his touch.

He let the door open to air out the space. Off to the west, the last rays of sunset silhouetted the dark, rocky islands. A rain squall dragged its heavy belly across the horizon. He switched on the lights and was rewarded with a soft red glow from the gauges. He pressed a large black button. There was a whine and thump from somewhere beneath his seat. A needle measuring hydraulic pressure twitched as the rubber lines filled with oil. *So far, so good.*

Two worn steel handles wrapped in black electrical tape sprouted to either side of the seat. One elevated the boom, the other swung it in an arc. A rocker switch built into the end of one controlled the hook block. A squeeze trigger in the other opened its jaws. A red button on the end was the emergency stop switch. He reached overhead, switched on a spotlight and aimed it on the yellow hookblock. He squeezed the trigger to unlock its jaw, then gingerly moved the handle to raise the boom.

Far out at the bow, the heavy block trembled, then lifted free. There was a troubling vibration that rumbled up through the hull and deck, as though the beams that tied the crane to the ship's keel were flexing. But this was an old vessel. Her bones were bound to be a bit loose.

Dawish pulled back on the other handle. The hydraulic motor whined. The boom started to swing to port, but then it stopped with a grinding squeal. Dawish moved the handle back. The boom refused to budge. He pumped it, and on the third try, with a heavy shudder, the boom moved, slowly at first, then faster. He yanked the controls to stop it. The boom kept moving. It would go all the way around. There was very little clearance between the hook and the deck house, and stretched out like a slingshot, none. It would tear right through the captain's cabin.

Dawish jammed his thumb down on the emergency stop.

The boom groaned to a stop with the yellow hook swinging wildly out over the port side. He could feel the ship heel.

Dawish angrily switched off the hydraulics. The engineer was enjoying his off-duty time in his tiny cabin, likely with a bottle.

That was going to change.

Ninety nautical miles to the northwest and sixty from the nearest land, Makayev woke up with his mouth parched and burning with open sores. It was so dark he had to touch his face to know if his eyes were open or shut. He felt a damp breeze flow over his feverish body. It carried the cool smell of rain.

He put his hand out and touched water. He snatched at the puddle until his fingers were soaked, then splashed his face.

The foul water reeked of diesel.

There was a distant thump and the world tilted. He started to fall, put an arm out and realized he was already on the ground.

No. Not *ground*. A steel *deck*. An oily drop fell onto his face. He struck out to feel something, anything, and scraped his fingers on sharp metal, and then he knew.

He couldn't see, but this was a steel floor next to a pair of double bunks, with crates of dried food over *here*, a hook with two blue uniforms over *there*, and a locked door to keep him a prisoner.

He remembered the box with its flashlight. He fought the impulse to panic and swept the invisible space with his hands until he found it.

With a twist of a barrel there was light. He pointed it to the door, and of course it was shut. Another drop of oily water fell. He pointed the light up and saw them arrayed across the roof. The vibration of the ship's engine seemed

266

labored. It made them glitter and dance. *Condensation*, he thought. *The sun has set and the metal is cooling. Another day nearer to Malta.*

If Hunter had been one of those exotic, light-generating organisms, the entire ship would glow from bow to stern like a nuclear reactor run wild. How many days were left before they pulled into port? They'd locked him away in this container, but locks and chains meant nothing to a virus. Air circulated in and out and Hunter would ride the almost imperceptible flow. The crew would breathe it in, the virus would land on fertile ground, find nourishment and explode into malignant life.

He felt his forehead. His skin was hot with fever. A few pustules had erupted from his brow, small and round and hard as lead shot.

Phase one was fever. The body tries to fight off the invaders. Phase two begins when the last resistance is overcome. The fever breaks and the virus comes storming in, converting the cells of Makayev's body and bending them to its own purpose: frantic reproduction. All meaningful distinction between Makayev and Hunter would vanish and he would die.

He was so thirsty.

Another drop of oily water fell on his face. He looked up. If only he could drink then perhaps he could think.

He staggered to his feet, gathered a blanket off the bottom bunk and used it to sponge down the walls. He was able to squeeze out only a tantalizing taste. But the roof. He had to reach those glittering drops.

267

He climbed the metal rungs to the top bunk. The effort left him dizzy. Dark, amebic shapes swam behind his eyes. He flopped onto the wet mattress, balled up the thin blanket and used it to swipe the ceiling. A deliciously cool shower, pure and with only a hint of salt, cascaded down onto his face, his blistered tongue, his open mouth. He put the wettest corner of the blanket into his mouth and sucked it dry.

Makayev stopped. The drops were distributed evenly across the corrugated ceiling, except in one place. There, a small rectangle remained dry. It was close enough to touch. He reached up.

It flexed, not like steel but like fabric.

He pushed again. No. Not *like* fabric. It *was* fabric. He pushed hard and a corner yielded, then another. Cold wet air showered down. He got onto his knees and ripped the fabric away from the little escape hatch. It had been taped over well, but the sun had dried the adhesive. First his hand went through, then his head, then his shoulders, and soon he found himself looking out across the roof of the container. It was night out here, the sky low and dark without moon or stars. He turned around and saw the glass eyes of the bridge glowing dim red.

The ship buried itself in a wave, rose, then dipped. He turned. Ahead, off the bow, a shimmering gray curtain was draped across the sea. It grew larger, taller. The freighter plunged through, ripping it open, releasing the rain hidden within. He put his head back and opened his mouth, letting the storm wash his face, soothing him.

He remembered the chart on the computer

screen. Pale blue to dark. Deep water was somewhere ahead, and close.

Think! The ship ran on diesel oil; a fuel that was deliberately hard to ignite. *Fire won't work. But water?*

The engines were like his body; cooled with water. Not fresh, but salt. That meant pipes full of ocean. Pipes that could be opened with a valve, or if not, broken open with an ax.

The engine room.

He dragged himself to the edge of the container roof. It was a long drop to the deck.

The engine room.

He eased one leg over, then the other and though he tried to hold on, his weight pulled him over. His legs collapsed under him and he toppled out against the wall of the container.

He was in a kind of elevated alleyway. The cargo holds were under him, full of pallets stacked high with sacks of dry cement.

Let in the sea.

He got his feet underneath him and stood. Makayev felt a kind of exhilaration flow through him. Locks and chains meant nothing to Hunter, but they'd kept him a prisoner. Now, though he knew what was coming and how it would end, like the virus itself, Makayev was free.

CHAPTER SEVENTEEN

CQB

K-335 *Gepard*
off South Point, Andikithira Island

'Ready?' said Senior Warrant Officer Anatoly Dobrin. He wanted the full attention of all four of his torpedomen. And their strength. 'Heave!'

The green plastic capsule looked light but it wasn't. Thirty feet long and two and a half in diameter, it contained a weapon that weighed close to six thousand pounds. Once it started to roll it was hard to stop. The cylinder smacked against the guide blocks and rocked back into place.

'Fuck your mothers!' Dobrin cursed. 'That's a *rocket!*' Unlike the boys he commanded he'd been around long enough to know what mishandled weapons could do. Let Leonov watch his clock. Dobrin was going to do this the right way.

The four sweaty young men set to work unbolting the straps that held together the two halves of the green shell.

The forward bulkhead was studded with eight bronze hatches, each leading to a torpedo tube. Six more tubes lived between *Gepard's* inner and outer hulls. It made the mere four that armed a *Los Angeles* seem laughable, though as any submariner will tell you, *one* smart torpedo coming

270

your way is *way* too many.

The breech door marked '1' was unlocked and opened. The tube gleamed with polished metal streaked with grease. Plastic inserts were fished down its length to guide the oddly shaped weapon.

Dobrin had good reason for his mistrust. The VA-111 *Squall* was an underwater rocket that flew through the sea in a cocoon of bubbles at over two hundred miles an hour. There was no evading it, no defense against it. At such tremendous speed even a fast ship might as well be dead in the water. But it was also a delicate, cantankerous device filled with poisons, chemicals and fuel so viciously flammable even the ocean couldn't snuff it out; once lit, the rocket burned until its fuel was exhausted or its four hundred pound warhead was triggered.

Dobrin had spent an evening drinking with the leading torpedo chief in the Northern Fleet. When the bar at the Murmansk Club for Mariners and Submariners grew quiet, he'd filled Dobrin in on what the admirals knew but would not say about the *Squall:* forget all the lies about collisions with American submarines. Static electricity had ignited the rocket's engines while still inside *Kursk,* setting off a cascading series of thunderous explosions that doomed the huge submarine and her crew.

Not on my ship, he thought. 'Peel the shell and get it stowed!'

The *Squall's* storage shell was removed, revealing a tapered gray cone machined to a jewel finish and unmarked by any ridges, seams or fins. The torpedomen nudged it into the waiting tube. It swallowed the nose, the midbody. When only the wide bell of its main rocket motor showed, the torpedomen stopped.

Two cables dangled from the tube's open mouth. One transmitted target data to the *Squall's* guidance computer. The other ignited its rocket booster. It was Dobrin's duty to plug them into the tail end of the missile.

The torpedomen stood back as Dobrin grasped the two cables. They ended in metal caps. The data wire was first. He looked up into the mouth of one large, and eight small rocket engines. The small ones got the *Squall* moving from its tube and powered a gas generator. The big one, well, when it lit this bastard *really* moved. He started to reach in, but then stopped and pulled out a medallion with Saint Nicholas, patron saint of Russian sailors, from under his shirt.

He kissed it. *Fuck the Lion, the Turtle and his friends.* Then, Dobrin touched the medallion to the bronze tube door.

A bright blue spark leaped across the gap with a tiny *snap!*

The torpedo room was silent as Dobrin plugged first one, then the other cable in, then slammed the breech door shut and locked it. 'Captain?' he said into the *kashtan.* 'Tube One is loaded.'

'Seven minutes fifty-two seconds,' said Leonov. 'You're running behind.'

'Understood,' said Dobrin. *But we're alive.*

'All stop!' said Steadman.

'All stop, aye,' said the sailor at the helm's outboard control station. He twisted the knurled knob of the engine telegraph from *FLANK* to *STOP.* A moment later the maneuvering room aft acknowledged that Steadman's order had been carried out. 'Maneuvering answers all stop.'

Portland had sprinted down the east coast of Andikithira. The island's southern tip was three miles off the starboard bow. With a Russian boat around, Steadman wanted her slow, stealthy and rigged for ultra-quiet when she got there. 'Sonar, Conn. Any close targets?'

'Conn, Sonar,' said Niebel, who had the watch while Schramm grabbed a quick dinner. 'I'm holding Sierra Sixty-Two to the west, course and speed constant.'

'What about the *Akula?*'

'No contact yet.'

Who knows for how long? 'Very well.' Steadman wished Bam Bam were there on the scopes. He turned to COB Browne at the ballast board. 'COB? We'll surface with decks awash.'

'Decks awash aye,' said Browne, who would be responsible for blowing *just* the right amount of ballast from the tanks to bring *Portland's* sail out of the water, and not much more.

'Helm. Five degrees up on the planes. Take us up to sixty feet *slowly.* All stations make ready for periscope depth. Radio?'

'Conn, Radio, aye,' said Scavullo.

273

'Have you checked your links to Bravo?'

'We're dialed in,' she said. 'As soon as we surface we'll know how well it's working.'

Or if. Steadman clicked the 1MC. 'Surface detail to the main trunk.'

It takes time for a slick submarine to slow down. *Portland* planed up into the shallows bleeding off speed. She was nearly abeam South Point before Steadman walked aft to the periscope stand.

'Six knots and sixty feet, Captain,' said Pena.

'Up the number two scope.'

Steadman did a fast sweep, first looking out ahead, then swinging the scope around in a full circle. A tiny, distant star, low to the water, marked *Cristi's* masthead light. 'Down scope.' He heard voices out in the forward passage and saw men – SEALs and his surface detail – waiting around the ladder leading up to the main trunk hatch.

Portland's men wore bright orange or neon green float vests over their blue coveralls. The SEALs were blacked out from balaclava hood to boots. They carried silenced MP5s, side arms, knives, night-vision gear and climbing equipment. They looked like nothing so much as a gang of futuristic pirates straight out of a modern ship's master's nightmare.

Target, boarding party, position. There was only one thing left to do. 'Surface the boat,' said Steadman.

The 1MC boomed out *Surface surface surface!*

Browne's hands flew over the ballast board, blowing a little water out of this tank, adding a bit of trim weight to another. He even had time to call to the galley to make sure the gravy and the bug juice dispensers were secure against wave action.

There was no need to worry. *Portland* crept up slowly as a balloon lofted into an innocent sky. When her sail broke the surface, only the gentle rocking of the sea marked their arrival.

'Bridge is dry,' said Pena.

Steadman turned to the black-clad figures waiting in the forward passage. In war you never know what's right until after the fact, and sometimes not even then. You can only pray that in the end you chose correctly.

Jameson was right about some things. The country was at war with men who professed to love death as much as Americans loved life. Steadman had read the stories about mothers of suicide bombers proclaiming how grateful they were that their sons had been chosen to blow themselves to bits. That wasn't religion. That was evil, and it had to be fought and utterly defeated. *But does that end justify any means?*

Of that Steadman was far less certain. You might find yourself in a downward spiral, generating ever more enemies among the innocent as you tried to stamp out the guilty few. That was a war no country, no matter how many submarines, jets and divisions it fields, could ever hope to win.

'Captain?' said Jameson.

'Crack the hatch,' he said. 'Let's do it.'

K-335 *Gepard*

Like the great undersea predator she was, *Gepard*

275

could not remain still. Her engine, her nuclear heart, the mechanical lungs that manufactured air for her crew depended on constant motion. And so the submarine prowled the rim of the Hellenic Trench in wide circles, masked by the bulk of Andikithira Island.

'Sonar?' asked Leonov.

'No targets,' said Kureodov. This constant circling was making his job difficult. He had to keep switching between the hydrophones on the bow and the towed array that streamed behind *Gepard*.

A buzz sounded in Central Command, and Leonov plucked a *kashtan* down from the overhead hook. 'Captain.'

'Compartment One reports Tubes One and Two are loaded with Type 111s and ready to flood,' said Dobrin.

'Too slow,' said Leonov. Another clock was now ticking, for it was unwise to leave a *Squall* sitting in readiness any longer than necessary. 'Helm? Right full rudder. Maintain eight knots. Bring us around again.'

Leonov kept *Gepard* skimming the underside of the thermocline; a distinct change in water temperature. The layer can bend, even reflect sound, forming a kind of acoustic mirror beneath which even a noisy submarine can hide. And *Gepard* was far from noisy.

Kureodov switched his circular display to show signals from the towed array, not that there was anything to hear. He wished he could drink some tea, eat a fresh bun from the galley.

Gepard was halfway through her slow, stealthy orbit when he saw a faint line pulse on his screen.

The submarine was at the point when he would switch back to the bow arrays, and they were more reliable, and so he waited until their course steadied out again, and there it was. Not a flicker, not an echo, but a white spoke of light where there had not been one before. 'Single screw contact bearing three five zero.'

'The freighter?'

'A submarine!'

'That's too soon,' said *Starpom* Stavinsky.

Kureodov pressed his earphones against his head. 'Transients, transients! Target is blowing tanks! He's diving!'

Leonov took the headphones away and listened.

Too soon or not, the Termite was right. The long, sad sigh of air venting from a submarine's ballast tanks was unmistakable. Could it be *another* American submarine? Or was it the same one they'd followed here from the Straits of Sicily?

A few minutes later Leonov heard a very different sort of sound come through the sonar receivers: the waspish buzz of an outboard engine, though without the usual whine of high-speed screws. He turned to his *starpom*. 'The Americans launched a small boat. You understand?'

Stavinsky could scarcely believe a country that had been targeted by such men would now collaborate with them. But here was their submarine and there was that ship. What were the possibilities?

Leonov turned. 'Countermeasures. Switch on the *Sirena*. Helm. Turns for twelve knots.'

As the thudding of the active silencing system started again, the lieutenant at the ship's control station asked, 'What heading, Captain?'

'Three five eight. We'll pass behind the *Los Angeles*.'

It would put *Gepard* in the American's baffles; hard to detect and impossible to fire on. But the Americans would have a front row seat on the destruction of that freighter. The bandits would see that Russia was not a helpless giant. And, Leonov hoped, so would the Americans.

Bravo Squad

It was called a *CRRC:* a combat rubber raiding craft. It was a big name for a small, inflatable Zodiac boat loaded down with eight men, weapons, explosives, biological testing gear and motivated by a large pump jet outboard. The men carried no food and only a little fresh water. The raft's bladder tank held only enough fuel to make it to the target and back. Once *Portland* blew ballast and sank back down into the sea, the SEALs were alone with their target, and this was just as it should be.

Lieutenant Jameson had his weapons. He had his men. They'd been given the best training in the world. He was a warrior with an enemy that needed killing – not some asshat drug lord – and that enemy was steaming straight into an ambush. Holding hands, sucking up and playing word games with black shoe Navy pukes was not just a waste of energy. It was distasteful. The sooner he and the other seven men of Bravo conducted some business the better.

The pump jet engine loped, idling. Jameson watched the last bubbles rise from the diving submarine. Off to the northwest, *Cristi's* mast-head light burned feebly, low to the water.

Jameson swung his head mike into position. 'Comm check. One.'

'Two,' the XO whispered, though it was loud and clear in everyone's ears.

'Three,' said Wheeler.

'Four... Five... Six... Seven... Eight.'

'We're good.' He turned to Wheeler and said, 'Go.'

The outboard roared to life. Even loaded down with men and equipment, the CRRC accelerated fast, skimming across the water like a perfectly tossed stone, leaping from crest to crest.

Chief Wheeler was at the helm, his big hand on the throttle and steering bar. The pump jet outboard made a lot of noise up here, but without a spinning screw its underwater signature was remarkably quiet. The squad's equipment lay protected in the center well while the SEALs were astride the pontoons, one leg in, one out, like cavalry soldiers riding to the bugler's charge.

Cristi's light rose higher and grew brighter. Beneath it, the beginnings of a dark wedge of hull began to take on solidity.

When the small GPS receiver Jameson had strapped to his knee began to flash, he nodded to Wheeler and the chief throttled the water jet to idle. The raft settled with a final slap of rubber on water, and then, silence. All Jameson could hear now was the throb of a ship's diesel engine and the distant rumble of thunder.

279

He switched the GPS off to save the batteries. Between the radios, the nods – night-vision gear in special operations parlance – the global positioning system and the headsets that allowed them to speak in whispers from half a mile away, a SEAL squad went through a lot of batteries. Every man carried two dozen replacements.

Jameson nodded to Stepik. 'Steve? Let her know.'

The radioman clicked the PRC 112 twice to signal *Portland* they were in position.

There was no answer.

He clicked twice again. 'No comms to the boat.'

'Our problem or theirs?'

'Theirs,' said Stepik, offended. 'I should've checked her gear out.'

'Your wife wouldn't like you checking out her gear,' teased Pyro.

'Neither would Rosie,' said Jameson. 'She's a tough cookie.'

'*Rosie?*' said Kernal. 'I forgot. You dated her, right?'

'I went to language school with her, asshole.'

'That was wicked brave, skipper,' said Pyro. 'I mean, dating a frog hog who speaks better Russian than you.'

'She's no frog hog,' said Jameson. 'Stepik? Try the boat again.'

The radioman double-clicked the transmit bar, and this time the squelch was broken with two short clicks in reply. 'Acknowledged.'

'If you ladies are finished gossiping,' said Chief Wheeler, 'here comes our ride.'

Jameson looked off to the southwest. A distant flash of lightning froze the oncoming freighter, then released it to the night. But incompletely. A faint red glow remained at the base of the crane. *Fuck*. He flipped his nods down and switched them on.

The crane cab was bright green, and the boom was moving. 'Bad news. The Tangos are playing with the crane.'

'You want me to cap them from here?' said Anders.

'No. We'll take our time and do this the right way.'

Another rumble of thunder echoed across the flat water. When it fell silent, Jameson could hear the splash of the freighter's bow wake coming on. He'd chosen the jump-off point well. The target would pass a hundred yards to the south. He turned to Wheeler and held up a hand.

The squad chief nodded. He would wait for the lieutenant's signal.

The raft rocked in the gentle seas, a black rectangle on black water, deathly still. The ship's engine swelled, her hull low in the water, the deck agreeably close. Jameson considered coming in astern, then abandoned the idea. *Stick with the plan*. He could see the boom of the crane now. It was moving back to a fore and aft position. The blunt bow swept by. The sound of *Cristi's* sick diesel was rough and rasping.

Jameson extended the collapsed pole and ladder, locked it tight, then turned to Wheeler and nodded.

With a twist of the throttle, the water jet roared

281

to life. The raft seemed to explode from its own boiling wake, rocketing straight at the rising black wall of *Cristi's* hull.

MV *'Cristi'*

'Are you happy now?' said Ali, *Cristi's* engineer. His hands and face were filthy with grease and hydraulic oil. He smelled of unwashed sweat, stale cologne and tobacco. It was almost enough to hide the alcohol. He wore dungarees and a sleeveless mesh shirt through which thick chest hair poked through in tufts. The crane's emergency stop button lay on the floor where he'd cut it loose.

'What if we need to stop the crane?' asked Dawish.

'Stop it?' said Ali, exasperated. 'You wanted it to *go*. It *goes*.' The engineer jammed a cigarette into his mouth, then fished a steel lighter from his pocket. He stuck his thumb on the flint wheel.

Dawish covered it with his hand. 'There's too much spilled oil for smoking.'

'Who says so?'

'I do. Be careful, Ali. If you can't be bothered to keep the equipment clean and working we'll find someone who can.'

'You want some advice? Watch yourself. It's a long swim to Egypt and your uncle won't be around to fish you out.' He snapped the lighter.

'You'll be looking for another berth at Souda if you light that cigarette.' He could see a flash of real worry in Ali's dark eyes. 'Go aft and tell the captain you took the safety switch out. See what he says about it.'

'You tell him,' said Ali. 'I'm going to bed.'

'You mean back to your bottle.'

The engineer gave him a thumb's up sign, which in Egyptian parlance didn't mean everything was fine, but rather invited First Mate Somebody's Cousin to sit on it. Satisfied that he'd gotten the correct message across, Ali turned and started down the ladder.

USS *Portland*

Bam Bam came back to the sonar shack early. He had a mug of coffee in one hand and a CD in the other. A sweet roll capped the mug.

Niebel looked away from his screen. 'Can't stay away?'

'No.' Actually, Schramm was puzzled about something. He'd heard that other boats had encountered quiet Russian submarines up in the Barents. He figured it was lazy sonarmen. So what was *his* excuse?

All Russian submarines were noisy. First you picked up their screws, then the throb and whine of their machinery. Next, their flow noise which was always loud because they didn't know how to keep their hulls clean, and finally, if there was any doubt left, the 50 hertz hum of their electrical systems. Not just sometimes. Always. And from a long way off. In the right conditions, detection ranges of forty, even fifty miles were not unheard of.

Except for this *Akula*. Where had she come

283

from? How had she stayed hidden so long? It gnawed at him, for when it came to sound, Bam Bam knew the sea. It was filled with structures and peculiarities, with ambiguous echoes. Strange things happened. Sounds bent and bounced. They traveled fast in warm water and faster in water under pressure. All of these qualities varied with temperature, the time of year and salinity. Bam Bam's job was to pay very close attention to this watery chaos and make sense of it. The way this *Akula* just *appeared* bothered him. 'The Russian boat ever show up again?'

'No.' Niebel noticed the CD. 'Whatcha' listening to?'

Schramm slipped the disc into one of the sonar system's acoustic processors. It started to whir. *'Sounds of Silence.'*

'That's old shit.'

'This is the new version.' Schramm slipped into a chair. 'You know, our processors are good at finding stuff that's out there. But they're piss poor at looking for stuff that *isn't.*'

Niebel said, 'Huh?'

'Socks, the ocean is a noisy place. I got to thinking, what if we had the computers graph the extra *quiet* places? Like, quieter than ambient?'

'You are definitely thinking too much.'

Bam Bam fed the old sonar work tape through the spare processor, instructing the acoustic filters to pay attention not to the noisy signals, but to the quiet shadows. The screen went white. But there were a few dark patches drifting like clouds; random-looking spots where sound was muffled by changes in temperature, salinity.

The natural quiet places came and went, just as natural sounds came and went. There was no pattern, no rhythm to them. But one shadow looked different. It seemed to move with purpose. It maintained a constant bearing and distance dead astern, until it suddenly veered off.

Bam Bam watched the shadow dart away, then stop on a bearing of one nine four degrees. He froze the screen, then grabbed the intercom microphone and spun the growler to *Control*. 'Conn, Sonar.'

'Go,' said Steadman. Why was Bam Bam back in the sonar shack?

'What was that Russian boat's bearing when we picked her up?'

Steadman checked the contact evaluation board. 'One nine four.'

Schramm felt the blood rush to his head. There were things a submariner could count on. The ocean wanted to kill you. American boats were quiet. Russians were not. Something had changed. *That fucker's been trailing us for a while.* 'Captain, I think we've been had.'

Bravo Squad

Chief Wheeler angled the Zodiac in. When a collision with the sheer wall of the hull seemed imminent, he swung the steering bar over and paralleled the freighter's course from a few feet away.

Close in, Jameson could see that some imbalance in her cargo was causing her to ride stern low. Her white load line showed at her bow

285

but dived underwater aft. He sized up the angle, the tactical implications, and said into his head mic, 'Forward of the deckhouse.'

Wheeler twisted off a bit of throttle and let the rubber raft drift back along the hull, then expertly swung them in. The white foamy lane narrowed, the raft rode up over the turbulent wake, then bumped against the freighter's side, pinned tight by hull suction.

Jameson already had the caving ladder up. The grapple at the end caught a rail. He pulled down hard to set it. The SEALs of the second element trained their MP5s up to cover the deck in case someone chose the wrong moment to man the rails. Jameson turned to Anders, and the sharp-shooter swarmed up the caving ladder like he'd been launched.

Anders rolled out onto the deck and came up ready to shoot, but the deck was empty. A few seconds later Jameson appeared beside him with his silenced MP5 in his hands and gave the all clear.

Pyro clambered up the caving ladder slowly. The load on his back was heavy, even for him. He poked his head over the edge of the deck, and froze.

Jameson followed his gaze. A short man had just stepped off the catwalk between the pipe bundles and was walking to the rail.

Ali cupped his hands against the breeze and lit his cigarette. He leaned against the rail. He once had dreams of working for the Egyptian national airline, of fixing jets that were clean and modern, of traveling all over the world for next to nothing. His own sister was a stewardess and she'd been everywhere. Well, not since the world started looking at every Arab as though he had a bomb belt strapped on. She'd been to Europe, to America, while Ali was trapped on an old tub heading for the scrap yard.

He sucked the cigarette until it glowed bright, then held the smoke in his lungs. First Mate Somebody's Cousin was an idiot but he could get him fired. Then what would he do? The Greeks might be nice enough to throw him in jail, but the Americans, they had a base at Souda. They'd take one look at him, an Egyptian engineer, and put him on a one-way flight to Guantanamo Bay. The newspapers would be full of stories of Engineer Ali, a terrorist mastermind planning to blow up some–

A black shadow flitted in front of his face. He turned to see what had made it. Ali had only an instant to wonder when a hand clamped over his mouth, his nose, and a blade slipped swiftly, deeply into his back. He arched, trying to rise off that sharp point, but he couldn't. It kept driving deeper, deeper. He tried to twist away and the blade scraped bone. A jolt of electric agony sent his muscles into shock, into spasm. His hands jerked open and the lit cigarette flew away in a bright, incendiary arc.

First Mate Somebody's Cousin! he thought as he fell to the deck, a gloved hand still pressed tight over his mouth. His heart quickly pumped itself dry through two severed arteries and one great vein. Tiny black spots swam in front of his eyes.

They grew, gathered, merged. He didn't know which bothered him more; that Dawish had knifed him or that the worthless little snake would almost certainly get away with it.

Dawish was about to switch off the hydraulic pump when he spotted the tossed cigarette spark against the deck. *Fool!* He reached overhead and switched on the spotlight, then swiveled it. He found Ali sprawled on the deck with two black-clad figures kneeling next to him and a third with his head just peeking over the deck edge. All three looked up. There was a flash and a *pop!* The spotlight went dark with a tinkling of shattered glass.

Dawish might be young. He might be first mate because of his uncle. But he knew pirates when he saw them. They'd come from somewhere, likely an island, and figured this slow, plodding ship would be easy prey. *Think!* There was no time to alert the captain. No time for anything but to act. He was second in command and this was his ship.

He grabbed the control bar and squeezed the trigger to open the jaws on the hook block, then pulled back to elevate the boom off the wave shield. He grabbed the other bar and pivoted it smartly over the side.

Dawish wasn't sure what he hoped to achieve, but those pirates didn't fly onto his ship. They had some sort of small boat down there, and he had a ton of steel at his command. His thumb mashed down hard on the cable feed, and still swinging in its arc, the hook block plummeted below the edge of the deck, just as Lieutenant Sanders was leading the second element up the ladder.

He sensed the looming mass too late. Something struck him full in the chest and Kernal Sanders was flying. He only had a second to fill his lungs before he hit the water.

The sea was toasty warm compared to the chill waters off Coronado. He'd hit flat but he was drawn down deep. *Hull suction.* It pinned him against the freighter's side below the waterline. There was a clatter, a *thrum thrum thrum* in his ears, growing louder. He was a powerful swimmer but he couldn't stay here forever. He reached for the pull tabs on his emergency float vest and gave them a jerk.

The cells inflated explosively. The two CO_2-filled bladders brought him bobbing and gasping to the surface so near the hull he had to tip his head back to see the edge of the deck. *Not good.* He took a quick breath and felt a sharp stab in his chest. He had broken ribs for sure. That was something to worry about later. Right now he had to get away from the ship and swim for open water. Wheeler would have seen him fall. He'd come back. Then he could worry about broken bones.

The rumble of the engine and the slash of the propeller blades were overwhelming, like some great rapids on a wild and raging river just around the next bend. He was in the grip of a strong current, and it was heading someplace he very much did not wish to go.

Dawish felt the cable snag on something. He braked it to a stop, then worried it back and forth, up and down, hoping it was doing some good. Though if he sank the pirate's boat, would that make them more desperate? *Too late.* When it no longer met any resistance, he twisted out of the seat to go warn the captain.

He came face to face with the black hood and bright blue eyes of Tommy Anders. Dawish opened his mouth to scream, but the sound died in his throat when Anders punched him in the belly.

The pirate pulled his fist back, and only then did Dawish see the blade.

He felt warm blood stream down from his torn belly, over his belt, across his thighs, a pulsing red spray that seemed to have no end. He looked up and mouthed the word *Why?*

The pounding of the engine and the rhythmic swish of the propeller thundered in Kernal Sanders' ears. He put the pain of his broken ribs in a mental box, kicked off the hull and swam for his life. His vest kept his head above water, but the forces generated by thousands of tons of steel pushing the sea aside were stronger. The wild river drew him back against the hull. He bounced off once again. Barnacles slashed at his body. Before the pain could register he was under, accelerating down a chaotic chute of roaring rapids and turbulent foam, down deeper, deeper, directly into the blades of the ship's spinning screw.

CHAPTER EIGHTEEN

LIGHTS AND SHADOWS

USS *Portland*

'See these dark areas?' said Bam Bam, pointing to his screen. 'It's where the ocean's *way* quieter than it should be. Sonic dead zones come and go and shift bearing. Not this one.' He pointed to one dark area. 'This shadow's been stickin' to us like a burr. I think it's our friend the *Akula*.'

Shadow? thought Steadman. It was a good name. Submarine warfare was a lethal game of tag played in pitch darkness between opponents armed with rifles. Stay silent and you won't get shot. The first one to make a noise dies. American submarines were very good at silence. Now this Russian boat was, too. 'How long have they been with us?'

'I'll have to run the archive tapes.'

He could have been trailing us since Gibraltar. 'This is fine work, Bam Bam. But I don't much like a boat out there we can't see.'

'We're seeing him now. Besides,' said Schramm, 'if this guy's like all the other Russians, it won't be long before something breaks.'

'I've seen that movie, too. Your program. Can it run in real time?'

'Yes sir,' said Bam Bam. 'Well, almost.'

291

'How almost?'

'What we're doing here is trying to digitize the ocean in three dimensions, and throw out all the usual data points and use the gaps we always ignore to establish a baseline signal to noise–'

'Stop.' The last thing he wanted was to get drawn down the sonic rabbit hole where sonar operators lived. He wanted to know *what*, not *how*. 'How can I use it?'

'It'll tell you what he's doin' but not soon enough to target him, and only if we take two consoles off-line and soak up their processing power.'

Leaving us with barely enough to keep a normal sonar watch ... but like Jameson said, we're not here to do normal sweeps. 'Do it. And train Niebel here on the program so he can relieve you now and again.'

'I'll try,' said Bam Bam, relishing Niebel's scowl. 'It's not–' he stopped. The purposeful shadow on his screen was beginning to move off to the west. 'Sir? The *Akula* is moving.'

'Which way?'

'North. It looks like he'll pass astern of us. He might be going to give that freighter a once over.'

It would give the Russian boat a clear view to *Cristi*. And a clear shot. It would also put him astern of *Portland* and that Steadman did not like. He unhooked the intercom. 'Radio? Are you in contact with Bravo?'

Scavullo was cleared for Yellowstone and Banjo Gant was not, and so she'd evicted him from the radio room as soon as the SEALs went up the bridge trunk. Barring something unforeseen, she'd stay here alone until they returned. She had both antenna masts extended, and even risked raising them higher than was prudent to assure a good signal. 'The signal strength is erratic and we're starting to get some atmospherics,' she said, meaning *lightning*. 'But I can raise them.'

'Tell them a Russian submarine is headed their way. If they feel like shooting they're well inside torpedo range now.'

Would they? Scavullo had picked up a fair amount of Russian psychology along with the language. They had their own approaches to solving embarrassing problems. First, deny them, and if that didn't work, *annihilate* them. Russians seemed to believe that nothing hid the evidence of incompetence like a lot of high explosive.

'Lieutenant?'

'Aye aye, sir. I'll alert them right away.' She selected the frequency guarded by the SEAL squad. She wondered whether she should report only the facts, or her suspicions. The sizzle of frying bacon filled her headphones. She switched transmitters, got a clear sidetone through her headphones and clicked the transmit switch three times – the alarm signal – and waited for an acknowledgement.

MV 'Cristi'

Jameson ran the engine telegraph back to ALL STOP, and the order was answered a moment later by Chief Wheeler down in the engine room.

Wheeler had never set foot on a freighter like this before. The diesel was an East German

293

design with odd controls and markings. Someone had hung placards in Arabic script next to some of them, not that it helped. But the pipes were all color coded and Wheeler knew marine engines. The throb of the diesel soon fell silent and the freighter quickly lost way, drifting before a stiffening southwest wind.

'We'll try this again,' said Jameson. He was furious. A picture-perfect combat boarding had turned to pure shit and his XO was in the water somewhere astern. The sooner he yanked the truth out of this Arab's mouth, the sooner he could double back and pick him up. Kernal Sanders could tread water for hours but there were limits to everything and Jameson had reached his. 'Your name?'

'Ahmed Khanji. I am master.' A purple bruise spread across a cheek where he'd been thrown to the deck and trussed up like a chicken on the way to market, his hands bound behind his back by white plastic ties. There were three of these devils in his bridge and he had no interest in deceiving them. *Who are they?* They were close to Greek waters but these were no Greeks. The Israelis could show up anywhere, but Israeli commandos spoke better Arabic than *he* did. *Americans,* he thought. Simple people with simple ideas about the world, and the sooner he told them the simple truth, the better off everything would be. Why lie to save a cargo of rusty pipe?

'Where do you keep your logs *Master* Khanji?'

'Chart table. Top drawer. It's hard to open. You must hit.'

Jameson nodded to Anders, who backed his way

to the chart table, keeping his MP5 on Khanji. There was a thump, and the sound of metal sliding on metal. 'Where did you sail from?'

'Sukhumi. This is port in Georgia.'

'And from there to Sochi?'

'Sochi? Never. Very bad place,' said Khanji, and when the angry American seemed not to understand, he said, *'Mafiya*. You know?'

'You picked up some passengers. A Saudi, a Russian, a pair of Chechens. Are they on your ship?'

'No passengers. No Sochi. Check logs. Everything is okay.'

'No, everything is *not* okay.' Jameson strained to keep himself from kicking Khanji's teeth down his throat. A ship like this was full of places to hide. It could take days to search. *'Where are your passengers?'*

'Please. The cargo, the pipes, we load in Sukhumi. No stops. We take to Malta. That's it completely.'

'Malta is *west*. Why the *fuck* are you sailing east?'

'No, no. The company, they find new buyer on Crete and tell us to turn. They pay better for cargo. It's my fault?'

'Hey boss!'

Jameson looked up. Tommy Anders was holding two books, both bound in leather. One moldy brown, the other new and green. 'The log has a stamp from the port inspector in Sukhumi all right. But it's written out to a ship called *Nova Spirit*.'

'My ship!' Khanjo said proudly.

Nova Spirit? 'You see anything else in the logs?'

'Yeah. She collected another stamp when she

passed safety inspection at the Bosporus. That one shows her name as *Cristi*.'

Jameson leaned over and put his mouth close to Khanji's ear. 'Why did you change names?'

'This is not my fault! By company orders absolutely!' Khanji felt something cold and hard pressed against his skull, just behind his right ear and he shut his eyes, waiting for the blast.

'Sorry, Captain. But *everything* is your fault.' Jameson gave the muzzle of his Sig Sauer a hard shove. *'Where did you change names?'*

'Please! Company orders! Middle of Black Sea!'

'Your crew knocked my XO into the ocean with your fucking crane. Was that company orders, too?'

Dawish! he thought. *You've killed us!* 'No no no! You come aboard at night, who knows? Maybe pirates!'

'You're going to wish we were pirates.'

Stepik was guarding the frequency back to *Portland*. Three scratchy breaks in squelch got his attention. 'Bravo,' he said.

'Tell your CO a Russian submarine is headed your way,' said Scavullo.

'He's kind of busy for traffic reports.'

'He'll be a lot busier if they start shooting at you.'

Stepik said, 'Skipper? The Russians are back.'

Jameson could think of any number of ways a Russian submarine might screw things up and no way it might help. There was a mission to carry out, a SEAL in the water, and neither delay nor failure was an option. He kept the Sig Sauer pressed against Khanji's head and said to the radioman, 'Call Wheeler and see if he has any hits on the box.'

Stepik selected the low-powered tactical set and whispered something to the squad chief. The crew had been forcibly assembled in the mess with their arms tied behind their backs while Wheeler scanned them for smallpox. A 'hit' meant that one of the antibody-doped wires in the scanner had re-acted to a pathogen, changing the resistance ever so slightly, lighting up the scanner and making an alarm scream bloody murder. Stepik looked back to Jameson and shook his head. 'Clean.'

Jameson thought, *Goat rope*. Eight superbly trained men achieving in a matter of minutes what the whole fucking Russian military couldn't – or wouldn't – do. He had one man – his best Russian speaker – treading water with injuries unknown, an Arab captain playing games with names, no Saudis, no Chechens, no WMD and a Russian sub heading his way.

He *could* let this ship go. It wasn't the one he'd been ordered to stop. But it was a walnut in the shell game aimed at hiding the real *Cristi*. And if so, Khanji would put out the alarm the instant they departed. The *real* target would know they were being hunted and how the attack would come. *Smash the radios?* It would be too easy to miss a single satellite phone or shortwave set. *No.* He was here to deter and disrupt the terrorists and it was time for a little deterring and dis-rupting. 'Steve, call Pyro up on deck,' Jameson told his radioman. 'Meet at the rally point.'

While Stepik made the call, Jameson turned his attentions back to Khanji. The Sig Sauer is a double-action weapon. You pulled the trigger and it fired. There was just the smallest *click* when the minute slack in the take-up mechanism bottomed out. Jameson put the gun to Khanji's head and let him hear it up close. 'I'm leaving soon and I'd like to know a few things before I go. How about it, Captain? You up for it?'

Khanji shut his eyes. 'Please. Ask. I tell whatever you like.'

'The owners of this ship. They have another one just the same?'

'*Just* the same. Both Polish. Good ships but old. Nobody wants.'

You're wrong there. 'This other *Cristi,* she was on the Black Sea?'

Khanji didn't hesitate. 'She carries Russian cement. Captain is crazy black man from Africa.'

'Crazy?'

'God this, God that. Always God. He makes crew pray five times every day. Not me. This is a ship, not mosque. You understand?'

'I'm beginning to. Where did this other *Cristi* pick up that cargo of Russian cement?'

'You know this already.'

'Sochi.'

Khanji nodded. 'Very bad place.'

'Where is the real *Cristi* now?'

Khanji shrugged. 'We clear Bosporus before noon. She was behind, you understand? End of line. But same ship, yes? Slow. Maybe fifty, one hundred kilometers away now.'

Unless she made a little stop first. 'What name did your company have this crazy African paint on her?'

298

'This is not business for me to know.'

Nova Spirit. Jameson would lay odds on that. He relaxed his grip on the pistol and slipped it back into its holster. What he needed was to call back on a secure frequency and find out if anyone knew where a ship just like this one but not this one might be. He glanced at Stepik. 'How soon before we have a bird to bounce a signal home?'

The radioman checked his watch. 'Window opens in thirty-two minutes. But the bus could relay it for us now.'

'Okay.' He turned to Anders. 'Secure the captain. Make sure he's comfortable, then hustle back to the rally point. We're done here.'

'My ship okay?' said Khanji, relieved that he no longer had a muzzle pressed against his head. 'You go?'

'Yes,' said Jameson. 'We go.'

'God bless America!' said the Lebanese. He'd always been told that truth could be useful in the right circumstances. Didn't this prove it?

K-335 *Gepard*

'Periscope depth, Captain,' said Stavinsky.

Leonov got up from his chair and walked aft to a short ladder. It was just four steps up to the 'Pulpit' where the periscope was located but no one except Leonov was allowed to climb them. As though the sight of the outside world might be dangerous for anyone beneath the rank of captain, first rank. 'Bearing to target?'

'Zero three five,' said the Termite. Kureodov

saw the white line of the lumbering freighter fade. 'The ship's engines are stopped.'

'What about the small boat?'

'Contact was lost on the ship's range and bearing.'

So. *A rendezvous.* Leonov switched on the periscope's light amplifier, put his eye to the lens, grasped the handles of the instrument and twisted. It moved with the jerky gnash of reluctant motors and gears, the view, one of black sea and sky that flashed with sheets of emerald green lightning. There was nothing, and then a dark mass, a stern, swung into view. He checked the photos and silhouettes of the target transmitted with their new orders, then put his eye back to the scope, thumbed a switch and zoomed in. *Deck configuration, crane amidships. Wheelhouse. All the same. It's her.* Add an American attack submarine dispatching small boats and it was all Leonov needed. 'This will be a firing observation.'

Stavinsky shot a look at the Termite that said, *You'd better be right.*

'Target bearing zero three two. Range two thousand four hundred meters.'

'Transmit targeting data, Tubes One and Two.'

'Transmitting,' said Kureodov. The target's speed, bearing and range had to be loaded into the *Squall's* guidance computers, for there was no way to guide the missile once the main rocket engine fired. No ship could move very far in the few seconds between launch and impact, either.

The intercom squawked. It was Dobrin down in the torpedo room.

'Data received and accepted,' said Stavinsky.

Then, 'Tubes One and Two are ready to flood.'

'Flood One. Flood Two.'

Stavinsky clicked a stopwatch first, then pressed the red buttons to let the sea into the two torpedo tubes. A low rumble filled the hull as water rushed in to replace air. The factory that made the rocket torpedo said you could keep them wet for thirty minutes without any risk, but where were the factory representatives tonight? *Asleep in their beds.* He would cut their estimate in half. And, of course, there was no way to bring the *Squalls* back inside now. Not without risking *Gepard*. One way or the other, they would soon be flying *someplace*.

A second roar sounded as the next tube filled. The two red lights on the torpedo control console winked out, replaced by green. 'One and Two are flooded.' *Twenty seconds.*

'Open the outer doors.' Leonov called down from the Pulpit. 'Switch the intercom to ship's circuit.'

'Outer doors opening,' came Stavinsky's response. He checked the stopwatch. The torpedoes had been wet for fifty-one seconds. 'Ship's intercom is live, Captain.' Leonov's voice would be carried from the Pulpit throughout the ship. Stavinsky's only wish now was that any sermon would be a short one.

USS *Portland*

Bam Bam kept an eye on that determined dark cloud as it slid across his screen. Now that he knew what to look for, it was easy to spot. The little cloud's advance slowed, then stopped. It grew smaller, so much so that Bam Bam thought it might vanish altogether.

He glanced at Neibel's screen. It displayed a more normal sonar picture. He saw the white line that represented the old freighter. It, too, was faint, for her engines were shut down and she was adrift. But the relationship between them was both plain and ominous. 'Conn, Sonar.'

Steadman said, 'What is it, Bam Bam?'

'The *Akula's* got a clear shot at that, ah, target of interest if he wants to take it.'

Where are those SEALs? Steadman wondered. But now he had a more pressing concern: to move out of the line of fire. 'Helm! Right five degrees rudder! Course zero one five! Ahead two thirds and *do not cavitate.*' The Russians had torpedoes that homed in on the sound of a thrashing screw. Even if *Portland* wasn't in their sights, mistakes happened and Steadman didn't intend for them to happen to *him.*

Bam Bam watched the shadow's bearing drift as *Portland* shifted position. *Shit!*

'Conn! Sonar! Warning! I think the Russian flooded his tubes!'

MV 'Cristi'

'Anything from the boat?'

Stepik shook his head. 'I can't raise them now.'

So much for relaying messages. Jameson flipped his nods down and looked over the side of the

302

freighter. The crane boom was hanging over the port side. The hook block had really bashed in the hull, and all Jameson could hope was that his XO had not been caught between them. *If he did,* thought Jameson, *he isn't treading water waiting for a pickup.*

'We're set, skipper.' It was Battaglia, the squad explosives expert.

Jameson switched off his nods. 'Anything in the holds?'

'Zip. The tub's so top heavy it's a miracle she hasn't turned turtle. I left the watertight doors open. The captain say anything?'

'Yeah. We boarded the wrong ship.'

'Fucker would.'

'He's telling the truth. We found the logs. This tub left port as the *Nova Spirit*. They swapped names on us up north. The ship we want is still out there someplace. Bait and switch. We took the bait.'

'So then where's our target?'

It was silent for a moment, and then the rumble of thunder, louder than before, echoed across the freighter's deck.

'We'll find her.' Jameson looked to the northwest. A flash lit a towering wall of cloud. *It's coming on.* Chief Wheeler had stored the GPS coordinates when Kernal fell. Forget Russian submarines. He had to find his XO before the rain hit and dialed down visibility to pure shit.

'You want me to go below and retrieve the gizmo?'

'No. Set the squib for ten minutes.'

'But you said this is the wrong ship.'

303

'I didn't say the fuckers are innocent. If we let them go how long do you think it'll take before they phone home? Then when we find the *real* target, the one *these* assholes are protecting, the *muj* will give us a real AK hello. No thanks. This ship goes down.' He swung the radio headset mike to his lips and whispered, 'Extract, extract.' Then, to Battaglia he said, 'Set the squib then haul ass back on deck. We've got to find Kernal while we can still see him.'

USS *Portland*

A Russian boat in perfect firing position, and eight of our guys in the way. Steadman leaned back against the padded rail and searched the contact board for some answers. *He thinks we can't see him.* That was a tactical advantage, and Steadman was reluctant to give it up. But if the Russians were out to solve their runaway biologist problem with a torpedo he'd just as soon they wait until the SEALs were safely off.

COB Browne was at the ballast board and he didn't need a psychic to know what was going on inside the captain's head. 'Decoy?' Browne suggested. *Portland* carried torpedo decoys that made noise like a full-sized submarine. 'He might not fire if he thought he was shooting at *us.*'

The decoys took some time to set up, to load, to launch. This matter would be decided in the next few minutes. 'No.' He needed to give them something else to consider *right now.* 'Helm, right full rudder. Turns for twelve knots.'

304

'Right full rudder and turns for twelve knots.'

'Sonar, Conn.'

'Sonar, aye,' said Bam Bam.

'I'm going to put that shadow off the bow. Stand by to send an active pulse down his bearing. Max power. I want their full attention, Bam Bam.'

'Conn, Sonar, aye.' Schramm flipped up the switch guard that kept the SADS-TG active sonar from being accidentally triggered. He called up an on-screen menu and selected maximum power.

'Torpedo room, fire control. Make tubes One and Two ready in all respects and open the outer doors.' The *Akula* might mistake his ping for an act of offense, not defense. If so, Steadman wanted to be ready. 'Sonar, Conn. Stand by.'

Short range, clear water. Bam Bam's sonar was powerful enough to boil water. Focused into a tight beam and launched straight at that quiet Russian boat, it wouldn't just get their attention. No way. It was going to *thunder.*

CHAPTER NINETEEN

OUTBREAK

MV *'Nova Spirit'*

The sea was a mounded black landscape raked by lightning. The winds were steady at twenty knots with gusts to nearly twice that. The air was thick with foam and spray. Captain Warsame took the storm's measure as he stood on his bridge. The waves weren't big but the Mediterranean was famous for steep seas and tonight it was living up to its reputation.

He watched Hazil the helmsman struggle to maintain heading. The Pakistani was fighting the storm with large swings of the rudder. The ship was hogging over the sharp crests, surfing down into the troughs, sagging, staggering and rolling. The motions were complex and unpredictable. There would be no steering by autopilot tonight.

Warsame walked over to the engine repeater. It still showed 88 revolutions per minute. He could demand 122, but he thought about that hot seawater cooling pump down in the engine room. *Not yet.*

Nova Spirit heeled to starboard and rolled up the back of a sea. He'd picked Hazil to steer because he was a good man in bad weather, but he seemed oddly slow tonight. The ship began to lose way, the bow poised to fall away down the back of the wave, putting them broadside to the blow. 'Right rudder,' he warned Hazil. 'Full right rudder! What's wrong with you tonight?'

The helmsman swung the small wheel hard over. The bow paused, pitched down and plunged into the trough. The ship rolled hard to port, then steadied up. 'This heading, it is not so good. We should turn into these waves, Captain.'

'No. We're docking in Catania tomorrow. You're not sharp. That's the problem.'

'I ... I am not feeling so well,' Hazil admitted as he chased after the proper heading, over-correcting one way, then the other.

Warsame reached over to brace himself against the bridge windows as the ship rolled off to port again. Rain spattered hard against the glass. Another flash, another roll of thunder. The weather would get worse before it got better. They would have to turn into it at some point, and that would delay their arrival at Catania. *Salafi won't like it.* Not that there was anything he could do. 'Mark that heading and hold it!'

MV 'Cristi'

Jameson and Tommy Anders stood guard on deck as the men of Bravo climbed down the net ladder to the Zodiac. They'd left the freighter's crew tied up in the galley and the captain face down on his own bridge, but there were no guarantees they'd found everyone. Jameson was in no mood for another surprise.

Chief Wheeler took the Zodiac's tiller. He started up the pump jet. Its muffled roar settled to an impatient grumble. 'Bravo Three. Boat ready,' he said over the squad radio.

Jameson could still see a few stars off to the east, but the west was draped with low clouds that flashed and rumbled. The weather was going to complicate finding his XO. 'Bravo Five, this is One. Time check?'

'Eight minutes and change, skipper,' said Pyro.

'Six go.' Jameson nodded to the sharpshooter. Anders had been first up and now he was next to last down. He swung over the rail and dropped to the rubber boat below.

307

Fine drops of rain began to fall, turning the oily deck slick and treacherous. A gust of wind raised a cat's paw of whitecaps.

Jameson unhooked the net ladder and let it fall. He would slide down the crane's steel cable. It would tear up his gloves but so what?

'Seven minutes,' said Pyro.

Jameson put a leg over the rail when he heard something from among the piles of rusty pipes. Not a voice, but a faint sobbing. He swung back on deck, crouched low and flipped his nods down. The world came alive in shades of acid green.

"What the fuck, skipper?' Wheeler asked.

'Something's making noise up here.'

'Clock reads six and thirty.'

'Yeah. I know.' The fuel air weapon down in the hold would fill the hull with flammable gas, an explosive squib would set it off and *Cristi* would vanish in a cataclysmic blast in a little more than six minutes.

Jameson heard the soft crying sound again. Was the crewman Anders had taken down in the crane cab still alive? Or had a runaway biologist decided to crawl out of his steel spider hole?

There was a gap in the pipe bundles, a narrow aisle barely wide enough for his broad shoulders that led to the centerline catwalk. He brought up the silenced MP5 and flattened himself against the pipes, listening very, very hard.

'Five minutes, lieutenant,' growled Wheeler.

Wheeler's use of the word *lieutenant* told Jameson the old guy was pissed off. *So be it*. The hiss of falling rain merged with the static through his radio headset. He prepped himself curled his finger around the trigger to take up the slack in the firing mechanism, made sure of his footing, then hurled himself into the narrow alley.

Two brilliant yellow eyes stared back at him, bright as headlights on a dark road. His instinct did the rest, and even as his brain put a name to what he was seeing, the MP5 sent a stream of 9mm rounds into the rusty pipes. The heavy bullets caromed and sparked off into the night like meteors. Something struck his left shin. He was sure he'd caught a ricochet.

The weapon was silenced, but everyone down in the Zodiac knew the sights and sounds of an MP5 at work. Tommy Anders was about to claw up the side of the hull bare-handed but Chief Wheeler dragged him back down by the scruff of his Nomex suit.

Jameson felt blood on his shin. He reached down. Three strips of Nomex cloth hung from his leg with scratches to match. *Not a ricochet*, he thought. 'I found the noise. It was a cat.'

'A *what?*'

'A fucking cat!'

'Get your ass down in this boat, *lieutenant,*' said Wheeler. 'Or you and Pussy Willow will be flying overhead in about four minutes.'

K-335 *Gepard*

Captain Leonov reached up and pulled a *kashtan* microphone down. 'Range and bearing to target?'

'Three four six, range two thousand four hundred meters,' said the Termite.

'Torpedo room?'

Warrant Officer Dobrin answered for everyone in the torpedo room when he said, 'Tubes One and Two are ready. Absolutely.'

Absolutely? 'Jettison valves?'

'Armed.' Dobrin already had one hand on the emergency jettison valve. Pull it and a torpedo tube would fill with high-pressure air and pop the *Squall* out into the sea like a champagne cork. Ejecting a malfunctioning *Squall* was a risky proposition because it could get hung up in its guides. But a stuck *Squall* had put *Kursk* on the bottom. Dobrin had no desire to add *Gepard* to its score.

Leonov said, 'Ship ready?'

'Three knots, zero bubble. Ship is ready,' said *Starpom* Stavinsky. He stood at the firing console. Two green lights burned from a double row of reds. An old-fashioned rotary switch pointed to Tube One. A wide, flat button almost the size of his palm would initiate the complex series of actions needed to launch two undersea rockets. He glanced at his stopwatch. 'Both tubes have been flooded for fourteen minutes.'

Leonov clicked the *kashtan* to send his voice throughout the submarine. 'Men of *Gepard*.'

No. Not now, thought Stavinsky.

'We are about to strike back at a gang of bandit murderers. These barbarians are not just the enemies of our people, our motherland, but of civilization itself. Today we administer justice for Russia and for the world.' He dropped the *kashtan* and turned to Stavinsky at the firing console. 'Tube one! Shoot!'

Stavinsky moved his hand onto the cool curve

of the launch button.

The Termite was the first to see it coming. His sonar screen, fed by hydrophones on the submarine's hull, suddenly went white as an overexposed photograph. 'Captain! A–'

His voice was drowned out an instant later by the deafening roar of a great fog horn. The basso sonar pulse filled *Gepard,* resonating inside the steel hull like the tolling of an immense bell, tripping circuit breakers and making instruments buzz and needles vibrate in demonic harmonies.

In each compartment, men froze in fear, sure that something terrible was happening only to them. In the reactor spaces the compartment commander *knew* a stuck coolant valve had broken loose, stopping the flow, triggering the onset of meltdown. In Central Command, Stavinsky was just as sure a *Squall* had just blown up inside one of the tubes. He mashed his hand down on the launch initiator, swung the rotary switch to TUBE TWO and hit it again.

Warrant Officer Dobrin's hand was also quick. He pulled the emergency jettison valve on the first tube, then, with the ringing of *Portland's* sonar still echoing through the hull, he did the same with the second.

Dobrin acted fast but electrons move faster. The *Squalls* had already received their launch commands from Stavinsky's panel.

As the roar of high-pressure air took up where the sonar pulse let off, small, liquid-fueled booster rockets ignited, propelling two six thousand pound weapons along their launch guides. The slugs of air that chased them out gave

311

them an added shove.

Both weapons popped into the open sea. Their internal gyros aligned them to the preset attack course, and with a tremendous explosion of bubbles, both main rocket engines ignited.

A *Squall* flies through the water at better than seven thousand meters a minute. *Cristi* and all aboard her had just seconds left to live.

USS *Portland*

The subtle play of lights and shadows on Bam Bam's screen was gone, swept away by the powerful pulse of acoustic energy he'd blasted into the sea. Now, as the echoes of that pulse died away, he saw something different, something he'd never seen before. Two bright spheres of white noise burned where the dark shadow had once been, and they were moving fast; so fast he was sure it had to be his program going haywire.

But they were on Sonarman Niebel's screen, too. 'What the hell are those things?'

Bravo Squad

'Steer north,' said Jameson.

A flash of lightning, a low, heavy rumble of thunder.

'The winds are blowing the other way,' said Wheeler.

Jameson looked astern. The freighter had drifted broadside to the wind and was rolling heavily in the waves. 'You're right. Steady as she goes. We're getting close.'

The freighter's lights receded as the rubber boat took the seas bow on. A gust of wind caught the Zodiac at a crest, held it, then let it plunge down into a deep trough.

Another flash, this time showing a delicate tracery of fork lightning.

Jameson counted off the interval until the thunder rolled over them. *Five thousand feet. A mile.* The storm was coming on at something like twenty knots. They were running twenty knots straight for it. *Forty knots combined.* It was a toss-up whether they'd reach the coordinates where Sanders had fallen into the water before, or after the storm broke. It also occurred to him that riding a wet rubber boat with seven human lightning rods on board was not such a great place to be. 'Time check?'

'Two minutes six,' said Pyro.

Jameson concentrated on their progress across the glowing GPS screen. 'Slow down,' he said to Wheeler. He nodded to the other men. They took position on the pontoons, each with an arc of ocean to scan.

Wheeler throttled the pump jet back. The Zodiac settled.

No bioweapons, no biologist, no Tangos and we're down a man. 'Do we have commo with the boat yet?' asked Jameson. It was time to let them know there would be no need for elaborate decontamination, and a very great need to call Norfolk to find the real *Cristi*.

'Stand by.' Stepik broke squelch twice. Two

313

bursts of static came right back at him. 'Aye aye. Got 'em.'

'Tell them we're looking for a man in the water, that we're off the target empty-handed and we need a secure link back to Norfolk *now*.'

'Roger.' It took two tries but Stepik managed to make Scavullo understand that this had not been a good night's work and that they needed to relay a message back to higher authority.

Jameson used his nods to penetrate the mist and rain. Each SEAL carried a dazzling array of devices intended to make his presence known; pencil flares, star shells, chemlights, strobes. Sanders could see the freighter from here but he wouldn't know what was happening on board. He would stay dark to keep from alerting anyone who might still be a threat. But he would also hear the jet pump coming, figure the assault was completed and light *something* off any second now.

Tommy Anders straddled the pontoon at the starboard bow. He had sniper's eyes, and so it was only natural that he would see something different about the water fifty yards ahead. Anyone else might have dismissed it as nothing more than a mat of floating seaweed. Anders let his stare drift a bit off target, allowing the faint smudge of something to fall on the most sensitive part of his retina. A wave picked the object up, a whitecap framed it, and he recognized the straps and pouches of a SEAL's emergency inflation bladder. 'Contact!' He pointed a few points north of the bow. 'In the water!'

Wheeler shoved the steering bar over. The Zodiac clawed its way up the face of a wave, then surfed down the trough on the far side. It brought them right to the floating debris.

Stepik leaned over the gunwales and hauled the vest in by the straps. One bladder was full of CO_2, the other punctured. The tough webbing of a SEAL's suit harness was shredded. The shattered stub of a Sig Sauer pistol was still in its holster. A strong D-ring fastener was cut cleanly in half.

No one said a thing. No one had to.

Finally, Pyro checked his watch and said, 'Sixty seconds.'

Scavullo's voice erupted over Stepik's radio. Her words were shrouded by heavy static and almost unintelligible.

'Bravo, say again?' Stepik tried to listen through the interference. All he knew for certain was that she was worked up over something and that the radio link was shitty.

'What is it?' asked Jameson.

'She's having a hissy fit over something.'

'Hey! Over there! I got him!' Wheeler shouted. He stood up with his arm pointing straight west.

Everyone turned. There was a boiling commotion a hundred yards away, like someone splashing with both arms to draw attention to himself. When Jameson saw it he was so sure it was Sanders he let out a whoop. They'd been wrong! 'All fucking *right!*'

Wheeler gunned the engine and leaned on the tiller. The Zodiac carved a tight turn, but when it steadied the splashing was no longer a hundred yards away, it was *right off the bow,* and then it vanished beneath the Zodiac and reappeared astern so fast Jameson couldn't track it. The raft

315

was surrounded by popping bubbles, and the air had a powerful chemical reek.

Pyro sniffed. 'Smoke?'

A second trail of bubbles flashed by, this time to starboard.

Jameson had only begun to give up his hope that they'd found his XO when a dazzling white flash, not from the thunderstorm to their west, but from the east, froze them all in place.

Pyro knew his explosives by sight and scent and sound. He dived into the belly of the Zodiac as the first warhead detonated deep inside *Cristi*'s hull. Both sound and shock wave arrived in an instant later; a sharp *CRUMP*, a tall column of boiling white water and a great roar that echoed until a second blast eclipsed it with an even larger blast.

Ragged sheets of hull steel tumbled up into the sky. Pipes scattered like straws, propelled up-wards on a cumulus of fire and water and steam.

Wheeler checked his watch. 'Twenty-eight seconds early.'

'Nice work,' said Anders. 'You need a new watch or something?'

'That's not my fucking work!' Pyro protested.

Then, a small, bright star arced up from the torpedoed ship, trailing a tail of burning gas like a missile heading for orbit. The star slowed at the top of its flight, then expanded once, twice, again, growing wide and diffuse, a glowing nebula that spread itself over the dying ship from bow to stern. With a quick blue flash, the nebula erupted into a white hot sphere, flattened at the bottom, bulging at the top, snuffling out the lesser fires raging on *Cristi,* swiftly growing into a mushroom cloud.

'*That*'s my fucking work,' said Petty Officer Battaglia.

'Down!' warned Wheeler, and once more the seven men took what shelter they could find at the center of the rubber boat.

The shock wave swept over the Zodiac, briefly blowing the rain from the sky. Chunks of glowing metal splashed uncomfortably close.

The roar faded, the steel hailstorm stopped. Jameson raised his head. His nods were useless, bleached solid green by the overabundance of light. He flipped them up and saw the head of a mushroom cloud merge with the low overcast. Tendrils of flame flashed and coiled around dark snakes of smoke and ash. Its broad stem was pulled aloft by the dome of superheated air. Below, the sea gradually reappeared.

When it did, *Cristi* was gone.

CHAPTER TWENTY

GREMLIN'S JIG

K-335 *Gepard*

'Ahead one third,' said Leonov. 'Take her down.' *Gepard* dove beneath the thermocline. 'Silencing system?'

'*Sirena* is on,' said Sonar Lieutenant Kureodov.

It galled Leonov to have to slink away from the scene of a triumph, but the Americans had sent a

317

strong sonar pulse in his direction and who knew what might be following it? They knew precisely where he was, and the task before him was to put some distance between *Gepard* and that known point, all while making absolutely no noise.

'How could they see us?' asked *Starpom* Stavinsky. The echo of the powerful American sonar had faded. The memory of it had not.

'We don't know they did,' said Leonov. 'It could have been a signal to that ship. Some code. It could be anything.'

'Accident or not, they see us now.'

'I assume so. Run time?'

'Ten seconds,' said Stavinsky. 'Five, four ... three ...'

'One hit!' Sonar Lieutenant Kureodov sang out. He dialed the sensitivity of his sonar down to keep the roar in his headphones from deafening him.

'Two!'

Leonov looked up. The roar of half a ton of high explosive ripping through a small ship rumbled through the submarine. He'd known what to expect, but the speed of the *Squalls'* attack still surprised him. It seemed only a matter of seconds between ordering the torpedoes fired and the rolling thunder of their impacts.

The Termite reached for the gain control to turn it back up, but before he could adjust it another explosion, larger than the first two, poured through his receiver. He pulled the headphones away from his ears and said, 'Three?' He pressed the headphones to his ears. 'I have breakup noises.' He listened to the eerie groans and outraged metallic shrieks of a broken ship on her way to the bottom. They masked the fainter buzz of an outboard pump jet motor entirely.

Leonov said, '*Starpom*. Ahead now two thirds.' He turned to the screened-off radio cubicle. 'Kiselyev!'

Radio Electronics Lieutenant Kiselyev poked his big head from behind the blue curtain. There were crumbs on his fingers from a sweet cake. 'Yes, Captain?'

'Prepare a signal for Moscow. Tell them justice has been administered and we are standing by for further instructions.'

The attack boat moved steadily off to the northwest, putting the chaos of the triple explosions far astern.

'Sonar. What is the range to the American's last plotted position?'

'Nearly eleven thousand meters now, Captain.'

Far enough? Without the Sirena, possibly. With it? Leonov decided *yes*. 'Ahead dead slow. Turns now for four knots. Five degrees rise. Come to periscope depth. Radio?'

'Message ready, Captain.'

Gepard swam up to the shallows, extended her antenna and informed the Naval Command Center in Moscow that *Gepard's* mission was complete.

Moscow disagreed. For when its acknowledgement beamed back to *Gepard*, there were new orders appended to it:

1: CONTINUE TRACK AND TRAIL AMERICAN SSN AND REPORT

'Conn, Sonar,' said Bam Bam. 'I think we chased that *Akula* off. He just faded away. You want me to try reacquiring him on active?'

'No,' said Steadman. 'What do you know about the fish he fired?'

'They were swimming at *way* more than 200 knots.'

Rocket torpedoes. Steadman knew the Russians had them, but actually seeing them in action was unsettling. If they'd been fired at *Portland,* there would have been no escape. The time interval between detection and impact was too short. 'You're sure there were only two?'

'Aye aye. That third explosion was definitely on the surface. Maybe even *above* the surface. And it was a big 'un. Could be munitions that ship had in her holds.'

Or *Bravo.* What had Jameson promised? That the freighter would go down in little sterilized pieces? 'Any sign of our guys?'

Bam Bam leaned over and took in the sonic picture on Niebel's screen. 'They just showed up again on a zero one eight bearing, range six thousand yards. It looks like they're kinda' runnin' around in circles. And I may have that *Akula's* shadow out at twelve ... no, make it thirteen thousand yards. That's *extreme* range for this setup and the ocean's gettin' mighty noisy with wave action. It's hard to find any quiet places.'

'Helm, right five degrees rudder. Come to zero

one eight degrees. Turns for eight knots. Maintain fifty feet.'

'Right five degrees rudder, ahead eight knots and fifty feet, aye aye, sir,' said the helmsman at the inboard station. He turned his yoke until five degrees was indicated on the display before him. 'My rudder is right five degrees and maneuvering answers turns for eight knots.'

'Very well. Sonar, Conn. Any other close contacts?'

'The ship, I mean, the contact of interest is gone.' Bam Bam had actually heard the hull crunch when it hit bottom. You couldn't get any more *gone* than that.

'Radio, Conn. Are you back in contact with Bravo yet?'

'No!' said Scavullo, and she said it with all the annoyance she felt. 'They wanted a link and I can't make that work either.' She'd tried both antenna masts. They were supposed to permit instant communications with stations around the world, any time, any place, but tonight they weren't up to the challenge of talking with eight men in a rubber raft a few miles away. 'Atmospherics are ramping up. The frequency is buried in static.'

'Did you switch antennas?'

'Of *course.*'

'Broadcast in the blind. Tell Bravo we're proceeding to the pickup point.'

'She thinks the radio problem is outside the hull,' said Browne. 'I've got a tiger team of A-gangers to look at the masts.'

'Get your team ready to go,' said Steadman. 'Rig Control for red.'

The bright white lights went out, replaced by dim reds. Steadman wanted his eyes ready for the night-time conditions they'd find on the surface.

'Conn, Radio,' said Scavullo. 'Still no contact with Bravo.'

The SEALs had assaulted a ship that was on the bottom. Three blasts had put her there, two of them courtesy of that lurking Russian attack boat. But Steadman had to assume Jameson found something on *Cristi,* something he wanted to keep off *Portland* at all costs. 'COB? Call the surface detail to the main trunk. Tell Chief Cooper to rig a decon area on the weather deck and get his assistant ready to vaccinate. Have him hold off until he hears from me.'

'Aye aye, Captain,' said Browne, who'd already made both calls.

'Conn, Sonar, Zodiac is now two thousand yards dead ahead.'

'Surface the boat!' Steadman called out. 'Blow her dry.'

The 1MC rang out *Surface surface surface!*

Bravo Squad

As the squall line bore down on them the rain began falling in wind-driven sheets. Even with nods dialed up full the visibility was poor and getting worse.

None of this seemed to matter to Chief Wheeler. He steered the Zodiac in a careful search pattern, crisscrossing the sunken freighter's final course, north, then south, then north again, hoping for what each man knew was nothing short of a miracle.

The sea was littered with chunks of yellow insulation, wooden pallets, the stern of a lifeboat ripped so violently away that its fiberglass roots were just frayed threads. But miracles were harder to come by. Of Lieutenant JG Kernal Sanders, the first piece of evidence they'd recovered – the mutilated remains of his emergency flotation bladder – was also the last.

Anders spotted the white wake of *Portland's* radio mast. 'I have the boat,' called the squad sniper. By the time the other men of Bravo saw it, the antenna had risen clear of the sea and grown a dark base.

Jameson looked to Stepik. 'Still nothing?'

The radioman shook his head. 'Static.'

Lightning struck some unlucky piece of ocean a mile away. The crack of its thunder came just seconds later.

Jameson barely noticed. Somewhere out there was another ship, another *Cristi*. It had cleared the Bosporus behind the one they'd taken down. It could have made a beeline for the nearest Greek island. Or the Turkish coast. Or met up with another ship nobody knew anything about. He'd started the night with a great deal of misplaced certainty, and now the unknowns were swarming around him like wasps.

'What's the deal, skipper?' asked Wheeler. He was standing at the stern of the boat, oblivious to the risk of presenting an attractive target to a few million stray volts looking for something to hit.

Jameson shook himself out of his thoughts.

323

'Steve? We need to call back to Yellowstone and get an update. If we can't relay it through the boat then I want you to rig our own radio.'

'We'll have a bird overhead at 20 hundred hours,' said the radioman.

Chief Wheeler bent the Zodiac's serpentine course straight for the roiling sea that marked the surfacing submarine. Jets of high-pressure mist blasted skyward as the submarine's sail shouldered free of the waves. The sail grew taller. Far astern the shark fin of her rudder cut the sea, then the two were connected by the weather deck. Before any of the SEALs would have guessed possible, a brilliant searchlight stabbed the night, swiveling under the hand of someone already up in the submarine's open bridge.

Wheeler brought them alongside. Jameson leaped onto *Portland's* rubbed-coated hull and hurried to the side of the sail. He reached for the first rung of the ladder up to the open cockpit, but a man wearing head-to-toe mylar suit stopped him.

It was Chief Cooper, *Portland's* corpsman. 'I need to know what you guys found on that ship.'

'Not a fucking thing. It was clean.'

'No smallpox?'

'You heard me, chief. Now stand aside. I've got a critical message that needs sending *pronto*.' Jameson put his hand on the rung again.

Cooper stepped in front of him and now he had two other sailors in 'nuke suits' flanking him. Both were torpedomen. One was Red. 'First you wash,' Cooper said in the patient, firm tones of a teacher advising a child to clean his hands after going potty. 'Then you send messages.'

He could throw all of them into the water but it just might be faster to comply. Jameson let himself be taken aft to afterdeck. There was a kind of plastic tent there, made of tarps lashed to collapsible uprights. He piled his gear on deck, stripped and let himself be doused with a chemical that made his skin prickle. Not once, but twice. Finally, Cooper handed him a submariner's poopy suit to wear, a size too small, he noticed, and only then was he allowed to climb up to the cockpit.

Steadman turned up the small handheld radio he carried clipped to his belt. Had he heard Chief Cooper correctly? 'They didn't find it?'

'No,' he said, 'but we deloused him anway.'

'All right. Stand down the vaccination plan,' he said as he watched the SEALs toss their personal gear up onto the deck, then the pump jet motor, then came the Zodiac. He counted the dark helmeted heads once, twice, again. Bravo was short a man.

Jameson appeared at the lip of the sail, then swung his leg over and in. There was barely room for them both to stand in *Portland's* cockpit. The SEAL smelled strongly of gunpowder and bleach and the powerful chemical used to scrub down the galley griddles.

Four men crouched around the base of an extended antenna mast atop the sail's rounded cap. Three of them were from the Auxiliary Division. They had their tool rolls open. COB Browne stood over them with a powerful light aimed at where the antenna emerged from its well. All of them wore bright orange float vests.

'What happened out there?' asked Steadman.

'My XO was hit and ended up in the water. Someone fired a couple of fish. The Russians, I'm guessing. End of story.'

'There were no bioweapons but the crew fought back?'

'Lieutenant Sanders didn't kill himself. We were lucky to get clear before those torpedoes hit. They passed right under us.'

The sail locker came open easily this time. The SEALs carefully stowed the Zodiac and motor.

Steadman said, 'They fired two torpedoes. We heard three explosions.'

'Look, commander, before you tell me how we smoked a ship full of innocent tourists, you need to know that ship left port as the *Nova Spirit*. Somewhere up in the Black Sea they took out a paint brush and wrote *Cristi* on her. That wasn't by accident. The Tangos used her as a decoy.'

'I don't care if they painted *Queen Mary* on her. You said that if there weren't any hostiles on board you'd let them go.'

'They killed my XO. Is that hostile enough for you? Listen, right now I need to get a message off. If we're lucky, someone will have some idea where we can find the real *Cristi*.'

'Right now we've got antenna problems.' Steadman turned to Browne. 'COB! Anything?'

'Nothing yet.' Browne handed his flashlight to a sailor and climbed down from the top of the sail. His hands were covered in waterproof grease. 'I see two brand-new antenna masts, Captain. They look real good but I don't know what's happening on the inside.'

'Forget it,' said Jameson. 'We have a satellite window coming up in fifteen minutes. We'll use our own radios.'

Rain cascaded off the bill of Steadman's cap. Raising the masts to their full height to check cable continuity was not going to happen with a thunderstorm bearing down. A dazzling flash of lightning followed by the sound of ripping canvas an instant later settled whatever doubts remains. 'No. We'll dive and sail out from under this weather first. COB? Get everyone below.' He turned to Jameson. 'Your men, too, lieutenant.'

'Commander, I lost a friend tonight. It'll be for nothing unless we find the right ship and stop her. Someone back home might already know where she is. Your radios are tits up. We *have* to use ours.'

'You heard me,' Steadman said. 'Get below.'

'Sorry, but no fucking way.' Jameson turned to Steve Stepik. 'Steve! Bring the satellite radio up!'

'Belay that order!' Steadman shouted.

Stepik paused, looking between the two men.

'This is my mission and Bravo is my squad,' said Jameson. 'This is a war. You've got to take some risks if you want to win. If your guys are worried about a little rain then send them below.'

'This is your last warning, lieutenant.'

'Before what? You lodge a complaint?' Jameson pulled out his trump card. 'Feel free, commander. But remember, the President of the United States authorized me to act in his name and I say we remain on the surface until we get a message off.'

'A piece of paper signed by God almighty won't change my mind about who's the captain of this submarine.'

327

Browne spoke a few words into the handheld radio. Down on the afterdeck, Chief Cooper stopped, nodded, then spoke to the two torpedomen.

Red didn't need any encouragement. He and his mate grabbed Stepik from behind and hustled him to the escape trunk. Before the SEAL knew what was happening, he was looking up at a sealed hatch from the inside. In a few moments, Cooper and two pleased torpedomen joined Browne and two others from the Auxiliary Division.

'Have I made myself clear?' said Steadman.

'*Jesus,*' Jameson snarled. He stalked over to the open trunk, but not without delivering a kick to the steel wall of the open cockpit. The two A-gangers rolled up their tool bags and dropped down after him, with Cooper and the two torpedomen close behind.

Browne and Steadman were left alone in the open bridge.

A dazzling fork of lightning struck the sea off to starboard, ripping the air to shreds and leaving an eerie, green luminescence behind. The rain drummed down on the black rubber deck tiles. The sound of it swelled, gathered, then receded to an icy hiss of hail pellets.

'I believe that young lieutenant wasn't exactly telling you the whole truth about what happened,' said Browne.

'I know.'

'But he could be right about someone knowing more back home.'

'I know that, too.' Pea-sized hail bounced enthusiastically off his cap. 'The sooner we get out from under this storm the sooner we can–'

The hail was striking the lip of the cockpit and caroming back into the air where it came to a mysterious hover, levitating as though the laws of gravity were no longer in effect. Then, as Steadman watched, the floating pellets started streaming *up*, slowly at first, then faster. The piles that had collected on the deck joined in, pelting his face from *below*.

Browne had spent his entire Navy career in submarines, and while he'd seen his share of strange things hail falling *up* was not one of them. He grabbed Steadman's shoulder and pushed him in the direction of the bridge hatch. Then, as though a switch had been thrown, every hair on his arm rose. *Oh shit.*

The bolt struck an instant later. A solid column of incandescent energy fully ten feet across leaped from *Portland*'s sail up into the low clouds. The hull rang with a deep, indignant *clang*.

Steadman's ears were tilled with a furious buzzing. His fingers were claws, his limbs beyond command. He realized he wasn't standing any more, but falling. He landed on the deck like a carelessly thrown puppet, his left arm pinned beneath him. He struggled to roll to one side but he couldn't. He gasped for air. His lungs were not obeying him, either. He could feel his heart beating an ineffectual flutter. He realized that he was dying, drowning, not crushed in the depths of the sea as he'd imagined in those silent moments when he'd allowed fear to rise, but up here, on his own deck, under an open and hostile sky.

An avalanche of raw juice buried *Portland*'s exposed hull under millions of volts all looking for the quickest path to the earth. Half a dozen rubber deck tiles vaporized to mist and the surge of current flowed safely through the exposed steel, back into the ocean.

But the antennas were tall, metal and pointed as lightning rods. They were protected and grounded to the hull. But two cables had been damaged in their installation. Though it would take a microscope for a human inspector to find the breaks, the sea found them easily enough. Salt water infiltrated them, collecting down inside the antenna base unit. It corroded fittings, conduits and the welded grounding straps. The tremendous spark racing down the masts encountered the water and paused, even as more energy flooded down from above.

The temperature inside both antenna base units went from fifty degrees to fifty thousand – hotter than the surface of the sun – in a microsecond. Something had to give, and it did.

The water exploded into superheated steam, blowing the cables and base units apart and melting the welds right off the grounding straps. The pent-up bolt burst through the steam and found a new path to follow; one that took it around the grounding straps and down the shielded cables, straight into the part of the hull submariners call the *people tank*.

A storm was breaking over the boat, but the first sign Rose Scavullo had was the sudden blanking of her computer screens, followed by the explosive roar of an express train racing by over her head. She looked up.

A tremendous detonation seemed to suck the air out of the radio shack, and then, an instant later, every light failed, leaving only two battery-powered battle lamps and the dim, glowing circles of a few old 'steam gauge' dials to light the space. As she reached up to connect the radios to the emergency battery buss, the dials suddenly lit up again, no longer dim, but bright as so many round portholes that gazed into a raging furnace.

The glass covers shattered, the foul, metallic smell of burning electronics exploded into the compartment, and the elusive gremlin she'd been hunting for came crashing in full force.

White-hot tennis balls flew from the faces of the broken dials, bouncing from bulkhead to overhead to deck and back, spinning, floating in the air, shooting off joyful blue sparks. Some dashed themselves to death in splashes of liquid light. Others merged, grew larger, changing color from white to blue to green. One came to rest in midair not two feet from where Scavullo sat, hovering, as though deciding where next to take its mischief. It grew an orange fringe around a hot blue core.

Scavullo thought, *The gremlin!* No longer hidden away inside the circuits of the submarine's radios, but out in the open for all to see. The sharp, electric taste of ozone was on her tongue. Her finger was still on the buss switch, and even as her brain registered the fact that this was not too smart, the ball pounced.

It struck her body with a *snap!* and shattered, enveloping her in a brilliant shower of cold, white light. The surge flowed up her arm to the console where her hand was only now moving away from the metal toggle. It leaped the gap with a spitting spark that threw Scavullo to the deck and sent all her paper radio logs flying.

As she lay staring at the metal overhead, the last glowing ball splattered against a steel conduit with a soft *pop*. The 4MC emergency intercom circuit buzzed, and the engineer of the watch sent his voice throughout *Portland:* 'Rig the ship for reduced power!' The intercom went silent, and then, barely one breath later, the clamor became just one voice: Chief Farnesi, sitting at the ballast control panel up in Control, said, 'Corpsman lay to the bridge!'

CHAPTER TWENTY-ONE

BOLT

USS *Portland*

Choo Choo Watson might not be the officer you'd select to lead men into battle, but he was the obvious choice to take command of a disabled submarine. He knew casualty drills better than anyone aboard *Portland* and was famous for devising devious combinations to test the crew's ability to react properly and automatically.

But when a hundred million volts struck *Portland,* when a tidal wave of electricity surged right by the very devices meant to protect her, Watson acted neither properly nor automatically.

Had they struck something? Was it an explosion? Fire? A Russian torpedo? His brain skidded like a tire on black ice, seeking traction, looking for an answer because the obvious one was just about impossible.

One moment he was standing in Control, the lights soft and red, the boat surfaced, everything as it should be. Then Lieutenant Jameson climbed down the bridge trunk and stomped off angrily in the direction of the forward ladder. The XO was about to call out to find out what was going on when a stabbing brilliance flooded down the trunk, followed by a huge *crack!* that seemed to come from outside the boat, inside the hull, from within Watson's own chest. Then, darkness.

As the battle lamps winked on, new alarms began to sound: power distribution failure, atmospheric controls, the O_2 generator. Critical systems tripped off-line, a reactor scram alarm was shrieking. It was an emergency drill he might have thought of himself.

Watson stood rooted in the control room, methodically eliminating possibilities. If it had been another Russian fish he wouldn't be standing here asking what had happened. They hadn't struck anything. They were in deep water with engines at *All Stop*. He was still on his feet. A small explosion? Possibly, but where, and why? Had a careless SEAL dropped a 'flash crash' grenade? But then what about the reactor scram? The O_2 generator trip? He sniffed. *Ozone?*

The evidence was clear. The explanation was

not, for there was nothing on earth so lightning-resistant as a steel pipe floating in the perfectly-conductive ocean. The bolt should have flowed into the hull and dissipated harmlessly into the sea. Why didn't it?

It fell to the chief of the watch at the ballast control board to break the spell and ask the far more important question:

'Hey, did the skipper and COB make it below?'

Chief Farnesi waited a fraction of a second for the XO to respond, then grabbed the sound-powered IC mike. *'Corpsman lay to the bridge! Corpsman lay to the bridge!'*

Chief Cooper raced back to the bridge trunk. Bursts of light still flashed down the smooth, steel barrel from above. He reached for the ladder just as Watson came to the conclusion that, probabilities aside, they'd just been struck by lightning.

'Hold on!' he said. 'I can't order you up top!'

Cooper looked up the trunk, then at Watson. 'With all due respect, XO, you don't have to.' He swarmed up the rungs and disappeared.

Watson re-established contact with the reactor control space. He didn't know what malady had befallen his boat. Or its captain. But he knew reactors, and he knew that bad things happened quickly to nuclear boats when the kettle went cold. 'Engineer! Reset the reactor scram breakers and run the hot start checklist!'

Soon, the engineer of the watch reported 'All rod groups in the power range!' And a few, very long minutes later, 'Reactor in the power range!'

The lights came back. But then Chief Cooper's voice came echoing down from the bridge with the words no sailor ever wants to hear: *'Man overboard to port! Man overboard to port!'*

Watson thought, *Hollywood?*

The rescue diver dragged the bulky canvas Man Overboard Bag to the bridge trunk and flew up the ladder like a rocket heading for orbit.

'XO?' said Chief Farnesi.

Watson turned.

'Lieutenant Scavullo's calling on the 4MC.' The sound-powered emergency intercom. 'They must have taken a bad hit in the radio shack.'

'Have the messenger escort her out and then get Banjo in there.'

Chief Cooper heard the swish and pound of someone coming up the bridge trunk in a *big* hurry.

A head covered with black Neoprene emerged. 'Where?'

'Over there!' Cooper shouted, and pointed off where a strobe bobbed up and down on westerly swells. The rescue diver's portable searchlight flared, freezing drops in midfall, then released them to the night. The beam swept over the whitecaps, then came to a stop at the brilliant orange of COB Browne's float coat. Or half of it, anyway. One side had inflated automatically, the other had not.

Lines were secured, fins and goggles donned. Only when Cooper was sure the diver had COB in his light, he returned to the work of saving his captain's life.

He'd found Steadman crumpled beneath the forward lip of the bridge. Wisps of acrid smoke still rose from the cuffs of his khakis. His orange

335

float coat was charred, its CO_2 cylinder blown apart and the small strobe that clipped to the harness simply gone.

Chief Cooper had never been trained to deal with lightning strikes, but every submarine puts electricity and water in uncomfortably close proximity. Electrical burns and temporary heart arrhythmias were easily treated. With whole-body shock you had to be quick. A man's heart could flutter for hours but a few minutes without air would kill him dead.

It was time for DR. ABC to roll up his sleeves and get to work.

D was for *Danger*. Well, Zeus was still throwing thunderbolts and the top of a sail made an inviting target, but there wasn't much Cooper could do about it. He'd volunteered. And while a lot of juice had just hit the boat and its commander, none of it remained in Steadman's body.

R stood for *Response*. 'Skipper? Can you move?' Steadman's eyes were glassy and unfocused. His arms and legs trembled.

ABC. Airway, Breathing, Circulation. Steadman's pulse was strong but racing. One arm was pinned underneath his side, the one Cooper could see was flash burned and his face was an ominous blue. *Oxygen!*

Cooper ignored the crash and bang of thunder, the pelting rain, the very real threat of another lightning strike, and pulled out a ventilator tube and began filling the captain's lungs with air. He waited five seconds, then did it again. *Come on, Breathe!*

Steadman's body tingled, his ears rang. What

336

vision he had was blurred. He felt his lungs inflate with Cooper's breath, and as the air sighed out into the rainy night he formed the word *'COB?'*

'We'll get him. First you gotta' breathe for me, okay?'

Steadman didn't seem to hear or understand, so Cooper took another deep breath and sent it into the tube. A light flashed in the corpsman's eyes and he snarled at the errant line handler who'd done it. The beam shifted and Cooper saw two black footprints on the deck where the soles of Steadman's sneakers had partially melted. Each dark outline was dotted where bright steel showed through the non-skid paint. *How many amps does it take to vaporise a shoe?*

Steadman's chest rose, and now he felt the pain come rushing in. His chest muscles had spasmed so violently the ligaments had torn from his ribs. He'd fallen on one of his arms and it hurt. He tried to move but he couldn't. What was going on, and where was he?

The last clear memory he had was of a kind of sizzling, elastic band that had stretched across his chest, then *snapped*. His head throbbed like he'd been hit with a sledgehammer and he *just could not* keep his mind tracking. He was at sea. He could smell it. His face was upturned to the rain. He could feel it. Someone was breathing air into him. No. Not *someone*. Chief Cooper. As he choked out his borrowed breath he said for the third time, 'COB.'

Browne reflected that the water felt a lot colder than the Mediterranean ought to off the coast of

Crete. *Flash burns,* he figured. The skin on one arm was burned raw. He could feel the sting of salt. It wouldn't kill him and might even help. But something was wrong with his float coat. The vest wanted to roll his face over into the water. The waves weren't steep but they seemed to be coming at him from all the points of the compass. He couldn't brace against their sudden slaps.

And the damned rescue strobe wasn't blinking. There was nothing more difficult than rescuing a lone man on the open sea in broad daylight. And at night, in rain and wind without a strobe?

Browne reached for the pocket that held a whistle, found it, and started to blow for all he was worth. Something seemed to be wrong with the whistle, too. No matter how hard he blew, it didn't make a sound.

Now what? Command Master Chief Jerome Browne had spent his whole career not showing fear at things that would terrify any young sailor. It was his duty, his *calling,* not to panic, to never let on that a problem was beyond solving. If a tight ship ran on *automatic,* problems had their automatic solutions, too. There were checklists to follow, steps to take.

Browne had just fallen off the checklist. He felt his body sink deeper as the soft air bladder slowly collapsed. The ocean seemed to be telling him he was a piece of nature cast adrift where it didn't belong. The sea was completely indifferent to his fate. There would be no special dispensation for sea duty, for years served. No voice divine. No shining light. And *that* was a surprise. Strobe or no strobe, by now the crew should know where he *wasn't*. Why the *hell* weren't they sweeping the water with a light to find out where he *was?*

Brown put his hand before his face. Nothing. He twisted around. He couldn't see the waves, the whitecaps. Not the lightning-stitched sky. Not the boat. Not anything. Either every last particle of light was sucked out of the world by that lightning blast, or else he was stone blind.

He tried to sense the rhythm of the waves and take quick, gasping breaths. Sometimes he found air. Sometimes water. He felt a stream of bubbles rising against his hand and discovered where the float bladder was losing pressure, though there wasn't a damned thing he could do. There was an inflation tube but he was having a hard enough time breathing. He had no air to spare.

He tried the whistle again. Still nothing. *Blind and deaf.* Was Steadman in the same condition? Was he in the water, too? Had they *both* been blown off the bridge? Browne knew his Bible about as well as he knew *Portland,* and the words of Lamentations 2:13 came to him.

For vast as the sea is your ruin. Who can restore you?

That was the big question all right. Where was *Portland?* And how could he find his way back to something he couldn't see? He twisted around again, hoping for some glimmer of light, some familiar sound. The slosh of water through the boat's vents, the whine of the radar bar or the tinny squawk of voices over the bridge intercom.

A wave struck him, the damaged bladder collapsed and his head went under. He tried to cry out, but when he opened his mouth he swallowed a slug of cold water. The feel of it, the taste of it, triggered an angry, defiant response. He spat it out, swung his arms and kicked with his feet. His head broke through to the air and he gasped a quick breath, then yelled, *'Hey! I'm over here!'*

Silence. Darkness. And the steady, quiet trickle of hope taking its leave.

Well, the ocean was mighty big and even a senior chief was small. Maybe the boat had drifted away. Maybe they were too busy with their own worries to tackle his. It was possible they didn't even know he'd gone over the side. And he couldn't wait much longer.

Lord, he thought as he struggled to keep his head above water, *we've had a bunch of one-way conversations over the years and here's another one:*

there's a good captain and a good boat that needs Your help and I believe they could use mine if it suits Your needs. But if these are your standing night orders, I will carry them out.

The water surged and a wave lifted him. He seemed to hang there suspended, weightless, and then a pair of arms closed around him. For a moment, he thought his one-way prayer had been received, but angels don't wear swim fins. He felt a powerful kick, the drag of water reluctantly letting go of him as he was being towed on his back.

Thank you, he said as he bumped hard against *Portland*'s steel hull a lot sooner than he expected. It couldn't have been more than ten or fifteen yards away. A surge tried to pull him back but those arms never let go. They were joined by another pair, and together they dragged him up to where Browne had a good submarine under him once again. No faces, no voices. Just anonymous arms belonging to the boat's rescue diver and a brawny line handler from the deck division.

'We got him!' a voice yelled down the open trunk.

Watson watched Chief Cooper guide the stretcher with Steadman on it down the ladder from the bridge. The words were prescribed, and they came out quickly and without a hint of triumph: 'I'm relieving Commander Steadman. Take him to his cabin. I've got the command. Damage to the bridge?'

'Some tiles got blown away and both antenna masts are still up. They have holes melted through them,' said the deck div sailor.

Watson pictured the complex machinery that raised and lowered the masts, the external hydraulics, the cable bundles. The antenna masts themselves were just two, telescoping steel pipes wrapped by a teardrop fairing to smooth the flow of water. At the bottom of each was a base unit, and beneath *it* was a hull fitting. Broken antennas were a nuisance but problems with the through-hull fittings could let water in where it didn't belong.

He felt the boat roll. Swells were coming in from the west; a sign of the ocean's unease. *Dive, or stay on top?*

Browne eased down the bridge ladder with Cooper's steadying hand to aid him. One arm of his blue overalls was torn, revealing skin that looked angry, red and blistered. Water puddle at his feet.

'Glad to have you back aboard, COB,' said Watson.

341

Browne didn't react.

'What's wrong with him?'

'He can't hear you,' said Cooper. 'He's flash-blinded, too.'

'Use my stateroom,' said Watson. 'Who's left up on the bridge?'

'Nobody!' the rescue diver said, 'I'm the last man down!'

'Secure that hatch until we figure this thing through.'

'No! Wait!'

Jameson and his radioman were at the ladder to the bridge. 'We need to get a message off and we've got a bird overhead *now*.'

'XO?'

Watson turned away from the demanding SEAL. It was Banjo Gant, the radioman. 'What is it?'

'Lieutenant Scavullo says I'm not cleared into the radio shack. She won't let me in.'

'She won't *what?*'

'The door's locked from the inside, sir. I'll have to bust it down.'

'Can we go up, XO?' asked Jameson.

'No!' Watson reached for the sound-powered set and rang up the radio shack. 'This is the XO. Open that door and let my radioman in.'

'I'm... Conn, this is Radio. He's ... not cleared,' said Scavullo weakly. 'Where's ... where's the captain?'

'I've got the command, lieutenant. Now open that door.'

Silence.

'Ah, sir?' It was Jameson. He nodded at the

microphone. 'Mind if I put my oar in?'

Watson handed the intercom over.

Jameson nodded, but didn't speak.

'Well?' said Watson.

'Yes sir. I was just thinking that while I'm helping out down here my radioman can go up on deck and get that message off.'

'I can't assure his safety on deck.'

'No need to.'

'All right.' Watson nodded. 'Do it.'

Jameson shot a look at Stepik and the radioman disappeared up the bridge ladder. He waited, then put the mike to his lips. 'Hey Rosie! *Podnimi tvoyu zatnitsu!*' he said. '*Atkroi yob anuyu dyer!*'

You heard your captain! Open the fucking door!

Scavullo stared at the sound-powered intercom. Her arm muscles trembled. Her finger bled where a shard of shattered instrument glass had pricked her skin. The deck was littered with papers, manuals and drops of blood. All the radio consoles save for one were dark. The air smelled of burned insulation, scorched paint and melted wires.

'Open up, Rosie,' said Jameson. 'They'll just bust the door down if you don't.'

Rosie. A memory from when they were both studying Russian at the Defense Language Institute. Sitting by the window in her apartment in Monterey, the sun just breaking through the morning fog, a textbook on her lap opened to the chapter on Russian verbs of motion, Jameson emerging from her shower wrapped in a towel. She'd made him memorize all the words that meant *to go;* by foot, by motor vehicle, one-way and round trip, before she let him drop it.

'Rosie? Come on. Open the door.'

She slowly got to her feet and walked to the door. The deck was littered with glass and crunched like old snow that had melted in the February sun, then refrozen at night. *What happened to Steadman?*

She threw the bolt, opened the door and stood back.

A figure stood outside, indistinct in the dim glow of the battle lanterns. Not Jameson?

'Hey, lieutenant,' said Banjo. 'Let's go get that hand bandaged.'

The MST-20 Plus was the latest and the greatest in military satellite communications. It provided Bravo Squad with a clear, secure link from anywhere in the world to Yellowstone; a continuously manned duty desk inside a steel vault on the Pentagon's Fifth Deck. Heady stuff, but from an operator's point of view, the radio was seven and a half more pounds to hump, not including its umbrella antenna, and a real pain to maneuver up a submarine trunk.

Steve Stepik had to shoulder out of the rig and pass it up through the open hatch ahead of him. Next, he pushed the umbrella antenna through, and only then could he climb up himself.

It was raining hard now, and some of the waves were large enough to roll over the submarine's spherical bow. He crawled under the forward lip of the cockpit to find a bit of shelter. The air still smelled of burned rubber and plastic and ozone.

He unfolded the antenna and stood it up on the

deck. It was so light the wind threatened to pick it up and throw it over the side. And if lightning were looking for a place to make another appearance this would be the place. But if the CO asked Stepik to jump over the side, swim to the nearest island and find a pay phone, that was what Stepik would do.

He put a boot onto the base frame, got the approximate tilt and azimuth set and plugged it into the satcom. A few minor adjustments later, the 'handshake' light glowed; Steve had found the satellite. The submarine's radios might be toast, but Bravo was connected.

Stepik picked up the mike and said, 'Yellowstone, check-in.' He wondered how they would take the news that they'd hit the wrong ship and the Russians had, too. *Good thing they fired those fish,* he thought, *or else they'd try to hang us for it.*

The reply was remarkably clear and strong.

'Roger, Yellowstone. Go ahead your check-in.'

Stepik told the anonymous voice what had happened to Kernal Sanders, what they'd found on board the wrong ship and how the Russians had charged in and just about shot the freighter out from under them. He passed along Jameson's urgent request for updated intelligence, perhaps on a vessel that might have *Nova Spirit* painted on her stern.

'Copy all. Put your CO on.'

Stepik thought, *Well fuck you very much.* They could have said *Sorry about Kernal.* 'Stand by.' He swung his headset mike to his lips. 'Hey LT,' he said into the squad radio. 'Yellowstone wants a word.'

345

'On my way.'

Jameson popped out of the trunk hatch a few minutes later. The two big men, the MST-20 and its unfolded antenna filled the submarine's cockpit and then some. He took the mike. 'Yellowstone, Bravo One.'

The clear voice said, '*You have something to write with?*'

Jameson reached into his soaked flightsuit and fished out a grease marker. As Yellowstone spoke, he furiously scribbled letters and numbers onto the steel walls of the submarine's cockpit. *Deep Blue ... source intel,* then, *distress call ... lat/long 36/18,* and finally, *Catania.* Jameson repeated the message back just to make sure he had it right.

'*Read back correct. Execute.*' The 'handshake' light went dark.

'What's the deal?' asked the radioman.

'The Greeks monitored a distress call yesterday from up near Kithira. They called themselves the *Cristi,* then canceled the SOS in a weird way. Yellowstone says she's bound for Catania now.'

'You don't look happy.'

'Yellowstone's source is a Saudi national.'

'Shit.' The implications of *that* piece of information were clear to Steve Stepik. You never knew what to believe from the Saudis. 'Sounds like an accident waiting to happen. How about we call in an air strike?'

'You can't tell what's on a ship from twenty thousand feet. Or find out if they passed the bugs off somewhere up the line.' Jameson stood up. Rain streamed down his face. He leaned on the lip of the bridge, looking out to the northwest. It was possible the Saudis knew about the theft, the bioweapon, all along. And it was also possible he and his men might be walking into an ambush of their making.

'What now?' asked Stepik.

'We get the CO to drive us to the scene of the accident.'

CHAPTER TWENTY-TWO

THE TIP OF THE SPEAR

MV 'Nova Spirit'
Ionian Sea

Salafi stretched out on his bunk and closed his eyes. *One more day.* They would dock at Catania, he would walk off the ship, be met and driven to the nearest airport. A private jet would fly him to Riyadh. To a clinic, to civilization, to his friends. *One more day.* Adnan and Musa would find the martyrdom they craved, though perhaps not the one they expected. *One more day.*

It promised to be an uncomfortable one. The smooth sea had turned treacherous and unpredictable. Days had passed when the freighter seemed motionless and the world beyond his two portholes scrolled slowly by. Tonight, the freighter was falling into invisible holes. The deck pitched down, the bow buried itself with the deep *boom* of a great drum, the engine throbbed and they'd stagger back out. There was no rhythm to these holes, no way to brace against them. And they were coming more often.

Salafi smelled the curry being prepared down in the galley. It was not a pleasant aroma. He knew there were good reasons to feel queasy. Anyone holed up inside a small cabin at sea in storm had every excuse to feel sick. Yet each time his stomach sloshed one way while the cabin rolled the other was like the ringing of an alarm bell. Was this how the Russian disease began? Would this room with its pale green metal walls, its cracked linoleum floor, its two black eye sockets for windows become his prison, his coffin?

The ship plunged into a deeper hole than usual; deep enough to send his shoes sliding across the deck. Salafi saw the leather briefcase slip out from underneath his bunk. He made a grab for it and ended up on the floor, clutching the Vuitton to his chest. Another *boom!* and the ship trembled as though some great jaw had closed around it and given it a good shake. He could smell the stink of chlorine from the briefcase. *It can't be them. It can't be.* Still, he would not open it. He would not let it go. He fell back into bed and curled his body around it. *One more day.*

The blustery winds grew stronger and the waves rose higher as the ship and the *gregale* converged. Up in the ship's bridge, Hazil could feel the swells surge up from the port beam and roll under the keel. The deck went through a complex series of rolls in response, almost a shiver. The sea would pass, the bow would fall, and then it would happen all over again.

But the waves kept growing. Hazil would have preferred to turn the bow into the storm but Captain Warsame had ordered him to hold course for Catania no matter what, and this was what he would do.

The engine beat a steady 88 revolutions per minute. That was usually good for fourteen, sometimes fifteen knots. A glance at the GPS screen showed them struggling to make six.

Hazil was struggling, too. His forehead was hot. His fingers tingled as though electricity flowed through the ship's wheel. As the ride grew rougher, the rolls and the shivers more pronounced, he found himself holding onto the wheel as much as steering with it. He wished he could go to his bunk and sleep. He checked the ship's clock. Where was his relief?

With Assad the engineer on duty, Hazil at the helm and three men belowdecks on safety patrol keeping an eye on the ship's doubtful seams, Warsame had no choice but to hold evening prayers in two shifts. Only six men were present as Rafik, the Pakistani boy who cooked and served and cleaned up, busied himself at the galley stove. Warsame wondered where the Saudi and his two Chechens were tonight. The Chechens, especially. They'd never missed prayers.

He dismissed the first shift with *'La ilaha il Allah, Muhammad-ur-Rasool-Allah!'* None has the right to be worshipped but Allah, and Muhammad is the Messenger of Allah! 'Go find the others,' he instructed them. 'Tell them it is

349

time to pray. I will wait.'

He went to the dark porthole and cleared away the steam on the glass. Outside, the sea seemed to be pulling itself apart. Sheets of spray spattered angrily against the portholes. He turned to Naim, a twenty-five-year-old sailor from northern Pakistan. 'Go up and relieve Hazil.'

Naim nodded and left the galley, heading for the interior ladderwell to the bridge. Halfway up, he felt the ship rise up; a smooth, strong roll directly from the port beam. He waited for the ship to find its way, to come level, but it did not. It kept on rolling. He grabbed the handrail as the sound of loose objects slid and crashed on the deck below amid the alarmed shouts of the men in the galley.

Fifteen, twenty degrees. He held his breath. Push hard enough and the lights would blink out and the water would come roaring in.

Not this time. She slowly righted herself. Before she rolled off in the other direction, Naim scrambled the rest of the way up to the bridge, calling out, 'Hazil?'

Makayev didn't know what the forward holds were like, but the aft Number Three was filled with towering piles of canvas sacks full of powdered cement. The sacks had been secured with steel rope, but some of them had snapped, allowing the stacks to topple, forming a labyrinth of blind alleys, tunnels and caves. Some of the sacks had burst and spilled their powder to mix with water coming in through the hull. Gray liquid concrete inched across the decks and down into the bilges.

The hold lights were on and Makayev could watch the heavy gray sludge advance on his hiding place. The motions of the ship were growing increasingly wild. The wet cement oozed like lava, pausing, piling up into dams, then breaking through. The sludge engulfed the fine, comb-like bones of some small animal that had died down here; a fossil some future paleontologist might puzzle over.

Makayev was dying, yet he felt furiously alive. Frantic energy coursed through his body like the buzzing of a great, disturbed hive. The disease had moved into its end stage. It no longer had to waste time fighting his immune response. It no longer had to go looking for fresh cells to invade. It was everywhere and the only thing that mattered was to multiply. Makayev's cells had been hijacked and were churning out replicas of Hunter. His body burned with the waste heat of their manufacture. His clothes were completely soaked through and wisps of steam rose from his arms.

Makayev poked his head out from his canvas bunker. The aft bulkhead with its watertight door to the engine room was close. Twice this night he'd heard voices and hidden himself deeper as men with flashlights came through the hold. At first he thought they were searching for him, but they seemed more interested in turning their lights on the hull. Makayev soon learned why. Each hollow boom of a wave, each sea washing over her decks and hatch covers above was accompanied by a shower of cold, salt water. Somewhere below his feet, a bilge pump cycled on and off, trying to keep pace with the leaks.

He crawled all the way out from his cave on his hands and knees, getting covered in wet cement for his trouble. His skin was hot and drawn tight by thousands of pus-filled lesions. The raw cement was cool and astringent. He gathered a handful and smeared his neck, his face.

He listened for voices again, and when he heard none, he pulled out a heavy wrench he'd found hanging at the bottom of the hold ladder. He staggered to his feet, reeling as the deck tilted one way and his brain another. A sack tumbled from the top of a pile and landed with the sodden *splat* of a suicide.

He listened to the groan of old steel, the hard *thump* of waves. It was possible that nature had her own plans for this ship. But he was far beyond possibilities now. Only certainties would do. He would fix what he had broken. Stop what he had started. Seize one final chance to live for something real, something meaningful, even if it meant his certain death.

Makayev stepped into a thick porridge of wet cement and headed for the watertight door leading into the engine room.

Naim climbed out onto the bridge. There was no sign of the helmsman. Leaving the bridge when you had the watch! And look! Hazil hadn't even set the autopilot. The small wheel was spinning on its own, the wind and the waves taking control. He ran to the helm and found the helmsman sprawled on the deck. His forehead bled where he'd struck the sharp edge of a metal table. Naim reached down and touched hot skin. A wave rolled up the hull and sent him staggering back.

Hazil could wait.

Naim pulled himself up to the wheel and spun it hard. The world beyond the bridge windows was one of rolling black hills streaked in white foam. He had to swing the bow into the wind and take those hills head on. But the engine was weak and the wind was strong. The ship didn't want to turn, even with the wheel hard over.

'What's going on up here?'

Naim looked back and saw the captain rushing up the ladder. 'Hazil fell and hit his head! The ship, I can't bring her around!'

Warsame shoved the young sailor away and took the wheel. Wallowing, his ship had lost way. He needed more power to turn her bow in a direction the wind did not wish it to go. The engine gauge showed 88 RPMs. They could turn 122 in an emergency. He grabbed the telephone and rang up the engine room. 'Assad?'

The engineer answered immediately. 'What's happening up there?'

'Never mind. How many turns can you give me?'

'One twenty, but she's running hot.'

'I need it all. Wait for my signal. Be ready.' Warsame would have to let the ship sled down the back of one wave, then use both power and momentum to swing her bow around before the next one rose up and rolled them over for good.

The hull pitched and slammed. Warsame brought the rudder amidships. The deck began to roll as the next swell came up beneath them. The starboard bridge wing seemed to be reaching down for the water. When he judged the moment was right, he swung the engine telegraph to *All Ahead Full*. 'Assad! Now!'

The needle on the engine repeater quivered as the diesel roared. *100 ... 115 ... 122* revolutions. The ship churned up the side of the wave, hung for a moment, then pitched down into the following trough.

The freighter picked up speed, and Warsame swung the rudder hard over, right to the stops.

USS *Portland*

Jameson let Steve Stepik stow the satcom radio while he hurried below. He dropped to the bottom of the trunk ladder and almost stepped into the control room without asking permission. But the look on Tony Watson's dour, disapproving face reminded him that he was among Navy men again. 'Permission to enter?'

'Granted,' said Watson.

'We need to have a little talk.'

'See me in the wardroom when–'

'I haven't made myself clear, XO. I mean *right now*.'

'Very well. Make it brief.'

They gathered around the chart table aft of the periscope stand. Jameson snatched a pencil and quickly plotted the latitude and longitude relayed from Washington. When he put a dot on the paper, it was a good hundred and fifty miles from *Portland*. He looked up. 'How fast can you get us up there?'

Watson bent over the chart. 'We're speed-limited on the surface. I'd say twelve knots. Ten hours. What's the rush?'

'The ship we hit was a decoy. This one is the real deal,' said Jameson, tapping the chart with his pencil. 'There's a good chance they'll be waiting for us and I want the odds stacked in our favor. That means hitting them when we can see and they can't. We've got nine hours of darkness left. I want to find that ship in the next four, board it at five, blow it out of the water by five thirty and be back aboard the boat by sunrise. I know you can sail a lot faster dived.'

'Sure, but we can't pull the masts down and if the fittings at the bottom are damaged we could have a flood. That's a serious risk.'

'*Portland* wasn't built to move humanitarian supplies. She's a warship and we're at war. This,' he said, jabbing his finger on the chart, 'this is the enemy. I need you to get us there the fastest way you can.'

Watson saw his point, but minimizing risk was built into a nuclear engineer's soul. You don't spend years repeating the mantra *If the ship's not safe the reactor's not safe* and then go throwing it all away. And nothing trumped keeping the reactor safe. Nothing. 'If we did get you into position you might have to board that ship in the middle of a gale.'

That's right, thought Jarneson. *I might have to. Not you.* 'Good. Maybe the Tangos will be too busy puking to shoot.'

'If you're convinced that ship is the right one, why not call for help? You could put her under aerial surveillance, send out helicopters, a couple of frigates, or even have her met at her destination by the police.'

He's fucking wasting my time, thought Jameson. 'Sir, there are no helicopters close enough to lend a hand. And flying out in this weather would be as risky to them as boarding is for us. By tomorrow night that ship will be riding at anchor in Catania. We could alert the police and have them waiting, but the Tangos might decide to use the weapon they stole. All they'd have to do is crack open a vial and wave it around in the breeze. And remember, there's an airport there. Once it's loose the virus could be anywhere in the world in hours.'

'Then why not have someone put a missile into her tonight?'

'Because nobody knows if the weapon is still on board. And if it isn't where we have to go to find it.'

'Submerging might put this boat at considerable risk.'

'I'll take a possible risk over a definite failure any day. Look, XO, cards on the table. I'm operating under the direct authority of the President of the United States. Piss in my pocket and you'll be pissing in his. And if you waste time worrying about a few leaks while that ship starts an epidemic, maybe *more* than an epidemic, you'll be flushing your command-at-sea star down the head and that's a no-shitter.'

Watson wished he could send a signal back to COMSUBLANT. He wished someone would take this off his plate. Dive a boat with questionable watertight integrity? It went against everything Watson believed in as a submarine officer and totally against Navy regulations.

The United States Navy had a term for it: *hazarding the vessel*. Let your keel drag a sand bar and you were hazarding your vessel. Fumble a reactor startup and you were hazarding your vessel. Do something that your squadron CO didn't like and you would discover that you'd been hazarding your vessel.

Of course, every boat underway did *something* against regulation. It was only when bad things happened that it came back to haunt the captain. *Captain*. *Portland* finally had a good, sensible engineer in command and yet Watson's first decision was not about how to reduce risk, but how much to add.

Steadman and this SEAL are two of a kind, he thought with a scowl.

'Sir?'

Watson weighed his choices. Play it safe and defy the President of the United States. *Not good.* If he dived and something bad happened, the Navy would want to hang him but he could tell them to take it up at the White House. Framed that way, the choice was clear. He turned to the chief of the watch. 'Rig for dive. Helm. Stand by to answer a flank bell.'

'Thanks, skipper,' said Jameson, knowing exactly how that word would resonate in Watson's head. 'Where's Lieutenant Scavullo?'

'What do you want with her?'

'My exec is dead. She's the best Russian linguist I have left.'

'You can't just Shanghai one of my crew.'

'Actually, she's not exactly one of your crew, is she?'

MV *'Nova Spirit'*

Adnan unlocked the forward watertight door leading out of the iron house to the cargo deck. He opened it enough to put his head out into the wind and the rain.

'Where are you going?' asked his brother Musa.

'To check on the *kaffir.*' The unbeliever.

'How far can a dead man walk?'

'He wasn't dead when I left him.' Adnan stepped out and let the wind slam the steel door behind him.

There was a raised catwalk between the double row of containers lashed on deck. Foam rushed first one way and then the other as the deck rolled and pitched. The foam was light and easily driven between the wind, but beneath it was water. Sometimes a sheet. Sometimes enough to rise to his knees. Adnan knew ships were made for the sea. But water so far up made him nervous.

The catwalk was still higher than the waves and the alley between the containers offered some protection from the wind. The Chechen had no trouble making his way to the front of the blue SEALAND container. He unlocked it and started to pull it open, but then he thought better of it and took out the knife, wickedly sharp and with a serrated edge for sawing. When he was ready, he pulled the door wide.

The interior was dark and smelled of rot and

mildew. And something else, something both sharp and sweet. Had the *kaffir* died in here? It was important to know. If he and his brother had one week, then they would travel leisurely and thoroughly. Rome, London, New York if possible. Even if it meant being arrested. What good would iron bars do against a germ? But if they had only a few days, that was also important to know. They would use the time God gave them very differently. Paris, say. At the international terminal. Waiting for a flight that would never come while thousands hurried by to catch planes leaving for everywhere.

And on those swift, gleaming planes would ride an invisible army, delivered to the enemy by ... the enemy.

Had not the Lions of September used this same strategy?

He was about to turn his flashlight on when he noticed water streaming out from the floor of the closed container. A lot of water. And wind. Wind?

He turned the light on, sweeping first the bunks, the floor, then the shadowy corners. Then up. The circle of light came to rest at the hanging flap of canvas at the back. Rain sheeted off it and gathered in pools on the floor, where the deck's pitching sent it sloshing one way, then another.

The secret door was to have been their escape hatch when the container was offloaded at the port of Valetta. Their way out.

It would seem that the sick Russian had already discovered it.

Assad scurried among a vibrating forest of fuel

lines, checking for leaks, cracks, for anything amiss. The Polish-built diesel rumbled like a big contented cat when it was happy. Now it clattered as though someone had dumped a fistful of coins into the crankcase. And the heat! The engine room was always hot, but Assad knew without having to consult the gauge that they were at the edge.

He let his hand linger on one cylinder that felt hotter than the others. Too much heat and the piston would stick and weld itself to the sleeve. At slow speeds the engine might just bend a rod and clank to a stop. But with masses of iron and steel moving in a blur at maximum revolutions, the stopping would be more violent.

Assad kept a small bound notebook at the end of a chain clipped to his belt. He pulled it out and jotted down *122 RPM, hogging in seas, #4 hot.* He thought about that, then added *very hot.* He slipped the book into his back pocket and turned in time to see an apparition standing on the open mesh catwalk: a ghost, a demon risen from the waves, still dripping ocean and smeared in gray slime.

A dead man, lost overboard, was standing with a Number Twelve iron wrench in its hand.

Assad screamed, though in the cacophony of the engine room only he could hear it. He fell back against his beloved engine as the dead gray arm covered in mud from the bottom of the sea brought the big red wrench down once, twice, a third time.

It worked! thought Warsame. Rudder and engine together had swung his ship's bow into the swells.

True, they were sailing in the wrong direction and they'd miss their scheduled docking tomorrow. But arriving late was better than not arriving at all. And in any event, this storm was God's doing, and who could say what He had in mind by it?

The bow struck a steep sea and buried itself to the wave shield. The ship nearly came to a stop as foam surged back over the deck and drained off the scuppers. His ship would beat itself to death unless he slowed. He swung the engine telegraph back to *Ahead Half,* then picked up the telephone and rang the engineer. 'Assad? Give the engine a rest.'

He waited for the engine room to answer. There was no reply. The decks still vibrated under the strain of full power. And the needle on the engine repeater remained steady on 122 revolutions.

Makayev climbed down to the bottom of the engine room. He knew he was looking for a pipe that cooled the engine with sea water, and it was likely a big one. But there were dozens of pipes, all sizes and colors. Green ones, blue, brown, yellow and red ones.

A large green one emerged from the open mesh deck, then bent forward to connect with some kind of pump. Makayev touched it. His wet fingers sizzled. The green pipe was cold going in, warm going out. He found a hinged panel next to where the green pipe emerged from the deck, and when he opened it he found a large wheeled valve. Below it was more green pipe, though it was covered in white corrosion. It seemed to go straight through the bottom of the hull. He

361

reached down. *Ice cold.*

He turned the wheel. It moved stiffly as the valve closed off the flow of water to the straining diesel. Immediately, the pump vibrated in protest. No doubt it would burn up, and without cooling water, the engine, too. Neither one would put the ship on the bottom. That took more water, not less. Enough to flood the engine room. Enough to rush through the watertight door he'd left open to the Number Three hold.

Four big nuts secured the sea water intake to the pump. With the valve shut there would be no water pressure to fight. The pipe would come loose, he'd open the valve again and let the ocean roar in. He wrapped the jaws of the wrench around the first nut and leaned. The wrench, slick with blood and scalp and tufts of hair, slipped and the sharp edges of the metal mesh decking sliced his knuckles.

Makayev didn't feel pain. He adjusted the jaws, got them on the nut and cracked it loose. Soon, it spun off and fell into the pool of filthy bilge water, oil, and blood below. He sat back, breathing hard. *Three more.*

The ship pounded into the swells on a full bell, the engine driving her blunt bow straight into the oncoming waves. They were breaking right over the bow in great tumbling cataracts. Warsame knew they would lose the shield and then their deck cargo if they didn't slow down. 'Something's wrong with Assad,' Warsame told Naim. 'Go below and throttle back the engine. You know how this is done?'

'Yes, Captain.' The young Pakistani was still kneeling beside the injured helmsman. 'What about Hazil?'

'Leave him. Report from the engine room on the telephone. Go!'

Naim stood and was about to head aft to the ladderwell when he felt a short, sharp vibration that rattled the old freighter right to her bones before subsiding. 'What was that?'

Makayev felt it, too. It was louder, stronger, but then he was only a few meters away from its epicenter deep inside the number four cylinder. The piston had swollen in the raging head and was no longer able to slide freely. It caught, slid, and caught again. Stopping the engine might save it, but there was no hand on the throttle.

Makayev leaned on the iron wrench. The second fastener was welded to the flange with corrosion. He pushed harder. All his weight now. It refused to turn. He was about to rap it with the wrench when a loud *thud* sounded from behind. Another deep shudder coursed through the decking.

He turned in time to see the number four head blow off the engine case, followed an instant later by a piston the size of a small drum. It was glowing red, dripping tears of molten metal and chased by the fractured stump of a connecting rod. It arced across the engine room, snapping off fuel and hydraulic lines as it went. The ruptured lines sprayed flammable mist into the air. The red-hot piston torched it off and became a comet that smashed through the engine control panel and came to a stop against the hull plates.

There was a moment of the most intense silence, then the *whump!* of a small explosion, followed by an angry boil of orange flame that engulfed the whole of the fidley level.

Makayev watched it, stunned. He'd come down here to drown a ship. Instead, he'd started a fire that flashed from within a pall of oily black smoke and filthy steam.

It became very quiet. Makayev thought the explosion had deafened him, but then he heard the hiss of escaping steam, the *boom* of waves against the hull. He looked at the seawater intake, wondering how he could pry the frozen bolt off in time, for surely the crew would be coming down here to investigate. There Makayev, an atheist to his bones, saw something that suggested the possibility of a God: the shock had broken the pump free from its pipe, and the ocean was boiling in.

CHAPTER TWENTY-THREE

INTO THE GULF

MV 'Nova Spirit'
Ionian Sea

Naim unclogged the watertight door to the engine room only to have it fly back into his face in a blast of hot steam and oil smoke. He took a quick breath of clean air and charged back in.

Burning pools of oil sputtered down on the

bottom level, the flames fed by ruptured fuel and hydraulic lines. The main lights had died with the ship's generator, but the battery-powered lamps were on and it didn't take long for Naim to see that the engine had blown itself apart. Pieces of blackened metal lay scattered across the fidley deck. The motor control panel behind Assad's desk hung from its wires.

Nor did it take long to find Assad. The engineer must have been leaning over the engine when it let go. He'd taken the full force of it with his face. It was battered and bloody, as though someone had taken a hammer to a bag of raw meat and pounded it flat.

Naim yanked on the red handle to trigger the ship's fire alarm. It still worked, thanks to God. He could hear distant clanging from somewhere overhead. He was about to return to the cargo hold to get help to knock the flames down when he heard a different sound: the roar of water. *The hull!* He looked once more at Assad's body to assure himself that he *must* be dead, then raced back out to the passage and slammed the water-tight door shut. He swung the locking bar all the way down, then pushed a big steel railroad spike through the hasp, freezing it in place.

Warsame heard the clanging fire bell and felt his ship begin to slew sideways to the wind and waves. A fire at sea was a matter of the utmost seriousness. So was an engine failure in bad weather. He had both to contend with, and not much time.

'Captain!'

Warsame turned. It was Naim. 'What happened?'

'The engine! It's gone!'

'Gone?'

'It blew up!'

'Where's Assad?'

'Dead! The room is still on fire!'

'Why aren't you down there fighting it?'

'The space is flooding! I could hear it come in! I sealed the door!'

At least that will put out the fire, Warsame thought grimly. But a flooded engine room was not much better than a burning one; let it fill and it could pull the whole ship under. 'Shut down the blower and seal the engine room ventilator. Then check the aft scuttle and make sure it's tight, too. Do you understand?'

'Yes!'

'Then do it!' Closing off the engine room from above wouldn't keep water from coming in below, but it might slow it down. No matter. Warsame knew that his ship was no longer under his command. Or anyone else's, for that matter. It was a slave to the wind, the waves and the inexorable invasion of the sea. He glanced at the GPS screen, memorized their position and ran back to the radio cubicle. He switched on the yellow shortwave set, dialed channel sixteen and spoke.

'Mayday! Mayday! This is the *Nova Spirit* eighty kilometers south east of Catania! Uniform, Bravo, X-Ray Fox!' UBXF was the international call sign that signified the *Cristi*, not *Nova Spirit*. But they might all end up in the water before long and Warsame had neither time nor interest in games.

'Calling any ship near Catania! This is UBXF! We are on fire and adrift!'

Makayev climbed up to the fidley deck on his hands and knees. The steel mesh cut him and the red trails of blood that spattered the rusty metal were so hot with virus they should have sizzled. Instead, they dripped silently to the rising pool of water below and vanished.

The sea was coming in through the broken cooling water pipe, surging around the shattered engine. He could see the water rise, claiming the stairs tread by tread until it lapped at his heels.

How long before this ship died? The waves were striking her side. Each one heeled the ship over and the water below would slosh and crash in a curling, interior wave. Then slowly, slowly, the ship would stagger upright. Was there an hour left? Thirty minutes? Would he die before the ship went down, or ride to the bottom inside this steel box?

He felt a growing sense of unease. He had no wish to die down here, alone and trapped like an experimental animal in a cage. He'd seen the results of failed experiments taken to the lake at Pokrov. Monkeys, rabbits, dogs, still locked inside their cages and tossed in. There would be thrashing, bubbles, then nothing.

What it would feel like to drown? He knew the answer from the biological point of view. A man of greater courage might open his mouth and let his soul flow forth. But Makayev knew the water would cover his head and he would hold on to every last bubble of air. Twenty seconds later, maybe forty, surely in less than a minute pure instinct would force open his mouth. He would gasp a desperate breath and drag water into his windpipe, his lungs. The real drowning would begin in earnest.

Whether his vocal cords clamped down to keep the fatal breath from flooding his lungs or not, his heart would starve for oxygen first. It would labor, beat erratically, then stop. The brain, hoping for a miracle, would shut down in a kind of suspended animation, waiting for a rescue that would never come. After fifteen minutes, hope and brain and Makayev would all be dead.

But what would those few minutes of perfect, awful consciousness *feel* like? Would they be like the warm embrace of the womb? A euphoric sensation that tucked him in beneath soft blankets as the world gradually dimmed? Or would it be a shuddering, thrashing panic? A wave of fear that would rise up to a height Makayev could not possibly imagine?

He took a deep breath of smoky air and coughed. Drowning was better than he deserved. He'd been a fool. A virus meant to end the world was safe only in the hands of men who did not wish to die. The Soviets, the Americans, they'd stared at one another through gunsights for decades without pulling a trigger. Why? Because they were sane, at least by comparison. And now?

Makayev could die a fool. But not a mass murderer.

He crawled up to the fidley and looked down over the railing. The lower level emergency lights were underwater, still burning. It would be so easy to simply stop here, to let the sea bear him up and carry him away. Easier than struggling up these steps, surely.

Makayev reached the fidley three steps ahead of the flood and utterly exhausted. The water was deep and dark now, and even with the emergency lights he couldn't see its bottom. He turned to face the door he'd entered from the cargo hold.

Someone had shut it. He leaned against it.

It didn't move.

He looked up. A ladder climbed the bulkhead beside the sealed door. It rose up to some sort of a hatch. Something cold touched his ankles. The water had crept up through the steel grate of the fidley deck. When the ship rolled, the level shifted, then surged back, higher. *Stop here,* Makayev's body told him. *There's nothing more to do. Rest.* But when the ship rolled back and the water drained away, his mind said, *This is a trap. A cage. Climb. Open that hatch. Escape.*

Makayev reached up and grasped the oily rung. He pulled his body up as the water rushed and swirled around his legs. He pulled himself onto the ladder, and let the rising water drive him up.

'Mayday! Mayday!' said Warsame. 'This is *Nova Spirit* calling on Channel Sixteen. We are broken down and adrift! Does anyone hear?'

The shortwave radio crackled with the energy of the electrical storm. But then it resolved into a voice.

'Ship on Channel Sixteen near Catania, this is the USNS *Apache*. Say again your position?'

USNS? What was that? 'We are eighty kilometers southeast of Catania. We have a fire in the engine

369

room! We are broken down and drifting north!'

'Stand by, *Nova Spirit*.'

Warsame waited for only a few moments, but in that time all the ground he'd gained in turning the ship into the waves was lost. She was broadside to the storm again and rolling hard. He could hear the stomp of running feet below, then,

'This is *Apache*. We're only fifty miles north of your position. It's a hell of a night for a fire. Can you put it out or will you have to leave?'

'I don't know this yet.' Ships – even broken ships – had a way of staying afloat a lot longer than you'd expect. There was an old maritime wisdom that the smart sailor always steps *up* to his rescue, never down. 'We have only one life boat and one raft.'

'How many souls on board?'

'Thirteen. No. Sixteen.' He'd forgotten Salafi and the two Chechens.

'Are you able to rig your ship for a tow?'

'If we are afloat. How soon can you be here?'

'You're headed for the Gulf of Noto. It gets shallow up in there. We'll have to beat against the weather to find you before you run aground. Say, three or four hours. Are your lights still working?'

'No. The generator is gone. We're on battery power only.'

'Better post lookouts with a flare gun. We may only get one shot at hooking on. What's your cargo, anyway?'

'Powdered cement. And we will post lookouts at once! But what kind of ship are you, *Apache?* Can you pull us into port?'

There was a soft chuckle. 'We can tow aircraft

370

carriers. We're a United States Navy seagoing tug and salvage is our business. We'll relay your mayday to the authorities. Hold on. We're coming.'

United States Navy? 'We will wait for you.' Warsame put the microphone down. Perhaps his luck wasn't so good after all. A United States Navy ship meant that he and his crew would not just walk away and vanish into a crowded port. There would be questions asked, lists consulted. If *Nova Spirit* didn't trigger an alarm Warsame's name surely would. Chances were good that he would end up like his brother: swallowed up, sitting in a cell.

But that was better than being swallowed by the sea, wasn't it?

As though to settle the matter, there was a *boom!* as a wave struck the ship's sides. The bridge wings dipped low, first one way, then the other, like the stroking arms of a swimmer flailing across the waves. Water and foam poured right over the cargo deck. When the ship rolled back level, the blue SEALAND container was gone.

USS *Portland*

Banjo bandaged up Scavullo's cut, helped her stretch out in her rack, then, when the obnoxious SEAL lieutenant showed up and told him to take a hike, he headed back up to the radio shack to sort things out.

It wasn't a pretty sight. The smell of burned wires and the blank stares of the indicators told him that the gremlin might be gone but he'd left a larger problem behind. He pushed the strewn

371

radio logs into one pile, the shattered glass into another, then tried to coax some of the electronics back to life.

The boat had redundant communications systems, multiple channels, transmitters and receivers fed by several antenna arrays. The masts that had taken the direct hit were backed up by antennas on the periscopes, by a floating wire streamed behind the boat, and at a pinch, by an antenna that could be brought up from storage and mounted on deck.

But they all relied on a common distribution device; a dedicated computer that routed signals like a traffic cop to their proper destinations. It was called the Antenna Distribution System, and it was no longer a traffic cop: it was a scorched pothole.

As he flipped switches trying to come up with a way to work around it, he noticed a dim light glowing up on the ELF panel; the floating wire was picking up some kind of a signal. Someone wanted to talk to *Portland*. But how would they answer? Banjo figured they'd have better luck strapping a message to a pigeon and letting it–

'Banjo?'

The radioman swung around to face the door. 'Oh. Hey, XO. Some mess in here, huh?'

Tony Watson took in the disarray. 'Get it squared away.'

'Aye aye.' *Like I'm not?* 'We might have an ELF light.'

'Might?'

'It could be just a fused circuit. I can't tell yet. I'll have to rig up some kind of workaround.'

'Do it later. We're going to dive. I want you to keep an eye on the overhead.'

Banjo looked up as the fluorescent tubes buzzed awake. 'What am I looking for?'

'You may see a little seepage from the cable fittings. If you do, holler out and we'll stay shallow to keep the pressure off.'

Seepage sounded a lot like *leaks*, and the XO was taking the matter of a *leak* pretty casually. He thought about something sonarman Niebel had said: *If we don't get the bitch off the boat she'll put us all on the bottom.* How much water had to come in to be just a *little* seepage?

'Are you listening, Gant?'

'Yes, sir,' said Banjo. 'I sure will keep an eye on the overhead. What about the ELF signal?'

'How long will it take you to restore comms?'

'Sir, I'm not sure they *can* be restored.'

Watson glowered. A *lightning strike* could damage a rich man's yacht. It could set a wooden ship on fire. But this was a nuclear-powered, twenty-first-century warship and for reasons he was not able to understand much less explain it had been thrown back to the nineteenth. The boat could see what her lookouts could see, hear what her sonar operator could detect. The Navy, indeed, the rest of the *world,* might as well not exist. 'I don't care if you have to rig up a tin can and string. Get something functional. And let me know if you see anything out of the ordinary in the dive.'

'Yes, sir. I'll *definitely* let you know.'

'No way,' said Scavullo. 'You're out of your mind if you think I'm jumping into a raft.'

'Come on, Rosie,' said Jameson. 'You don't have to ride the CRRC. I just need you on the other end of a radio in case there's some translating that has to happen fast. I need you to be there for *me*.'

'For *you?*' His words threw a switch inside her. 'When you needed help with Russian, I was there for you. Right?'

'Sure.'

'And when you got lonely?'

'Rosie–'

'I rented a car, packed it and stood outside the gates waiting for you to show. We were going to drive down to Big Sur for the weekend. Where were you?'

'Headed for Iraq. There was a war. It's not my fault. I didn't have time for long goodbyes.'

'You had time to get wasted with your froggy friends.'

Shit. He'd gone pub crawling with the other special operators attending language school for a last night out before going to war. But how did she know about that? 'Okay. I screwed up.'

Scavullo was less than impressed. 'And what exactly happened with that ship? You said you were going after terrorists with stolen WMDs. Where are they? *Oops! I guess there aren't any.* You're no better than the CIA.'

'Hey, there's no reason to start calling names.'

'Isn't there? I know you didn't find smallpox up there but you still blew that ship up into...' she paused, 'what was the expression? Little sterilized pieces? What was *that?* Another screw up?'

'The Russians put that ship down. Not us.'

'Two torpedoes. Three explosions. Add it up. I can.'

'There *was* a good reason not to let that ship go on its merry little way. You've got to trust me on that.'

'Why?'

No doubt there was an answer but Jameson couldn't quite think of it under fire. 'Look. Just stand on the bridge and patch in to the squad freq. Steve will set you up with one of our good radios and–'

'You told the captain you were fluent. So? Go fluent yourself.'

'You know my Russian. That's why I need some help.'

'Where have I heard *that* before?'

'Can you *try* to keep this professional?'

'Absolutely. Thanks for your vote of confidence, Lieutenant Jameson. Request denied.'

'I don't have to ask. You're attached to Yellowstone. I can throw you into the raft and your captain will back me up.'

'You mean Watson? I'm surprised he didn't come up with the idea in the first place. Or was that the plan?'

'Quit acting like the world is out to spoil your day, Rosie. The plan is you provide translation if we find Russian speakers. The plan is you serve your Navy, your country, not just your feminist ego.'

'My *what?*'

'And if you don't step up to the plate I can guarantee you'll never get another shot. That will be it. For you and for every woman who wants to go out on the boats. When the going gets rough, the girls go off and do their nails.'

Scavullo swung her legs out of her rack so fast she nearly kicked Jameson in the stomach. She stood up in the narrow passage. 'Thanks.'

'For what?'

'For reminding me what an asshole you are.' She stormed off, heading for the forward ladder.

'Where are you going?'

'To do my nails.' She turned her back to Jameson and climbed up the ladder, heading for the upper deck, and officers' country.

'It's just like I told you,' said Niebel. 'Chief Remson loses a hand, COB and the skipper get zorched up on the bridge. You really want to wait around for the last act?'

'I hear you,' said Bam Bam. He was honestly troubled. You might explain some things away as pure, or impure, chance. But there was no denying misfortune had found a home on *Portland*. 'I don't know what there is to do about it. She'll be with us until we put in somewhere.'

'Unless we find a way to get her off our backs for good.'

'That kind of talk will put you in a brig, Socks.'

'A brig is better than the bottom of the fucking ocean, which I guarantee you is our next stop if she has–' Niebel stopped.

'What?' asked Bam Bam.

Niebel nodded at the open door of the sonar shack.

Bam Bam turned. Lieutenant Scavullo was standing out in the passage, her back to them, facing the door to Steadman's cabin. She knocked, and went inside.

Steadman was sprawled on his bunk with Chief Cooper kneeling beside him, stethoscope in hand.

One look and Scavullo knew she wouldn't be having any conversations over her duties to the Navy, the country or to womankind. His burned khakis lay in a heap. His chest was bare. Angry red welts snaked across his skin, emerging from a bandage that encased his right hand, along his arm, across his neck and down his sides. 'Is he–?'

'Yeah. Probably. What I can see won't kill him,' said Cooper as he listened to Steadman's heart. It was still fluttering, though more strongly.

'What about COB?'

Cooper stared at her. 'You lonely, lieutenant?'

'Okay. I get the message.' Scavullo left the small stateroom and paused out in the passage. She considered going aft to the radio shack, but she'd have to cross through Control and Watson was in there. She heard the rush of compressed air, the rumble of water rushing into *Portland's* ballast tanks, and then the almost imperceptible tilt of the deck as the submarine slipped beneath the waves.

She decided to head down to the middle deck, walk aft and come back up on the other side of Control. She might as well help Banjo clean up the radio shack. She came to the forward ladder and unhooked the chain that guarded it.

The steel rail was cold and slick with skin oil. Some of the crew liked to slide down without touching any rungs, but she wasn't out here to show off. She shifted her weight to step across, and instead found herself slammed hard against it.

She bounced away before she could grab the rail. And then she was falling. She shot out one hand, two, trying to grab something to break her fall. She knew it wasn't smart. It was a good way to have your arm broken, but a broken arm was preferable to a broken skull.

She nearly made it to the bottom before a leg, not an arm, caught between rung and rail. She could feel her knee try to bend the wrong way, up, not down, heard the crackle of protesting bone and ligament. Her knee was about to snap when suddenly, mysteriously, she came to a stop in mid-air, her hair touching the linoleum deck plates.

'Hey, hey hey,' said Jameson as he untangled her from the ladder. He'd caught her in both arms with her head low, her legs high. Another half second and it would have been a toss-up whether she'd break her skull on the deck or her leg in the ladder. 'Take it easy, Rosie. You slip?'

'I didn't slip, asshole. I was pushed,' she said. 'Put me down.'

Jameson helped her stand, then he looked up at the ladderwell. It was empty, of course. 'Maybe the world is out to spoil your day after all.'

She started to shake.

'You gonna' be okay?'

'Sure. Thanks. I mean for catching me.'

'No sweat.' He smiled. 'So. Can we be friends?'

'No,' said Scavullo. 'Just allies.'

'I'll take that,' said Jameson.

CHAPTER TWENTY-FOUR

THE TEST

USS *Portland*

Tony Watson and the lieutenant in charge of damage control made a fast tour of the boat from the forward elliptical bulkhead to the engine room aft. They spent a long time poring over the 'Bomb' in the Auxiliary Machine Room; the device that made *Portland's* air was a temperamental beast. If provoked it could bite back.

Watson was in his element. He knew *Portland's* complex systems at least as well as his senior watchstanders, if not better. He found a hairline crack in a high-pressure hydraulic line that supplied the antennas, radar masts and periscopes that even the leading A-Gang chief had missed. He took nothing for granted.

And so when Lieutenant Kelso, the amiable sonar officer told him that everything was perfectly normal, Watson walked into the sonar shack to see for himself. What he saw under those soft blue lights was very far from normal. Only Niebel sat before a recognizable display. Two of the other four screens were blank and the last, Bam Bam's, was filled with incomprehensible white noise.

'What is going on in this space, Mister Schramm?'

'We're using a new acoustic program to keep track of that *Akula*, sir.' Bam Bam knew it sounded lame even as he spoke the words. More so, given that the shadow he'd been watching had slipped away to the north and disappeared.

'What new program? Who sent it down?'

'No one sent. I wrote it.'

'And it's running? Who the hell authorized *that?*'

'Commander Steadman,' said Lieutenant Kelso, thinking that he was coming to Bam Bam's aid.

Watson thought, *That figures.* Steadman was like one of those weekend sailors who thought channel buoys were for others, who wondered what all that 'brown water' might be and went aground for his curiosity. 'All I see are two dead consoles and garbage on yours. Niebel is the only one sitting a real sonar watch as far as I can tell.'

Niebel gave Schramm a raised eyebrow, then turned to his screen.

'Well, I know it kinda' looks that way, but the program soaks up a lot of the BSY-1's distributed computing power. We have to switch off some of the consoles and gang up the racks to get it to play in near-real time. If I can just tell you what it does then I think you'll–'

'I don't want to be *told*. I want to *see* and what I'm seeing is your home-brewed program disables half our sonar suite. Correct?'

'It doesn't disable anything. I shut those consoles down. My program allows us to hear things the system misses. Like that *Akula*. That's why the CO gave me the green light.'

'The light just changed.' Watson peered over

Schramm's shoulder and tried to make sense of the onscreen blizzard. He knew sonar and whatever this *mess* was it was definitely *not* sonar. 'Where's the *Akula?*'

'He was paralleling us from about eight thousand yards for a long time, then moved off, fired those two rocket torpedoes and–'

'And now?'

'He scooted off to the north and we lost him in the surface noise. He's way quieter than any *Akula* I've heard, XO. I was playing with the signal-to-noise algorithm to reacquire him when you walked in.'

'In other words, you're playing and half the world's best sonar system is switched off. Does that about sum things up?'

'I can find him again. The program hunts for quiet zones and up here there's just too much wave noise to pick him out of the weeds.'

Watson took out his list and made a few notes, then glanced at Kelso. 'This is a warship. Not a video arcade. The sonar suite is not installed for your amusement. It's been tested and found to be the finest in the world. Restore it and heaven help you if you can't.'

'I can.' What had Steadman said as they were threading the needle of Gibraltar? *The day will come when you get to tell me I'm full of shit.* That day was *now*. Bam Bam sat up and said, 'But XO? I don't think it's a good idea. Our sonar may be the best in the world but it didn't pick up the *Akula*. My program did. If you want to track him you'd best let it run.'

'And *you* had best recognize an order when you

hear one.'

'Sir, with all due respect, if I do what you're asking that *Akula* can sneak up and bugger us again whenever he feels like it. We'll have no idea what's coming our way. That's just dumb.'

'Fine.' Watson's jaw tensed. 'You're relieved. Kelso? I'll come back in ten minutes. Make sure I like what I see.' He spun on his heel and left.

'Forgive me Jesus for I have sinned,' muttered Bam Bam.

'You heard the man,' said Kelso. 'Make it look right.'

'Even if it's wrong?'

'It's not wrong if the XO wants it.'

'Bullshit.' Bam Bam ejected his CD and powered up the other sonar stations. Passive broadband, narrowband, demodulated noise, active intercept. Bow, flank and towed arrays. Choo Choo was right: put them together, sit a group of United States Navy blueshirts in front of them and you'd the best sonar system in the world. But he was also wrong. Bam Bam had seen enough of that lurking Russian boat to know that even the best in the world would not be good enough.

'It's a simple deal. Sign me off as fit for duty or get someone who will,' said Browne. He sat up in Tony Watson's bunk and threw off the thin blanket Cooper had arranged for him.

'COB, it ain't that simple,' said Chief Cooper. 'You're lucky. You got knocked away from the juice before it fried you. You have your ears back sort of and your burns aren't that bad. But your eyes—'

'A chief has more than eyes goin' for him. I

don't need *eyes* to know what's happening around here.'

Yes you do. The duty corpsman held up his hand, all five fingers splayed. 'How many fingers?'

Without a moment's hesitation Browne said, 'All of them.'

'Okay.' Three came down. 'Now?'

Browne squinted. Being a fearsome poker player could only take him so far. The room wasn't pitch black the way it seemed when he first arrived. There were areas of light and dark gray, and some of them even seemed to move. But fingers? Hands?

'How many?' Cooper persisted.

Browne scowled. 'Damn it Coop, my ears came back.'

'We're not talking about your ears.'

'We're talking about a submarine that just took a hit. We're down a captain and last I heard we had Russians shooting off rockets in the neighborhood. *Portland* needs every able hand.'

'That's right. Able.'

'Hell. What's every nub sailor got to do to earn his dolphins?

'A blindfolded walk through the boat. What's your point, senior chief?'

'He's got to find his way through a submarine, locate and repair critical systems, all without using his eyes. Correct?'

'Sure, but–'

'No buts,' said Browne. He swung his legs out of the bunk and pressed the soles of his feet to the deck. It felt good. *'The eyes of the blind shall be opened and the ears of the deaf unstopped.* That's what Isaiah says.'

'What does Isaiah know about submarines?'

'Nothing. But I do and I *know* you're not saying I can't hack what a non-qual nub can hack.'

Cooper sighed. 'I'll put you down for limited duty.'

'LIMDU is better than NODU. Take me to the skipper.'

'The XO's surveying the boat for damage.'

'I don't mean the XO. I mean Commander Steadman.'

'He's sedated. He'll be down a couple hours.'

'I ain't sittin' around waiting for the grass to–' Browne stopped.

A moment later, the roar of escaping air and the rush of water filling *Portland*'s ballast tanks rumbled through the hull.

K-335 *Gepard*
East Ionian Sea

'Contact re-established,' said Kureodov. *Gepard*'s sonar officer pressed the black headphones against his ears, then reached up to adjust the circular display. 'The American submarine is diving. I have screw noise, but it's very faint.'

'Enough for a turn count?' asked Leonov.

'Turns for sixteen knots. Range nine thousand meters. Bearing change consistent with a course of two hundred sixty-eight degrees.' Kureodov looked at his captain. 'He's coming our way.'

Leonov was unimpressed. 'Surface contacts?'

'None.'

Though an American hunter-killer submarine was moving closer, Leonov was pleased. He'd administered justice to criminals who'd been certain they'd escaped it. And he'd done it despite the American's attempts to distract him with a noisy active sonar pulse.

'He could pass close,' said *Starpom* Stavinsky. 'He could hear us.'

'He'll hear us, Oleg. But not yet.'

You're up to something, thought *Gepard*'s exec.

'Range still closing,' said Kureodov.

'*Sirena?*'

'Active silencing is on, Captain.'

'Very well.' Leonov trusted it to keep *Gepard* invisible for the moment. There were limits, of course. At some range the Americans would detect him. What was that range? Find out and he could trail them and never fear discovery. 'Helm? Five degrees down on the planes. Make your depth two hundred meters. Ahead dead slow.'

The stealthy *Akula* slipped silently through first one, then another thermal layer, using them to muffle and distort the stray sounds *Gepard* radiated into the sea.

'Signal is very weak,' said the Termite. 'Still moving this way.'

Stavinsky shot a questioning look at his captain.

Leonov read his assistant's expression. 'We'll let him pass, Oleg. Then move in and pull his tail and see if he barks.'

Barks? They'd fired two rocket torpedoes and destroyed a ship. Perhaps with Americans on board. What would their captain think if he looked in his rearview mirror and saw *Gepard* creeping up from behind?

Accidents had put both American and Russian submarines on the bottom. Some were true accidents. *Thresher* on their side, *Kursk* on his own. Others, like *Scorpion* and *K-129* – a missile boat the American Navy not only sank but then had the nerve to send the CIA to pick up the pieces – were not accidents at all, but more like convenient explanations to cover very dangerous truths.

And so as *Gepard* stalked the American boat, it wasn't the dog's bark that worried Stavinsky. It was his bite.

USS *Portland*

Banjo stared at the overhead. *A little seepage my ass.* How would it come? As a stream? A spray? A explosion of foam and water, a white avalanche his eyes would barely have time to register before he was up to his neck in ocean looking for air?

He watched, waited, and then it came: a single drop slid down a loop of exposed antenna cable, paused at the bottom, shivered, then fell to the deck with the singular *plop* of a leaky faucet. A minute passed, and then another *plop*.

Banjo grinned. 'Well, shit.' He found a white ceramic coffee mug Scavullo had left behind, put it on the deck beneath the drip, then went to work. The ELF light was still on. Someone was trying to talk to *Portland*. He didn't know how he was going to do it, but he was going to find some way to hear what they had to say.

386

The sonar shack door opened onto the Control room, and Niebel had no trouble leaning back to hear what was going on without benefit of the intercom.

'Depth now one hundred fifty feet,' said the Dive Officer.

'Steady on two eight zero,' said Watson. 'Radio, Conn. What's your status?'

Niebel leaned back in his chair to hear better. Whatever Banjo said must have been good enough, for Watson replied.

'Sonar, Conn. Is the BSY-1 back on line?'

'Conn, Sonar, aye. System is restored.' Niebel glanced at the passive broadband display. *Portland* was swimming through clear waters with good sound propagation.

'What have we got for layers?'

'Upper layer is at three hundred feet,' said Niebel. 'The second one's down at five fifty. Got a third deep at nine hundred. No contacts.'

'Helm,' said Watson. 'Make your depth four hundred feet. Turns for twenty-six knots. We've got an appointment. Let's not be late.'

K-335 *Gepard*

Sonar Officer Kureodov watched the dim spoke of light that was an American hunter killer submarine shift around his screen. It grew brighter, brighter, then it began to fade. He looked over his shoulder. 'Target is passing two thousand meters on the port beam, Captain. Range is opening. He missed us.'

Leonov winked at his executive officer. 'Helm. Left five degrees rudder. Course two six zero. Let's go have a close look.'

Leonov had heard stories of how American submarines performed underwater acrobatics around slow, stupid Russian targets. The Americans were undetectable, malevolent ghosts that haunted Russian ships until they were safely tied up to the pier.

'Range now four thousand meters.'

American captains earned a certain cowboy fame for their ability to 'underhull' Russian ships, daring to extend their periscopes and *film* their exploits so that their peers could look on and laugh. He thought of the American commander out ahead. *He* would become famous, too. But not in quite the same way. Leonov sat down in his ceremonial seat of command. When would they hear *Gepard?* How would they react?

'Range now six thousand meters.' Kureodov.

'Make turns for twenty-eight knots,' said Leonov. The Americans were confident there was nothing threatening in these seas.

And they were wrong.

USS *Portland*

Okay, Lord. I know this is a test, thought Browne as he climbed down the forward ladder to the middle deck. *I asked you for it. You gave it to me. I can hack it.*

'How you doing down there, COB?' asked Cooper. He was watching Browne's movements very closely from above.

Browne stepped off the bottom rung. He tilted his head up to where he figured Cooper was waiting, gave him a thumbs up and stepped back.

'Down ladder!' Cooper slid down the rails like a fireman answering a bell.

The Goat Locker was just a few steps forward and Browne made it there without difficulty. He went in and began rummaging through his gear. His hand closed around a cool, metal object: a spare handheld radio he could use to communicate with men throughout the boat. He'd lost his to the sea and it had left him feeling a bit naked. He clipped it to his wet belt.

There was a knock at the door. 'Permission to enter?'

'Come!' he called out. Browne heard the sound of feet. He could see a dark shape masking the lights from the passage beyond. But he could not make out a face. 'Well?'

Cooper saved him. 'Hey, Bam Bam.'

'COB,' said Schramm. 'I need to talk.'

Browne leaned against his bunk. 'I ain't got the time to play twenty guesses, son.'

'I came up with a program that lets us see *real* quiet boats.'

'Like the *Akula*.'

'Yeah. The XO had me pull it and go back to a normal watch. I told him he was wrong and he told me to take a hike.'

'The XO relieved you?'

'He said our sonar was the best in the world. So how come it didn't pick up that *Akula?*'

'Anything more to this story?'

'That *Akula* put two fish into a ship. You ever hear of a Russian boat pulling shit like that right in front of an audience?'

'Not when they knew they *had* one.'

'Exactly. He took the shot even though we had him nailed on active. This guy's yanking our crank, COB. He thinks he has us beat and I got a bad feeling he isn't done playing games.'

Browne respected Bam Bam's feelings. They were grounded in hours of long and careful attention to the sounds of the sea. 'You told all this to Mister Watson?'

'He didn't want to hear shit from me.'

'A good engineer ought to appreciate what works.'

'A good captain did,' said Bam Bam. 'COB, if that *Akula* is still around we're meat on the table.'

'Let's hope the Russians have other places to be.'

'Yeah? Where would *you* be in his shoes?'

Browne didn't hesitate. 'Sailing right up our ass.'

CHAPTER TWENTY-FIVE

THE KNOCK DOWN

K-335 *Gepard*

Leonov spun around in his leather swivel chair to face his sonar operator. 'Range to the *Los Angeles?*'

'Nine thousand meters, Captain,' said the Termite. 'They're above the upper layer.'

And running away at twenty-six knots. They still had no idea *Gepard* was there. 'Helm, make turns now for thirty knots.' It would close the gap, but not quickly. 'Sonar, start calling out the range every five hundred meters. Watch him very closely. He'll react suddenly when he hears us.'

The *Akula* boiled straight up *Portland's* wake.

'Range eight thousand five hundred.'

Leonov wondered about the American captain out ahead. You learned a great deal about a man from how he sailed his ship. Captains of missile submarines were timid as mice. Russian, American. It didn't matter. Turn on the lights and they fled for the shadows.

British attack boat commanders were more aggressive. They were like wrestlers, all maneuver and tactics. He wasn't there to dazzle you with technical competence. He was there to knock you down and pin you to the mat. Nothing more and nothing less.

'Range now seven thousand meters.'

American attack boat captains were a blend of the two. Aggressive when they held the upper hand, timid when they did not. Leonov was sure that it came from their training. The American Navy demanded engineering expertise on a par with a specialist who had nothing better to do than tend to a submarine's nuclear plant. Leonov was convinced this was a mistake. Submarine warfare wasn't just one machine pitted against another. It was also man against man. Leonov relied on his chief engineer to know the ins and outs of *Gepard's* reactor. But solicit him for advice on how to fight his ship? Ridiculous.

391

'Range now six thousand five hundred meters.'

No, *Los Angeles* captains were like snipers. They'd keep you at a safe distance where they could shoot you in the head and never risk being shot *at*. Put them in your sights at close range – at *knife* range – suddenly and without warning, and what would they do?

That was what Leonov intended to find out.

'Range now *four* thousand meters,' said the Termite.

'Arm the active sonar, Kureodov. Set for continuous pinging.'

The Termite flipped up the switch guard on the MGK-503 active sonar. He remembered his fear when the American sonar had thundered through *Gepard*. This would pay them back and more.

Leonov thought, *We're chewing on his tail and he still doesn't see us.* 'Kureodov?' he said. 'Activate.'

USS *Portland*

Niebel swallowed a mouthful of cold coffee, then leaned back to take in his passive sonar display. It was quiet enough down here beneath the upper layer, but the waves were perking up on the surface, with the irregular splash of light made by breakers showing up in all quadrants. *Fucking storm at sea,* and he thought, *that bitch is a total shit magnet.* They'd gotten mauled by waves, struck by lightning. What would hit them next? A tanker? An undersea mountain? Or would it be something bigger, something worse, like a fire, a reactor casualty or–

'Hey, we lost the tail,' said Lieutenant Kelso. He sat before the screen fed by *Portland's* towed sonar array; the tail. It was pure white.

Niebel sat up and leaned over as a piercing, crystalline *ping!* washed over *Portland* from stern to bow. The volume rocketed from annoying to painful in his headset before the automatic filters cut in. It dazed him, and then, as he reached for the microphone, a second *ping!* struck, a third. A fourth.

'Sonar, Conn!' Watson snapped. 'Secure from pinging!'

'It's not us! It's a Skat set and he's close!'

'A Russian sonar?'

'With an *Akula* attached!'

Watson was used to picking up Russians from forty, even fifty thousand yards away. Poor acoustic conditions? A lazy sonarman? Some malfunction in the BSY-1 brought on by Bam Bam's tinkering? All possible, alone and in combination.

Ping!... Ping!... Ping!

Watson had no headset to muffle the sharp pulses of sound pouring through the hull. He'd put his fingers in his ears but he'd be damned if he would let his embarrassment show. But a red flush appeared at his neck and quickly moved north. Like a thermometer left out in full sun.

Chief Farnesi was at the ballast board and he didn't care who thought what about him. 'He's driving right up our ass, XO. We've got to do something.'

'I'm aware of that, chief.' There were iron rules

in this business. Russian boats did not creep up on American boats. They were incapable of it. They were *targets*, not *hunters*.

Ping!... Ping!... Ping!

And another iron rule: it was *always* better to evade detection than torpedoes. Especially torpedoes that ran at two hundred knots. Unfortunately it was too late to avoid detection. Would he fire on them? *Now what?* He could turn, maneuver, try to shake them. But get into a cat and mouse game and it could go on for days. They'd never find Jameson's ship by dawn.

Ping!... Ping!... Ping!

'What's *Akula* mean, anyway?' asked one of the young sailors at the helm.

'Shark,' said Lieutenant Pena.

'I guess we're the USS *Sharkbait* now,' said another.

Ping!... Ping!... Ping!

Dive below the second layer. Run silent. Hide and hope he makes a mistake. 'Rig the boat for ultraquiet! Right full rudder! Full down on the planes. Make your depth five hundred feet.'

'Jesus, he had us knocked down and *nailed*,' said a torpedoman.

'The XO kicked Bam Bam out of the sonar shack,' said Red. 'You want to guess who's on the scopes?'

'Socks? Shit. That grape wouldn't hear a train if his head was on the tracks.'

'The train's coming and the whole fucking *boat* is on the tracks.'

Ping!... Ping!... Ping!

The torpedo room was large by submarine standards, but that still meant the torpedomen had to work around, even step over the men of Bravo squad.

They huddled around Lieutenant Rose Scavullo under the acoustic onslaught. She tried on one of their head mikes. It screened out the sonar's damning sound.

Stepik switched it on. 'Feel okay?'

She nodded. 'It's not as bad with these on.'

'Maybe the XO'll pass out ear muffs.'

Jameson walked over to the torpedo breech doors and whispered something in Russian.

'I hear you fine,' she answered.

Jameson took off his headset and returned to the conclave held beneath the portside torpedo loading tray. 'Okay. Let's hope the thunder and lightning are behind us. You'll be up on the bridge and–' but then he stopped.

The deck was rolling hard to starboard. Scavullo reached out and grabbed a torpedo tray as the submarine pushed over into a steep downhill plunge and the 1MC came alive: *'Now rig the ship for ultra quiet.'*

Portland dove away from the *Akula* like a pigeon who'd glimpsed the shadow of a hawk, seeking the protection of the deep thermocline. The pinging grew noticeably fainter, then stopped though why no one knew. Active sonar that close could burn through any layer.

'Maybe it broke,' said Chief Farnesi, but he was thinking something else. *They're toying with us.*

The subdued hum of normal operations swiftly

395

died away. Quiet became dead silent. Voices fell to whispers. Fans switched to their lowest setting. The big pumps circulating coolant to the reactor were shut down. Natural, noiseless convection would keep the nuclear kettle from overheating now.

A *Trident* missile boat is the gold standard when it comes to silence, but a slow, stealthy *Los Angeles* boat doesn't make much noise, either. Watson wished to remain hidden, and it was a matter of absolute faith that no one could find a well-run *Los Angeles* that wanted to hide.

'Depth now five hundred feet.'

Chief Farnesi hovered over the lights and indicators of the ballast control board. They'd dived for cover good and fast but it was a black mark on any submariner's soul to be ambushed. It wasn't supposed to be possible. Someone had screwed up and he didn't need to wonder too long to know who.

'Zero bubble,' said Watson. 'Maintain depth. Steady on heading one five zero.'

'Steady on one five zero, aye.'

Seven thousand tons of low-magnetic steel gradually lost forward speed until they were barely making knots against the prevailing current. Watson watched the gyro course repeater. When 150 showed, he said, 'Rudder amidships.' Momentum had brought them around and now the world's most sensitive submarine sonar was aimed right at the oncoming *Akula*.

'Sonar contact!' Niebel sang out. 'Bearing one eight zero, zero rate change and he's *close!*'

'Close isn't a range, Niebel,' said Watson.

'Inside two thousand yards. I'm starting to pick up flow and steam and tonals. He's an *Akula* for sure.'

'Speed?'

'Better than twenty five knots. He'll pass us to starboard.'

He had us, thought Watson. *But I shook him.*

K-335 *Gepard*

'Contact lost astern,' said Kureodov.

Leonov chuckled. 'Did you record everything? We'll want his soundprint in our library.' Recording an American submarine's acoustical signature was the modern equivalent of collecting scalps.

'The entire sequence is on tape, Captain.'

'Excellent. When we return to base we'll all have a story to tell. When someone whispers the Americans are unbeatable, you may feel free to correct them. Ahead dead slow. Let's give them a chance to catch up and then we'll burn their ears again.'

'Captain?' It was Kiselyev, the radio officer. 'We're coming up on a scheduled seance.'

He'd pinned the Americans to the mat. They were immobilized for the moment. *We might as well use it.* 'Helm? Five degrees rise on the planes. Come to periscope depth.'

Leonov jotted down a quick message as *Gepard* swam up to where the waves rocked her usually steady decks. He could well imagine what was going on aboard the American submarine. A Russian boat had come out of *nowhere* (unheard of!), forced the Americans to freeze in terror and then, as mysteriously as it had appeared, vanished. The Americans were not used to such rough treatment. What would they think? How would they explain it to themselves?

He handed a short, exulting note to Kiselyev:

1: ASW OPERATIONS SUCCESSFUL AGAINST AMERICAN SSN THIS POSITION

2: SIRENA COMPLETELY EFFECTIVE AT RANGES GREATER THAN 4000 METERS

3: UNLESS OTHERWISE DIRECTED, WE WILL CONTINUE TRACK AND TRAIL SSN AT COMBAT RANGE

The antenna rose, the radio officer sent Leonov's message up and copied a new broadcast from Moscow. Then, as the *Akula* sank back down to the quiet deeps, Kiselyev went to work decoding it.

'He might not be waiting for us back there,' said *Starpom* Stavinsky.

'He froze like a frightened rabbit,' said Leonov. His men smiled and slapped hands in appreciation for an unaccustomed victory. But it was curious. He'd half expected a more aggressive response. The American captain had been audacious enough to send an active ping his way. To be pinged, ranged, targeted. That was a bold move. This time the American had been timid.

'Captain?' it was Kiselyev. 'New message decoded.'

Leonov expected congratulations. Instead the new orders contained surprising information, and ended with a clear rebuke:

1: RADIO VOICE TRAFFIC INTERCEPT FROM TARGET UBXF *(CRISTI)* LOCATED NORTH IONIAN SEA, 80 KM SE CATANIA

2: TARGET REQUESTING RESCUE FROM AMERICAN NAVAL SHIP APACHE

3: LOCATE AND CONFIRM *CRISTI*'S STATUS

4: IF AFLOAT, DESTROY *CRISTI* PRIOR TO LANDFALL OR ANY, RPT, ANY RENDEZVOUS W/VESSELS OF ANY KIND

5: ALL MEASURES REQ'D TO COMPLETE THIS MISSION ARE AUTHORIZED

6: YOUR 'JUSTICE DONE' PREMATURE. DON'T STEP ON THE SAME RAKE TWICE

North Ionian Sea? thought Leonov. *Still afloat?* 'Kureodov. Is there any surface contact with the freighter we attacked?'

'The ship was destroyed, Captain. I heard her go down.'

Was there a second Cristi *out there?*

'Contact regained with the Americans, Captain!' said the Termite. 'Range fifteen thousand meters. Still moving northwest.'

'He's heading for the Ionian Sea,' said Leonov. He turned to Stavinsky. 'And so are we.'

399

CHAPTER TWENTY-SIX

THE WORDS OF FAITH

MV 'Nova Spirit'

When Musa heard they were going to be rescued by an American naval vessel he hurried to their small cabin and quickly shut the door. 'We're not going to Sicily any more, brother.'

Adnan opened one eye. He was feeling heavy and slow, and the constant pounding of the ship in the waves had given him a terrific headache. 'Malta?'

'Guantanamo Bay.' He explained their hopes to strike the enemies of faith would be thwarted, not by bombs and bullets but by the idiotic generosity of the Americans themselves. 'When they find out who we are they'll put us all in cages.'

So what if they did? Adnan was sure the invisible army they would bring along in their blood and breath would not stay locked away. But there was a more troubling possibility: quarantine. *They could keep us on this ship until we die.* He sat up in his cot, wincing against heavy, liquid pain that sloshed against the inside of his skull. 'If we can't bring this weapon to them, perhaps the Americans will take it for us.'

'How?'

'By trusting in God and using the right words.'

'What words, brother?'

'The ones our faith commands of us. Come. I will show you a library full of them.'

Captain Warsame stood atop the ladder that once led down to the fantail deck. No more. The stern had settled and green seas and white foam rushed around the base of the ladder now, burying the deck and the engine room hatch cover. The corroded jackstaff with its Tongan flag had long since been carried away.

To Warsame it seemed the sea had been transformed. Gone were the rolling black waves raked with white spindrift. They'd become sheer, looming cliffs, white avalanches that exploded like bombs against his ship. He looked up at Walid, the lookout he'd sent up to watch for the Americans.

Walid huddled against the radar mast and waved back, but weakly. The young able-bodied seaman from Karachi had never been seasick in his life, but he was sick tonight. He'd emptied his stomach onto the wheelhouse roof. The rain and spray washed the deck clear but left him feeling no better.

The motions of the ship were more violent up high and he was fully exposed to the elements. It was all he could do to keep his cigarette lit against the wind and rain. His head felt heavy and his throat burned with bile. Though the rain was cold his neck and shoulders were hot. His fingers tingled with strange electricity.

Once, when the ship rolled especially hard Walid felt an almost irresistible urge to let go, to fly off into the night. Was that yielding to God's will, or defying it? It scared him so badly he took off his belt, wrapped it around a stay and fastened it to his waist.

Warsame's eye told him they had no more than a few hours left, and that was only if the hull stayed together. They were taking the seas hard: the whole ship had pivoted around until she took the brunt of the storm from astern. It steadied the freighter's drunken pitches and rolls. The men gathered in the galley might appreciate it but Warsame was worried. Seas were breaking against the engine room hatch. If it failed any air trapped beneath would escape. The stern would flood all the way up to the main deck and they would almost certainly go down before *Apache* could arrive. Would it?

God knows.

Warsame sensed someone standing behind him. He was surprised when he saw who it was.

'*Will it get any worse?*' Salafi had to shout above the shriek of wind and the tumbling roar of the waves.

Warsame wasn't sure what the Saudi meant but there was one answer that covered most of the likely possibilities: '*Of course!*'

Salafi ducked back into the aft bridge door to shelter from the rain. He'd seen foul weather before. Desert cloudbursts, sand storms that could strip the paint off a brand-new car in minutes. Blizzards in the Alps that trapped him inside a well-equipped and agreeable chalet.

But a storm at sea was built to a different scale. Or even, he thought, an *indifferent* one. The waves, the wind, the way the ship was thrown about said that what happened to the freighter, to this crew, to him, was utterly beside the point. There was no shelter, no negotiations, no deals. No anxious concierge calling to reassure him that workers were busy clearing the snow. Here was something far beyond anything Salafi had ever seen, felt, tasted. Or feared. He leaned outside and shouted, *'How much longer until they come for us?'*

'Just finding us will be difficult enough, and then–' But Warsame stopped, turned and listened hard. There was a new sound, the muffled *crack!* of the hull starting to split. *'Go to the lifeboat and wait!'* He pushed by Salafi and ran to the top of the ladderwell, listening.

'What is it?' asked Salafi.

'Go to the lifeboat!' said Warsame, and he turned his back and charged down the ladderwell to the cabin deck.

Salafi waited. The ship didn't seem in any more danger now than a few moments ago. And surely a radio would be a useful thing to have? He scooped up the shortwave set, wondering how fresh the batteries were, but he didn't wait to hunt for new ones. Salafi figured that a captain ought to know when the time had come to run.

He opened the door to the bridge wing where their one and only lifeboat hung from rusted davits. The open door funneled in rain and wind and spray. How were they going to lower it? And how would they keep it from capsizing in these seas? It seemed much smaller tonight than it had yesterday. Would they all even fit? He shut the door and waited for the others to come.

And wait he did. When too much time had

passed Salafi began to wonder if they'd found another way off the ship. Had they all jumped into a raft on the protected side? Had they left him behind? He could keep an eye on the boat from here. But not the captain.

He abandoned his post and went to the ladderwell. The iron house was blacked out. Even the emergency lamps were dead. He started down, feeling his way. It was like negotiating a cold, dark crypt in a violent earthquake. When his hand touched the edge of a wall, he turned and found the railing leading down to the galley.

The thump and crash of waves striking the stern were louder now. So were the angry voices coming from the galley. Its comforting smells of food and warmth were gone. In their place were sharp, rancid odors of bile, sweat and oil smoke.

Salafi paused at the door and looked inside.

The room was dimly lit with a single kerosene lamp. Eight sailors were gathered at the single long table. Warsame was bent over, listening to one of his crew speak. Salafi recognized Gul Hassan, a rough, boisterous oiler from the engine room who took offense easily and settled matters with his fists. Rafik the cabin boy was actually wiping down the metal counter as though it could possibly matter now.

Two other sailors were huddled beneath the carved wooden bar. Hazil the helmsman was unconscious, his legs drawn up, Naim, the sailor who was to have relieved him at the wheel, dabbed at his hot forehead with a cool, wet rag.

Shadowed faces looked up, eyes glittering in the flickering yellow light. They didn't look frightened. Or at least, not *only* frightened.

Captain Warsame said, 'Your two men tried to shoot Gul Hassan. He is not very happy about it.'

'The little one with his fancy beard tried to put a bullet in me,' said Gul Hassan. 'The fool forgot that bullets bounce off steel decks. He pulled the trigger and it flew around the cabin like a hornet. Too bad it didn't sting him.'

'But why would he shoot at you?'

'Go ask him,' said Gul Hassan.

'Where are Adnan and Musa now?'

'Maybe they went for a swim. Like your Russian friend,' said Gul Hassan. 'Come. Let's take a walk on deck and we'll look.'

A steep wave struck the stern hard enough to send something more solid than spray against the iron house. There was something large and hungry out there and it was hammering to get in. Salafi had no desire to go meet it.

'Where are Adnan and Musa?' Salafi asked again.

'The fifth cabin. They broke in,' said Warsame. 'We need help from the Americans and they're arming themselves to fight.'

Salafi thought, *Americans?* 'You said there was a ship coming.'

'A United States Navy ship,' said Warsame.

'Navy? But that's impossible.'

'For all our sakes, I hope you're wrong,' said Warsame.

'The sheep is afraid of being locked up with wolves,' Gul Hussan snarled.

No. Salafi had larger worries than being locked up with Adnan and Musa. A Saudi national with diplomatic papers could talk himself out of anything. Oil calmed even the stormiest waters.

But the American military had a simpler view of right and wrong. You couldn't solve problems with an envelope stuffed with cash. You couldn't call up a friend who would whisper to an admiral that one of his ships should sail the other way. No. Some American captain would wonder why a Saudi was riding such a ship, and with such men. There would be no room for maneuver, no chance at whispered threats. Salafi would be on his way to Guantanamo Bay. And if the Americans didn't think this way at first, Adnan and Musa with their holy war would make sure they would.

Unless I speak to the Americans first.

What would they make of news that their good friends in Riyadh were reaching for a biological weapon to hold against the world's throat? A kind of nuclear deterrent in a glass vial? Or *four* glass vials?

The more he thought about it the more sensible it seemed. An American military hospital would be as good as any in Riyadh and unlike the House of Saud, the Americans would have an excellent reason to keep him alive and talking.

Sami Salafi had made a career of serving the interests of the highest bidder. Radical, conservative. Wahhabi, Shiite, believer or infidel. It made no difference. Naturally, the Saudis had the deepest pockets on earth, but if the Americans wanted to save him, why should he stand in their way?

'Go talk to them,' said Warsame. 'Tell them to throw the weapons into the sea or we'll leave them to fight their war alone.'

'No,' said a new voice.

Adnan stood outside in the dim passage. He wore a seaman's dirty khaki pants and a dark overcoat that seemed oddly padded with solid-looking lumps. Ammunition? Grenades? He had a pistol thrust in his belt. The knife was somewhere; he never went anywhere without it.

Gul Hassan could hardly contain himself. 'Look! Here is the holy warrior brave enough to shoot at an unarmed man. I wonder how brave you'll be shooting bullets at a battleship?'

'You're still alive,' said Adnan. He looked at Warsame. 'How long before the Americans come?'

'An hour, maybe less. Finding us in these seas will be hard. Rigging a tow will be harder.'

'Perhaps we can save them the trouble,' said Adnan.

USNS *Apache*
North Ionian Sea

Captain Albert Hunt, master of the Fleet Ocean Tug *Apache,* climbed back up to his spacious bridge with a fresh mug of coffee. Normally, a source of pleasure but tonight it reminded him of the crew of the stricken *Nova Spirit.* Riding a sinking ship in a gale, no power, no heat, no hot food. *If they're not already in the water.*

He walked over to the barometer and wind gauges. *Pressure's still falling and the wind is starting to back to the southeast.* That didn't surprise him. The center of the *gregale* was near, and the latest

407

satellite imagery even showed the beginnings of a small eye; a scale model hurricane sized for these smaller waters. *We'd better rig that tow fast.* The winds and waves would likely kick up. 'Gene?' he said to the second mate at the ship's wheelstand. 'Ring all ahead full.'

'All ahead full, aye.' Gene Morrissey ran the engine telegraph handles forward. Two big General Motors diesels sent their distinctive crackling roar up the twin stacks.

Hunt walked over to the spinning clearscreen and looked down on a world of steep, breaking waves that rose up and burst around *Apache's* high bow.

At two hundred and forty feet long, forty-two in the beam and displacing just over two thousand tons, *Apache* was built along the sturdy lines of an oilfield workboat. She was about the same size as the disabled *Nova Spirit*, but that was their only similarity. She was one of five oceangoing tugs leased to the Military Sealift Command to support the ships of the United States Navy. *Apache* was bulldog tough, powerful and equipped with tow gear able to haul anything afloat through nearly any weather.

Other than a .45 automatic kept locked away in the captain's safe and an old M14 rifle used to protect divers from inquisitive sharks, she was unarmed. Navy divers occasionally rode her but tonight, the sixteen men of her crew were all civilians.

'Anything from La Mad?' asked Morrissey. By that he meant the United States Navy base at La Maddalena, Sardinia.

'Small, old, Tonga-registered and Lebanese-owned,' said Captain Hunt. 'And they can't send out a helicopter until tomorrow morning.'

'She could go down before then,' said the second mate. 'What about the Italians?'

'They might send out a cutter tomorrow if we still need one.'

'That's bullshit.'

'That's the Italians. Radar working?'

'Got Cape Correnti to the northwest but nothing looking south. Tom looked her up in *Lloyd's List*,' he said, meaning *Apache's* Chief Mate Tom Stone. '*Nova Spirit's* a small target on a good day. Not much above the waterline except a cargo crane. Basically, she's junk, but I'll take her.'

'What's that supposed to mean?'

'I missed out on that rescue you guys made last year by *one week*.'

Apache had pulled four civilians off a sinking sailboat out in the middle of the Atlantic last year. This was a simpler matter, so long as they found the ship in time. The open ocean was not *Nova Spirit's* only concern. The gale was pushing her into the Gulf of Noto. It was a shallow bay named after a Sicilian city, but with another and more appropriate meaning: *Gulf of the South Winds*. It was surely living up to its name tonight. 'How far out do you figure they are?'

'No more than twenty miles.'

'Maybe we'll get lucky. Light 'em up,' said Hunt. Finding a whole ship in these seas was hard enough. Finding lifejackets and bobbing heads would be a real bitch. *Apache* had a rigid inflatable ship's boat that could handle these seas but Hunt didn't look forward to using it.

The second mate switched on an eighteen-inch million candlepower spotlight mounted atop the bridge, reached up, grabbed a brass handle and swept the white beam across a black and angry sea.

MV 'Nova Spirit'

A faint light sparked at the edge of Walid's vision. His first thought was that the captain had caught him with his eyes shut against the wind and salt spray, but when he shielded his face he saw it again, and more clearly.

The crescent moon had ripped a ragged slit in the low, scudding clouds. It grew brighter, then dimmed, then vanished as the hole knitted itself shut. Was the storm passing? The wind still moaned through the radar mast but it was no longer trying to push him over the side. That was good, because Walid wasn't sure that he had the strength to get down off this high deck and... *What?*

Another light! It seemed to probe and sweep. If it wasn't a lighthouse, if they weren't about to run aground on some rock-jawed shoal, then it was a *ship!*

'Allah u akbar!' Walid yelled. *God was Great*, and never had he meant the words more. He grabbed the flare pistol, raised it high over his head and pulled the trigger. *'Allah u akbar!'*

An orange spark flew off into the wind. Walid was sure it would be swallowed by the storm, the

410

rain, the clouds, but then it blossomed into an intense white fire bright enough to cast the shadow of his frantically waving arms onto the deck.

'*Allah u akbar!*' There were men out there who would save him. He would see his family again. If Walid couldn't find the words to give thanks for that, then what was God for?

USNS *Apache*

'Flare,' said Gene Morrissey. 'Two points off the port bow. Radar's starting to pick up a return out there, too.'

'Let's see if their radio's working.' Hunt took the microphone down from the overhead clip and pressed the transmit bar. '*Apache* calling *Nova Spirit*. *Apache* calling *Nova Spirit*. We have your flare in sight. Are you guarding Channel Sixteen?'

'Yes!' It was Warsame. 'Thank God we can see your light!'

'What's your situation with fire and flooding?'

'The fire is out and the flooding is under control. But we have no power and there are many injured!'

Hunt looked at his second mate. 'You hear that?'

'Don't let Hub know. He'll grab his bag and swim over there like a Saint Bernard if you'd let him.'

'Hub' was Third Mate Francis Hubbard. He'd been a hospitalman in the regular Navy and had put in papers to leave the merchant marine to attend medical school. *Apache* was too small to

411

have her own doctor, but Hub was the next best thing. Two of the four sailors they'd pulled off that sinking yacht were half-dead with hypothermia. Hub saved them.

'The injured, they are in a bad condition!' Warsame pleaded.

Captain Hunt didn't answer. He was glad to rig a tow and keep that ship off the rocks until the Italians could send out a cutter. But taking injured men on board in bad weather was a risky proposition. He clicked the mike. 'How many casualties, *Nova Spirit?*'

'My engineer is dead and my best helmsman, he is unconscious. We have six hurt. We can lower our lifeboat and bring them over to you.'

Hunt didn't answer.

'It's your call, Captain,' said Gene. 'If you ask me, you let a few guys come over the whole crew will jump in with them.'

The radio speaker came alive. 'Are you still there, *Apache?*'

'Get the tow gear ready, Gene,' said Hunt. 'We'll back down on them from the south, put her in our lee and fire a line. I want to take a real close look to see what we're in for before I decide about any visits.'

'Aye aye, skipper,' said the second mate. 'But if we do send the boat, I'd sure like to take her over.'

Warsame said, 'Are you there, *Apache?*'

'Stand by, *Nova Spirit,*' said Hunt. 'Put all your able bodied on deck at your bow. We'll fire a line over. You'll have to haul in the cable bridle through your bow chocks and make the ends fast to something good and solid. Can you do that?'

'Yes, but our injured! What about them?'

'Once we have you on tow we'll figure that out.'

There was a pause, then Warsame said, 'God is great! America is great! We are blessed! Thank you!'

Hunt hung the mike back up. 'Steer one seven zero.'

'One seven zero aye.' Gene spun the wheel and the powerful tug charged across the breaking waves.

Hunt grabbed a pair of binoculars. 'Put the light on him. Not the bridge. He's got enough problems without being blinded.'

The beam lanced out. Hunt followed it with his glasses and caught *Nova Spirit as* a wave rolled up her fantail and broke against her aft house in a billow of wind-driven foam. The walkie-talkie squawked. He put the glasses down. 'Bridge.'

'Bridle plate's bolted up. Deck's ready for towing.' It was Tom Stone, *Apache's* chief mate down on the low work deck aft. It was a wet place to be tonight. 'Are we backing down on them?'

'That's the idea. As soon as we put them in our lee, fire the line. They'll be waiting at the bow.' He thought about the wave he'd seen break right over her stern. 'Better rig the cargo net, too. Someone might end up in the water. Who's down there with you?'

'Hub, Delfus, Rankin and Polacco.'

'All right. Stand by.' Hunt put the radio down and took up his glasses again. 'Steer one eight zero. Engines ahead half.'

'One eight zero on a half bell. You know what, captain, this is gonna' make some real good PR.

413

Especially after all those stories about how we torture prisoners. Apache *Saves Arab Crew from Certain Death.*'

'No one will believe a word of it.'

Apache shouldered her way by the derelict ship close enough for Hunt to see crewmen scrambling to the bow to receive the tow line.

'I count four guys at the wave shield.'

'Captain's in his bridge, one dead plus six casualties. That could be every one he's got left.'

'Steer one nine zero. Ahead one third.' He put the walkie-talkie to his lips. 'Tom? You set?'

'Cargo net is out. Rig is set. Deck is ready.'

Hunt turned to his second mate. 'Okay, Gene. Spin up the thrusters.' *Apache* had two powerful auxiliary engines for close-in maneuvering. Tonight he would use them to keep his ship oriented to take the wind and the waves so that *Nova Spirit* would not have to.

Hunt gauged the distance between the two ships with a practiced eye. Too close and they might be driven together and collide. Too far and they'd never get a line across. The wind-whipped water between the two ships subsided as the tug took the brunt of the storm. 'All right. She's falling in our lee. Secure the engines. Switch to the thrusters.' *Here we go.*

CHAPTER TWENTY-SEVEN

CONTACT

USS *Portland*
Sicilian Escarpment

'Sonar contact bearing three five zero,' said Niebel. 'Twin screws making twelve knots. Designate him Sierra Sixty-Three.'

Merchant ship, thought Watson. And not the right one. *Cristi* was single-screw. 'Range?' he asked, though without much interest.

'Outside seventeen thousand yards. No rate change. We'd need to run a few legs to know for ... stand by.' Niebel had sent the new contact through their soundprint library, searching for a match. The computer found one. 'Archive has a match. Evaluate Sierra Sixty-Three as a Navy fleet ocean tug of the *Powhatan* class. Could be any one of five hull numbers, though. They all have similar sound cuts.'

'A Navy tug?' said Watson. 'What's she up to out here?'

'They carry a civilian crew,' said Chief Farnesi from his perch at the ballast board. 'I knew a diver who rode one. I bet Bam Bam could come up with a hull number for you.'

'We don't need a number,' said Watson. 'Nav? How much water do we have under the keel?'

'A good thousand fathoms,' said Pardee. 'We'll have deep water so long as we keep this side of the Sicilian Escarpment. The Gulf of Noto is due north and it shallows up pretty fast.'

'Conn, Sonar. Still no bearing change. Signal strength is growing. Range now estimated at fifteen thousand eight hundred yards.'

He's coming right at us, thought Watson. 'Helm. Right five degrees rudder. Steady on new course of zero one zero.'

The new course put the tug on a divergent bearing. The vertical line of sound that represented her on Niebel's broadband screen shifted and *Portland's* fire control computers made quick work of calculating a solid, solution.

'Conn, Sonar. Sierra Sixty-Three's range now confirmed at twelve thousand yards, course one eight five, and he just cut engines.' Niebel listened hard. The tug's engines had died but she was making *some* kind of a noise; it sounded like nothing so much as a giant blender starting, stopping, and starting again inside some hollow, echoing chamber. *Boomy* is what Bam Bam would call it. *What is that thing?*

'He's just drifting?' asked Watson.

'He's running *something* but I can't figure out what.'

'XO?' said Chief Farnesi. 'Maybe we ought to have–'

'All right,' said Watson. 'Have the messenger of the watch go wake up Mister Schramm and have him listen in.'

Bam Bam had been expecting some kind of

summons ever since he sidled into his rack and pulled the blue curtain shut. People did dumb things on submarines all the time. But Bam Bam had never heard of an American boat getting pinged without knowing it was coming. In other words, someone screwed up. Sooner or later, word would get out.

It was the XO's fault. The question in Bam Bam's mind was, how was he going to convince anyone back home? There'd be a 'lessons learned' investigation that would be run by some gold-braided Academy graduate who'd make sure Choo Choo came out better than he deserved. He'd be called a victim of 'unforeseeable events' or a 'communications breakdown' that would hand half the blame to Schramm.

Well fuck that. If they tried to blow sanitaries on *him* Bam Bam would open the ball valve wide and let it all fly. Academy ring or no, Watson was going to be wearing some shit. He dialed up the ship's country and western audio channel and was listening with half an ear to Garth Brooks when the curtain was yanked open.

'Hey, rise and shine,' said the messenger of the watch. 'Skipper wants you back in sonar.'

'How come?'

'Mister Watson didn't say but there's a target up there that's acting weird.'

'Is there.' Schramm catapulted himself sideways out of his rack, remembered to put on his shoes and socks, and hurried up to the sonar shack.

'What's going on?' he asked Niebel.

'Take a listen.' Niebel offered his headset.

Bam Bam took his own custom phones down

from the bulkhead, jacked in and listened. 'What is she?'

'Sound cut archive matches a fleet tug.'

'That makes sense. She's using thrusters to maneuver. The *Akula* ever show up?'

'Nah. We lost him.'

How would you know? 'Play the work tape for me.'

Schramm listened to the entire encounter from the moment the tug appeared on the northern horizon. He heard the out-of-synch swish of the tug's twin screws. He heard something else, too. Faint, and easily overlooked against the backdrop of a noisy, turbulent sea. But every time that tug's screw's *swished* a fainter *swash* came echoing back a few seconds later.

'Sonar, Conn,' said Watson. 'Any idea what that tug is doing?'

Niebel was about to answer but Schramm took the mike. 'Conn, Sonar. That buzzing noise is coming from a pair of thrusters. I think the tug is keeping station on something.'

'We're not holding any other targets.'

You didn't see that Akula, either. 'I'd lay odds she's not alone.'

Tony Watson thought, *Another ship?* 'Why aren't we hearing it?'

I am, asshole. 'She could be adrift, XO. Maybe the tug is coming to her assistance.'

And maybe, thought Watson, Bam Bam is building more elaborate scenarios based on hot air. He was about to tell him to stick to what he knew when he thought, *What if he's right?* He knew there would be questions to answer about that

Akula. It wouldn't do to add any more fuel to that fire, and if he could keep track of all the times Bam Bam used *guesswork* instead of *evidence,* well, that would make them easier to answer, wouldn't it? He turned aft. 'Nav? How far are we from the search track on that target of interest?'

'Still twenty, thirty miles away, XO,' said Pardee.

Radar sweep, he concluded. They'd rise up shallow enough to see if there really *were* two ships, and if they found one adrift he'd take a closer look. He reached up and took the 1MC microphone and clicked it. 'Lieutenant Jameson to the Conn.' He paused, then clicked it again. 'Secure all gear adrift. Stand by for heavy rolls.'

He smiled. They were almost the exact words that had brought *Portland* to near calamity in the Atlantic. But this time would be different: Watson would do a professional job. He turned to the Chief of the Watch at the ballast board. 'We'll go up twenty thousand pounds heavy and maintain depth control with planes and power.'

'Twenty K it is, XO,' said Farnesi.

'And have the messenger of the watch make sure Commander Steadman is strapped down. We may have a bit of a rough ride.'

'I'll do that.'

Watson turned. COB Browne stood at the forward port side door. Chief Cooper, the boat's corpsman, was with him. 'I wish our radios healed as fast as you, COB.'

'Thanks, XO. It's nice to be back, too,' said Browne. 'Mind if I have a look at things?'

'Come ahead.'

419

Browne knew the layout of the control room right down to the smallest detail. He could *run* through this space blindfolded. He made a slow, deliberate circuit, seeming to check everything as he went.

'Chief,' he said to Farnesi as he stopped at the ballast board.

'Good to see you back, COB.' Chief Farnesi noticed that he looked a bit glazed, and that he didn't comment at the handwritten note *twenty K heavy* he'd posted above the ballast board.

Browne turned to face the padded rail where he expected Watson to be, but was not. 'What about that *Akula?*'

'Gone.' Watson was looking into the AVSDU repeater, a few feet away from where COB's head was pointed. 'I haven't consulted any crystal balls but I think we've seen the last of him.'

Browne shifted slightly. 'Be nice to *know,* wouldn't it?'

USNS *Apache*

A good tow is a low tow, and *Apache's* work deck, where her winches, cable spools and cranes were mounted was built low and flat to the water. There was scarcely anything between a sailor's feet and the sea. Tonight, despite the tug's bow taking the brunt of the waves it was a cold, wet place to be.

Tom Stone, *Apache's* chief mate, watched the helpless freighter loom out of the night as the tug backed down on her. He could feel the deck vibrate under his boots as the thrusters fought to keep them properly aligned. It was working; the sea between the two ships was no longer raked white by the wind. 'Delfus! Get ready!'

Seaman Delfus was at the rails with the line thrower; an M-14 rifle with a cable can attached below the muzzle. Inside it was several hundred yards of very light, very strong Kevlar line attached to a finned projectile equipped with a chemical light. Delfus was safety-clipped to the rail, and with good reason; when the tug took a wave badly he was up to his knees in foam.

Third Mate Hubbard was back at the cable spool checking the shackles and chains on the triangular flounder plate. The braided steel lines of the bridle were bolted to two corners of the plate. A shackle at the end of a yellow haul line was snapped to the third. Its other end was connected to the line-thrower's light painter. True to form, Hub had a large, waterproof medical supply bag strapped to his back.

Seamen Rankin and Polacco were fighting to keep the haul line in a neat coil but each time a sea surged over the gunwales it shifted dangerously around their boots. It would be very easy to find yourself pulled over the side on a night like this.

The chief mate huddled under the ship's rigid inflatable boat, using it as a wind block. The wide avenue of sea that separated the two ships narrowed. Two football fields. One.

Closer, he could see that *Nova Spirit's* stern was a surf zone. Waves were breaking hard against the iron house. From the low vantage of *Apache's* work deck, the freighter's bow seemed to be

421

climbing an invisible wave into the sky. Dim yellow light flickered through a few portholes. He unclipped his radio. 'Bridge. Deck. We're coming in good.'

'Your call, Tom,' said Captain Hunt.

One hundred fifty yards.

Hub gave the thumb's up. The bridle was ready.

One hundred yards.

'Rankin! Polacco!' he yelled to the two seamen. 'Stand clear!'

The two seamen jumped away from the nylon haul rope and scrambled up beside Stone.

Eighty

'Fire!'

Delfus raised the M-14, pointed it at the looming shape of the dark freighter and pulled the trigger. There was a loud *crack* that the wind quickly sucked away, and the green glowing dart flew out across the water trailing Kevlar line. It struck the freighter's wave shield and caromed high into the air. The wind caught it and streamed it right over the hull and into the water on the far side.

The men on the stricken ship grabbed it and started hauling.

'Bridge,' said Stone. 'We're in business.'

USS *Portland*

Jameson joined Watson at the navigation table. 'It's too soon.'

'Our chief magician thinks he heard two ships up there and I think we're obliged to rule it in or out.'

422

Jameson acknowledged the point. 'How sure is he?'

'Bam Bam is always certain about his guesses.'

Jameson smiled. 'How long will it take?'

'One radar sweep,' said Watson. 'But we'll have to conic to periscope depth.'

'If it's *Cristi*, that Navy tug is in for some trouble.'

Watson snatched the 1MC mic. 'All stations prepare for periscope depth. Radar operator. Stand by to raise your mast.'

Steadman was still sleeping off the effects of Cooper's sedative. The corpsman checked the bandaged burns on his right hand, listened to his heart, took his blood pressure and pronounced him still alive.

'What's it going to take to get him on his feet?' asked Browne.

'A miracle.'

'I'm serious, son. The boat needs him. Can't you bring him out?'

'Look, COB, he took more juice than you did. He was the wire connecting Zeus with planet earth, okay? If it were up to me we'd be flanking to the nearest port with a good hospital.'

'You tell the XO that?'

'Mister Watson ain't callin' the shots. The SEALs are.'

'Son,' said Browne, 'that's why I want Commander Steadman back on his feet.'

CHAPTER TWENTY-EIGHT

BATTLE STATIONS TORPEDO

USS *Portland*

'Eighty feet,' said Lieutenant Pena. 'All stations ready for periscope depth.'

Watson turned to Farnesi. 'Chief?'

'We're at plus twenty thousand pounds.'

Good. Steadman hadn't ballasted down enough in the Atlantic. Watson would show how this evolution *should* be done. 'Helm? Five degrees up on the planes.'

Jameson stood beside Watson at the forward railing of the periscope stand. Two officers of the deck, not one.

'Seventy feet.'

There was a shudder, the deck heeled, then righted.

No matter the storm's developing eye, or that it was perfectly capable of sinking *Nova Spirit*. A Mediterranean *gregale* is no Atlantic hurricane. When *Portland* rose up into a Force Eight gale, the ride was uncomfortable, not cataclysmic. There were steep pitches and hard rolls, but nothing compared to what she'd already survived.

'Sixty feet.'

'Make turns for four knots.'

'Four knots, aye,' said Lieutenant Pena.

'Radar operator, extend the mast,' said Watson, though he wondered if it would. The split hydraulic line he'd found had been repaired. But there were a great many similar pipes and valves buried up beneath the sail that he could not physically inspect. Would the external hydraulics function?

An Electronics Technician sat before the radar console. His hand went to a rocker switch with RAISE to the left and LOWER to the right. He snapped it to the left. 'In-motion light is illuminated,' he said.

The hydraulics are good, thought Watson.

The radar console was dominated by a large glass screen, a few controls for setting range rings and scales, digital range and bearing windows. The screen was dark one moment, and then, with a green flicker, it came alive. The tip of the mast had broken the surface. Then, 'Radar target bearing three five zero at nine thousand six hundred yards. Designate Romeo Five.'

'Just one ship?' said Watson.

'Single target, XO.'

So much for Schramm's theories. 'Sonar, Conn,' said Watson. 'Any more guesses you'd like to share with us?'

'I guess not, XO.' *So where did that echo come from?*

'Radar operator. Retract the mast,' said Watson. 'We're done.' He turned to Jameson. 'Looks like you can stand down your team.'

The radar ET's hand went back to the rocker switch. This time he snapped it to the right. The red RAISE light went out. But the green LOWER

425

stayed dark. 'Ah, something's hung up,' he said. 'The mast appears jammed.'

'Rock it until it frees.' Why did he always have to do their thinking for them? As the operator clicked the rocker back and forth, Watson called up a mental blueprint of the complex hydraulics that operated the mast and pondered how much pressure to shunt up there to overcome the binding.

But as his mind was filled with schematics and option trees, the radar head kept up its steady sweep.

USNS *Apache*

The wide, staring eyes of Hunt's big binoculars were focused on the flounder plate as it emerged from the water at *Nova Spirit's* bow. He followed the darting figures of her crew as they made the bridle cables fast. *Seas fifteen feet at twelve seconds,* he thought. It was vital to let out the proper length of tow line. Get it wrong and the two ships would be 'out of step' with one another and the stress would snap the tow line. 'They're on tow. Secure the spinners. Right full rudder. All ahead half.'

The second mate swung the wheel over and advanced both throttles. White foam boiled at *Apache's* stern as the tug bustled off.

Hunt opened the log and jotted down. *Freighter Nova Spirit on tow forty miles east Cape Correnti, steaming south, seas fifteen-twenty, gale Force Eight.*

Watson was about to summon the A-Gang leading chief to find out how much additional hydraulic pressure the external loop could take when the radar operator shouted out,

'XO? Radar now holds *two* targets.'

Watson went over to the radar console. The operator was right: it had changed: the one large radar target was now two smaller ones. Watson felt a ghost of his past hesitations return. How could it happen? What was the technical explanation? He walked aft to the starboard Type 18 periscope. They were already at the correct depth. There was no reason not to take a look.

'Snap visual. Up the search scope,' he told the quartermaster of the watch, who trained the rising scope into a three five zero bearing.

Watson crouched low as the periscope rose. The break between water and sky was a lot more subtle at night, and the waves blurred it even more. But when the surge of roiled water fell away and the view through the eyepiece cleared, the night-vision circuitry built into the Type 18 left little doubt. Watson was seeing two ships, not one.

He pressed the trigger to put it all on tape, then dialed in as much magnification as the dim light would allow. 'Down scope. Helm. Make your depth four hundred feet. Turns for six knots.' He turned to Jameson. 'You'd better take a good look at this.'

USNS *Apache*

Hunt clicked his walkie-talkie. 'Tom? Pay out two hundred and set a soft brake. Let's see how they do.' He figured two hundred yards would make a nice catenary loop that would absorb the freighter's motion like an underwater shock absorber, and it was in the ballpark for keeping both ships in step in these seas. Though they were separated by hundreds of yards, both ships had to rise and fall together.

The tow line steamed and smoked as it ran out through the chafe sleeve at *Apache's* stern. The tug drew quickly away from *Nova Spirit*. When Hunt's eye told him the right moment had come, he ordered a turn into the wind.

'Left full rudder.'

'Left full rudder, aye.'

'Rudder amidships. Put the spot on her bow.'

The second mate trained the brilliant spotlight onto *Nova Spirit's* blunt bow.

There! A white line of foam marked the freighter's bow. She was coming along. *This is going to work,* thought Hunt. 'Ahead two thirds.'

The tow line drew taut. The tug shuddered and strained. Then the screws dug into the sea and caught. *Nova Spirit's* bow swung around to the south into the seas.

USS *Portland*

There was a knock on Steadman's door. Browne shouted, 'Come!'

428

It was Bam Bam.

Browne nodded to Cooper for a little help. He knew *someone* was standing there but he sure didn't know *who*.

'Hey, Bam Bam,' said the boat's corpsman. 'What's up?'

'I was hoping to talk to the skipper.' He looked down at Steadman.

'Talk to me,' said Browne. 'What's on your mind?'

'COB, I think we're getting into some deep shit again. The XO called me out of my rack to listen to something. Sonar picked up a fleet tug, twin screws. Not our target. But I kept hearing echoes.'

'The *Akula?*'

'Not unless she was sitting on the surface a couple hundred yards from a US Navy fleet tug.'

'So what's making that echo, Bam Bam?'

'Another ship. Real quiet, like maybe drifting with his engines off.'

'Keep talking.'

'The XO said I was full of it, but he went up and did a radar sweep.'

'Let me guess,' said Browne. 'Two ships?'

'So close the radar painted only one at first.'

'We know who she is?'

'The freighter the SEALs were supposed to take down off Crete. They're having a powwow in the wardroom now. Look, I'm no fan of those guys, but if that Russian boat's still around the SEALs will be walking onto another target. Only nobody knows shit because the XO won't let me run the sonar program that will let us see what the *Akula* is up to. You know what happened a

429

few hours back, right?'

He pinged us. 'I do.' Browne managed to say just two words and mean, *And it was disgraceful.* Browne turned to Cooper. 'Chief? How's the skipper coming?'

'Heart's good, pressure's good. His burns are dressed but they'll hurt like the worst sunburn he ever got when he wakes up.'

'Broken bones? Internal injuries?'

'No bones broken but I can't *see* inside him, COB.'

'I can,' said Browne. 'And what I see is this: *Portland* needs a good captain right now more than she needs a good engineer.'

'You're asking me to wake him up?'

'I'm telling you to.'

Chief Cooper opened his bag, pulled out a small glass vial and a disposable needle. He uncapped the plunger and the tip, plunged the needle through the vial's rubber cap and sucked down a dose.

'What about that sonar program, COB?' asked Bam Bam.

Browne turned. 'Once we're on the roof to let those SEALs off, sonar's not going to be worth shit. Not in those waves.'

'So?'

'Get that program ready to run the *instant* we're surfaced. Run the work tape through it. Find that *Akula.*'

'On what authority?'

'Commander Steadman's.'

'Hang on, COB,' said Chief Cooper, 'You don't know when the skipper's going to come out, or

430

what condition he'll be in. And you *sure* don't know what he'll say.'

'That's true. There's a lot I believe in that I don't *know*. Faith carries the load when knowledge falls short. The Bible says that's the very definition of faith.'

'But it could be hours. This stuff isn't science, COB. It's art.'

'And that,' said Browne, 'is the very definition of *command*.'

Jameson followed Watson down to the wardroom and shut the door. Watson pointed a remote at the flat screen and clicked it.

The screen made a soft crackling sound and came alive with a startlingly clear view of a tugboat's high, flared bow and some of her port side. She was facing the periscope but it was clear she was turning away, her hull elongating until it was possible to see all the way to her aft deck.

'Hull number 172,' said Watson. 'That makes her the USNS *Apache*, a Military Sealift Command ship. Not quite Navy, not quite civilian. Two hundred twenty feet long, forty-two in the beam. She displaces 2300 tons and she can make sixteen knots. Crew of fifteen though she can carry twenty more in a pinch.'

The view shifted to the right.

It was very nearly a copy of the ship they'd assaulted off Andikithira: the same blunt bow, the same tall cargo crane amidships, aft house and single stack. Even the same rust streaks weeping from her portholes and scuppers. But there were several differences. This ship's decks were clear of cargo and she was so down by the stern that waves washed right up over her fantail.

'Why is that tug messing around with my target?' asked Jameson.

'Your target's drifting and down at the stern. If she sent out a distress call the tug captain was obliged to respond.'

'Respond how?'

'By rendering assistance. Pumping water from flooded spaces, putting out fires. Saving the crew if she starts to sink.'

Save the crew? The tug and her crew would be easy pickings for a few hard-core *muj*. Jameson would have a hostage situation on his hands. Some, maybe all of the tug's crew would die, and keeping a lid on Yellowstone would become, if not impossible, a lot more difficult. 'If he brings *jihadis* on board his ship he's fucked.'

Watson pursed his lips. 'It's possible he's only rigging a tow.'

'Then we hit that freighter before he has a chance to do something fatally stupid. What about the Russians?'

'There's been no sign of them for hours.'

'You're sure?'

'I checked in with sonar myself. Don't worry. The *Akula* is gone.'

Jameson looked at the screen. 'Is there any way you can warn that tug off once we're on the surface?'

'With my radios out? Sure. With a light gun.'

'Start flashing lights and the Tangos will be waiting for us.' But he thought, *I wonder what kind of radio gear the merchies use?* 'Which way are they headed now?'

'South, into the weather and not very fast.' Watson clicked the remote and the periscope video vanished, to be replaced by a nautical chart showing the southeast coastline of Sicily – from Cape Passero Island north to the port of Syracuse. The land was displayed as a featureless outline; only lighthouses, points and bays were called out in detail. After all, there was little chance of *Portland* missing the Gulf of Noto and straying off into the foothills of the Monti Nebrodi. But the sea bottom was shown in vivid detail, from the dark blue of the deep Ionian Basin, the gradual upslope of the Calabrian Rise, to the abrupt, scalloped cliffs marking the beginning of the Sicilian Escarpment.

Once in the Gulf of Noto everything would change for the worse. It was full of shoals and shallows, not to mention a few wrecks.

'What will you need from *Portland?*' asked Watson.

'Put us over the side with decks awash two thousand yards out ahead of them. We'll man up our CRRC and take it from there. You can stand off and wait for our recovery signal. *Any* of your radios working?'

'They will be,' said Watson.

'Lieutenant Scavullo's got one of ours. She can monitor the squad frequency from your bridge.'

'I'm uncomfortable with having anyone up in the bridge in this storm. Unless we blow our tanks dry we'll ride low. Waves could break right over it. The last thing I need is to explain why I let her fall over the side.'

'She's been seconded to Yellowstone,' said Jameson. 'You won't have to explain anything to anyone. That's the beauty of it, XO.'

There was a knock at the wardroom door, and Banjo Gant put his head inside. 'XO? I might have some good news.'

'Well?'

'All those surge-protected boxes, well, I hope the Navy can get its money back because they are *fried*. I had to jump the HF transceiver around the antenna base units. I terminated the jump with a coax cable on one side and the teletype on the other.'

'The *teletype?*'

'I figure it's better than nothing. We'll need to rig the emergency whip antenna up on the bridge. I'd like a few A-Gangers up there with me. But we might have you connected to Norfolk again.'

'If it works you've got to warn off that tug,' said Jameson.

Watson dearly wished to return to the comfortable, electronic fold. 'All right. Go find someone to help you rig that antenna, Mister Gant. Make sure you both stay attached to the boat no matter what. Plan to follow Lieutenant Jameson up to the bridge in fifteen minutes.'

'The antenna's thirty feet long when it's extended, XO. I could use more than one extra pair of hands.'

'You'll have them,' said Watson. 'Lieutenant Jameson will volunteer one of his guys.'

'Who?' said Jameson.

'Scavullo.'

'Blade count shows turns for four knots, Captain,' said Kureodov. 'Contact is moving slowly to the south, bearing now three four one.'

Two screws, thought Leonov. *The ship we're hunting has just one. So whoever this is, it's not the right ship. Unless Moscow was wrong.* He examined the big circular sonar display. The American submarine had come near the surface, then dived away. It had moved first to the east, then back to the west. What did it all add up to?

He turned away from the Termite's console. 'Helm. Make your course zero one zero. Prepare for periscope depth. I'm going to look at this ship myself.'

USNS *Apache*

'Four knots, one eight zero aye,' said the second mate.

Hunt clicked the walkie talkie. 'How's the rig, Tom?'

'On the step, Captain. I only had to let out fifty yards to drop strain. I've got Polacco standing hawser watch. By the way, Hub wants to know when he gets to make his house call.'

'Stand by.' Hunt went to the radio and made sure they were still on Channel Sixteen. *'Apache* calling *Nova Spirit.'*

'We are here, *Apache*. The tow, it is working very well but the men! My helmsman, I think he is now dead.'

'How the hell did his helmsman get caught up in an engine room fire?' asked the second mate.

'Small ship, short crew,' said Hunt. He clicked the radio. 'Do you have a Jacob's ladder, Captain?'

'Yes! We have this!'

'Put it out amidships port side. We'll send our doctor in a boat.'

There was a pause, then Warsame said, 'Your boat is okay?'

'For what?'

Another pause, then, 'The seas.'

Apache's rigid hull inflatable could take much heavier weather than this. But Hunt guessed *Nova Spirit*'s master might have other reasons for asking. 'I wouldn't send it out if it weren't.'

'Then we will set out the ladder and wait, but please hurry.'

'I'll signal when we're ready.' Hunt clicked off the radio.

'You don't suppose they're hoping to all ride back here, do you?' asked the second mate.

Hunt thought, *I would be.* 'Who's best with the shark rifle?'

'Delfus, but Polacco outweighs him by what? Got to be a hundred pounds. It depends on whether you want a guy nobody will screw with or someone who shoots straight.'

'Polacco. Think he'd be willing to ride shotgun?'

'You'd have to chain him to a capstan to keep him on board. I'd still like to take that boat over, Captain. If you're willing.'

'Glory hound.'

436

The *Akula* outweighed *Portland* by nearly three thousand tons. Once Leonov had her at twenty meters depth not even the pull and surge of wave action could upset her. He climbed the ladder up to the Balcony where the command periscope was mounted. He used the motor control on the handle to swing it onto three hundred and forty degrees; the twin-screw contact's last sonar bearing. He put his eye to the lens and triggered the control to raise the instrument.

At first Leonov saw nothing but the soft green glow of the illuminated crosshairs. He pivoted the head up, thinking he might be seeing only waves. Still nothing. He pushed the handle to swing the periscope again and this time the view changed.

A misty white line scribed the right edge of his field of view. A shoal? Breakers? There were no islands, no shallows here. Then it appeared again, this time dead center. When the faint, linear glow showed up a third time Leonov knew he was seeing the foam rush of a bow wake.

And there is no bow wake without a bow. 'Three five zero! Bearing and mark!' he called down angrily. Everyone would know that was a different bearing from the one Kureodov had provided. The Termite had fouled up again, and this time badly.

'But Captain, I show the twin-screw contact passing through three three five,' said Kureodov. 'Still moving south at four knots.'

Leonov snorted, and to prove Kureodov was an

impossible idiot, he swung the periscope to three three five degrees. He was about to tell the sonar operator to come find his target when he saw the ship.

She was showing plenty of lights. Leonov didn't need the scope's night vision to see her high bow, boxy bridge, twin stacks and low, flat deck aft. A tug. Not a small one meant for harbors, but a big one meant to go anywhere, to pull anything. *That* explained it! They were *towing* something. But what?

A hot white spotlight flared from the wheel-house. Leonov felt his heart jump, but the beam swung away from *Gepard* and pointed down the ship's wake. He pushed at the handles again, moving the scope back to the north to see what was back there.

The spotlight was frozen on a ship's bow. And Leonov had seen its like before. '*Dermo!*' he cursed. '*Starpom!* Come up here.'

By the time Stavinsky climbed up to the Balcony, Leonov had the image intensifier switched on. There, in the eye of the periscope in shades of green, was a small ship. Silent, unlit. And while it was down at the stern, there was no doubt about *which* ship it was.

Stavinsky put his eye to the scope. 'The target?'

'Without lights, half sunk and a twin of the one we sent to the bottom. Now swing south to three three zero.'

Stavinsky started. The tug's work lights were almost painfully bright. 'Another ship.' He switched off the night vision and examined the ship more closely. 'An American fleet tug?'

'Exactly so.' Leonov pulled down the *kashtan* microphone and clicked it. 'This is the Captain. Battle stations torpedo!'

CHAPTER TWENTY-NINE

THE ONLY EASY DAY

USNS *Apache*

'All ahead slow,' said Hunt

'Ahead slow, aye,' said Tom Stone. The chief mate ran both throttles back to STOP, then forward a notch. *Apache's* stern settled as she made only enough speed to keep the tow properly in tension. 'Gene sure wanted to make this run in the worst way.'

'He missed that rescue last year by what? A week?'

'Do you remember the name of that yacht?'

'I do,' said Captain Hunt. Four amateur sailors caught up in a hurricane, their boat sinking, hauling them through the waves like the catch of the day. He hadn't forgotten. 'The *Bossa Nova II*.'

'And now the *Nova Spirit*.'

Lightning flashed on the southern horizon. 'We'd better get a move on.' Hunt clicked the handheld. 'Deck? Put the boat over.'

'Aye, Captain. I'm lifting now.' Seaman Rankin sat at the crane's controls in the lee of the tug's blocky superstructure. He raised the rigid inflatable boat off its blocks.

Apache's ship boat was no elegant watercraft; just a utilitarian, U-shaped inflatable with orange fabric pontoons for gunwales and a fiberglass deck in between.

When Rankin swung it over *Apache*'s aft work deck, the wind caught it and spun it like a kite. He had to be careful not to snag a pontoon. The wind died for an instant and he used the brief lull to drop the boat alongside.

The waves were running fifteen feet and sometimes more, and the small inflatable, secured only by the crane's 'pelican hook', bobbed well above deck level, then vanished below the gunwale. Second Mate Gene Morrissey, Third Mate Francis Hubbard and Seaman Anthony Polacco, all in orange exposure suits and float vests, timed the rise and fall and stepped directly across, dead level.

Gene Morrissey got the inboard started. The boat had a small cockpit at the stern with throttles, a compass, a GPS and radar. Morrissey had equipped himself with a portable radio clipped to his belt and the captain's old .45 in his survival suit pocket. It felt like an anchor in there and he vowed to throw it into the sea if he ended up swimming. A microphone was fastened to his float vest. He turned away from the wind to keep it from drowning out his voice. 'Words of wisdom, Captain?'

'Don't bring any guests back if you can avoid it. The paperwork would sink us.'

'What if they rush the boat?'

'Have Polacco stand guard at the ladder. I don't

think they'll want to push their luck.'

'Weather's coming on pretty fast.'

'If that freighter looks like she's about to sink then you'll have to bring them across. We'll deal with the paperwork later. Get going,' said Hunt.

'Aye aye, Captain. We're set.' Gene turned to the brawny sailor standing at the bow. 'Polacco! Captain wants you to block the ladder and make sure no one gets by. Look fierce, okay?'

'Got it.' Polacco cradled the M-14 rifle in his arms and gave the second mate a thumb's up.

'Right. Let's go,' said Morrissey.

Third Mate Hubbard reached up and released the pelican hook that connected them to *Apache*. He had his big medical kit safe between his knees. Morrissey gunned the engine, and the pontoon boat angled away, curving back down *Apache*'s wake.

K-335 *Gepard*

'New sonar contact, Captain,' said Kureodov. 'Bearing and range match the American tug.' He pressed his headphones tight to his ears, then turned. 'It sounds like a small boat engine.'

'Again.' Leonov looked at his executive officer with an expression that said, *You see?* 'Range to the *Los Angeles?*'

'Holding steady at twelve thousand meters northeast.'

It was a difficult matter to arrange a rendezvous at sea. And yet here was an American submarine, there an American ocean-going tug. And in the

441

middle? A ship filled with stolen weapons and bandits who had murdered Russians to take them. What *else* could any thinking person see but a coordinated plan? Perhaps the ship had broken down. Perhaps it was all part of the plot. Either way, Leonov knew what he had to do. He took down a *kashtan* and clicked it. 'Torpedo room. Are Tubes One and Two ready?'

'Loaded with SET-60s. Checkout is complete. The breeches are sealed and the outer doors are shut,' answered Senior Warrant Officer Dobrin. SET-60s were big, wire-guided torpedoes armed with a warhead sized to break the back of an aircraft carrier.

'Sonar, bearing and range to the freighter?'

'Bearing three four eight, range eleven thousand meters.'

'Target select, Tube One,' said Leonov.

Kureodov spun a trackball, highlighted the sonar return that represented *Nova Spirit,* and selected it by pressing down. A red 'kill box' appeared with *Nova Spirit* dead center. The kill box represented the passive acoustic homing range of the SET-60 torpedo, and the American tug boat straddled the southern limit.

'Captain, there are multiple targets now inside the kill box.'

'Inhibit the seeker. Take over manual command.'

The *starpom* controlled these options from his firing panel. 'Seeker is disabled. Ready to steer the weapon,' said Stavinsky. Though the guidance wire was fine and easily snapped. If it did, the weapon would start looking for a target on its own, and that could be dangerous.

'Transmit targeting data, Tube One,' said Leonov.

A few moments later, Dobrin reported Tube One ready.

'Sonar, bearing and range to the American submarine.'

'Zero one five, range ten thousand meters.'

'Target select, Tube Two.'

Kureodov turned. 'Captain?'

'Target select, Tube Two, and be quick about it.'

Kureodov spun the warm, rubber ball until the cursor sat atop the American *Los Angeles*. He pressed down and a second red box flashed onto his screen.

'Transmit targeting data, Tube Two. Stand by to open Tubes One and Two.'

USS *Portland*

Jameson and his men gathered at the base of the ladder leading up the bridge trunk. They spilled into the control room, the sonar room. They'd have filled Steadman's stateroom, too, but the door was shut. The narrow passage just couldn't contain seven special operators bulked up and weighed down with the lethal tools of their trade: weapons, ammunition, explosives and breaching gear. Their faces were masked by black balaclavas. There'd been no time to dry their flightsuits. A noxious blend of strong cleansing chemicals and salt water pooled on *Portland's* freshly waxed deck.

'Sonar, Conn. Any close contacts?' asked Watson.

'Conn, Sonar,' said Niebel. 'None.'

The seven SEALs were joined by Rose Scavullo. She wore an orange float coat over her blue submariner's coveralls and a SEAL radio headset on her head. Scavullo edged a bit nearer to Steve Stepik, the SEAL radioman. She was uncomfortably close to the ladder where someone had given her a push.

'Helm?' said Watson. 'Surface the boat with decks awash.'

The 1MC rang out with *'Now surface, surface, surface!'*

Chief Farnesi sent air from the high pressure blower into the ballast tanks, and the boat filled with their turbulent thunder.

Browne didn't need eyes to know they were headed upstairs. A few moments later he felt the distinct change in pressure that signaled the cracking of the bridge hatch. Then the heavy *thunk* of the clamshell falling open. He knelt beside Steadman's bunk. 'Captain? It is *definitely* time you got up.'

Steadman's eyes fluttered and his left hand clenched.

'He can't hear you, COB,' said Cooper.

'Faith, Cooper. Faith. Captain?' Browne took Steadman by the shoulder and gave him a good, strong shake.

Steadman shifted, his lips parted, and he made a sound that anyone might have taken for a sigh.

Browne wasn't just anyone. He heard, *'COB?'* and answered, 'Right here, skipper.'

Another whisper, clearer and stronger.

'*How ... is ... my boat?*'

Browne grinned and said, 'She needs a captain.'

The control room might belong to Tony Watson but the sonar shack was Bam Bam's. Even though the XO had been kind enough to cut his balls off in full public view, none of the junior sonar operators dared to ask him what he was doing back on the scopes when his scheduled watch was hours away.

He slipped into his familiar seat, loaded the CD with his acoustic program into a drive, called up the 'work tape' filled with hours of sonar data and began shutting down displays one by one until only two were left: one with normal sonar data streaming down the green glass like poured sand, and one in front of Bam Bam.

As the program drew on the combined computing power of *Portland's* BSY-1, his screen began to fill with white snow. Like an old rabbit-ear TV trying to pull in a faint signal, the snow shifted, lines appeared, flickered and vanished. Dark shapes that represented quiet zones drifted across the screen and faded away to white noise.

Even with the BSY-1's nearly full attention, the job was too big and the time too short. The SEALs were already on their way up the bridge trunk. Bam Bam's program could only step through one ten degree sector at a time and there were 365 degrees of sectors. *One minute a step, half an hour to check all the way around.*

The maths didn't add up.

What did COB say? If I was that Russian I'd be

445

sailing right up our ass. But where would the *Akula* be if she wanted to put a fish into that freighter? Not astern. No. Off the freighter's beam, in ambush.

He stopped the computer and forced it to concentrate on the most likely bearings.

The first ten degree sweep revealed nothing. The amorphous dark clouds appeared and evaporated. Nothing had the staying power of a real – and far too-quiet – submarine. The second sector was no better. He heard the *clang* of the clamshell swinging open.

The SEALs were on their way.

He was about to check the third sector when Niebel showed up at the door to the sonar shack.

'Hey. You're not on for another six hours. What gives?'

'I'm checking the work tapes,' said Bam Bam.

'For what?' Niebel walked over and looked at Schramm's display. 'Not that shit. You're hunting ghosts again?'

'What if I am?'

'Better not let the XO catch you.'

'I'm trying to work here.'

'Hey, I'm just saying, okay? For your own good.'

For my own good there better be an Akula out there. 'What are you doing hanging around? You're off watch, too.'

'The XO volunteered me for special duty.'

'You? Extra *work?* Don't let me stop you,' said Bam Bam. It was strange that Niebel should volunteer for anything. He always seemed allergic to work. But Schramm had other things to think about. And so he went back to hunting for

Russian ghosts.

Stepik moved aside and let Scavullo climb up the bridge trunk ahead of him. When she emerged, the tight cockpit was already empty. The SEALs were already over the side, the fairing locker down on the weather deck was open and the inflatable assault boat was out and taking shape.

The sky flashed with sheet lightning, illuminating a world of foam-streaked waves and low, scudding cloud. Both sky and ocean were rushing north in a big hurry.

'We'll check comms from the CRRC,' said Stepik. 'See ya in a few.' The squad radioman pushed her aside and all but dived through the small ice door set in the side of the fairwater. She started to call after him but remembered her radio headset. 'Good luck,' she whispered.

The rain stung her face. The waves broke against Portland's exposed sail as though it were a steel tower set adrift in the open ocean. The wind picked up the spume and sent it tumbling up and into the cockpit, drenching her.

Standing on Portland's weather deck, the SEALs were calmly working up to their waists in water. The CRRC was ready, they tossed their gear aboard then jumped in after it.

Jameson pulled the radio headset down tight and secured it with a black knit balaclava. He popped the earpiece into his left ear and adjusted the filament microphone so it just barely brushed his lower lip, then ran the commo wire down to the Motorola and switched it on. He heard the open frequency sizzle and dialed down the

447

squelch to make it go away. He looked up and saw Scavullo. 'Hey, isn't it pizza night tonight?'

Jameson's voice seemed to come from inside her head. Saturday was pizza night on *Portland,* though it seemed an odd thing to be worried about. 'I guess so. Why?'

'Make sure they save us five slices each with everything. When we come back we'll be hungry.'

'Okay. I'll make sure they know. Hey Smooth Dog?'

'Yo.'

'Take it easy out there. I'm running low on allies.'

'The only easy day was yesterday,' said Jameson. 'Comm check. Bravo One.'

'Three,' said Squad Chief Wheeler.

'Four,' said Steve Stepik.

'Bravo Five,' said Pyro, loaded down with his breaching tools, a Remington shotgun and the last cylinder of explosive gas.

'Six,' said Tommy Anders, who had eyes that saw things no one else could.

'Seven.' McQuill, the other sharpshooter.

'Eight.' Flagler, the medic.

The frequency fell silent, and they all looked up at her in unison.

'Nine?' she said at last.

'Okay, Rosie. Don't call us. We'll call you. And don't forget the pizza.'

'Hey Nine, no anchovies on mine,' said Pyro.

'Got it.'

A lot sooner than she would have guessed possible she heard the roar of the CRRC's pump jet, and they were skimming across the waves, disappearing into the gray curtain of rain.

'Bravo Three, Channel Sixteen listen-only,' said Jameson.

'We're on.' It was Stepik's voice.

Other than a bacon fat sizzle of interference, there was nothing.

And then there was.

'Apache, Apache. *How do you hear?*'

The answer came back loud and strong.

'Got you loud and clear, Gene. How me?'

'Clear. We're coming down their starboard side. The hull's glued together with rust. I could stick my thumb through. I don't see the – wait. Okay. I see the ladder now.'

'Tell Hub to be careful.'

'Okay. They tossed down a line. We're tied on.'

There was a *click*. 'Everyone hear that?' It was Jameson.

It fell to Pyro to sum up all their feelings. 'Shit. Now what?'

'Stick to the script,' said Jameson. 'This is *not* hostage rescue. The *muj* are number one. Number two, the material. Number three, the Russian. Four, any documentation he brought out. Someone comes at you with a weapon, they go down. Period. If they come at you with a weapon *and* a hostage, take the head shot if you can but don't suck up a round to do it.'

Scavullo heard a raspy, metallic noise and turned in time to see Banjo Gant emerge from the bridge clamshell. He was carrying something that looked like a length of pipe. He turned. Someone passed up a second pole, a third, and then a fourth.

449

'Hey, lieutenant,' he said. 'You join the SEALs now?'

A wave *boomed* against the sail. Another white flash of lightning.

'What are you doing up here?'

'Rigging the emergency whip. We'll run it through the spare through-hull down to the radio shack. I got the teletype working.'

'The *teletype?*'

'It's about the only thing that didn't get fried and if it *doesn't* work the XO will fry *me*. You game to help out?'

'I'm not raising a lightning rod in a storm.'

Banjo handed her the threaded cap of a coaxial cable. 'Don't worry, ma'am. I brought my own spark arrestor for that.'

'Who?' But then Scavullo saw a figure crawl up through the open clamshell hatch.

It was Sonarman Niebel.

Bam Bam was in a race. There was still no sign of the *Akula*. Eventually, the XO would find out he was here and pull him off for good. Then what? He glanced at the screen on Niebel's console; the only one displaying a normal looking sonar picture. It came alive with the buzz of the SEAL's outboard motor. They were on the way. To what? A ship? Or a target for a pair of Russian rocket torpedoes? He remembered those white hot balls streaking across his screen. *Game over.*

The system was chewing through the fifth sonar sector when he saw a dark cloud that maintained itself against the screen's white snow. He watched as it held together against the backdrop of noise. At first dead astern, but then it began to slide across the screen until it was ahead of *Portland* and directly astride the freighter's course. He heard a sound from the doorway to the portside passage. He turned.

'Mister Schramm?' said Tony Watson. 'You want to tell me what you think you're doing back here?'

CHAPTER THIRTY

MERCY FOR MERCY

MV *'Nova Spirit'*

'Remember,' said Gene Morrissey, 'look fierce.'

Seaman Polacco gripped the rifle at quarter arms and made a face. 'How's this?'

'You look constipated.' Hub put his arms through the handles of the rubber medical bag, wearing it like a backpack. He grabbed the stiff, tarry ropes of the Jacob's ladder and began to climb. It was just four rungs up to the scupper. He swung himself over and stood on deck.

Only three men were waiting. Hub wouldn't have been surprised to see the entire crew poised to jump. One was short and his face was properly smeared with oil. He looked like a sailor. Another looked too clean to be anything but a passenger. He even wore a little tape player connected to a tiny earset. The last of the trio, a black man in pink plastic beach sandals, stepped forward.

'I'm Mohammed Warsame, ship's master.'

In pink sandals? Though Hub was too polite to say anything. 'I'm Frank Hubbard, Third Mate of the *Apache*. I'm more or less the local doctor. Where are your injured?'

'We thank God you have come. My men, they wait for you inside.' Without a word of explanation nor invitation, Warsame turned and walked to the centerline catwalk and headed aft.

Polacco heaved himself onto the deck. When he stood he effectively blocked the ladder with his body. The M-14 was just extra incentive.

'Fierce,' Hub reminded him.

Polacco bared his teeth.

Hub took off after the captain. He noticed the hatch covers weren't in great shape. The deck fittings were torn, bent in half, missing. It looked like something with a taste for iron and rust had been gnawing away at the ship for some time now.

He followed Warsame aft. The going was distinctly downhill. The bridge atop the aft house was dark, the radar bar motionless, the portholes black. The last thing Hub wanted was to get lost wandering around inside an unlit, foundering ship. 'Hey! Wait up!'

Warsame stepped over a coaming and into the iron house.

'I will show you the way.'

It was the too-clean sailor with the tape player and earphone.

'Thanks,' said Hub. 'What are you listening to?'

'*The Challenge of the Koran*. What do they call you?'

452

'Frank Hubbard. Third Mate. But they call me Hub.'

'Hub,' Musa repeated. 'Like the wheel?'

'Something like that. How about you?'

'Musa. They are waiting for you inside, Mister Hub.'

USS *Portland*

'Frankly, I'm disappointed,' said Lieutenant Commander Watson. 'I thought you had a better head on your shoulders. Now pull that program and get the hell out of the sonar shack. You're on report.'

'But I found the *Akula*,' said Bam Bam. 'She's ten thousand yards off the port bow and–'

'So you say. I don't see it.'

'I was right about that second ship. I'm right about *this*, too.'

'A busted clock is right twice a day,' said Watson. 'Being right isn't enough, Schramm. Your thinking was,' he paused, searching for the most damning word he could summon, *'unsound.* Now pull your little video game and take off before this gets out of hand.'

'XO, you let that *Akula* trail us up here. You know what they did to that other freighter. The SEALs are in danger and you've got to tell them.'

'I won't be lectured by an enlisted man on tactics. Least of all by one who can't follow orders. Procedures get results. Hunches and *impulses* can lead you anywhere. That's the point.'

'You're going to let those SEALs die to prove it?'

453

There were times that Tony Watson wished submarines had the space for a proper brig. Any surface ship worthy of the name had a real cell with bars and locks. And though it would have to wait, this stubborn petty officer would see the inside of one when they put in to port. 'You deliberately disobeyed me, Mister Schramm. You placed yourself above the boat. You put us all at risk.' Watson savored his words. They had the ring of a proper indictment. 'I'm not out here to chase shadows.'

'Worried you might find one?'

Watson stiffened as though he'd been slapped. 'You just earned yourself a date at Captain's Mast.'

'Excuse me, Mister Watson, but you might want to ask the captain about that first.'

Watson turned. Browne was out in the portside passage. 'COB?'

'I'm the one who told Bam Bam to fire up that program. And if he says there's an *Akula* in the neighborhood, I sure would be inclined to check it out before I turned my back. Again.'

'What is this? A conspiracy from the rates? The men may think you're God's representative on earth but the commanding officer of this submarine gave Schramm an order. He ignored it. If you had a hand in that then you'll have to answer at mast, too.'

'I'll stand at mast and tell the captain what I'm about to tell you, XO. The *rates* are the ones who make sure your orders get carried out. The *men* are the ones who keep your machines looking pretty and working right. Now they aren't

454

Academy graduates, but it's a fact that without them you aren't going to get anything done.' He stopped and turned, looking back over his shoulder, hoping that the sounds he'd heard were the *right* ones. 'Now, as for what the commanding officer has to say,' he said to Watson, 'you might want to ask him.' Browne stepped aside.

Commander Steadman stood next to Chief Cooper. His eyes were open, his burned arm was in a sling and he was clearly having trouble taking deep breaths. 'Tony,' he said. 'Thanks for filling in.' He looked at Bam Bam. 'Now where's that *Akula?*'

'Nine thousand yards on the port bow. She's laying for that freighter, Captain.' He looked at Watson, then back. 'And you can take that to the bank.'

That was good enough for Steadman. He leaned out of the sonar shack and shouted, 'Helm. Ahead two thirds.'

'*If* that *Akula's* not another figment of Schramm's imagination,' said Watson, 'you're driving us right at her.'

'That is exactly what I'm doing, XO.'

MV '*Nova Spirit*'

Hub trailed Musa through the watertight door into a narrow passage lit by a weak, flickering light. His nose was assaulted by a combination of rancid smells; one part oil, another smoke, a third curry, a fourth raw sewage, and finally, a rank, sweet smell like nothing he'd ever smelled.

455

Jesus. What a stink.

The smell grew worse as he approached a lit doorway. He peered in. *Crew's mess.* Six small, dark and very scared-looking sailors were gathered around the long table and a boy – he couldn't have been more than twelve – was hiding out in the galley.

The ship's master stood over a body slumped in a corner. 'My helmsman Hazil,' said Warsame. 'He's in a bad condition.'

He smells like he died last week. Hub shut his nose, breathed through his mouth and went to the unconscious helmsman who lay face down, legs drawn up. The sickly sweet smell drilled right through. A filthy rag lay in a bowl beside his head.

Hazil was shivering and his breath came in dry gasps. Hub knelt down and felt the back of his neck. *Jesus!* It was like touching a roast fresh out of the oven. *Way north of 105,* he thought. *Infection? Meningitis? Allergic response?* No matter. If he didn't bring it down he would die. Hub handed the empty bowl to Musa. 'Fill this with cold water.'

'Me?'

'With ice, if you have any.' He rummaged through his bag for the liquid aspirin. It was strange. They'd said the boy was caught in the engine room fire. So where were his burns? The singed clothes? And why spike this high a fever?

Hub gently turned Hazil over so that he could squeeze some aspirin down his throat. He froze, staring, part in shock, part in horror, part in absolute amazement, for Hazil's skin was pebbled with small, hard lumps.

At first he thought the boy had taken a face full

of buckshot. But other than a nasty cut on his forehead, there were no open wounds. No blood. Whatever was going on was coming *up* from inside, not *down*.

Musa put a bowl of tepid water down, then, without a word, he turned and left.

Hub soaked the rag and spread it over Hazil's brow. 'How long has he looked like this?' he asked Warsame.

'Maybe one hour only. Do you know what's wrong with him?'

'It looks like an allergic reaction.'

'Can you help him?'

Not here. He'd already decided that. He soaked the dirty rag again and washed Hazil's burning cheeks. 'What did you say happened to him?'

'He fell and hit his head.'

Hub could give the boy something to bring down his fever. And he had injectable anti-histamine for the allergic shock. But there was something going on here, something bigger, something he'd never seen.

'What will you do?' Warsame asked.

That was an easier question to answer. 'He needs a helicopter and a hospital. Anyone else this sick?'

Warsame thought about Walid. He was not looking so well when he saw him last. But then Walid had been up on top of the bridge roof for hours in the wind and the rain. 'My engineer is dead. Hazil is the worst.'

'We've got to bring him back to our ship.'

Warsame smiled. 'God is great.'

Seaman Anthony Polacco was one of those big

men who were slow to anger and whose very size kept him from having to prove it. And so when Adnan walked up to him flanked by two of *Nova Spirit's* Pakistani crew, he was curious, not worried.

'Mister Hub. He wants to see you now,' said Adnan.

But here was a dilemma. This guy obviously had been sent by the third mate. *Hub* was like a password. But if he didn't stand watch at the ladder, who would?

'He said you must hurry,' Adnan urged.

'Shit.' Polacco turned and called down. 'Hey Mister Morrissey!'

Gene looked up from the rigid hull boat.

'Hub says he needs me inside.'

'Then what are you doing out there?'

'Okay.' Polacco made sure the M-14's safety was clicked on, then said, 'Where is he?'

'Please,' said Adnan. And he led Polacco to the centerline catwalk, just aft of the crane.

Polacco could feel the deck plates deflect under his weight. The only surprise was that the ship hadn't snapped in half when the stern flooded.

The three men stopped at the base of the cargo crane. One Pakistani crewman moved to Polacco's right. The other did the same on his left. Adnan remained in the middle, motionless.

Polacco was slow to anger but there was nothing slow about his wits. This was a setup, likely to open the way to the boat for the rest of these raghead assholes, and he was quite sure that they had made a mistake by choosing to fuck with him.

He brought the stock of the rifle up and swung

458

it like a club at the guy to his right. It connected with the solid, heavy *crack* of a well-struck ball and the little Pakistani flew off his feet and performed a nearly perfect backflip.

The other two were on him now, clinging to his arms, his neck, but Polacco still wasn't concerned. Put them together and he still outweighed them. He would knock their fucking dentures through their rectums, but he needed his fists free. He let go of the M-14. The rifle clattered to the deck as he began to shrug them off. The Pakistani slipped to the deck and Polacco planted a kick that sent him tumbling.

But the other one had him around the neck, riding his back like a fucking monkey. Polacco suddenly dipped, trying to bring Adnan over his head. He leaned too far and they both fell. He felt a ticklish, feathery touch beneath his chin. Like a blade of grass.

The sting came an instant later. He roared, but it came out a wet gargle as a flood of warm blood spurted from his throat. One of the others was back, sitting on him, pressing him down to the deck.

Adnan flipped the sharp blade around, brought the serrated edge to bear against Tony Polacco's throat, and began to saw with swift, sure strokes.

Polacco tried to yell, he tried to breathe, but everything was drowned in an ocean of blood. He heard them shouting, *'Allah u akbar!'* Then, more softly, *'Allah u akbar!'* And then, with the strange sensation that someone was pulling at his hair and that he was looking on the scene from elsewhere, he heard, faintly, a distant whisper:

459

'*Allah u akbar.*'

A bright flash silhouetted the hull, and Gene Morrissey began to count. He heard the low rumble of thunder at twenty.

Five seconds a mile. Four miles away. That was close. And it must have seemed that way to Hunt, too, for the third mate's radio came alive.

'Gene? Hub and Polacco back down yet?'

'No. You want me to go and find them?'

'No. Better stay with the boat.'

'Aye aye. I'll–' Morrissey heard scuffling and looked up. 'Hub's back and he's got a crowd. Stand by.' Morrissey cupped his hands to his mouth. 'What gives?'

'Got one bad injured we're bringing back.'

Then what are all the others doing there? he wondered. 'Where's Polacco?'

'I thought he was with you.'

'You said you needed him.'

'No way. Who said so?'

'One of the crew.'

Hub looked at Warsame.

'We'll carry Hazil down to your boat now.'

Hub leaned over the deck edge. 'Someone's going to look for him. We're coming down with the injured.'

'Wait for Polacco. He can carry the guy over his shoulder.' *And that will keep the rest of them off my boat.*

Hub turned to Warsame. 'Second mate says wait.'

Warsame issued a sharp command to one of the crew, and then, as the man hurried off, he said to

460

Hub, 'He comes now.'

Bravo Squad

'Any time you're ready, chief,' said Jameson.

Wheeler eyed the rise and fall of the waves across the freighter's waterlogged stern, and as the water began to pour back out through her scuppers, he twisted the throttle bar to full.

The pump jet roared and the raft charged forward, launching over the crests, flying over the troughs and slamming hard into the rising wall of the oncoming sea.

Jameson flipped his nods down and scanned the freighter's stern one last time. *Nobody on deck, nobody on top security. Bridge is dark.* The wind was blowing their sound away, and that was good. But they weren't being subtle about their intentions, and all it would take would be one *muj* taking a leak over the side at the wrong moment and they'd have to fight their way on board.

But the fantail, the bridge wings were empty. There were no lookouts posted. And so, as the sea began to heap up over the freighter's stern, there was no reason to stop. And then, no way to.

A wave heaved the CRRC above the freighter's deck level. Wheeler swung the rudder over and they surfed it right onto the ship's fantail.

'Bravo, go,' said Jameson.

The SEALs tumbled over the black pontoons and onto *Nova Spirit's* deck even before the raft bottomed out on a deck hatch. They instantly formed up into two trains while Chief Wheeler

461

secured the CRRC and began to unpack the 'bug boxes'; the portable virus detection gear.

Jameson took Anders the marksman and Stepik with his radios up the ladder to the dark, deserted bridge while McQuill, Flagler the medic and Pyro Battaglia stormed up the slanting deck. Once the ship's topsides were clear, they'd go through the accommodation deck, then work their way forward. With Tommy Anders up in the crane cab with his match grade M25, any *muj* hiding belowdecks would be forced up and picked off like gophers rising from a dirt mound.

That was the plan. And like most plans in combat, it lasted exactly as long as it took to find the enemy.

Gene Morrissey looked up to the corroded wall of the freighter's hull. What was taking them so long? He felt the first big drops begin to fall. A few at first, then more. He wiped the water from his eyes. It stung like salt. 'Hey Hub! What gives?'

Hub saw a figure in an orange survival suit step out from behind the legs of the cargo crane. He had a bag in one hand and a rifle in the other. 'Get your ass back here!' he shouted.

Polacco raised his hand and started for the edge of the deck. Two crewmen were with him.

Hub leaned over the side. 'That big dumb asshole went souvenir hunting. He's coming.'

'Tell him to get a move on.' But Morrissey thought, *Souvenirs?* What could a person find on a ship like this worth saving? And it wasn't like Polacco to go wandering off when he'd been told to stand guard, either.

462

Hub knelt down beside Hazil and felt the heat rising from the flushed, pebbled skin of his throat. Rain pelted down on his back. It bounced off the deckplates in a lively silver dance. He felt for a pulse and it was there, weak and fluttery. *I'm losing this guy.*

He felt the deck vibrate with footsteps. 'Fuck of a time to go on a tour, Polacco. Help me lift this guy. You get his legs.' Hub grabbed Hazil by the shoulders and waited for the brawny seaman to do as he was told.

A black drop fell to the deck, swirled in the rain and streamed off through the scuppers. Another. A third. More.

Hub looked up. The front of Polacco's survival suit was sprayed with fresh blood. 'What–'

It wasn't Tony Polacco, but Adnan. And the bag he was carrying was not a bag, but Polacco's head. The Chechen heaved Polacco's head over the side. It landed with a splash next to *Apache*'s inflatable.

Gene Morrissey thought it was Hub's medical kit. He reached over the side to retrieve it. He managed to catch it and drag it close. He lifted it Out of the water.

What the fuck? The bag was too small, too heavy, and the handles weren't handles, but hair.

He screamed and dropped it back into the water. This time Polacco's head landed face up, his eyes open, gazing back up at Morrissey as it sank below the surface and disappeared.

Squad Chief Floyd Wheeler, Bravo Three, had taken part in every special operations deployment from the green jungles of Panama to the dusty alleys of Baghdad. Each year they sent him out with 'new and improved' gear. Counted individually, it was always lighter, more capable, more lethal. But when you threw all the crap in your cruise box it always, *always* weighed more.

Batteries not included had become the bane of every SEAL's life. *Battery, PRC-112, twenty each* had grown to cases full of D-cells, C-cells, double and triple As. You could stock a hardware store.

Wheeler knew it was supposed to be amazing to be able to shove a small cartridge the size of a deck of cards into a rubber-coated attaché case, uncap the inlets, turn on a circulator and know within a few minutes if there were any bioweapons floating around. No doubt when some salesman dog and ponied the Bug Box – or Antibody-Doped Nano-wire Array as they called it – there was a nice convenient wall socket to plug into. Wall sockets were in short supply tonight, and four pounds of big, fat D-cell batteries were required. Put it all together and the 'light, man-portable biological detector' was a fucking pig.

He pulled out a cartridge from an insulated bag and slipped it carefully into the opening in the side of the rubberised case. It seated with a soft *click*. Inside it were hundreds of incredibly fine wires, each of them coated with antibodies tuned to respond to specific biological organisms. Turn on the circulator and air would be drawn through them. If an organism triggered an antibody response, a specific wire would change its electrical resistance and a window would flash with the appropriate message.

He uncapped the inlet and outlet ports and was about to switch on the small fan that would draw in the first air sample, when the message window flashed with *V. MAJOR*.

Well shit, he thought. How much virus had to be in the air to trigger a reaction *before* the fan drew in a sample? He whispered into his radio headset, 'Hey skipper. Bravo Three. The Bug Box is screaming smallpox. I didn't even take an air sample before it screamed. Where are you?'

'Bravo One's coming up on the bridge.'

The first train of SEALs – Jameson, Anders and Stepik – swept into the dark, empty bridge. Jameson went left, hugging the wall and sweeping the deserted space with his MP5. 'Bravo One. Clear. Six, go starboard.'

Anders burst in and hugged the right wall. If anyone had been there they'd be caught in two overlapping fields of fire. But there was no one. 'Six, clear!'

Jameson eased out through a door to the port bridge wing. Stepik guarded the rear while Tommy Anders headed for the other.

He slipped out into the rain, scanned the decks below and saw why the bridge was empty. 'Bravo Six has multiple targets. Main deck amidships,' he said into his radio headset. His nods revealed that two of them were wearing orange survival suits with *Apache* stenciled across the backs. The others were armed. The situation was clear but the implications were complicated. 'Looks like a pair of hostages and a posse of *muj*. AKs and one M-14.' The AKs were expected. The M14 was a surprise; his own match grade M25 was developed from it.

'Bravo Seven has the two hostages in sight. I'm on a target,' said McQuill. The sharpshooter was somewhere down on the main deck with an infrared 'death dot' on one of the armed men. 'Seven has the starboard AK. Ready.'

'Bravo Six has the portside AK. Ready.'

'Bravo One, no target,' said Jameson. 'Six and Seven, take 'em.'

The shadowy figures on deck moved. Anders shifted the telescopic sights of his M25 rifle, recentered the glowing death dot, let out his breath and pulled the trigger.

The two muffled shots came so close together they were like one elongated report. Rafik's head snapped back, and some deep, sailor's instinct sent him staggering away from the deck edge. Instinct was not enough to save him. He was dead when his blown skull struck rusty steel.

Gul Hassan's AK exploded from his grip as though he'd grasped a bare high-voltage cable. The weapon flew up, then arced over the side, and only then did Hassan realize that he was following it, and wondered how this could be happening, even as the sea rose up and struck him in the face.

Tommy shifted to the third armed *muj* with the M-14. 'Six is on the Tango with the 14. Ready.'

'Six, go,' said Jameson.

Warsame barely had time to register the fact that something very wrong was happening. Two flashes, two muffled *pops* and two crewmen were down. He took one step for the bridge then

466

changed his mind and ran for the Number Two cargo hatch scuttle. It was closer and would lead directly down into the bowels of his ship.

Adnan had the same idea, only he had something to do first. He pulled out the big, serrated blade still glistening with Polacco's blood and, as Hub slowly turned to see what was happening behind him, he drove it into the American's stomach.

Third Mate Francis Hubbard tried to pull the blade out but only succeeded in slashing his palm.

Adnan flicked the knife point up and then twisted. Blood spurted from Hub's survival suit. The more blood the better, for each drop was like a suicide bomber driving straight into the heart of the enemy. He pulled the blade out, threw the American down to the deck and ran for the cargo hatch scuttle.

Hub landed across Hazil with his head partly over the edge, face down. He could feel the steady, strong pump of warmth from his slashed belly and could guess the reason. *Liver, spleen, pancreas, descending aorta.* A good surgeon in a good trauma hospital might be able to save him, but out here?

Then he spotted Gene Morrissey down below, and he knew there was something that needed doing. Something that only he could accomplish. 'Gene! Get going!' he shouted, though the effort seemed to tear his insides apart.

The Second Mate didn't hear. Or couldn't. He was swatting the air, rushing about the small cockpit as though trying to escape a swarm of hornets.

467

'Gene! Up here!'

The second mate stopped his frantic rush and looked up.

'*Get out!*' He felt a warm flood fill his belly. '*Now!*'

Adnan pounded by Warsame and dove for the open scuttle that led down to the number two hold. Warsame was right behind until a sandal fell off and he slipped.

The Somali captain got to his knees, but then a great wave seemed to break over him, driving him to the deck. He gripped a torn deck fitting and held on. A sea. It had to be a rogue sea. It would roll over the ship, then pass. If he held his breath long enough he would live.

He waited, then gasped for air, but his lungs refused to inflate. As fast as he drew in a breath it whistled and bubbled from the ragged crater in his chest. A heavy weight pressed down on him. More feet pounded by. Wraithlike figures dived into the open scuttle and vanished below.

He tried to rise but he might as well have tried to pull his ship out of the water by yanking on the radar mast. He felt the open wound, saw his own blood stain his fingers red. Warsame knew what every Muslim must do and say in the face of death, and everything, eternity itself, depended upon it.

'There is ... no ... God...' he gasped, 'but ... Allah.' He gulped another mouthful of air. 'Mohammed is ... is...' He ran out of breath and tried to swallow more air, then spit it out through his mouth. 'And Mohammed is ... is ... is...'

Every Muslim knows that when the angel of death comes, he gently removes the souls of true believers. It emerges from the dry husk of the body as easily as a drop of water spills from a glass. A believer's worldly deeds are recounted to him in warm, friendly tones; like a mother whispering lullabies to a child. Unbelievers are relieved of their souls by red-hot iron tongs, and the angel is harsh and mocking.

'Mohammed ... is...'

This was his last moment. Warsame ached to finish the prayer, to see that bright window open onto Paradise. Try as he might, the air, and the words, would not come. Instead of light, there was a terrifying darkness. Instead of sweet voices, silence. And when he gathered a final breath to say the words that would unlock eternity, *'is ... his ... his...'* they were swallowed up by the wind and the rain, and swept away.

If Hub's scream to get out didn't penetrate the second mate's shock, the flash of gunfire and the sudden appearance of black-hooded men running along the deck edge did. He yanked the painter free from the Jacob's ladder and dove for the stern, striking his hip on something solid and sharp. It cut the tough fabric of his survival suit and gouged his skin. He didn't feel a thing.

Morrissey started the inboard, swung the tiller hard over and put his stern to the horror that was *Nova Spirit.*

Tommy Anders tracked the boat with his scoped M25. He didn't know if this was a target or a hostage making a break for freedom, but that didn't stop him from placing the red death dot on the back of Morrissey's head. 'Bravo Six has a boat taking off with one soul on board. He's in an orange suit, skipper. You want it stopped?'

Orange suit. Probably a crewman of that tug. Though Jameson could imagine a few other, less pleasant, possibilities. Whoever he turned out to be, he would have to be vaccinated, isolated, quarantined, along with everyone he came into contact with. But that was not top on his to-do list. He had a Russian doc and his stash of virus to find. 'Six, let him go. We'll deal with that problem later. Set security on deck from the crane cab.'

'Six, roger.' Tommy Anders let the red dot linger for a moment more, then swung it away.

USS *Portland*

The submarine charged straight into the teeth of the wind and waves. Surfaced and with her decks awash, the seas broke high and hard directly against the sail.

A black wall of water rushed out of the night, rolled over *Portland's* bow and smashed into the sail with an explosion of water and foam.

'That's one!' yelled Banjo Gant. The breaking wave filled the cockpit to their knees. Niebel was crouched low, wedged in a corner with a death grip on a steel hand hold. When he was slow to let go, Gant gave him a kick, and together they went back to raising the emergency antenna whip.

Scavullo rubbed her fingers together and felt fine sand mixed in with the water and foam. Had it come in on the wind, or from the sea? *How shallow are we?*

Thirty feet below their feet, mess specialists were spreading tomato sauce on pizza to serve at the midnight meal. But up in the submarine's bridge, Banjo, Niebel and Scavullo were marooned together on a half-submerged steel barrel in the middle of an angry sea. With *Portland* ballasted down and decks awash, the bridge rode right at eye level to the crests and every sixth wave was higher.

Another dark shape mounded up off the bow, rolled over the hull and smashed against the sail.

'Two!'

Scavullo tugged the nylon safety belt that tethered her to the deck, then spoke into the headset radio. 'Steve, do you copy? The *Akula*'s back, over.'

'–off the freq. We're busy.'

'Hey! The cable!' Banjo yelled. A clip holding a coil of heavy coaxial cable together had snapped and one end of it had found a scupper. The wire was streaming through it and into the sea.

Scavullo jumped on the cable and stopped it.

Gant gave her a thumbs up and said, 'Way to go!'

Niebel gave her a filthy look.

Boom!

'*Yeehah!* Three!' Banjo yelled out.

'I can't believe you're enjoying this,' Niebel sputtered.

'They'd charge a fortune for a ride like this back home!' said Banjo with enough innocent enthusiasm to annoy even Scavullo.

K-335 *Gepard*

'Captain? The *Los Angeles* is moving in our direction,' said the Termite. 'She's making turns for twelve knots on the surface.'

'On the surface? You're sure, Kureodov?'

'I hear hull slap. If they continue they'll pass between us and the target.'

A dangerous place to wander. *Unless it's deliberate.* Had they detected *Gepard* somehow? *No. It has to be chance.* 'Turns for ten knots now. Stand by to flood Tube One.'

USS *Portland*

An old fleet boat from WWII was as much a creature of the surface as the deeps. She could slice through waves as cleanly as a drawn knife. Not *Portland.* She could run silent and deep clear around the world, but she was out of her element on the surface.

The boat shuddered, pitched up, then over. Steadman braced himself by holding onto the back of Bam Bam's chair. He was in a great deal of pain. His chest burned with every breath. Every nerve felt studded with glass. It hurt like hell, but it helped him to think. *We have to get in that Akula's face,* he thought. And to do that he would have to maneuver without respect to the seas. The cockpit was going to get very wet. He took down the phone off the bulkhead. 'Bridge ... this is the captain.' His words were slow and slurred. Anyone listening would guess he'd been drinking.

'*Commander?*' The surprise in Scavullo's voice was just as palpable. 'Is that you?'

'Are you in contact with the ... with Lieutenant Jameson?'

'With his radioman. Yes sir. I'm on the squad frequency. They're pretty busy right now.'

'We'll be maneuvering and you're going to take some waves into the cockpit.'

'We're already soaked. And sir? There's sand coming in with the waves.'

Steadman leaned over and pretended to examine Bam Bam's screen. Raw electricity shot right up his arm and he couldn't keep from wincing. The pain seemed to clear his mind, and he stood back up and reached for the intercom. 'Nav ... what ... what do we have for a bottom?'

'We're over the crest of the Sicilian Escarpment, Captain. We'll have six hundred feet for the next couple of miles but it shoals to less than two hundred in the Noto Gulf.'

'Fucking *aye*. I've *got* you!' Bam Bam shouted. He jabbed his finger on a flickering white line on the scope still showing a normal waterfall display. 'Screw noise bearing two one eight.' He jacked him with his homemade headphones and listened to a faint *thrum thrum thrum*. 'It's either the *Akula* or her twin!'

'What range?' asked Steadman.

Bam Bam shook his head. 'It was a weak direct path contact, skipper and sonar conditions suck up here on the surface. He could be real close.'

'Where's your evidence, Mister Schramm?' said Watson.

'Sitting on the bottom off Andikithira Island, XO.'

Steadman clicked the intercom. 'Bridge? Tell Bravo the *Akula* is close. Who ... who do you have up on there with you?'

'Banjo and Niebel.'

'Niebel?' said COB Browne. 'What's *he* doing up there?'

'Lieutenant?' said Steadman. 'Make ... sure you're all secured to the boat.' He put the microphone back and staggered out to the passage leading to the control room. 'Helm! Left ten degrees rudder. Turns for fifteen knots. Steady on course two one five.'

'Captain?' said Watson. 'You put on all those turns and you'll bury the bridge in green water.'

Steadman could already feel the drunken motion of the boat change. They were pitching less and rolling more. He took down the microphone again. 'Torpedo Room, Fire Control. Make Tubes One and Two ready in all respects but *do not open the outer doors.*'

'Commander,' said Watson. 'We're not here to hunt *Akulas*. Firing on a Russian ship could start a war.'

'Too bad nobody told the *Akula*,' said Bam Bam quietly, though plenty loud enough for Watson to hear.

'I'm not firing,' said Steadman. 'But he doesn't know that.' With that, Steadman pushed by Watson, heading aft for control.

The deck beneath their feet seemed to shudder, then lean. The water at their feet sheeted and sloshed across the cockpit.

'What the fuck?' said Niebel.

'We're turning,' said Gant. 'Check your tethers, ladies and gents. We'll be taking seas broadside. The management assumes no responsibility for any items you may have brought along! Be advised this ride is going into *overdrive*.'

CHAPTER THIRTY-ONE

THE TRAIN

K-335 *Gepard*

Kureodov smelled the yeasty aroma of baked bread rising from the galley and thought, *bulichki;* sweet rolls. The officers would be served first and anything left over would be handed out to the crew. Of course, nothing good was ever left over. Sailors were here to work, not eat. The sonar officer checked the time and saw he had only fifteen minutes to go on his watch. He wondered if the success of this operation would be enough to propel him to Moscow. *Twisting the tail of a* Los Angeles? *Destroying a bandit ship? Yes.*

'Stand by to flood Tube One,' said Leonov.

'Ready.' First Officer Stavinsky reached over and let his finger rest against the flat blue button that would flood the torpedo tube in preparation for firing. Inside Tube One was a SET-60 heavy torpedo with a derelict freighter burned into its electronic brain. He was happy to be shooting old, reliable '60s. They might not fly through the sea like a rocket, but they weren't so delicately dangerous either. He smelled the baking bread, and it reminded him of home.

From the outside, the six-story apartment building looked like all the others: an unpainted ruin eaten away by cold, wind and neglect. The electricity was unreliable. The foundation had settled and the tiles in the hallway were cracked. But open the door to his own flat and it was like entering one of those magic worlds built inside an egg; warm, cosy, decorated with colorful fabrics. All his wife's doing, of course. He looked at the sprig of birch she'd given him the day of the departure. He'd kept the water in the glass fresh. It had grown a halo of fine roots.

'Seeker?' asked Leonov.

Stavinsky's mind was pulled back inside the steel world that was *Gepard*. 'Inhibited.'

The Termite watched the cluster of sound that was an American submarine shift across his screen. 'Captain? The *Los Angeles* is directly between us and the target again. He's stopped.'

'Still on the surface?' Leonov asked.

'It seems so.'

Leonov thought Kureodov had an unnatural liking for the word *seems*. It was lazy, slippery and undefined, not unlike Kureodov himself. Leonov stalked over to the sonar position, looked and then swore under his breath. Kureodov was correct. The Americans had stopped exactly in the wrong place. 'Helm. Right full rudder. Make your depth one hundred meters. Steady on course two eight zero.'

Another dark wave rolled up the hull and smashed against the sail with a heavy *thud* and a billow of spray.

'That's two!' said Gant.

Scavullo tugged the nylon safety belt that tethered her to the deck, then spoke into the headset radio. 'Steve, do you copy? The *Akula's* back. We're trying to block them.'

'–off the freq. We're busy.'

Niebel looked half-drowned. He leaned close to Scavullo as the next wave rolled up and smashed against the sail. 'Why am I not surprised that this is totally fucked?'

'I'm not conning the boat.'

'You weren't conning the boat when the COB wrestled a fish barehanded, or when the radios went tits up or when your boyfriend got zapped up here. You don't have to do anything. Shit just happens when you're around.'

'You'd better hope I'm not doing it,' she bristled. 'If I could call down lightning strikes your ass would be toast.'

He didn't seem to hear her. 'You know what else?' He leaned close and whispered. 'The ocean's going to get us unless we get rid of you first.'

'What are you worried about? Rats are good swimmers.'

The next wave smashed against the side of the sail. The wind sent a sheet of dirty spume against

477

their faces.

'Three!' said Banjo. 'The last bolt, guys.'

The emergency whip was nearly secured. That left connecting up one end of the cable to a through-hull fitting and the other to the base unit. It sounded simple, but trying to do it while riding a roller coaster that wanted to alternately throw you off its back and drown you complicated the matter considerably.

Boom!

'Four!'

Gant threaded the mounting bolt into the base unit and began cranking it down with a socket wrench.

'Bridge, Conn,' said Steadman. 'Have they acknowledged?'

'No, Captain,' said Scavullo. 'They sound too busy to talk.'

The fifth wave struck and sent solid water rising straight into the wind. It curled back over and showered them with dirty foam.

'Big one's next!'

There was a pause, then Steadman said, 'Try Jameson again.'

She pressed the push-to-talk switch on the Motorola. 'Steve? How do you hear?'

This time Stepik's voice came back loud and clear. 'Hey Nine, we got a ship full of bugs and Tangos, okay? So can it wait?'

'No. The *Akula*'s back!'

There was static, then, '...few more minutes. Bravo out.'

Banjo Gant saw the sixth wave rush out of the night. The wind streaked its broad slope white.

The crest was an undulating line that Gant was looking *up* at. 'Big one! Hang on!' He ducked down below the lip of the bridge and grabbed the antenna base unit. Sonarman Niebel had already hogged the handhold Scavullo was reaching for.

Thanks. She found a fitting on the trunk hatch just as the wave struck. *Portland* didn't ride up to it so much as through it. The cockpit was buried in green sea. Scavullo lost her grip on the fitting. Her head was under. She felt pressure in her ears as her feet rose from the deck plates. She was floating away. She grabbed at her safety line and hauled herself in as the cockpit burst up through the surface.

She listened to the hiss of water draining through the scuppers. She looked up into the low clouds. Cold rain never felt so good.

'Hot tub party!' said Banjo. 'Where's the bubble switch?'

MV *'Nova Spirit'*

Tommy Anders climbed up to the slanted roof of the crane cab, found a place to sit and settled in. From here, he could cover the entire ship from the wave shield at the bow to the watertight door into the iron house. He saw a flicker of light on the deck and swung his scoped M25 to check it out.

There was a lot of trash and loose gear strewn around: chains, ropes, mangled pieces of old cargo containers. He put his scope on the light source and saw that a small ventilation hatch at the forepeak had been flung open. Someone was

479

crawling out.

The figure flopped onto his belly and rolled, keeping low to the deck. He might as well be wearing a sign that said *Shoot Me First*.

Anders shifted his M25. The Tango was hiding something under his body, though his nods didn't have the resolution to identify it. A rifle? A bomb belt? That classic *muj* conversation-starter, the RPG-7 grenade launcher? Whatever it was, the figure had turned himself into a target. He swung his headset mic to his lips. 'Bravo Six has a Tango low-crawling at the bow.'

'POI?' asked Jameson. *Person of Interest.*

'Just a raghead hauling a bag.'

Explosives? 'Take him, Six.'

'Roger.' Tommy Anders placed the death dot on the target's forehead, exhaled and squeezed off a single 7.62 round. There was a sharp *crack!* and Rafik, the Pakistani cabin boy, tumbled back onto the jumble of trash and debris at the wave shield. The pillowcase he'd brought along to wave his surrender had been a grimy gray. It fluttered to the deck with sprays of red that streaked and bled in the rain. 'Tango's down. Clear deck.'

'Roger, clear deck,' said Jameson.

The two SEAL trains swept through the blacked-out iron house. Jameson, Wheeler and Stepik cleared the superstructure from the bridge down. Pyro, Flagler and McQuill worked up from the cargo deck. There was no time for finesse. When Jameson came upon an unarmed crewman standing in a passage he simply threw him to the deck and ran right over him. It fell to Wheeler to flip him over, search him for weapons and flex-cuff his hands behind his back.

Jameson's train cleared the cabin deck one space at a time. The first three were empty. Two cabins were left.

The train piled up outside the door marked '5'. Jameson could hear a low, scraping noise of metal on metal like a knife being honed. The cabins were dangerously small. They'd have to go in one at a time. His finger curled through the trigger of his MP5. 'Bravo One. Ready.'

'Three is on set,' said Wheeler.

Stepik said, 'Four, ready.'

Jameson kicked the door open and burst into the space, hugging the left wall. Stepik rushed in behind him and went right while Wheeler covered the passage behind.

'Shit.'

The cots were heaped with empty green canvas sacks. Boxes of ammunition stood on the deck, ripped open. The air smelled strongly of gun oil. Two rocket grenade launchers were propped against the rear wall, hastily abandoned. One was fitted with a round. The other conical grenade rolled across the deck with the motion of the ship.

'Careful,' said Stepik. He'd seen dead Iraqi children turned into boobytraps by rigging their bodies with grenades.

Jameson picked up the loose grenade and tucked it back into a canvas sack. He looked to Wheeler. 'Hot?'

The squad chief glanced at the window on the ADN detector. He'd run four new cartridge decks through the machine. Each time the *V. MAJOR* message popped up instantly. 'This

481

vial? He wrapped them back up, closed the case and passed it to Wheeler. 'Give this a sniff.'

Wheeler yanked the old cartridge and inserted a new one. Once more *V. MAJOR* illuminated on the display before he could turn the sample fan on. 'Same deal.'

Jameson faced Salafi. 'What were the brothers trying to do?'

'They were going to infect themselves, then carry the virus out to the world. Only something happened. The virus escaped. The ship and everyone on it is contaminated. I am. You are, too.' He swallowed, painfully, for his throat was dry and sore.

The only thing Jameson believed was that the ship was teeming with virus and that the brothers would like to see it spread. 'We may have a solution to that problem.' Jameson grabbed Salafi's laptop computer, snapped the lid shut, tossed it to Stepik then said to Wheeler. 'Cuff him.'

'No!'

Wheeler pulled two plastic flex cuffs from the nest fastened to a snap-ring dangling at his waist.

'*No!* We must get to a hospital quickly! All of us!'

No, we have to sterilize you and this tub quickly. He turned and the MP5 moved off Salafi. 'Chief?'

Salafi uncrossed his legs. 'I have diplomatic credentials issued by His Highness Turki Al Faisal, our ambassador in Washington. You can't do this to an accredited diplomat. It's against international law.'

'So is fucking around with smallpox. But don't worry. We'll let his Highness know where to

e, skipper.'
ple vials, thought
xcept they were
what did she say

u want to talk to

oor marked '4'.
o a thin line of
he closed door.
He sniffed, and

ne.
and around the
slowly, silently.
mechanism take

elled occupied.
ne inside could
th Stepik and
ith a silent nod.
icked the door
. It was bright
s nods. Stepik
n attaché case,
intel inside; the
one numbers,
ondence, not
, dressed in a
crossed like a
lafi. His shoes

said in BBC-

airdrop the flowers.'

'You don't believe me? I can prove this.' Salafi had never encountered a situation his green Saudi diplomatic passport could not fix. And he was desperate. Even now his throat was sore and with every breath came a strange, metallic taste. He reached into the pocket of his blazer. 'You don't want to make the ambassador angry. Trust me. Your President understands our special relationship and–'

Wheeler reached for his MP5. 'Watch it!'

A silenced MP5 is a marvel of engineering. The *clack clack clack* of the weapon's internal workings was louder than the sound made by the exploding cartridges.

Six nine-millimeter rounds thudded into Salafi's chest and sent him flying, arms out-stretched as though he'd given up on talking and had taken wing. He struck the bulkhead behind his bed and collapsed as the dark green passport wallet fluttered to the deck.

Jameson picked it up. It was embossed with the crossed swords and date palm of the Saudi royal family. He tossed it to Stepik. 'There goes the price of unleaded.'

USS *Portland*

The dark cloud of coherent silence that was the *Akula* slipped across Bam Bam's chaotic white screen. Though it took a lot of interpretation, he had a good idea where it was going, though not why. *He'll be in shoal waters if he doesn't watch out.*

485

'Conn, Sonar. The *Akula's* moving northwest at ten … no, make that twelve knots. The freighter's five thousand yards dead off his bow. He may be trying to duck underneath her.'

Steadman sat down heavily and gripped the chrome rail surrounding the periscope stand. He didn't have the strength to stay on his feet. He wondered if he really was ready for this. He knew that every man in control was likely wondering the same thing. *Hands shaking, can't stand up, can't take a deep breath without coughing and can't cough without doubling over or passing out.* If this were a test cruise to see if a prospective commander had what it took, Steadman knew what his answer would be.

'Commander?' said Watson. 'If you don't need me I should probably go...'

'No, Tony. Stay here. I want you ready to take over.'

'Conn, Sonar,' said Bam Bam. 'The *Akula* is now four thousand yards off the freighter's port beam.'

He can't vanish any more, thought Steadman. *But we can.* 'Helm?'

Lieutenant Pena turned, a worried look on his face. 'Skipper?'

'All stop.'

CHAPTER THIRTY-TWO

THE FLOWERS OF PARADISE

MV 'Nova Spirit'

'Steve?' said Jameson. 'Signal the boat. Find out if she has comms back to higher authority yet. We've got the samples and a computer with a hard drive. It may be everything worth grabbing.'

Steve Stepik pressed the push-to-talk on the Motorola. 'Hey lieutenant, how do you hear Bravo?'

The frequency was drowned in sizzling static.

'Signal's blocked,' said Stepik. 'You want me to go up to the bridge? I'll have line-of-sight to the boat from there.'

'Now, we can–' Jameson began, but he stopped and listened as the rattle of automatic weapons fire sounded from below.

'AKs,' said Chief Wheeler. 'Two of them.'

Jameson whispered into his head mic, 'Who's shooting?'

'Bravo Five is getting shot *at*,' said Pyro. 'Two Tangos are holed-up in the aft cargo bay. Touch the door and they crank up on full auto. If they were shooting armor piercing I'd be hamburger.'

'Charges set?' asked Jameson.

'Yeah,' said Pyro. 'But we can't leave the gismo unguarded with *muj* around. They might come

487

out and monkey with it.'

The ship will run aground someplace. No. They would have to dig the *muj* out of the hold before they could set the fuel-air charge and blow the ship. 'Okay Five. Rattle the door when I give the word. We'll pop the deck hatch while they're busy shooting at you.'

'Thanks.'

'You're welcome. We'll drop two grenades. Burst in shooting after the second one. You sweep low and starboard. We'll take high and port.' It would catch anything in between in opposing fields of fire, and in theory keep the SEALs from shooting one another. 'Okay with that?'

'Sure,' said Pyro. 'What about hostages?'

'We don't know there are any and we don't have time to deal with them if there are. Hey Six, the deck's still clear?'

'Still clear,' said Tommy Anders.

'Keep it that way,' said Jameson. 'We're coming out.'

USNS *Apache*

Gene Morrissey curved the rigid hull boat in and struck the side of the tug hard enough to bounce off. It was terrible seamanship and Seaman Rankin couldn't help but notice.

'What's his problem?' he asked Tom Stone.

Apache's Chief Mate had come down to the work deck to help control any of *Nova Spirit's* crew who might be coming back. But there were no extra bodies on board the rigid hull inflatable. Indeed, there were too few. 'Where's Hub and Polacco?'

'I don't know. Here he comes again,' said Rankin.

This time the second mate managed to catch the pelican hook and snap it onto the boat's lift bar. It was hardly secure before Morrissey scrambled up the cargo net and flopped onto *Apache's* deck face first, heaving like a landed fish.

'Where's Hub and Polacco?' asked Stone.

Morrissey didn't answer. He got to his feet and started for the bridge ladder.

'Hey, slow down!' said Stone. 'Where'd you leave them?'

The second mate didn't turn, didn't pause. He walked straight into the tow cable reel, caromed off, found the ladder going up and rushed up as though something was chasing him.

Something's not right. Stone looked up at the bridge windows and saw Morrissey and Captain Hunt. He was about to radio the bridge to find out what was going on when the rumble *of Apache's* engines fell silent. The tow cable that had been drawn tight sagged.

'We're stopping,' said Rankin.

Stone's walkie talkie chirped. He plucked it from the holster. 'Work deck. What's going on, Captain? The cable's way slack.'

'We're dropping the tow. We're dropping it *now*. Stand clear. I'm springing the hook.' The tow cable was secured to the tug by way of a large hook with a powered latch. A switch up on the bridge released it.

'What about Hub and Polacco?'

'Stand clear!' said Hunt, and he pressed the

489

emergency release.

There wasn't much tension left in the cable but several tons of braided steel could not escape the pull of gravity for long. When the jaws sprang open the tow cable buzzed and whipped like a wounded snake, streaming through the chafing gear at the stern so fast it smoked. The pad eye at the tail bounced along the deck, gouging it before it was pulled over the stern and into the sea.

K-335 *Gepard*

'Passing beneath the target now, Captain,' said Kureodov.

'And the *Los Angeles?*'

'Still to the...' but Kureodov stopped. He watched the circular display as the computer stepped from sector to sector. 'The tugboat is speeding up and moving southwest ... but the target is not!'

Tow line snapped. 'What about the *Los Angeles?*'

'He ... was there a moment ago. Let me check.' But the American submarine had vanished. 'No contact!'

Submarines do not evaporate. *He's out there and up to something,* thought Leonov. What were his intentions? To trade torpedo for torpedo? One old freighter full of criminals for the finest warship in the Russian Northern Fleet?

Leonov had come to think of the American captain as two men: one who took risks when the odds were stacked in his favor, the other timid when they were not.

490

Which captain was in command now?

MV 'Nova Spirit'

Jameson knelt at the cargo hold hatch with Wheeler and Stepik beside him. He pulled two grenades from his vest and placed them on the deck; one high explosive, the other a fragmentation round. The hatch was dogged down with four rusted latches. He grasped one of the handles. 'Bravo One on set.'

'Five is ready. Say when.'

'Six?'

The sniper came back with a terse, 'Bravo Six, deck clear.'

Jameson turned to Stepik and Wheeler. He got two nods. 'Okay, Pyro. Shake and bake.'

Petty Officer Battaglia grabbed his sledge hammer and smashed it against the steel door. The effect was instantaneous as the out-of-synch *pop … pop pop … pop pop* of two AKs lit off.

Jameson grabbed the hatch handle and turned. Stepik and Wheeler did the same. At first it seemed rusted in place, but then the hatch yielded. The staccato flash of automatic weapons lit his face. A billow of acrid cordite smoke rose from the hold. He pulled the pin on the HE grenade, let the handle fly, counted to two and dropped it.

A brilliant flash, and the grenade went off with a terrific roar that shook the deck plates. Jameson dropped the fragmentation round into the smoke rising from the first. It detonated with a smaller,

491

sharper *crack!* followed by the whistle and ping of a million flying shards.

The silence pressed in on Jameson's ears. *Did we get lucky?* 'Pyro, go!' He slid his nods into place and dived down the ladder, using his gloved hands to brake the fall. He landed on deck, rolled and came up with his MP5 firing high and portside. An instant later Pyro kicked open the door and blasted away with his Remington 870 shotgun.

The hold had *ambush* written all over it. The space was a maze of cement stacks and narrow passages. One look and he knew that if the grenades hadn't taken the Tangos down finding them and killing them was going to be a bloody business.

Jameson saw something move and instinctively squeezed off three rounds as Pyro's shotgun raked the sacks from the far side.

'Hold your fire!' said Pyro. 'One Tango down!'

'So where's the other one?' grunted Chief Wheeler.

That was a good question. Jameson listened to the muffled boom of waves hitting the hull and the drip and slosh of water moving in the bilges. He heard a metallic *twang.* Wheeler and Stepik heard it, too.

Almost at once, *Nova Spirit* began to swing her broad sides to the wind and waves.

'Tow line snapped,' Wheeler whispered.

How far are we offshore? Jameson wondered.

'Hey skipper,' said Pyro, 'you better come take a look at this.'

Jameson rose from behind a pile of cement

sacks shredded by grenades and cautiously made his way to where Pyro stood.

Musa lay sprawled on his side across a thoroughly aerated bag of cement. He wore the green headband of a martyr-to-be. Limestone dust leaked from rips in the canvas, mixing with water and blood.

Wheeler sniffed. 'What's that? Perfume?'

A coroner would face a challenge determining Musa's cause of death; he'd taken all three of Jameson's rounds in his chest. They made a tight, fatal triangle: belly, lung, heart. He'd taken shotgun pellets to the face and neck. The fragmentation grenade had stitched his bloody back full of steel needles. For all of that, he still had an earphone on through which faint music still tinkled. Though that wasn't what drew Jameson's eye.

Two Kalashnikovs lay beside the body. Musa still had his finger through the trigger guard of one. The other was not a foot away.

'The fucker was shooting two-handed,' said Pyro.

Wheeler knelt beside the dead Chechen and wrinkled his nose. 'And he's wearing perfume.'

Jameson looked up at the underside of the cargo deck. One brother was accounted for. Where was the other one?

'Hey, check this out,' said Pyro. He'd found the tape player under Musa's hip. A testimony to Japanese manufacture: it was still turning. Pyro stopped and ejected the tape. *'Allah Helps you Grow.'* He tossed it to Jameson.

He flipped it and saw the other side. 'The perfume is flower water,' he said. 'The *jihadis* wear it so that they'll smell good when they show up in paradise. What we have here is some serious *Taqiyya*.'

'Tequila?' asked Wheeler.

'*Taqiyya*. The Muslim doctrine of deception.'

'You mean one guy shooting for two?' said Stepik.

'No.' He showed them the other side of the tape cartridge.

It was Michael Jackson's *Blood on the Dance Floor*.

'Man.' Pyro looked genuinely horrified. 'This dude was twisted.'

Jameson thought, *Materials secure, a computer full of good shit. We're done.* 'Set the gizmo,' he told Pyro. 'Rig the timer for ten minutes. Steve? Tell the boat we're coming off target.'

'I'll have to go up on deck to get a signal.'

Jameson nodded. 'Bravo Six, this is Bravo One. Keep the deck clear. Everyone else back to the rally point. We're outta' here.'

Adnan separated the rusted slats of the steel louver and peered out. A gust of wind spattered them with rain and drove the sweet, fresh smell of acacia into his nostrils. He'd brought a small bottle of scented oil for just this moment. It came from southern Jordan, harvested by a tribe directly descended from Nuh; the prophet Christians tried to steal by calling him *Noah*. It was the sweetest, most fragrant variety of acacia, and he'd poured the entire bottle over his hair.

The gardens of paradise would smell even sweeter. There Adnan would bathe in rivers of water incorruptible, drink from rivers of milk, wine and honey pure and clear. Eat fruits which tasted beyond any earthly description, and receive the infinite Grace of God.

Had He not shown His trust in Adnan this very night? After all, it was normal to place the louvered intake at the front of the false stack where fresh air could be directed down to the engine room. But it was God's hand to put a soldier of the cross directly in his sights.

From his vantage inside the ship's false stack, Adnan could look over the top of the bridge to the roof of the crane cab. He had no night-vision equipment, but the occasional flash of lightning and the dim glow of coastal lights to the west was enough to illuminate the dark shape of a man crouching atop it.

It angered Adnan to think the American's 'rescue' had been nothing more than a lie to cover their assault. But when a snake bites, what was that but a demonstration of its true nature? Now all their lies had been exposed. He'd heard the furious firefight break out in the cargo hold. He'd felt the thump and crack of explosions. The shooting had stopped. No doubt his brother was dead. Adnan was sure he'd taken a great many with him.

The holy words of the Koran rose within him like the sweet scent of a fresh blossom: *'Against them make ready your strength to the utmost of your power. Strike terror into the enemies of Allah!'*

He and Musa had unleashed a power that would shake the world of disbelief to its core and with any luck, bring it down. And who had done this great thing? It briefly troubled Adnan that no one would know, but that was false pride. Who was unknown to Allah?

He raised the barrel of the AK and slipped the muzzle soundlessly out through the open louvers. He waited for a flash, and it came; a double stroke! As though God had said *Here. Let Me guide you.*

Adnan shifted the AK to automatic fire, put his sight on Tommy Anders, raised the barrel to offset the drop of the bullet, whispered, *Allah u akbar!,* and pulled the trigger.

The AK hammered against his shoulder as Adnan hosed the crane cab with 7.62 millimeter bullets. He could hear the smash of glass and shouts from somewhere close by. They did not deter him. He fired the magazine empty before pulling the smoking barrel back in. He put his eye to the louver to see.

When the lightning flashed again, the dark figure was gone.

USS *Portland*

'Captain?' said Scavullo. 'I lost contact with Bravo.'

'What about the new antenna?'

'It's up. We have one last connection to make.'

Banjo's blue coveralls were soaked through and his face dripped salt water. But he was grinning. He fished around and came up with the other end of the cable. 'Here you go, lieutenant.' He handed the other end to Scavullo. 'Thread this puppy on and we can go below.'

She took it and started aft to where the through-hull fitting was mounted. Her safety line went tight. She turned, thinking Niebel had stepped on it to be annoying, but no. Even with her arm extended, the belt was a foot and a half too short.

'What's wrong?' asked Gant.

'Nothing.' She knelt down and unclipped the safety line as a wave slapped against the sail. She climbed up and noticed a dim glow on the western horizon. *Lights?* 'Hey, I can see the coast out there.'

'Forget it,' said Banjo. 'Just hurry.'

MV 'Nova Spirit'

Jameson was at the watertight door leading out onto the deck when he heard the shooting over-head. 'Bravo Seven! Can you see where the fire's coming from?'

'I think we got a Tango up on the bridge,' said McQuill.

Shit, thought Jameson. He should have posted another sniper up there to cover the aft end of the ship. 'Bravo Six, you on?'

There was no reply. Just the sizzle of atmospherics.

'Tommy, do you copy?'

Silence, again.

'Bravo Seven, hustle up to the bridge and clean it out. Then set security forward.' Jameson turned to Wheeler and Stepik. 'Steve? You secure the ladderwell. Chief? Watch my ass. I'm going to find Anders.'

Wheeler nodded and flattened himself to the side of the door. Stepik went aft to guard the ladderwell going up to the bridge.

'Seven?'

'Almost there, skipper,' said McQuill. The sharpshooter hurried up the ladder from the half-drowned fantail. He paused at the door to the galley, listening, then burst in. The space was deserted.

He went back out and took the final flight up to the bridge. Before he went in through the door to the radio room he examined the old lifeboat carefully. The canvas cover was undisturbed. He looked up. The stubby smokestack was set nearly flush with the aft edge of the bridge roof. 'Bravo Seven's at the radio shack. You see anyone up high?'

'Negative. Bravo Five has your back,' said Pyro.

'Bravo Four is at the ladderwell,' said Stepik.

'Seven's going in.' McQuill entered the dark bridge through the aft watertight door. The radio cubicle was empty. So was the bridge. The two wings were deserted. He looked up. *Got to be up there on his belly.* There was just one ladder bolted to the outside of the wheelhouse, but how did you climb into the face of an assault rifle?

One rung at a time. 'Bravo Seven's going up to the bridge roof. Keep an eye on the stack. If he's up there he might try to slip around the back.' He put his sniper rifle over his shoulder and drew his Sig Sauer pistol. One rung. Two. The next would put his head over the lip. 'Bravo Seven, ready.' The pistol had no safety but it did require taking up the trigger slack before it would fire. He squeezed the trigger mechanism shut. The slightest pull and it would fire.

'Bravo Five, clear,' said Pyro, then, in case they needed reminding, he added, 'Be advised eight minutes on the timer.'

'Bravo One, out the door in three, two, one and *now.*' Jameson flung open the forward watertight door, hoping the noise would draw fire from above. The door clanged against its frame. There was no other sound. Jameson scanned the cargo deck with his nods. *Tommy's out there someplace.* He eased out of the iron house, flattened himself against the wall, waited one beat, two, then made a dash for the crane cab. He leaped off the catwalk, dodged left, then right, then back up the center in a random pattern he hoped would spoil some Tango's aim.

McQuill exploded up the ladder. He swept the bridge roof with his Sig Sauer. Up here the ship's stack was only a little taller than he was. The roof was empty. 'Seven! Clear!'

'Bravo Four's coming up,' said Stepik. 'Don't shoot.'

McQuill hurried to the forward edge, looked down and spotted Jameson kneeling at the base of the crane cab.

Tommy Anders had taken two rounds. One had cratered the back of his body armor and would have left him bruised and amused. The other was something they jokingly called a 'Golden BB'; an unlucky shot that found a narrow, unprotected zone above the armor and below his helmet. A few inches to either side, up or down, and Tommy

499

Anders would be laughing. Instead, he was dead.

'One, this is Eight,' said Flagler, the squad medic. 'I'm coming out.' He was equipped to treat gunshot wounds, to stop bleeding.

'Hold your position,' said Jameson. Whoever shot Tommy Anders was still around. 'Where's that fucking Tango, McQuill?'

'I don't see him. What about Tommy?'

There was silence on the squad frequency, then Pyro said, 'Seven minutes thirty seconds.'

CHAPTER THIRTY-THREE

THE SIXTH WAVE

MV 'Nova Spirit'

Steve Stepik clambered up the ladder, rolled over the edge of the roof and stood. 'Shit. We're cutting this deal too close.' The Sicilian coast was a luminous fringe to the north, the west, the south. Only the east was dark. *Somebody's going to see this ship blow.* 'Where's the Tango?'

Adnan could hear the soft scrape of footsteps on the rough, rusty roof of the bridge. He could hear McQuill whisper into his radio headset. He slowly raised one of the louver's slats. Adnan found himself doubly blessed. He reached for a fresh magazine.

Stepik pressed the push to talk on the Motorola. 'Hey ma'am. How do you hear Bravo now?'

The reply was strong and clear. 'Great! We were getting worried.'

'Yeah. The tow line snapped and we're adrift again. We're coming off target. Meet us at the recovery point. We should be there in–' Stepik saw McQuill freeze. 'What?'

McQuill's finger was tight on the pistol trigger. 'You smell something?'

USS *Portland*

'Captain?' said Scavullo. 'Bravo says the tow line snapped. They're drifting north. They're leaving the ship and they want us to meet them at the recovery point.'

The recovery point is east, thought Steadman. With tight waters in all the other quadrants, east was a good direction. 'Tell them we'll be there. What about the emergency antenna?'

'Almost done.' Scavullo put down the intercom and scrambled up onto the top of the sail to finish threading on the antenna cable. Her safety line dangled uselessly behind her. The boat rolled and shuddered as though trying to flick her into the water. *Niebel would throw a party.*

Lightning flashed and Banjo saw a wave heap up off their port side and it looked like a big one. 'Forget the cable! Get back down!'

'It's ... *done!*' She gave the fitting a final twist, then jumped back down to the cockpit. She snapped her tether ring to a hard point on the deck just as the sixth wave struck.

The instant before her head went under she

501

realized the wave would have swept her right off the top of the sail if she hadn't grabbed something solid. And then the world became cold, gritty water, surging, black and heavy. She let out a few bubbles. How long would it last? The boat dropped away beneath her feet the way it always did. As it fell, so would it rise, eventually. She grabbed her tether to reel herself back in. One hand, two, a third. Her hand closed around the metal end fitting.

It wasn't attached to something solid. She wasn't attached at all.

She dropped it and flailed with her arms, reaching for something, anything connected to the submarine. Her knuckles scraped metal but there was nothing to hold. Her float coat took hold and began tugging her up and away from the deck. The water roiled and surged around her. Her inner compass spun. Her lungs began to burn. If the wave didn't pass in time she would have no choice but to kick for the air. But which way was the air? The floats! *They* knew. And so she stopped struggling against them and let the floats pull her up, but then there was a *whumf!* of another breaking wave. She felt herself caught in a powerful current surging over a steel cliff.

Something sharp struck her in the stomach and blew her breath out in an explosion of bubbles. She scrambled to push away from whatever it was and found herself sprawled half over the side of the sail. The water fell away in a tumble of white foam. She tried to edge back into the cockpit but the boat took a roll and she went over.

Before she hit the surface she came to a sudden

and painful stop, her harness cutting into her skin. She gasped for air, wondering how she could be hanging in the air looking *down* at the waves.

'Hang on!' said Banjo. He was holding the metal ring of her tether, and her life, in his hands. He started hauling her up the side of the sail hand over hand. He was strong but the angle was poor. The rope slipped and he stopped her fall with his hands jammed against the lip of the sail. He turned. 'Socks! Quick! Help me!'

Niebel didn't move.

A wave rolled up the hull, reaching for Scavullo, then receded.

'Shipmate! Help me!'

'I'm coming.' Niebel grabbed the socket wrench he'd been using and swung it down hard across Banjo's knuckles.

Scavullo couldn't see what was happening in the bridge. All she knew was that Banjo was yelling and the water was reaching for her. And so she grabbed her tether, got her shoes on the smooth steel side of the sail and started climbing up, hand over hand.

MV *'Nova Spirit'*

Adnan slipped the fresh magazine into his rifle. It seated with a satisfying *click*. He reached for the slats to move one aside, but then he heard a rasp of rusted metal; not from the two devils walking around outside on the roof, but from down by his feet.

He looked down.

The floor of the false stack was littered with chalk white bird droppings and brown chunks of rusted steel. But there was a hatch set into it as well. A hatch with a handle. And as Adnan watched, the handle moved.

'Six minutes forty-five,' said Pyro.

'McQuill, Stepik,' said Jameson. 'Rally point now.'

There was no answer and for a moment Jameson thought he'd lost another man; maybe two. 'McQuill?'

'Stand by,' McQuill whispered. He stood absolutely still, his senses dialed up full. He could hear the rumble of thunder, the pounding of waves against the hull, the hum of wind through the stays, the creak of the old ship's bones as she was driven before the wind. Indeed, he could hear the *rush ... rush ... rush* of blood in his ears. But against all of that he had heard something very different.

'What?' Stepik asked again. He had his MP5 up and ready, though he could see no reason for McQuill's alarm.

McQuill held his hand out palm down to signal silence. There were only so many things in this world that could make the soft, metal-on-metal sound of a magazine being pushed into a receiver. And Petty Officer McQuill, Bravo Seven, was not seeing any of them.

He craned his head up to survey the whole of the mast, from the antenna at its top, the small platform where the radar bar stood motionless, down its bare, spindly legs all the way to the deck.

His gaze paused at the metal slats of the short smoke stack. The air intake? Could the wind have shifted a slat? Yes, but then he caught a detail he had overlooked: the air intake was set in a frame, and the frame had a handle.

What was the point of a handle that didn't open something?

'Hey assholes,' said Pyro. 'Six minutes thirty.'

'Let's get off this tub,' said Stepik. He started for the ladder. One step, two, and then they *both* heard it: a heavy thump, a curse, a clatter and thud of something heavy falling against thin metal.

McQuill opened up on the stack with the Sig Sauer. Then Stepik unleashed his MP5, first on three-burst, and before the third round left the muzzle he'd slipped it into full auto.

Unlike the Soviets, the Gdansk yard had used decent steel plate when it welded up the ship's false stack. But decades of salt spray, diesel exhaust, bird droppings and neglect reduced it to a kind of sandwich made of equal parts old paint and new rust. It offered little resistance to the torrent of 9mm rounds. Thirty heavy bullets ripped through the stack, sending jagged pieces flying off into the night.

McQuill charged up to the gaping hole where the air intake had been with his pistol already reloaded. He saw something move and nearly fired, but caught himself just in time: the shape sprawled inside the stack wore an orange survival suit with USNS *Apache* stitched across the back.

As he watched, dark red welled up through the letters.

'What's going on up there?' Jameson demanded.

'Hostage down!' said Stepik, but then McQuill rolled the body over with his boot.

'That's no fucking hostage,' he said.

Adnan's bushy beard was slicked down with his own blood, and his mouth was set in a grim smile that McQuill found unnerving.

Then, the corpse arched his back.

McQuill swung the pistol to Adnan's head and was about to squeeze off a shot but he was stopped by a hiss and gurgle of wet air escaping under pressure. A steam cloud spurted out from beneath Adnan's riddled body as the fidley hatch beneath him cracked open.

'Six minutes!' warned Pyro.

McQuill dragged the body off the hatch and let it fall open. A gust of oily fumes and water vapor rose, and then, a dark shape. It took them both a moment to realize what it was: a head, a face, a neck. Hair plastered down with gray cement and almost every square inch paved over with pea-sized blisters. By some fluke of biology, only the eyelids remained clear of them. They were two, pale crescents of smooth skin, though puffed up as though they were subject to a great pressure.

'Jesus,' said Stepik.

The face was barely recognizable as ever having been human. But then the two eyelids opened, blinked in surprise, then recognition, and a tear dribbled down, wending its way among the cracked channels and weeping blisters. A wide crack split the pebbled pavement, a mouth

opened and three words struggled free: *'Menya ...
zavoot ... Makayev.'*

I am Makayev.

USS *Portland*

A wave rolled the submarine to starboard. The
weight dangling from the tether eased as the
motion moved Scavullo in the right direction.
Banjo used it to hold Scavullo with one hand and
fend off Niebel with the other. But then the boat
came level, the weight returned and the tether
slipped. He had to grab on with both hands to
stop it.

Niebel had figured Banjo to be stubborn but
not stupid. He would see that shedding the
source of *Portland's* problems was just good
sense. But cracking his knuckles with a wrench
had not educated him sufficiently. Indeed, here
was a new problem: if Banjo wouldn't go along
with the program *now*, what might he say *later?*
Niebel's thinking evolved and expanded, and so
he took the wrench and swung it again, this time
at Banjo's head.

Gant ducked the blow as another wave rolled up
into the cockpit. He felt the tether jerk as Scavullo
climbed up hand over hand. A few seconds more
and she'd be up over the lip, Banjo could let go
and they could face this crazy sonarman together.

'Let her go!' Niebel screamed.

'No fucking way.'

Niebel swung again and connected with
Banjo's shoulder.

A raw spasm sizzled down his arm, his fingers shot open. The tether swept over the lip of the sail.

Niebel knew that one more would end it. 'Asshole,' he said. He raised the wrench over his head and brought it down in a vicious arc.

Gant tried to protect his head but the wrench struck above his left eye with a solid *crack* that doubled his vision. He toppled back to the deck. He was looking straight up as a great wave crashed over the cockpit, burying them all in an avalanche.

He struggled to his feet before it receded. His head was bleeding and two broken fingers were swelling up into sausages. He felt something thrashing against his legs and reached down to yank Niebel up by his hair.

He found Scavullo instead. She'd ridden the wave up and into the cockpit. He pulled her to her feet as the invading sea hissed out through the cockpit drains. When the deck appeared, they both saw one end of Niebel's tether still clipped to a deck ring. The other end, and the sonarman who'd predicted the ocean would get him, was gone.

She went to the side to see if she could spot him. *Portland* was leaving a curving white wake across waves black and streaked with foam. If they didn't find Niebel now they likely never would. She reached for the intercom to make the man overboard report, but Gant's uninjured hand closed over hers and he said, 'No,' he said. 'Wait.'

CHAPTER THIRTY-FOUR

REVELATIONS

MV *'Nova Spirit'*

'Five minutes thirty.' There was an edge to Pyro's warning, and with reason; in three hundred and thirty seconds the ship they were riding would become an incandescent ball of vaporized steel and flame.

Jameson was ready to leave, his mission as complete as possible and with two of his men down way too costly. But both McQuill and Stepik were talking over one another, jamming the squad frequency with their voices.

'...the ... down. The shooter ... is–'

'...Russian–'

'Everyone, *shut up!*' Jameson yelled. 'Steve, go.'

'We've got the Russian. Do you copy? We have Makayev.'

'Makayev? You're sure?'

'That's what he called himself. He's saying something else. Wait.'

'One, this is Seven. The Tango is down,' McQuill filled in. 'It's the other brother.'

'Okay,' Stepik said. 'I don't know what the fuck he's talking about. It's just two words. *Ohotnik* and something that sounds like *fermented* .'

Ohotnik meant *hunter.* But fermented? Jameson

had no idea what that was about. 'Bring him down. We'll haul his ass off in the raft and have a talk after we sterilize the target.'

'Ah, I don't think so, skipper,' said Stepik. 'You better come up and see for yourself. He ain't going anywhere.'

'How bad do we need Makayev?' asked Chief Wheeler.

It was a practical question and it demanded a practical answer. Jameson had the virus samples that probably came from Russian weapons stocks. He had a computer that might have useful information on its hard disk. It was nice to know that the Saudis, those staunch American allies in the war against terror, were playing around with bioweapons. It was especially interesting that they would entrust them to Salafi and a couple of *jihadis*. But it would be a whole lot better to be able to prove all this. What connected all those dots? *Makayev.*

Jameson made up his mind. 'Pyro, abort the timer. We'll command detonate the package when we're clear.'

'Shit. You could have told me that a minute ago.'

'Bravo Four, this is One,' said Jameson. 'I'm coming up.'

K-335 *Gepard*

'Contact regained!' crowed Kureodov. 'The American submarine is on the surface. It seems to be coming in our direction again.'

Seems! Leonov had tailed the best ships of the American Navy without being detected. He'd closed to firing range and withdrawn only because he knew he could return when and where he chose. There could be no doubt now: they could see him. Was his ship emitting some kind of signal, some new noise – a 'sound short' – that he could not hear but the Americans could? Or had they come up with something that rendered the invisible visible?

Submarine warfare was just the latest match in the eternal struggle between offense and defense. You have arrows? We have chain mail. You have crossbows? We have guns. You have guns? We have tanks.

You have active silencing? We can detect you.

No doubt this encounter would have to be studied closely. But that could wait. Right now, Leonov had a target in his sights and an American submarine that was getting in his way. A submarine commanded by a man who'd been easily frightened, easily cowed once before. '*Starpom?*' he said. 'Flood Torpedo Tubes One and Two.'

Stavinsky pressed the flat blue button marked One, then did the same for the second tube. The rumble of rushing water echoed through the silent submarine, and into the sea beyond.

USS *Portland*

'Bottom sounder's flashing, Captain,' said Lieutenant Pena. He'd set the safety limit at five hundred feet. Plenty of water under the keel when the boat was on the surface. But it would feel quite different should they have to dive. And from here the Gulf of Noto grew only more shallow to the north, south and west.

'Reset the limit to two fifty,' said Steadman. That was a good hundred feet *less* than *Portland*'s own length.

'Just how far are you going to take us in?' asked Tony Watson.

He's got a point, thought Browne. He'd kept silent as *Portland* maneuvered to block the *Akula*. But while his vision was still blurred, his thinking was not. The boat was in dangerous water.

Before Steadman could answer, Bam Bam shouted, 'Conn, Sonar! Transient! The *Akula* just flooded tubes!'

'Captain, you've got to pull back,' said Watson. 'Give him the ship. We don't want to have to run from a rocket torpedo.' This was sound advice, for only a fool hears the click of a rifle being cocked and waits around to see what happens next.

Steadman knew that turning away from the *Akula*'s likely target was the safe move. You didn't want to be anywhere near a smart weapon hunting for prey; they sometimes did very dumb things. Safe, but wrong. The Russians seemed to think they could gun down ships whenever and wherever they pleased. He hadn't been able to stop them then. He could now. 'Torpedo room, fire control,' he said, 'make tubes One and Two ready in all respects. Sonar? Range and bearing?'

'Range eighteen thousand yards, bearing two six eight.'

'Firing point procedures, Tubes One and Two.'

'Captain–' Watson began, but Steadman was not interested.

'Log your objections as you see fit.' He took down the intercom microphone. 'I'm not running.'

Gepard's challenge had been accepted, and met.

MV *'Nova Spirit'*

The idea that Makayev would forge a link of evidence that joined Pokrov with Riyadh lasted only a little longer than it took Jameson to climb up to the bridge roof. Up there he could see the glow of towns on the Sicilian coast, dangerously near and bright. It cast enough light to silhouette Stepik and McQuill as they stood together at the edge, about as far from the bullet-riddled stack as possible. A dark stream of blood spilled out onto the bridge roof. It swirled and spread as the ship pitched and heeled under the impact of the wind and waves.

'Where's Makayev?' he asked them.

Stepik pointed to the false stack.

Jameson took one look at it and figured they'd shot up the Russian biologist, too. He hurried to the shredded air intake. When he grabbed the handle the entire panel came off in his hands. He tossed it aside. It was dark inside, and he swung his nods down and dialed them up to full, acid green.

Adnan's body had been dragged to one side, and though Jameson trusted Stepik and McQuill, the sight of the bloody orange survival suit still gave him a shock. Having to explain why you

513

killed a Tango was hard enough these days. Think Abu Ghraib. But a hostage? An American? He turned. Makayev looked more like a pile of old rags tossed from a speeding car than a man. He moved closer.

'*Damn.*'

Jameson had seen recent photos of Makayev, but there was no way he would have identified him from the nightmare staring up from the littered floor of the false stack. His first, second and third thoughts were *run, run* and *run* again. Whatever this thing was, whoever it had been, it was no longer. It was horror. Nothing more, nothing less.

Blisters crowded nearly every square inch of visible skin. Neck, cheeks, lips, ears and forehead. They even erupted from beneath Makayev's hair. Only his eyelids remained clear. Then those two unblistered crescents blinked, the swollen slash that had once been a mouth cracked, and Jameson heard, faintly, a soft hiss. It became a word. A cobbled tongue flicked across the lips, then the word was spoken again.

'*Ospe … ospe.*'

Jameson had done many dangerous things with the Teams that went far beyond the definition of merely *heroic:* jumping from blacked-out jets high over a dark ocean, swimming through icy waters to a North Sea oil platform the IRA had thoughtfully rigged to blow, assaulting booby-trapped caves high in the Hindu Kush. Things that demanded the utmost disregard for his life as well as an almost religious faith in what he and his men could accomplish.

But what it took to step out of a jet flying at

thirty thousand feet was nothing compared to this. He felt a force radiate up from Makayev that repelled him in a way that dug down deep beneath his consciousness, even his training. Jameson had to make himself turn back, crouch down, put his ear close to those horrible lips and listen.

'*Ospe!* ... *ospe!*'

'Smallpox,' said Jameson. He switched to Russian. '*Ot Pokrov?*'

'*Da* ... *da.*' The eyes blinked, the deformed tongue licked, the chest rose and Makayev whispered, '*Ohotnik* ... *ohotnik...*'

'Hunter?'

'*Ohotnik* ... *dolzhan* ... *omeryat* ... *v'more...*'

Jameson's Russian wasn't up to Kernal's standards and far below Scavullo's. The individual words held meaning. *Hunter must die in the sea.* Together, they did not. Who was this hunter?

Makayev sensed Jameson's confusion, and he said again, '*Ohotnik* ... *ospe* ... *dolzhan* ... *omeryat* ... *v'more.*'

'*Ohotnik eta smallpox?*' A guess, but quickly rewarded with a nod.

'*Da* ... *da. Ohotnik* ... *smallpox. Ot Pokrov.*' Then, another word: '*Fermenty...*'

Fermented? Beer and wine were fermented. But he doubted the Russian was asking for those. '*Shto eta fermenty?*'

Makayev sucked in a breath. It rattled in his chest, then he said, '*On* ... *namervayetsye* ... *kuda* ... *vwi ideti* ... *ohotnik posdedyet* ... *za.*'

Where you go, Hunter will follow.

'They did *what?*'

'The *Los Angeles* just flooded two torpedo tubes, Captain,' stammered Kureodov. 'I can't ... it's not certain because the conditions are very poor. There's a great deal of background noise on the surface and–'

'Never mind the conditions. How far away is he? Exactly!' Leonov caught a glance from his *starpom.*

'Seventeen thousand meters.'

They couldn't see us from beyond five thousand before. Or did they only mean for us to think so?

'The Americans have men on that ship,' said Stavinsky.

'There are bandits who murdered Russians on it, too.'

'But if the *Los Angeles* can see us they can target us. If we fire on that freighter they might–'

'I know what they might do,' said Leonov. *What I don't know is what they will do.* A drifting freighter with a stolen strategic weapon. An American submarine sitting near the firing bearing, its own weapons at the ready. How could he destroy that ship without allowing the *Los Angeles* the chance to shoot back? 'Range to the freighter?'

'Nine thousand meters and slowly closing,' said the Termite, happy to be asked a question he could answer definitively. 'They're being blown back at us.'

Nine thousand. An old, reliable SET-60 ran at a little more than twelve hundred meters per minute. It would take more than seven minutes to

516

strike the ship; long enough for the American captain to hear the torpedoes swimming and launch a counter-attack. Leonov needed to strip away time and force the American to withdraw, to evade.

Was there an answer?

Central Command was nearly dead silent. Only the distant thud of the *Sirena* active silencing system and the soft click of the pumps and the whir of cooling fans could be heard.

Starpom Stavinsky looked at the sprig of green birch he'd brought from home. It was in a glass of water on a bookshelf above the firing console, wedged between two thick manuals. American torpedoes had excellent guidance systems. Even if the submarine that launched them didn't know precisely where the target might lay, their torpedoes stood a good chance of finding it. Wisdom said they should back away. Once the American submarine was gone they could finish the job of sinking the freighter. And if they failed? If a stolen Russian weapon fell into American hands? Well, there were worse hands that might wish to grasp it. He looked at Leonov. *He's decided something.* 'Captain?'

'Secure Tubes One and Two and close the outer doors.'

Thank God. Stavinsky let out his breath.

But Leonov was not finished. He pulled down the *kashtan* microphone. 'Torpedo Room. Dobrin?'

'*Michman* Sotnikov listening, Captain,' came the tinny answer from Compartment One. 'Dobrin has left the watch.'

Sotnikov was one of the younger warrant

517

officers on board *Gepard*. 'Sotnikov? Make Tubes Three and Four ready with Type One Elevens.'

A *Squall* would shrink those seven minutes down to barely sixty seconds. 'It took Dobrin ten minutes to load a pair of *Squalls*. Do it faster.'

'Start your clock,' said Sotnikov.

MV 'Nova Spirit'

The squad frequency came alive with Steve Stepik's worried voice. 'Skipper, the boat says the Russians are setting up for a shot.'

'Area security is their goddamned job,' Jameson snapped. 'Find out how much time she thinks we've got.' He stood up. 'Pyro. The charge is set for command-detonate?'

'Rigged and set. We're leaving?'

'We're leaving.' Whatever Makayev, or what had *been* Makayev, might be trying to tell him, it wasn't worth riding this bitch to the bottom.

But before he could leave, Makayev reached out and grabbed Jameson's ankle. His grip was surprisingly firm. *'Vwi … ne dolzhni vuiti.'*

Jameson pried Makayev's fingers off. He could feel the hard nodules of virus move under his hot skin.

'Skipper?' said Stepik. 'Your old girlfriend says they're in a Mexican standoff. *Portland*'s flooded her tubes and the CO says he'll shoot if the Russians do.'

'The XO? I don't believe it. Wars are against Navy regulations.'

'You talk to her then. I'll patch her through.'

The squad frequency filled with heavy static that only partly cleared. Jameson said, 'Rosie?'

'Yes! I'm...' her voice dissolved, then re-emerged. '...for now. If the Russians change their minds you won't have much time to get clear.'

'Is Watson serious about firing on that *Akula?*'

'Not ... Watson ... Steadman has the conn and ... serious.'

Steadman? Jameson was still angry about that little tiff over radioing back for an update. 'I got a Russian speaker here who's not making any sense. You want a shot at him?'

The static swelled, then fell away. '...ready.'

'*Ne mozhit vwi pogurit Russkovo?*' asked Makayev.

Jameson was about to say Makayev was damned well *looking* at the only Russian-speaker around, but that was not exactly true. He looked down into that horrible face and saw something in Makayev's eyes, determination, desperation, pleading.

'*Da.*' Jameson slipped the boom microphone off his head and put it to Makayev's lips. '*Vwi poprosidi Russki diktor?*' You want a Russian speaker? '*Zdyez adna. Pogovoritye!*' Talk.

Makayev could feel his body collapsing like an old brick wall in a violent earthquake. He was running out of chances to keep Hunter contained and everything, absolutely everything, depended on this idiot who could speak words without understanding them.

'Hello? Are you Makayev?' said Scavullo.

Her words were very clear, her voice reassuring and warm. Makayev was surprised. Not that he was somehow speaking to a civilized human

519

being, but that he could still feel a faint flicker of something almost like *hope*. 'Yes. I ... am Makayev. But who ... who are ... you?'

'My name is Rose, doctor. I have a few questions.'

'*Rozah*. Your Russian ... *is* ... quite...'

'Thank you but first, what were you trying to tell Lieutenant Jameson? He didn't understand you.'

'Jee ... ime–ee–zon...?'

'Please. We don't have much time. What were you trying to tell him?'

'*Ohotnik...*'

'Hunter?'

Makayev sucked in a breath, then said, '*Da ... Da. Fermenty.*'

'Do you mean the biological process of fermentation?'

'*Nyet*,' he said weakly, dejectedly. Here was another chasm that beckoned him to jump, to surrender. The man she'd called Jameson was just a soldier. What could he know about microbiology? He was dying aboard a dying ship, surrounded by dying men, and she'd offered him the hope of being understood. There was nothing more important in all the world, and in the end, she had not.

Fermenty, thought Scavullo. It was a cognate, a word imported into Russia from another language. Sometimes cognates retained their meanings, sometimes not. What was Makayev trying to say? Why was it so important? What hidden meaning did it hold?

Makayev was a biologist, and *fermenty* was a

biological process of breaking down, of changing things from one form into another. Memories of high-school chemistry and biology struggled into focus. What changed things? 'Dr Makayev?' she said. 'Do you mean *katalyzor?'* Catalyst.

Makayev turned his head as though she'd whispered the word straight into his ear. *'Catalyzor ... protein ... change.'*

'Proteins? Like *enzymes?'*

Makayev's eyes shot open. *'Da! Fermenty!'*

Enzyme. 'Why are enzymes important?'

'Fermenty ... inserted ... into genes.'

Oh shit, she thought. 'What kind of enzymes? 'What for? *Buistra!'*

'Virus ... modified ... enzymes ... with ... interleuken-4...'

'I don't know what that means.'

'Vaksina upornaya ... panimayu?'

She felt the hammer of Makayev's words beat against her with the dull thud of a lead mallet. *Vaccine resistance.* 'How resistant is it?'

Makayev tried to answer but he had almost no strength left. His lungs were melting, his organs dissolving into a slurry of thick fluids and a rising flood of virus. He felt a searing pain clamp down around his chest, then another, a third, and only then, as his heart began to quiver in uncontrollable spasms did he find a final reserve of energy. *'Vpolne.'*

Total.

His vision grayed. The furious energy inside him was dimming.

My God, thought Scavullo. Did Makayev really mean to say the virus had been engineered to be immune to vaccines? 'Why did you bring something like that out?' Her voice was no longer warm. 'Didn't you know what could happen?'

'My reason ... can't ... be used ... who ... would dare?' His words came out in gasps. 'Can still ... stop ... not ... too ... late. You...'

He heard a new voice. Her accent was very different and also very familiar.

'Lonya? You're still awake?'

'I'm scared, mother. Is it too late?'

'Don't worry about time. You did the right thing.'

'But does she know?'

'Close your eyes. She knows.'

He did as she told him. He sensed something leaving his skin in waves, rising up like some evaporating vapor. His worries? Or was Hunter abandoning him, too? Rising up to hunt for new bodies to conquer? He was dissolving, his skin a patchwork of hot and cold, wet and dry, alive and dead. The cells inside him were bursting, *storming* with Hunter. The tide that had chased him up from the belly of the engine room touched him, buoyed him up. He was floating. He was free.

His arm fell. The microphone clattered to the deck.

Jameson couldn't bring himself to touch anything that had come so near to Makayev. He slipped the Motorola from his hip pouch and spoke into it directly. 'Hey Rosie, it doesn't look like Makayev is gonna' be talking any more. What's up with this *fermenty* shit? Is he asking for a brew?'

'Dick... I ... can't...'

'You didn't understand him either?'

'No! I mean, *yes,* but ... I don't know if it's true!'

'What was it about?'

'I can't... I mean, who's listening?'

'Commo check,' said Jameson.

'Three's on and waiting for you down at the fucking boat, *lieutenant*,' said Wheeler. 'I got Flagler and Pyro with me.'

'Four's on,' said Stepik.

'Seven,' said McQuill the sniper. 'What gives, skipper?'

A wave struck the side of the sail and exploded into wind-driven foam. The boom sounded empty and hollow. The not-so-distant lights illuminated the gray bellied clouds as they hurried north. 'Makayev said the virus was genetically modified.'

'So?'

'It's designed to resist vaccine!'

'Okay, so how resistant is resistant?'

The frequency swelled with the bacon fat sizzle of static.

'Rosie? How fucking resistant?'

'Total.'

'Well, shit,' said Jameson. 'Flagler. Give me some options.'

'We've all had our shots,' said the squad medic. 'It stops normal smallpox cold. Even after a primary infection.'

'What about this bug?'

'Depends on if the Russian was telling the truth. If he was, we can do a surface decon, ditch our gear and burn our clothes. But if it really was designed to evade vaccine we'll be bringing Hunter out in our blood. To the boat, anywhere.'

'So we live in quarantine until we know for sure.'

'Where do we find a quarantine?' asked Flagler.

523

'This ship is drifting into a bay surrounded by people. If we run aground the bug gets loose. And if we blow it and return to the boat, we bring it with us decon or no decon. What will happen to us will happen to everyone on the frigging submarine, too.'

'So we blow it here.'

'What if something floats ashore?' said Chief Wheeler.

There was silence as the implications of this settled in. Then Jameson said, 'Any more ideas?'

The squad frequency sizzled and popped with atmospherics.

Jameson was a young man who lived his responsibilities to the fullest, who possessed an absolute faith that every man who wore the SEAL Trident, the so-called 'Budweiser Eagle', had an obligation to live up to them. Not just when he passed BUDS training, but every day of his life. Not for glory. Not for bragging rights. But to be able to pick up a radio and at the end of the day transmit two words: *Mission accomplished.* Anything less was failure, and failure was not an option.

'Okay, gents,' he said. 'Everyone understand what we have to do tonight?'

'Three's in,' said Wheeler.

'Five's not bailing,' said Pyro Battaglia.

'Seven ain't ending up like that Russian,' said McQuill.

Only Stepik remained silent.

'Steve?'

'Yeah. Okay. I'm in.'

'Rosie?' said Jameson. 'Do you have comms back to Norfolk?'

524

'I don't know! But they might have some idea how to–'

'Bravo Nine. Put your CO on,' Jameson said to her.

K-335 *Gepard*

'Hurry! *Buistra!*' Warrant Officer Sotnikov stood right behind the torpedomen as they unbolted the steel straps securing the six thousand pound *Squall* to its rack. With a grunt, they manhandled it onto the angled loading tray. It rumbled down the incline like a grand piano across a wooden floor, coming to a stop with a *crack* and a shower of green fiberglass splinters.

Sotnikov checked his stopwatch. *Seven minutes.* They still had to shove both weapons into their tubes and hook up the firing and guidance cables. *'Buistra!' Quickly!*

The torpedomen stripped the plastic shell away. Two of them started carrying it to the empty place on the storage rack. That was Dobrin's way, and it cost minutes Sotnikov refused to spend.

'Leave it for later! Get the ramp up to Tube Three now!'

They dropped the plastic clamshell to the deck. Their boots crunched broken fiberglass as they maneuvered the loading ramp into position against the breech door of Tube Three.

Seven minutes twenty seconds.

'Buistra! Buistra!'

The hydraulics whined, the ram pushed the *Squall* up the ramp and through the heavy bronze

525

breech door and into the open tube.

Eight minutes.

'Tube Four!'

The sweating sailors cursed and swiveled the loading ramp to open breech of Tube Four.

Eight minutes twenty seconds.

Now only the tapered tails of the *Squalls*, each dominated by a large central rocket exhaust surrounded by eight smaller ports and two red electrical connector blocks were visible.

Two cables dangled above each open tube. One transmitted target data to the *Squall's* guidance computer. The other ignited its eight small booster rockets. Both ended in metal caps. The data link that programmed the torpedo's course and depth was first.

Eight minutes thirty seconds.

'Move!' Sotnikov pushed the men aside and grabbed the data link, leaving the second cable that would ignite the eight small booster rockets for last. There was no reason to tempt fate. Those eight boosters looked small, but they had enough kick to propel the *Squall* out of its tube at nearly fifty knots. Only then, at a safe distance from *Gepard,* would the main engine ignite.

The metal cap was slippery in Sotnikov's sweaty hands. He wiped his palm on his trousers, grasped the connector cap and touched it to the receiver on the tail of the rocket.

'Do you think they'll send us home?' asked Stavinsky.

'Wherever they send us,' said Leonov, 'we're going to run firing drills until their hands bleed.

526

Look how long it's taken to prepare two weapons. I want the time cut by at least–' Leonov stopped, and turned.

Stavinsky felt a soft *pop* of pressure in his ears, like the shutting of an elevator door. He automatically looked up at the fresh air vent. 'What was that?'

Leonov was reaching up for the *kashtan* when a second, and larger, shock wave coursed through *Gepard*. The deck gave a sudden, violent jump. There was a crash of breaking glass.

Stavinsky looked down. The glass with the green birch sprig had jumped off the shelf and lay shattered on the deck. 'Captain!'

'Helm!' shouted Leonov. 'Full up on the planes! All ahead emergency!'

USS *Portland*

A cataract of white lines blossomed on the sonar screen to Bam Bam's right. 'Transient, transient! The *Akula's* goin' crazy!'

Steadman felt an ice-cold shower fall down his spine. The Russian captain had called his bet. He'd already decided what he must do. 'Helm, right full rudder and all ahead full! Fire Control, Tubes One and Two, match bearings and–'

'Conn, Sonar! Stand by!' Bam Bam yelled so loudly he could be heard in control without any intercom. 'Something weird is happening! The *Akula's* digging holes in the ocean with his screw and his plant noise is offscale! He's accelerating like a ... *whoa!*' The white lines suddenly brightened, then spread across the entire screen. A faint rumble sounded through the hull, and everywhere in *Portland* men looked up.

Bam Bam watched the white lines fade. The Russian boat emerged from them acoustically intact, her screw still making turns, her reactor cooling pumps kicked up to maximum circulation.

'Sonar, Conn. What was that sound?' asked Steadman. 'Something bad,' said Bam Bam.

K-335 *Gepard*

The *Squall*'s eight boosters lit off and the heavy weapon hissed down its launch tube until it banged to a halt against the still-closed outer door. There it stopped, rockets still burning, filling Compartment One with choking smoke. Sotnikov tried to slam the breech door shut but the heat drove him back. He briefly considered trying again, but the smoke was even denser and it was too late. He staggered to the watertight door in the aft bulkhead. Someone managed to open it, and it was the sudden release of pressure from inside the compartment that was felt throughout the submarine.

The eight booster motors cut off. There was a moment of the most awful silence, and then the *Squall*'s main rocket motor ignited.

The outer door still held, but the intense fire was too much for the tube. A cone of blue flame jetted through the heavy casing, breaching it. A fire designed to never go out, not even under-water, incinerated the sailors still alive inside

Compartment One. The watertight door had been left open, and toxic smoke and fumes roared aft into Compartment Two.

Just as the bow of the submarine began to rise under Leonov's emergency command, the blue flames broke through into Tube One. It still contained a SET-60, the tube was still flooded, the outer door open.

A hole half a meter wide now connected *Gepard's* inner hull with the sea. A raging river poured through the open watertight door into Compartment Two. Rocket smoke and steam spread through the air conditioning system. The air in Central Command grew yellow and poisonous despite the intervening doors.

Gepard was still pointed uphill, still heading for the surface, but the great submarine was dying. Critical circuits flooded out and shorted. The sheer weight of water in her bow slowed her ascent. Her screw spun furiously, but her bow began to falter, to drop. She came level for a few seconds, tipped over and started down.

Automatic sensors shut her reactor down. The lights blinked off, the emergency lamps came on throughout the ship. Steam still flowed through the turbines when her bow speared the mud.

The deafening, almost animal scream of bending, tearing steel ripped through the submarine. Equipment flew off mounts and crashed into piles against forward bulkheads. Men hung on to whatever they could find to keep from slipping, listening, wondering how they would get back to the surface, to the world of light and air.

Gepard furrowed ten meters of soft silt. The

outer doors of her torpedo tubes were ground off and mangled. The tubes collapsed to half their length.

Four of them contained live weapons ready to launch.

She stopped, bow low, stern high, balanced, and then, four torpedo warheads with the combined energy of nearly two tons of high explosives, went off.

The inner hull could take pressures of nearly sixty atmospheres. The solid bulkheads separating the submarine's nine compartments could withstand ten. Neither one could resist or even slow down the shock wave that ripped the bow from *Gepard* and crushed the rest of the hull in a furious white sphere made from fire, water, steel and men.

CHAPTER THIRTY-FIVE

HUNTER IN THE SEA

USS *Portland*

'Conn, Sonar,' said Bam Bam. 'Multiple explosions in the water. Bearing and range match the *Akula's* last position.'

There was no need to wear a headphone jacked into *Portland's* sonar. The rumble was strong enough to come right through the hull.

'Scratch one *Akula*,' whispered Farnesi.

'Conn, Bridge!' It was Banjo Gant. 'Man over-board starboard! Man overboard starboard!'

Steadman could feel the onset of information overload. He knew what he had to do but he felt as though every movement, every thought had to struggle its way out.

'Commander–' Watson began, but before he could finish COB Browne stepped forward, grabbed the 1MG, clicked it on and spoke.

'Man overboard starboard! Rescue swimmer to the bridge trunk!'

By the time COB's voice died away, Steadman had caught up. 'Helm, put your rudder hard over to starboard. Bridge, Conn. What happened up there?'

'We took a wave in the cockpit, Captain. Niebel was screwing down the last cable connector when it hit. His monkey tail let go.'

'Niebel?' said COB. 'I thought I heard Scavullo say she was connecting that cable.'

'She did,' said Steadman. 'Banjo, is Scavullo–?'

'She's here. I tried to grab Socks when he went over the side but I ... I couldn't hold on to him.'

'Where's that swimmer?' Browne groused.

Steadman wondered the same thing, then the rescue diver appeared at the bridge ladder, his bulky Man Overboard Bag beside him.

'Permission to go topside!' he shouted.

'Go,' said Steadman. The submarine's white wake curved away from her original heading. There was no longer a reason to worry about what the *Akula* might do. The rumble that still could be heard told him that something very wrong had happened to her. Had they tried to

531

take a shot at the freighter, or *Portland?* Run aground hard enough that one of her fish blew? One part of him said that either way they deserved what they got; the other that they were submariners, more like him and his crew than anyone else on earth. And the rumble meant that some of them, perhaps all of them, were dead. And any survivors were trapped.

'Conn, Bridge!' said the rescue diver. 'I'm on top. We need Chief Cooper *now.* Banjo's hurt bad. Do I have your OK to use a searchlight?'

Browne clicked the 1MC again. *'Corpsman lay to the bridge!'* He turned to Steadman. 'Captain? I can go up there and supervise this evolution.'

Steadman glanced at the multifunction screen. The freighter was miles away. 'Make sure to mark the spot with smoke. It's safe to use the light, too. And don't make it two men overboard.'

Browne turned and walked straight for the ladder. He nearly collided with Chief Cooper.

'Where do you think you're going, COB?' asked the duty corpsman.

'Where I'm needed. After you.'

When the boat had swung sixty degrees off her first heading, Steadman said, 'Helm, shift your rudder hard to port.' Whatever Chief Cooper had given Steadman was wearing off fast. He clutched the chrome rail surrounding the periscope stand as his boat pitched and rolled in the waves. The low rumble was gone but he swore he could still feel a vibration through the rail.

It wasn't the *Akula.* It was Steadman's nerves coming painfully back to life. The tingling rose up his arm, into his chest, down through his entire body. Every cell the lightning strike had touched and blasted to numbness was waking up. No. Not waking. *Screaming.*

'Conn, Sonar,' said Bam Bam. His voice was a hoarse whisper.

Then, from the duty radioman, 'Conn, Radio. The antenna's working! New message traffic from Norfolk received!'

'Commander?' said Tony Watson. 'You want me to go get that message?'

Steadman's eyes opened. 'Yes.' His skin was cold and covered with sweat. 'Bridge? Any sign of Niebel?'

'No sir,' said Browne. 'But you might blow a little trim so we ride higher. Five feet should do it.'

'Chief?' said Steadman. 'Blow a little fore and aft trim. See if we can give them five dry feet.'

'Aye aye, Captain,' said Farnesi.

High-pressure air forced ballast out of *Portland's* trim tanks. The submarine rose until the waves broke against her hull, not over it.

'Good blow,' said Browne. 'And Banjo is pretty beat up. Here.' Browne handed the microphone to Chief Cooper.

'Captain? COB's right. I need a stretcher up here.'

Steadman turned to Chief Farnesi. He was already summoning help. 'On the way.'

'I think he's got a concussion and broken. . . hey! What are you–?'

'Conn, this is Scavullo.'

Then, Bam Bam said, 'Conn, Sonar.'

Everyone was trying to talk to him at once, but Scavullo's voice cut to the front of the line.

'Stand ... stand by lieutenant. Sonar, Conn. What is it, Bam Bam?'

'I'm still picking up sounds from the *Akula*. She hit bottom hard but I can hear stuff rattling around like pots and pans. It could be deliberate.'

Survivors, thought Steadman. And if there were they would be trapped in the dark, with cold water rising around them inch by inch, the air growing thick and poisonous with carbon dioxide. It was a nightmare he and every other submariner shared. What to do about it? Radio the Navy base at La Maddalena? *They can't know we're here.* The demands of Yellowstone allowed for no exceptions. But time was also running short. Even if some of her compartments remained intact the *Akula's* machinery was dead.

The tug? At night in a storm. Chances were good they wouldn't have noticed the *Akula's* death. If Steadman could get word to Norfolk, Norfolk could bounce orders back out, stop them, turn them around. And an oceangoing tug would have salvage gear on board. Cranes, even rescue divers. And the water here was not too deep. *Yes.*

'Conn, Bridge! I won't stand by!' Scavullo's voice sounded panicky. 'Bravo's calling and ... they ... they've got to talk with you right now, Captain. *Right now.*'

'Coming up on twenty degrees off our initial course,' said Pardee. The navigator had marked the chart the instant the words *man overboard* sounded. The 'Williamson Turn' they were executing would bring them back, exactly, to that spot.

'Rudder amidships. Ahead dead slow.'

Steadman considered handing the search for Niebel over to Watson, but there was something in Scavullo's voice that worried him. After all, she'd been cool, calm and collected when *Portland* had collided with a Russian boomer. If something was going on up there that could rattle her, Steadman wanted to know what it was. 'Put Bravo over.'

'Wait,' she said. 'Let me try... COB? You hold it right there. All right. Can you hear me?' There was the sound of a microphone being scraped across fabric, then, 'Captain? I'm transmitting with the intercom next to the squad radio. Bravo should be on.'

'Commander?' said Jameson. 'How do you read Bravo?'

'Loud and clear.'

'You still holding the Russian submarine off us?'

'No. The *Akula* is ... she's gone.'

Jameson's reply was unexpected. 'Too bad. Listen. We got the right ship. We recovered the samples, found the Russian biologist and bagged a pair of hardcore *muj*. Okay? There is *no* room for doubt. Remember that when you hear what I have to say.'

'Well done, lieutenant.'

'Wait. This freighter is full of bugs. Every square inch. The detector screams smallpox before we even have a chance to take an air sample, okay? And we're running out of sea room. I can see the coastline. How far offshore are we?'

Steadman looked up at the multifunction screen over the helm. It showed *Portland* twenty-nine miles off the Sicilian coast. The freighter was

535

considerably closer. 'Twenty-three miles.'

'And we're drifting at what? Three, four knots? So in five hours this ship will beach itself. How much water do we have right here?'

'Two hundred eighty feet. But the ship won't beach. Not if you use your–'

'Stand by.' Jameson spoke to someone else, then said, 'Okay. My breacher says two eighty is enough. We can still handle this thing but we're going to need some help.'

'From us?'

'If we blow the ship with what we brought there's a good chance some pieces will wash ashore. Chunks of lifeboat, wooden pallets. All it would take is one fucking ping pong ball. We can't let that happen, so we're going to need a wee bit of a bigger bang.'

Steadman recalled the triple explosion off Andikithira Island. It just about vaporized that ship, though the Russians had helped. 'Why not just let it sink in place?'

'Because that golden ping pong ball might still bob up and float away. Look. This tub is hot with more than just ordinary smallpox. The Russians played with the genetics. Vaccine won't stop it. Even a combination of vaccine and antivirals.'

'Then your shots ... you're unprotected?'

'You catch on fast for a submariner. There *is* no protection against this bug. You could vaccinate everyone on the planet and it wouldn't matter. The same goes for *Portland*.'

'But then you–'

'Listen. There isn't time for *Q* and A. We're going to run out of sea room. If something

536

washes ashore then you can kiss Sicily goodbye. Then Italy. Then Europe. Then–'

'I get the idea. But you–'

'Forget that. *Every one of us* is going to come down with this thing anyway. *Hunter* is what Makayev called it. And you know what? I've seen what it does. No thanks.'

The outline of something huge and terrible took shape at the edge of Steadman's consciousness. Like some dim mountain made visible only by the stars it eclipsed. 'Go on.'

'The tug sent a boat over. The *muj* murdered two of their sailors but one got away in a small boat. Hunter is probably on their ship now. It can't be allowed to dock. Not ever. You understand what I'm saying?'

You want me to torpedo it? 'I'm not sinking a ship because something *might* be on it. How do you know your Russian was telling you the truth?'

'Hey Rosie,' said Jameson. 'You're the duty linguist. Was Makayev telling it straight?'

Scavullo knew the weight her words would carry. Get it wrong and people would die. The only problem was getting it right meant the same thing. She decided not to think, but to speak only what she knew to be true. 'He was telling the truth. But there's got to be another way. That tug is going to have to stay at sea until they know for sure if the virus is on it. Bravo could shelter with them until–'

'They catch Hunter for sure,' Jameson broke in. 'Someone back in Norfolk might have another–'

'There's no time for the tooth fairy, Rosie.'

'Lieutenant?' asked Steadman. 'What did Makayev say?'

The frequency popped and sizzled, then Scavullo spoke slowly, clearly, every atom of emotion drained from her voice. 'That the virus was genetically modified for total vaccine resistance. That where Bravo went, Hunter would follow and that it must die in the sea.'

'Okay, commander?' said Jameson. 'Now you know.'

Tony Watson appeared with a thick sheaf of teletype paper covered in dense black print. He held it up for Steadman. 'Norfolk's worried, Captain. COMSUBLANT wants to hear from us pronto.'

Steadman looked at the sheets, then away. *Portland* was no longer isolated, no longer removed from the dense network of communications that blanketed the globe. He could kick this thing up to Admiral Graybar. But where would that freighter be? *Run aground at some Sicilian fishing village.* Where would that tug be? *Putting in at an United States Navy base.*

That huge, dark mass he'd sensed rather than seen was not just some terrible dilemma, not just a problem for which there was no good answer. It sat there removed from certainty, beyond the scope of any checklist, immune to rational analysis. It was the full weight and responsibility of command itself, and no captain could ease himself out from beneath what was already in him.

Steadman faced Watson. The XO would demand proof, of course. He would question Scavullo's translation, ask for confirmation, and only when the accumulated evidence was overwhelming would he consider acting. The right response to an engineering casualty. And the wrong one now.

'Send a contact message to Norfolk. Tell them that tug out there may be infected with vaccine-resistant smallpox. They've got to stop it and make them drop anchor far from shore. She's not to make port, not to come into contact with anyone or anything until we know for sure it's safe.'

'But Sealift Command owns that tug. Norfolk can't just tell her to stop and drop their–'

'They will. And tell them we monitored an explosion aboard a Russian *Akula*. Copy her exact position from Bam Bam. The international submarine rescue service is right down the street from Graybar's office. If COMSUBLANT can't get them moving no one can.'

'Anything else?'

'That our mission will be accomplished within the hour.'

'You sure you don't want to send that yourself? I can take the conn while you–'

'No.' He was doing Watson a favor, not that he would appreciate it. For there was only one person who could do what was needed.

Steadman was correct. Watson only knew that he'd been dismissed, that Hollywood would die before he let anyone share in the glow that would inevitably surround the words *mission accomplished*. Well, Watson had a book stuffed full of Steadman's missteps that began with *hazarding the boat* and went up the ladder from there. A submarine should be run by the evidence, not gut reactions. By analytical decisions, by weighing options, balancing risk and gain. Not intuition. And while he had to admit the captain could bounce back from a bad situation, wasn't it smarter to avoid them?

'XO? Get that message off *now.*'

'What's the word, commander?' asked Jameson.

Steadman took a breath, let it out slowly and then said. 'This is *Portland,*'he said. 'Tell me what you need.'

MV *'Nova Spirit'*

Four of the six surviving SEALs gathered under a steady rain by the scuttle leading down to the midship hold. Jameson slammed the hatch shut and dogged it down tight.

Pyro was down below, personally tending the thermobaric explosive to make sure there were no glitches. 'One, this is Five. Screw that scuttle down.' This would be Pyro's greatest performance and he wasn't going to let an atom of high-explosive gas leak out and go to waste.

McQuill spotted a dim flash of light up at the bow. He swung his head and dialed up his nods. 'Skipper, Tango forward.'

A figure was wriggling out from the forecastle hatch. He flopped onto his belly and quickly got to his feet with both hands high in the air. The light flickered at his feet, and a second man emerged.

'Two Tangos. Wait. Three. Looks like a French victory parade.'

'Weapons?' asked Jameson.

'No.' The sniper raised his scoped rifle, but Jameson reached over and gently lowered it.

'Let 'em out. They probably could use a little fresh air.'

Another minute passed, and five of the ship's company were on deck, standing in a neat line, all of them with hands held high.

'Want me to go round them up?' asked McQuill. He was the only one who spoke some Arabic.

'No. Just tell them to relax and wait for the helicopter.'

'Got it.' With that, McQuill loped forward.

The sky flashed with sheet lightning. The squad frequency sizzled, then Wheeler's gruff, gravely voice came through.

'Bravo One, this is Three. I'm done back here. The raft ain't goin' nowhere.' Wheeler had done his work swiftly and professionally, using his stainless steel diving knife to put holes – one high, one low – in each of the CRRC's eight float chambers. 'When's the wetting down party?'

'Stand by. Bravo Five, this is One. You ready down below?'

'Just give me a thirty second warning.'

'Rosie? You still on the freq?'

'I'm here, Dick. We're about three miles to your southeast. The captain says he's ready.'

Three miles, thought Jameson. On a nice clear night he might be able to spot the surfaced submarine. Not tonight. Not in this weather. He looked up into the heavy bellied clouds. The wind was driving the rain in horizontal sheets again. The ship was settling, too. *The engine room must be completely flooded.* He found himself wishing for a clear sky, for a moon, for stars. It would be a prettier way to die, but the rain and

541

the mist and the clouds were more useful.

When he looked west, the lights of the coast had dimmed. Who would be out walking on a beach on a night like this anyway? It was possible no one there would see a thing, and certain they would never learn the truth about Yellowstone. None of it.

And that was the way it should be. In war, failures made headlines but openness generated casualties. Each extra person allowed into the circle exponentially increased the risk of a leak. Steadman had thought it was *responsible* to let some of his men in on Yellowstone. Would he have agreed to let the fucking *muj* in on it, too?

No, but to Jameson, do one and you eventually got smacked in the head with the other. And the next time the *muj* would be more careful. They were quick learners. He had to give them that much. They wouldn't use a ship. Or Chechens. Maybe it would be a nice European family on holiday. Maybe it wouldn't be a vial full of bugs, but a creaky old nuke swiped from someone's doomsday arsenal. Did the *muj* fight 'responsibly'? How was blowing up innocent men, women and children 'responsible'? How was sparking a smallpox epidemic that would kill soldiers and civilians alike 'responsible'? No. Fight terror 'responsibly' and you might find yourself on the inside of a mushroom cloud looking out.

Chief Wheeler walked up and squatted beside him. 'So what's the fucking delay, *lieutenant?*'

Jameson smiled. It was good to be able to count on some things. 'Hey Rosie, tell your CO we're a go, and give us a thirty-second count.'

Thunder rumbled, then 'Dick? I told him. Stand by.'

'Thanks. Hey, remember what I said before about taking off on you back at language school?'

'The captain says about four minutes.'

'I don't need *about* anything. I want thirty seconds *exactly*. So Rosie, I wanted to say I was wrong, okay? I couldn't let you know why I was leaving or where I was going. I mean, it was a war, right? But letting you stand there at the gate thinking we were going camping for the weekend? That was *cold*. I'm sorry.'

'Would you listen to that, ladies and gentlemen,' said Pyro. 'That was an actual apology. SEAL history has just been made.'

'You know, you didn't have to shoulder this. You could have weaseled out,' Jameson continued.

'How?' asked Scavullo. *Keep talking.*

'When your CO asked about Makayev. You could have said you didn't know. I mean, I was right here listening and I couldn't figure out what he was trying to say about that *fermenty* shit.'

God help me, I did know. 'You always needed help with Russian.'

'Well, it isn't like you didn't need help, too. Who's going to protect your sweet little ass from falling down ladders?'

'That problem was ... it's gone. Wait–'

'Rosie?'

'One's on the way,' said COB Browne. He'd sent Cooper and the rescue swimmer below. Now, only he and Scavullo occupied the tight confines of the open cockpit.

Scavullo felt the boat shudder again.

'Two,' said COB.

She turned west, though there was nothing to see out there now. Not even the band of distant lights. The clouds had drawn down around the freighter, the submarine. The world beyond no longer mattered. Just the voice in her ears. 'Dick, just talk to me, all right? Keep talking.'

But it was Stepik's voice that answered.

'Hey ma'am? This is Steve. How do you hear?'

'I hear you ... fine,' said Scavullo. Her eyes filled. Her voice caught.

'My wife's name is Julie. Julie Stepik. She teaches math at Tidewater Community College outside Norfolk. Got it?'

'I'll find her, Steve.'

'Tell her. You know what I mean.'

'I know. I'll be sure she knows, too.'

The intercom squawked. 'Sixty seconds run on One.'

'I can take over, lieutenant,' said Browne. 'You can go below.'

'No. Dick?' she said into the Motorola. 'One minute now.'

'Hey Rosie? You're wasting your time with these geeks. A little upper body development and you might even make it through Hell Week.'

'I'm no SEAL, Dick.'

'You're no quitter, either. If they can't appreciate it, fuck 'em. Give special ops a try. Someone lays a hand on you then, you break it off and feed it to him.'

The intercom sounded. Browne put an arm over her shoulder.

Scavullo clicked the squad radio's transmit bar. 'Forty seconds.' She realized she hadn't blinked for some time and the salt and the spray and her own warm tears made them burn. 'Dick?'

'About that Navy tug. If that virus got on board, you've got to make sure they don't sit on their gold-braided asses. There won't be time to collect information and evaluate the fucking situation. I know you can do it. Just tell them the truth, because–'

'Failure is not an option?'

'I knew you had what it takes.'

The even voice of a fire-control technician came over the bridge intercom.

'Rosie? Are you still there?'

Hot tears poured down her cheeks 'Thirty seconds, Dick.'

'Copy thirty. Bravo Five, Bravo One. Go.'

Scavullo listened for Pyro's answer. But if there was one it didn't carry to her ears.

'Say what? Where? Okay. I see it now. Damn! It's comin' on!'

'Dick?'

' ...portside. Look at those bubbles ... wait! There's two! All right! Rosie? Tell your CO good shooting! He can come out with us and plink beer bottles any time he gets the urge to bust out of his little–'

There was the sudden *click* of a thrown switch, a fragment of a voice, a slice of a great joyous whoop and holler of a boy riding a big roller coaster over the top, and then a brilliant white flash lit the western horizon. They were three miles from *Nova Spirit* but she felt a distinct pulse of heat wash over her face. Then, another. Fifteen seconds later, the rumble of the initial explosion arrived as the third and brightest flash scoured the sea with its light.

The shock wave drove the clouds back and in that instant Scavullo could see a hard blue ball of fire rising, rising, growing. As it merged with the overcast, when all that could be burned was consumed and the sea made pure once more, it flickered, dimmed to red and died.

The rain pelted down on them.

'COB,' she said, 'what if I was wrong?'

'Were you wrong?'

'I don't ... I didn't think so but–'

'If you were in doubt you should have called up someone who spoke better Russian.'

'There's no one else. You know that.'

'I also know you just answered your own question. Could you have been wrong? Sure. Even I've been wrong now and again. But if I'm the man on the scene with the right training, the rest doesn't matter.'

'But they died because–'

'Because some crazy ass killers wanted to spread a deadly disease around, and we stopped them. Not because you were the duty translator.'

'Makayev could have been lying.'

'And I could have come down a lot sooner on that jinx thing. I gave Niebel the benefit of the doubt. I made the call, and I was dead wrong.'

'You knew?'

'It's my job to know, lieutenant. I figured a word of warning would cool him off. I even smelled a rat when I heard he volunteered to help out on the bridge. I never did know Niebel to volunteer for anything. I don't imagine he had a sudden change of heart up here, did he?'

'No.'

'Then I expect there's not much point in looking for him.'

She stared out across the waves. 'No,' she said again.

'There will be an enquiry when we get back. Banjo got a pretty hard knock. He might need a little help *assembling* his recollections.'

Was Browne looking for evidence, or a way out of a larger problem? One that would taint Steadman forever as a captain who could steer his ship but not lead his men? A problem that would spread until everyone, Scavullo especially, was covered with it? 'I'll try, COB.'

'Good. Then you might want to put this where it belongs.' He held out the socket wrench. The sea had washed it clean of Banjo's blood.

She took the cold, heavy tool, turned and threw it as hard as she could. It splashed into the sea and disappeared.

'*You will cast all your sins into the depths of the sea. Micah 7:19.*' He smiled, then said, 'I think we've all cast enough sins into the sea for one night, lieutenant. Best get below.'

'Where will we go from here?'

'Where all ships go when their work is done,' said Browne. 'Home.'

EPILOGUE

La Maddalena, Sardinia

Senior chiefs know almost everything and a good COB had every reason to think he knew the rest. But in his last prediction, Jerome Browne would not be proven correct.

With Admiral Graybar's directive in hand and Steadman medicated and asleep in his stateroom, Tony Watson turned *Portland* away from the shallow Gulf of Noto, submerged and headed south. She hugged the hundred fathom curve off the southern tip of Sicily and turned west. Not for home, but for the naval base at La Maddalena, Sardinia.

The channel separating the islands of Sardinia, Santo Stefano and La Maddalena was thick with yachts sheltering from the *gregale*. Their white stern lights glittered across the dark channel when *Portland* rounded Cape d'Orso. She approached the NATO pier on the east shore of Santo Stefano in full darkness, picking her way through the anchored pleasure boats with rudder orders transmitted down from lookouts on the bridge in half-degree increments.

There, on the pier's south side, moored stern-to, was the submarine tender USS *Emory Land;* a floating repair yard and the flagship of Submarine Squadron Twenty-Two. *Oklahoma City,* the boat *Portland* had been called upon to replace, was moored to the tender's other flank, her mangled sail still hidden beneath a wrapping of blue tarps.

The CO of SUBRON 22, Captain Owen Fountain, had been informed that *Portland* was headed his way. His men had only begun their work on *Oklahoma City*. Its sudden arrival had been an imposition to his orderly world of crew rotations and scheduled maintenance. Why *another* Atlantic boat was snooping around the Med and why it required urgent care was a mystery, but submarine operations were not. He was a prudent naval officer and expected no less from *Portland's* CO. A prudent submariner would surely time his arrival for first light. And so Fountain was fast asleep when Watson brought the submarine alongside the tender at 0300 in the morning.

The brilliant work lights that usually burned from the tender's sides were dark. It was a delicate operation, but Watson performed it quickly and competently. Lines were passed over and made fast and a messenger was dispatched to wake Captain Fountain to inform him that prudent or not, *Portland* had arrived.

When Fountain showed up on deck, even the eagles on his collar looked ready to rip into something. The brow was lowered, and Lieutenant Commander Watson walked straight into the broadside.

What did he think he was doing, making an approach to the tender at night, without lights, without notice? Did Watson *really* expect him to drop everything and start work on *Portland* at

0300 in the goddamned morning? With none of the communications, none of the proper arrangements in place? Didn't he *understand* that major repairs demanded planning, requisitioning of parts and detailed scheduling of manpower? Tony Watson and *Portland* could get in line. When *Oklahoma City* was finished, work on *Portland* would begin.

An angry captain's shout is considerable, and Watson was in a tough position. Not because he felt like arguing, but because he agreed with nearly everything Fountain said. Indeed, he would have liked nothing so much as to help him make a stronger case.

But he kept his mouth shut. There was no point in wasting ammunition here in Sardinia. Admiral Graybar worked for other admirals with more stars. When the time came, Tony Watson would be heard.

And so would Graybar. When morning came and repair work had not yet begun, he fired a message from Norfolk that arced halfway across the globe and struck Fountain's desk with the impact of a flying Volkswagen. *Portland* was to get underway within twenty four hours. If Fountain couldn't fix what ailed the submarine by 0300 the next morning, he was to inform Admiral Graybar why not. In person.

When COMSUBRON 22 crawled out of the crater, he gathered his division heads and briefed them on some new priorities.

The tender's electronics, hydraulics and welding shops wiped their schedules clean, dropped everything and went to work on what

550

ailed *Portland.* Sparks fell in brilliant cascades from the top of her sail. Radio equipment was stripped from *Oklahoma City.* Inspection panels were removed and tangles of cables were pulled, patched and reinstalled.

What the sailors did for the boat the doctors at the base branch clinic did for Steadman, Banjo Gant and Browne. Some of *Portland's* damage was obvious, some of it subtle. What was true for the submarine was also true for them.

Time would mend Banjo's broken bones, but a concussion left him confused, irritable and unsure about what had happened up in the cockpit that night. He knew Niebel had tried to kill him, but he still wasn't sure why. There was no question about him going back to sea.

COB Browne was in better shape. The force that picked him up and threw him over the side had put some protective distance between his body and several hundred million volts of incandescent energy. His hearing was back. His flash-blindness had cleared. He was not only up to speed but able to perform the duties expected of a senior chief.

No one aboard the *Emory Land* knew where *Portland* had come from nor what she had done. But Browne immediately activated the chief-to-chief network, and cases of fresh fruit, vegetables and milk mysteriously vanished from *Emory Land's* refrigerated holds and reappeared in *Portland's.* Captains and commanders could argue all they wanted to. Sailors take care of their own.

Of the three, Steadman was in the worst shape. His burns were easily treated. The torn muscles in his chest would knit together. But the base doctors had no idea if the shock to his nervous system would ever heal. Half of all lightning strike victims suffered permanent numbness, pain, dizziness and exhaustion. Which half would he be in? All he knew was that right *now* he could either be awake in pain, or medicated and drowsy. Neither was acceptable for a commanding officer at sea.

There was nothing visibly wrong with Lieutenant Scavullo. No marks, no burns, no broken bones. Only a profound weariness that an infantryman coming back from the front would recognize as battle fatigue. Only her considerable stubbornness kept her going.

Her orders to separate from *Portland* arrived just before noon. A jet was arriving from Norfolk with Steadman's relief on board. She would fly it back for 'further assignment', whatever that meant. The orders were not unwelcome: she *did not* want to ride home with Tony Watson anywhere near the helm. Scavullo packed up her gear, stuffed it all into her seabag, slung it over her shoulder and walked over the brow to the *Emory Land*.

To Captain Fountain's relief the last welder's torch went out with a soft *pop* at 0100; two hours before Graybar's deadline. A radio technician from the tender hurried across the brow as *Portland's* maneuvering watch came topside to the main deck. Sailing orders were passed over, the brow was lifted and line handlers in green 'float coats' took their positions.

Steadman was not supposed to leave his stateroom aboard the tender but Browne had sent word of the boat's imminent departure. *Portland* would sail at 0230. He would be there to see her leave if he had to crawl. He stood at the rail, holding it tightly to steady the shakes he could not seem to stop, watching his crew make the boat ready for sea.

Three flags shifted in the warm Mediterranean air. The stars and stripes fluttered from a short gaff at the submarine's stern. *Portland's* commissioning pennant hung from a mast atop her sail, and forward, at the bow, the rattlesnake jack with the defiant *Don't Tread on Me*.

He thought of the new captain the admiral had dispatched. He was the CO of the *North Carolina;* a *Virginia*-class submarine still under construction. As befitted the captain of a ship sitting on blocks in a building shed, he was a meticulous, engineering-oriented man who left no detail to chance. He and Watson would get along just fine.

He also thought of the men who'd hoped to unleash a cataclysmic virus on the world. This was no 'clash of civilizations', no struggle between competing religions. This was a war against pure, unadulterated evil. It had been met and stopped, this time, and at a cost. Jameson, his squad. Perhaps the crew of the *Apache*. Not even Browne could find out what had happened to them. Niebel. The butcher's bill was bearable only in comparison to what would have happened if they'd failed. What had Jameson said? That there were seven other plants just like Pokrov? Would the Russians improve security or bury their heads in the sand?

Steadman saw motion up on *Portland's* bridge: her new CO and Tony Watson. *Good luck to you both,* he thought. *I brought them out. I brought most of them back. May God help you do the same.*

'Stand by to single off all lines!' came the amplified command from the submarine's bridge.

Browne told me Niebel was washed overboard working alongside Banjo and Scavullo, thought Steadman. *But I could see something else in his eyes. He was giving me an easy way out of something unpleasant. We'll award Niebel a medal, though I think it might be a travesty. May it brighten his memory.*

'You're up early today, commander.'

Steadman turned. It was Captain Fountain. 'I wanted to see her get underway, sir. I hate to see her sail without me, but she looks good.'

'From here. If you ask me it's nothing more than a hundred yard paint job,' said Fountain with a sour look on his face.

'Cast off lines one, two and three!'

'You know,' said Fountain, 'I've asked around. You've developed quite a reputation, Mister Steadman. They say you're the most expensive officer in the submarine force. We give you good boats and you bring them back in pieces. *Portland* spent a year in the yards last time. That's a three billion dollar asset out there. I wonder if you have a sufficient appreciation for that fact.'

'I have a good understanding of what she's for, Captain.'

'Do you? Submarines are expensive and some folks think they're not good for much now that the Soviets are gone.'

'They changed their flag. They're not gone.'

'Even more reason to keep our hulls safe and functional for more than a few weeks at a time, wouldn't you say?'

'Excuse me, sir,' said a third voice from behind them, 'but I heard someone say that a harbor is a safe enough place for a ship, but that wasn't what ships are for.'

Both men turned. It was Lieutenant Scavullo.

'And here's another little mystery,' said Fountain, ignoring the challenge in Scavullo's remark. 'It's been some time since we saw a Russian linguist pass through. Is Moscow up to something in the Med?'

She glanced at Steadman, then said, 'With all due respect, I'm not at liberty to discuss duty assignments.'

'CNN seems to think the Russians are having problems.'

'Problems?' said Steadman.

'There's a report out this morning that one of their boats is overdue. An *Akula*. She was on her way home from a courtesy call in Syria and missed a scheduled check in. The Russians aren't calling her lost, but they are saying that if she did go down we must have done it.'

'Don't they always?' said Scavullo.

'Yes, but then there's that.' He nodded at *Portland*.

'We were hit by lightning, captain,' said Steadman.

'Maybe lightning hit the *Akula*, too.' When neither Steadman nor Scavullo spoke, he continued. 'And there's a fleet tug that was due in here from Naples. The *Apache*. They dropped anchor out in the middle of the Tyrrhenian Sea. Any idea why?'

'I wouldn't know,' said Steadman.

'An *Akula's* supposed to be a pretty good boat. Very quiet. Very hard to track. *Apache's* got heavy-lift salvage cranes and divers. I'm adding two and two here, Steadman. The numbers making sense?'

'We can track an *Akula,'* said Steadman. *Thanks to Bam Bam.*

A narrow stripe of black water opened between *Portland* and the tender's side. The deck crew was still hanging on to a thick mooring line attached to a recessed cleat on *Portland*'s stern.

'Well, since neither of you seems to know much, I'm going back to bed,' said Fountain. 'But before I go, allow me to make one last observation: I hope you made the most of your command at sea time. You're two for two. You'll be lucky to command a desk next time.'

'Well, Captain,' said Steadman, 'sound procedures can take you only so far. After that it's all luck. Maybe I'll be lucky.'

Fountain didn't believe in luck. He turned to Scavullo. 'What about you, lieutenant? Still hoping to ride submarines?'

'No sir. I'm going to try for a language school slot.'

'Teaching?'

'Studying. Arabic, this time.'

'There aren't many Arabs at sea and there are *no* submarines in the desert. You're also two for two. I see a desk in your future.'

'Maybe I'll get lucky too, sir,' she said, sending a quick smile in Steadman's direction.

Fountain snorted, turned and bustled off.

Steadman watched the graceful screw at *Port-*

land's finely tapered stern thrash the water to foam. The slim black hull began to edge backwards.

'Make fast the number four line!'

The propeller stopped. The stern line held fast. The bow slowly angled out away from the pilings until she was pointed at the open channel. Only a few lights twinkled on Isola Caprera on the far side.

The amplified voice ordered, 'Cast off number four!'

As the last tether holding the boat to the *Emory Land* fell away, *Portland*'s ensign and jack fluttered down. The commissioning pennant at her sail was replaced by the stars and stripes. The screw churned, the boat began to move away from the tender on her own power.

Portland was a ship, built from machinery, computers and weapons, but also from men. An engineering marvel, but a marvel built to go in harm's way. Steadman had taken her there and brought her back. That's how it would read on some dry report on Yellowstone that would immediately be classified beyond the reach of a select few in the innermost circle of the Pentagon.

'Can I help you back inside, commander?' she asked.

'No thanks. I'm fine right here.'

She paused. 'Sir? Do you think he was right? About you never commanding another boat?'

'They don't hand out medals for banging up submarines.'

'How about for saving the world?'

He didn't answer. She sensed that Steadman

557

wanted to be out here alone, and she turned to leave.

'Lieutenant? Wait.'

She stopped. 'Sir?'

'What's it going to take to bring women onto the boats?'

'A CO, an XO and a COB who are behind it one hundred percent. Two out of three isn't good enough. And next time don't send out one woman. Send *three*.'

He chuckled. 'I'll pass your thoughts along.'

'Good night, commander. And sir? If we both get lucky I'd consider it an honor to sail with you again.'

'Thanks. And good night to you, lieutenant.' She stepped through a watertight door, and Steadman turned to watch *Portland* grow smaller, her hull blending into the predawn darkness. Black on black, a shape, a shadow.

Portland was a ship, and all ships needed a captain. He'd been that captain. He'd taken her out and he'd brought her home. Letters of commendation or reproach were beside the point. He'd commanded a warship at sea. He'd kept faith with his country and most of his men. And no matter what they did to him, no matter where they sent him, there was nothing better, nothing more honorable, than that.

The white light at *Portland*'s stern was visible the longest, and then, as she made the sweeping turn at Point Fico, heading for the open sea, it flickered once, twice, and then disappeared.

The publishers hope that this book has given you enjoyable reading. Large Print Books are especially designed to be as easy to see and hold as possible. If you wish a complete list of our books please ask at your local library or write directly to:

Magna Large Print Books
Magna House, Long Preston,
Skipton, North Yorkshire.
BD23 4ND

This Large Print Book for the partially sighted, who cannot read normal print, is published under the auspices of

THE ULVERSCROFT FOUNDATION